# Dark Matter

## Weird Stories and Poetry

# DARK MATTER

## Weird Stories and Poetry

Carl E. Reed

Foreword by S. T. Joshi

Hippocampus Press

New York

Dedication: To the 1970s Chicago public schoolteachers whose love of literature and encouragement of my fledgling writing efforts opened up illimitable horizons: Gloria Brock, Jim Conway, Bob Smith. I keep the faith you kindled, nurtured by the most powerful intoxicant in the universe: the power of story.

Published by Hippocampus Press
P.O. Box 641, New York, NY 10156.
www.hippocampuspress.com

Cover art and design © 2024 by Daniel V. Sauer.
Hippocampus Press logo designed by Anastasia Damianakos.

First Edition
1 3 5 7 9 8 6 4 2
ISBN13: 978-1-61498-437-5 trade paper
ISBN13: 978-1-61498-441-2 ebook

# Contents

# Foreword

It is exceedingly rare for a first book of short stories to exhibit such assurance and panache as this one, but this is only one of the many virtues we find in Carl E. Reed's *Dark Matter.*[*] Reed has in fact been writing for at least the past twenty years, but he has been more intent on perfecting his craft than in throwing his work out to all and sundry; and his quiet but relentless diligence now pays dividends in this scintillating volume.

Reed approaches the genre of weird fiction as a well-versed veteran. His awareness of the long heritage of supernatural and psychological terror is displayed in story after story. H. P. Lovecraft is a dominant influence, as "Cold Tickle" amply demonstrates; and "A Matter of Debt Concerning the Gentleman in Baltimore" points to Reed's devotion to the pioneering work of Edgar Allan Poe. More broadly, Reed recognizes the lingering potency of age-old weird motifs such as the vampire, the werewolf, and the haunted house; but he understands that these venerable tropes must be reinterpreted to retain their potency in our time.

In other stories Reed goes back even further to the realm of myth and legend. Celtic lore is at the heart of "Samhain Eve," while Norse myth is pungently brought into the present day in "Come Haltingly, on Lame Feet." Native American legendry is made chillingly real in "Motauqwa Means Mountain."

But Reed does far more than merely resurrect ancient weird elements. His skill at portraying the figures of our own muddled era is exceptional, and it is here that he brings both empathy and sardonic satire into play. Children are the focus of the plangent tales "Night Terror" and

---

[*]Strictly speaking, this is Reed's second short story collection, as a volume of his stories appeared as an ebook in 2015.

"Haunted House"—but the pestiferousness of young hoodlums-in-the-making is uproariously etched in "The Strange and Curious Tale of Prof. Robert Howard Wilson." Psychological horror reaches an almost unbearable level of grim poignancy in "The Water Is Warm, Mommy" and "Pulp Writer." War and politics mingle forebodingly in "The Candidate" and "The Final Flight of Major Havoc." As for "The Möbius Strip Trip," this expansive novella reveals a staggeringly vivid imaginative scope that makes for a compulsive reading experience.

More than a few words need to be said for the poetry Reed has generously sprinkled throughout this volume. His verse is taut, compressed, and evocative, whether it be a free-flowing ballad or a sonnet. Not many writers in our field can boast virtuosity in both poetry and prose, but Reed is one of them.

For all his many years of experience as a writer, Carl E. Reed has only begun to reveal to the world what he has to say in the weird mode. We can relish it thoroughly with the knowledge that further baleful delights are to come in the future.

—S. T. JOSHI

# Night Terror

Seth Freeman awoke with a scream, heart hammering in his bony chest like a panicked sparrow who'd flown into an enclosed space and now found himself trapped. He could not find his way out again. The imagery of the dream was already fading like faerie, though he recalled swooping through an inviting hatch that opened into a shadowed tunnel that twisted—turned—looped—and dropped . . .

"Mommy!" Seth called out. "Daddy!" Cartoon-character bedsheets were knotted around his sweat-soaked gnomish frame. Over-large eyes glimmered from a moon-pale oval of a face crawling with nervous tics and twitches beneath a black widow's peak of clammy hair.

Seth Freeman was a good boy who thought himself a very *bad* boy. And that, in the words of a certain New England rustic who wrote deceptively simple, unflinching poems on the dark sorrow at the heart of things, "made all the difference."

*"Mommy! Daddy!"* Seth called again, more insistently.

A light went on in the master bedroom at the back of the house. Heavily refracted illumination filtered through the kitchen and down the hallway, turning the darkness of his bedroom into a garish-gray sickscape of pallid light.

Snatches of dream returned. He'd transformed from a sparrow into a loin-clothed, black-maned warrior: dagger in hand, hacking away at anthropoid monsters that thrashed and moaned. A tongue of flame stabbed at his face. Detonations in the dark . . .

Seth was wide awake now. He noted the humped-up form in the chair-desk opposite him, a pair of doll-like forms flanking the digital alarm clock atop the dresser an arm's-length away from the foot of his bed, the closet door ajar beside the bureau nestled against the chair-desk. The green luminescent numerals of the digital alarm clock atop the dresser glowed 2:35 A.M.

He blinked and attempted to focus his vision in the grayish darkness. Surely that was no dozing hellhound, but rather his wadded-up winter jacket jammed into the chair-desk? As for the doll-like forms atop the dresser leaning against the wall on either side of the alarm clock—why, those were dolls: his "battle buddies," in fact: an M-60 machine-gun-toting American Marine in jungle camouflage keeping comradely company with a black pajama-clad Viet Cong guerrilla clutching an AK-47 assault rifle. As for the closet door . . .

The closet door concerned him, to be sure. But that uneasiness was as nothing compared to the terror that caused his breath to hitch in his chest when he considered the thing coiled beneath mattress and box frame—for he knew, with the absolute certainty of conviction that gripped small boys who awakened in the dark witching hours of early A.M., that a monster lurked under his bed. A diabolical, calculating monster waiting for just the right moment to spring up and inflict terrible wounds.

"Seth," called a muffled voice through mattress and box springs.

"Shut up!" said Seth.

"Be reasonable. I'll get you. I mean, all I have to do is reach up here, grab your arm and"—a pale, long-fingered hand spider-crawled into view and began to tug at his covering sheet and comforter—"clamp down hard and *yank!* Why make it harder on yourself?"

"Shut up; shut up; *shut up!*" sounded Seth's prepubescent alto.

"Now is that any way to talk to your monster?" *Whump!* went the hand thumping Seth's mattress. *Crump!* a cold fist on the sheets.

*"MOMMY! DA—"*

"We're here, darling."

The hand snaked back under the bed.

Mrs. Freeman glided into view with regal finishing-school grandeur: a statuesque, slim-hipped woman of hawkish nose and shoulder-length hair advancing in the uncertain light of the darkened bedroom. Hard on her heels followed Mr. Freeman: a shorter, thicker form with bald round head. His hunched shoulders and muscled, free-swinging arms exuded the violent energy of a below-decks disciplinarian stalking the aisle between rows of recalcitrant galley slaves.

Relief flooded Seth's body: a warm and welcome rush of narcotizing euphoria.

"Look out! There's a monster under my bed!" Seth fought the entangling sheets, struggled to sit up against the headboard. "It tried to grab my arm!"

"Stop speaking in exclamation marks," commanded Mr. Freeman. "You were bred better than that. One would think you were naught but a common little vulgarian."

"But——"

"You had a nightmare, darling." His mother's voice was soothing balm to his frazzled psyche. "That's all it was. A nightmare."

"A very *bad* nightmare," Mr. Freeman elaborated. "I'll grant you that. A night terror: a vivid, heart-rate-elevating oneiric experience of adrenalized terror and suffocating horror." He nodded vigorously. "Quite common at your age. Upsetting, to be sure; but nothing to be overly concerned about. God knows you've had enough of them this summer."

Seth caught little of this. Not that it mattered. He'd come to the realization long ago that his father spoke primarily for himself and not his son's—or anyone else's—benefit. Yet Mr. Freeman's rich, warm baritone conveyed inarguable parental certitude and authority. That was something—especially on dark, scary nights like this when one longed for a higher authority to dispel the monsters hiding in one's closet or lurking under the bed.

Mrs. Freeman dropped to her knees beside Seth and opened her arms. "Poor baby, come to Momma."

Seth strained forward into the proffered embrace and allowed his mother's arms to encircle and hug him. How curiously cold her breasts were! Like her arms: a bone-chilling, mausoleum-marble cold. And the bulk of her seemed somehow . . . not all there.

"You're cold, Mommy," noted Seth. "And rather lacking in mass."

"Hmm? What's that?" said Mrs. Freeman. "I hadn't noticed. You're rather cold and insubstantial yourself, I'm afraid. The quick-silver lightning—"

"Glenda," warned Mr. Freeman.

"—burned so as it licked my throat. I was *very* warm then; so very warm."

Seth wriggled out of her embrace. His heart was going ba-*DUM!*, ba-*DUM!*, ba-*DUM!* and that was very curious indeed; because there was no reason for his heart to start banging away in his chest again—no reason at all.

"We don't blame you, Seth," Mrs. Freeman said. "You must remember this: it wasn't your fault. I ascribe it to temporary madness brought on by night terrors."

"You had the knife," elaborated Mr. Freeman. "I went for the gun in the nightstand."

"You were sleepwalking," Mrs. Freeman rushed on, putting hands to her throat. "Wild-eyed, gibbering. Hacking away."

"Enough." Mr. Freeman pulled his wife to her feet and nudged her toward the door. "You're overstimulating him."

Mrs. Freeman drifted away, pulling disconsolately at her hair. She glanced back once before exiting the room, expression unreadable in the penumbral darkness. Slippered feet padded off, footsteps fading . . .

"Father," called Seth.

Mr. Freeman stiffened, paused in the doorway.

"Turn on the light."

"Yes?" Mr. Freeman turned to look at his son. "Are you sure that's what you want?" His hand hovered over the light switch. "What you . . . *truly* want?"

Seth considered. None of this made any sense.

He nodded—he had to *see.*

The world flared incandescent. Seth squinted against the brilliance as his pupils adjusted to the light.

Mr. Freeman stared back at him from the red ruin of his face. His left cheek was ripped open, exposing clenched teeth in a rictused grimace; his eye sockets were knife-ravaged, leaking holes. They bored into his son like troll-tunneled shafts plunging down . . . down . . . down to soul-devouring Avernus. "Get some sleep."

Seth emitted a strangled wheeze.

Mr. Freeman clicked off the light. Retreating footsteps sounded down the hallway, sounding fainter as they traversed the kitchen. Seconds later box springs creaked in the master bedroom.

Silence.

The light blinked back on.

Seth glanced at his war dolls atop the dresser. Immobile plastic figures: the Marine Corps machine-gunner and Viet Cong guerrilla. A flick of his eyes to the chair-desk: wadded-up winter coat jammed in between the wooden chair and fore-edge of the attached desk. Dart of his eyes to the closet: door ajar but nothing emerging from out that darkened space. Another flick of his eyes back to the dresser: the green luminescent numerals of the digital alarm clock glowed 2:35 A.M.

A high, keening wail broke from his throat.

"Crybaby," mocked the monster under his bed.

Seth's shriek became a series of shuddering, convulsive sobs.

"Now, now—enough of that." The thing wormed out from under the bed and sat down beside him. Seth was unsurprised to discover that it looked just like him—save for the fact that a quarter of its face and skull was missing. The remaining three-quarters of ghastly, bullet-blasted visage showed a bluish pallor through spattered blood and clotted brain matter. It laid a companionable hand on his shoulder.

"Night terrors indeed!" said Seth's corpse to his ghost. "After you pulled that boning knife from the block on the kitchen counter Daddy had no choice but to put you down with magnum force. Poor baby." The thing shifted its claw hand from shoulder to head; patted him as if he were a disconsolate dog. "You've been a *very* bad boy."

Seth screamed.

# One Who Walks Alone

The castle dark loomed tall & stark
upon the stony hill
where nothing green would grow but black
nettles, mold & chill

fungoid forms: mottled stalks
supporting toxic heads
mushroom in shape & weeping vile
ichors o'er undead

ghoulish forms entombed below
that neither laugh nor weep,
but shuffle-moan through crypt & tunnel
dank & fathoms deep.

I started up the flagstone path
a whisper in the night;
the blood-red gibbous moon above
shone down its fulgent light.

No stranger, I, to castle dark—
not guest, but rather, host
of many an eldritch ritual there:
warlock, scholar, ghost.

I wept & walked with straited gait;
I strode that path alone.
Burnt at the stake long ages past,
returned to claim my home.

# The Candidate

Is it that by its indefiniteness it shadows forth the heartless voids and immensities of the universe, and thus stabs us from behind with the thought of annihilation, when beholding the white depths of the milky way? Or is it, that as in essence whiteness is not so much a color as the visible absence of color; and at the same time the concrete of all colors; is it for these reasons that there is such a dumb blankness, full of meaning, in a wide landscape of snows—a colorless, all-color of atheism from which we shrink? And when we consider that other theory of the natural philosophers, that all other earthly hues—every stately or lovely emblazoning—the sweet tinges of sunset skies and woods; yea, and the gilded velvets of butterflies, and the butterfly cheeks of young girls; all these are but subtile deceits, not actually inherent in substances, but only laid on from without; so that all deified Nature absolutely paints like the harlot, whose allurements cover nothing but the charnel-house within . . .

—Herman Melville, *Moby-Dick*

"Get up." Voice a commanding baritone.

Pain erupted in my side.

"I said *get up*."

My eyes opened. The guy was dressed in blinding white: sharply creased trousers, *Mafioso*-style ankle boots, and leather trenchcoat. His close-cropped hair and goatee, though—black as the hole in the business end of a gun. Breath steamed from his nostrils in the chill morning air.

I groaned and rolled over, autumnal leaves crunching under my lanky frame. I'd crawled partway under a park bush to sleep for the night. And this was one derelict who intended to stay in bed.

"Go away," I said. A sour taste of vomit and cheap whiskey at the back of my throat.

Again the boot dug into my side.

17

"Up," Snow White repeated.

*Motherfucker.* I scrambled to my feet and swung for his face.

Snow White gave a dismissive sniff and stepped back.

Head whirling, off-balance, I stumbled and went down on one knee. I watched my tormentor through lidded eyes, bracing for his counterattack.

"Violence," he said. "Admirable."

I laughed. It came out a contemptuous grunt.

"You're hung over," Snow White observed. "Hardly a fair fight."

"Just wait till I get my hands on you." I stood up.

"Your name," he demanded.

"None of your goddamn business." I took a shaky step forward.

Snow White smiled a sly, fox-stole-your-dog's-chew-toy smile. "Your name," he demanded again.

"Get out of my face." I held my bomber jacket closed at the throat; the once beige garment now mottled piebald with stains. The zipper was broken—a defect in insulation partially compensated for by the logo-less sweatshirt I wore underneath. I poked him in the chest with my free hand. "What are you, park police? Advocate for the homeless? Cruising faggot?" I winced from the retina-scorching whiteness of his clothes. "From the North Pole?"

He stood hipshot before me, that mocking smile gone, measuring me with an insolent head-to-toe surveil. "It'll come to you."

Smug bastard. I'd forgotten my own name. But how could he know that?

"Get lost," I said and pushed past him, striding down the curving brick pathway of the park.

When I'd taken a good dozen paces away, I glanced back over my shoulder.

Snow White: still as a statue. Watching me.

"See you around," he called. Brought his index and middle fingers to his brow, snapped them away. Salute.

Noon found me in a bright yellow booth eating tacos of greasy meat, wilted lettuce, and oily cheese from corn shells that tasted like refried cardboard. Tepid water dispensed from a soda fountain a-swarm with buzzing gnats helped me choke down these sad mockeries of Mexican cuisine. Early twenty-first-century American fast food: cheap, ubiquitous, sickening. *USA! USA! USA!* A crudely lettered, comma-deficient sign taped to the soda fountain read: *Sorry ice machine broken sorry.* An elderly couple four booths distant sipped coffee from Styrofoam cups. Behind them, a teenaged trio perched atop stools carried on an expletive-laden conversation concerning school, their television-centered home lives, and the trials-and-travails of currently trending social media influencers.

It wasn't just my name that I'd forgotten. I couldn't remember where I lived. What I did for a living. Who might have been looking for me these past two weeks.

My jaws were busy working a mouthful of red-sauced gunk into a ball of congealment when Snow White sauntered up and slid into the facing booth seat.

"Has it come to you yet?" he asked.

"How much you irritate me?" I swiped my lips with a napkin, tossed the crumpled ball of sauce-stained paper onto the table between us.

"Your name," he said.

"This again. Seems to be an obsession with you. Why?" I studied his face. "I don't know you. Do I?" Classically sculpted features, high cheekbones. Predatory, hawk-like eyes close-set above a sharp dagger of a nose. Bit of an overbite and numerous pockmarks masked by that Ming-the-Merciless, tar-black goatee. "Nothing better to do? Cable out? Refugee from original-series Star Trek—that absurd *Mirror, Mirror* episode?"

"Cold, warm, warmer."

"Fuck off."

"You are the candidate of the new millennium."

"Well, why didn't you say so?" I shoveled the last bit of taco into my mouth, chewed, and swallowed. "That clears up everything."

"The first suicide of every new millennium is automatically considered a candidate for the office."

"Fascinating." I picked up the paper cup, sipped room-temperature water, set the cup back down. "One flaw in your supposition."

Snow White arched a brow.

"I'm not dead. And I've no intention of killing myself."

Slight head nod from Snow White, as if in sympathetic agreement. "You're alive—now. But I assure you, you'll die tomorrow. By your own hand. Once you realize what you've done."

*"I know where you were. I had you followed—you were with* him!" *Her eyes blazed with anger and hurt.*

A white-hot jolt of pain in my head. I doubled over in the booth and grimaced, hands to my temples. Waited till my galloping heart settled back down to a stately trot. Straightened up again.

"See you around." Snow White slid out of the booth, stood up and moved toward the exit.

I watched his retreating back. White leather coat bright as Arctic sun-prismed icicles.

I opened my mouth to call out something sharp and stinging, but the words died in my throat.

Snow White: gone.

I went back to the park after visiting a local liquor store where I picked up a pint of rotgut whiskey. The purchase left me dead broke save for a solitary crumpled dollar bill in my right front pants pocket. I'd lost my wallet somewhere, somehow during these past two weeks—or so I guessed.

*    *    *

*You didn't lose your wallet; you tossed it away. Along with your car keys and cell phone. When you awoke the next day in the park. Hung over, hurting, amnesiac. You didn't want to know; couldn't bear to know. Who you were and what you had done.*

Something tried to surface in my consciousness and I shoved it back down into the pincer-clawed, crawling depths where it could do me no harm. I pulled at the whiskey in a series of molten-fire gulps over the course of the next hour while I sat on the bench thinking as little as possible. A pleasant, depressive ennui hit along with the numbness. Perfect. Just what I wanted.

Children played in the park around me. Red-faced, screaming. Racing around. Whoop it up, spawnlings. Just wait till you see what's around the corner. A couple of barking dogs romped at the end of long leashes. Sharp looks from various people who passed as I sipped from the pint. Eyes to yourselves, assholes. A smartly dressed woman in pleated pants suit and pearl earrings halted in front of me when I was halfway through the bottle, face a rigidified mask of disapproval. She opened her mouth to say something.

I met her gaze and waited for the rebuke.

She walked away without uttering a word.

I finished the whiskey and tossed the bottle over my shoulder.

Fuck 'em. Fuck 'em all.

I'd dozed off on the bench when the wail of a police siren snapped my head up off my chest.

*"Good pinch, Jack."*

*I looked up from the paperwork I was filling out on the desk.*

*Double gold bars on the collar of a starched white shirt. Bannerman: precinct captain. Watch Commander this night.*

*"I hear the guy was dealing some weight. Ten kilos of blow. Belmont Cragin, right?"*

*"That's a roger," I said. "Behind the Brickyard. Third-floor walk-up. Dale and I kicked in the door—"*

Dale and I! Uniformed patrol officers of the C.P.D.

Again, the bolt of pain in my head. I threw my hands to my temples, thrashed and moaned.

When I straightened up again Snow White stood before me.

"Hello, Jack. Or should I say: Officer Evers."

I stared at him, breathing hard.

"Let's go."

Snow White had an apartment on the third floor of an old brownstone five blocks from the park. His domicile had a curiously unlived-in look. It was a space devoid of all domestic clutter—save for a couple of pieces of furniture low-slung and sleek as Ferraris, and hundreds of leather-bound volumes ranked upon bowed bookshelves along the shortest wall of the living room. The books were in numerous foreign languages. Though I couldn't translate the titles I recognized French, German, Spanish, Latin, and Greek—in addition to English—printed on the spines. The subjects covered—as far as I could make out amongst the English-language titles—leaned heavily toward history, religion, philosophy, and the occult. World literature was well represented in the mix. In addition to the aforementioned languages there were titles in dozens of other tongues, though what these particular languages were I couldn't tell. I was a cop, not a philologist or linguist.

"I like to read in my off hours," said Snow White with a shrug.

"Clearly."

"I have my favorites, of course: Dante, Milton, Melville. The Marquis de Sade. Nietzsche and Camus." His tongue darted out to moisten his upper lip. "The tragedies of Shakespeare. You?"

"I'm not much of a reader."

"Pity."

For some reason that stung. "When I do read I prefer the works of Mickey Spillane, Joseph Wambaugh, Don Pendleton. You know: The Greats."

Thin smile from Snow White. "May I take your coat?"

"No."

The door closed with an audible click behind us.

With a sinuous shake-and-shimmy Snow White removed his leather trenchcoat and slung it on a brass hook beside the door.

We moved deeper into the apartment.

The rest of Snow White's interior space was not so much apartment as stage set. And, as I might have suspected—the entire apartment was a blinding study in white: carpeting, ceiling, furniture. Facing walls of the living room were unrelieved expanses of polar opalescence, naked of any adornment save for 16′ × 8′ mirrors mounted in Baroque gold frames. The laws of optics and light being what they were, these giant mirrors opened the space up to impossible distances. The room doubled and redoubled again, in ever-diminishing size, out to infinity. Caught in that dizzying cycle of funhouse refraction, I was seized by a sense of vertigo. A thousand arms moved as I put a hand out to the wall to keep from falling.

"Take a seat," Snow White ordered.

I staggered to the couch and collapsed.

"I'll get you a drink."

He left the room accompanied by a myriad mirrored images.

*"I know where you were. I had you followed—you were with* him!" *Her eyes blazed with anger and hurt. "I've suspected for a while. That's why I hired a private detective. He texted me pics from your escapades tonight. You went to a leather bar on Halsted——"*

*"Dale and I——"*

*"—then a hotel."*

*"—were working undercover."*

*"Liar! Faggot!"*

*"Watch your mouth."*

*"Watch yours! Where's it been? On his cock or ass—or both?"*

*She'd been drinking. As had I.*

*"Ellen!"*

*"Don't 'Ellen' me!" She whip-cracked me across the face with a stinging backhand. "Liar!" she repeated. "Cheater!" She raised her hand to strike again—*

*And I stiff-armed her—both hands into her breasts, hard. She fell straight back, knocked off balance, arms flying up into the air. Her head hit the baseboard with a sickening flesh-dampened snap of bone. She sprawled there, limbs akimbo, head crooked at an impossible angle. Eyes glazing over in a fixed stare. . . .*

*"Ellen?"*

Snow White re-entered the room. He carried a diminutive cup and saucer with such fastidiousness and concentration it struck me as faintly ludicrous and theatrical. Which it was. He set cup and saucer down on a glass-topped coffee table—beside a .40-caliber automatic pistol. I recognized the gun: a seventeen-round Glock with green-glow front sight and black Parkerized finish. A pistol authorized by the city of Chicago for police use. The model of pistol I used. I leaned closer. My gun? Couldn't tell. . . .

"Triple shot of espresso." Snow White seated himself in a well-upholstered armchair opposite me.

"Pity." I mocked his snobbish, clipped vocal inflection. "I was hoping for whiskey."

"You've had enough whiskey. Drink the espresso. Sober up."

"Why?"

"We've things to discuss. Such as why you killed your wife."

"I don't know what the hell you're talking about." I shot to my feet. "If this is some kind of joke—"

Snow White scissored one trousered leg over the other with a sibilant hiss of fabric. He looked at me intently. His eyes were of the coldest aquamarine blue—flint-chipped bits of Antarctica set in a flawless, strong-jawed face. The high cheekbones and narrow, classical nose gave the man the arrogant beauty of a Renaissance prince; though that tar-black mustache and goatee ruined the effect, rendering his countenance comic-book sinister.

His mouth fell open and he imitated—perfectly—the vocal pitch and cadence of Ellen's voice: *"Watch yours! Where's it been? On his—"*

"Stop!" I cried, raising both hands, palms outward, in a warding-off gesture. The hair prickled at the nape of my neck.

"You killed her," Snow White stated flatly. "Though it must be noted: It was an accident."

"Yes," I whispered.

I knew who he was now. Had, in fact, suspected for some time.

"Sit down." Snow White gestured. "Drink the espresso."

Why not? Where could I go? Dead broke, buzzed, memory-impaired.

I sat back down, raised the tiny cup to my chapped lips, and sipped. The espresso was warm, not boiling hot. Watered down. Dissolved ice cube? I drained the cup; set it back into its saucer on the coffee table.

"After you killed your wife, you left the house."

I frowned. "Did I?"

"You did." Flat declarative statement.

The caffeine from the espresso hit my bloodstream, overcoming the depressive effect of the alcohol. My pulse sped up.

"I can't . . . I can't remember."

"Sure you can."

Another bolt of agony in the brain. I groaned, doubled over.

"Where could you go? To whom could you flee?"

*I stood on the concrete porch of the brick ranch, repeatedly jabbing the doorbell button.*

*It swung open.*

*"Jack!" said Dale. "What—"*

*"Let me in."*
*"It's three in the morning, for god's sakes!"*
*"I think I've killed my wife."*

"He let you into his home. You argued."

"No." I shook my head in emphatic negative denial. I was weeping now, detesting myself for the show of weakness but unable to restrain my emotions. Or further repress my memory. "No . . . no."

"Dale wanted to call a patrol unit to your house to investigate. If your story was true you'd need a lawyer. If Ellen was merely injured and not dead she'd need urgent medical attention. Correct?"

I made no response.

*"I said—isn't that correct?"*

"Yes."

"You'd both been drinking—everyone had been drinking that night. In addition, you and Dale had done a couple lines of Peru's finest white-flake export product earlier—back in the hotel, before the gymnastics."

I was sobbing now—chest-heaving, stomach-convulsing paroxysms of horror, guilt, and shame.

"In Dale's house the argument grew heated. Physical."

I recalled—in strobe-like, nightmarish flashes of images and sound—what happened next. Curses, gagging, drumbeat of heels against hardwood floor. Bulged eyes, white-knuckled hands around neck, protruding tongue.

"You broke your wife's neck; you choked Dale to death."

Agony: sudden, searing, white-hot. All conscious thought ceased as if a light switch had been flicked off. Or I'd hit a brick wall at Mach ten.

"Not that anyone cares about your sordid little sex games." Snow White sounded mildly apologetic. "That business was between you, your wife, and your lover. No, it's the pattern of lies, duplicity, and self-loathing leading to double-murder that renders you a fit candidate."

A long, keening wail broke from my throat.

"Rage—it's the first word of the *Iliad* in the new Fagles translation. Did you know that?"

I curled up into a fetal position on the couch and jammed my palms against my ears. I would hear no more.

"What a perfect candidate you are. Congrats! You're hired. Can't wait till you meet the staff—they're very thorough and experienced, I assure you." He shifted position in the chair; stroked his goatee in thoughtful rumination. "They have centuries of experience. In fact, millennia. *Sit up!*"

I continued to wail, hands clasped over my ears.

Snow White came out of the chair, grabbed a fistful of my hair, and dragged me upright on the couch.

"Stop that infernal caterwauling! It's most unseemly." He punched me in the face.

I barely felt it. The blow stopped my wailing, however.

He put a hand—dense and cold as mausoleum marble—on my chin and forcibly tilted my head up until our gazes locked. "You murdered the two people you loved most in the world. In so doing, threw your career—your reputation—your life away."

I stared at him blearily, numb as a corpse.

"What will your police comrades say? The in-laws? Neighbors? Mother?"

Snow White removed his hand from my chin, stepped back around the coffee table, reseated himself in the chair. "You'll be hot news—for a while. Till the next homicidal sex scandal knocks you off the front pages."

I picked up the pistol—ten thousand identical arms in front and back of me synced to my movement. The gun was light as a bit of wind-blown thistle.

"I know who you are," I said. I placed the muzzle of the gun against my temple. It tickled. "Only . . ."

Sharp look. "What?"

"Back there in the park. Your breath."

He chuckled: the burbling rumble of some dark river of Avernus over antediluvian stone. "Immortal, yes—but flesh nonetheless. As you shall be. The better to embody sin."

"Dead but . . . fleshed."

"Precisely."

"Monster."

He demurred.

"Demon," I said.

"Warmer."

More cryptic taunts.

"Enough." I was weary of the game.

"Say it!" Snow White barked. "Utter the two-syllable moniker that trembles on your tongue: the one beginning in a sibilant and ending in a phoneme that constitutes a voiced alveolar nasal. Acknowledge the reality of what is happening here."

I tried. My lips locked.

His studied the manicured fingernails of his left hand.

"You're—" I said.

He raised an admonishing finger of the right. "No, *you* are."

Yes. It was an office, not a proper name.

I pulled the trigger.

# Lycanthropic Howl

Is the eternal truth man's fighting soul
Wherein the beast ravens in his own avidity?
                              —Richard Eberhart

'Twas blinding rage & fury stoked white-hot
that gnashed my teeth, balled fingers into fists
long ere the upright wolf, werewolf begot—
it seemed I saw but dimly through black mists
of seething hate & killing woe: This Earth
marked & mauled the beast with rending claws;
bald babe become a child of cruel mirth
& fierce upholder of amoral law:
All is permitted if one have but strength!
I roam dark woodlands now by glowing moon
whose wintry silvered spears illume dense lengths
of fragrant pine & black loam; I typhoon
with hell-froth spatter foam & revel howls
red thrashing meat 'neath cold-eyed, circling owls.

# Haunted House

That damn furnace—I've got to get it fixed or replaced. There are cracks in the combustion chamber and exhaust piping; I've patched these up with duct tape. This jury-rigged repair will have to hold until I can get a repairman out here in the spring. Money is tight and Christmas fast approaching.

My daughter was the first to see them: flickering images that broke up into gray-white noise, like actors performing scenes on silver nitrate film stock in which three to four frames were regularly dropped; or characters in a sitcom broadcast to a television whose rabbit-eared antennae reproduced a picture that regularly shimmered, wavered, and scrolled. The image-people hissed and popped with static. They appeared with increasing frequency as time went on, only to disappear as suddenly as they crackle-popped into existence: the dark-eyed, oftentimes alarmed-looking *paterfamilias* with a touch of gray at the temples; his handsome, chain-smoking wife; their tow-headed boys, ages eight and ten—young countenances alternately fascinated, then terrified when—upon occasion—they seemed to become aware of *us*. The flicker-family's hairstyles were quite odd: short-cropped mannish hair on the woman, an unkempt tangle of Bohemian-like curls on the man that extended below his shirt collar, effeminate long hair on the boys. I suspected sharply constrained finances precluded frequent barbering. Their clothing was odder still: the woman wore fluorescent-colored pantsuits and skirts of, frankly, an indecently short length; the man sported garishly colored wide-collared shirts and broad ties. The boys dressed in white-splotched jeans that had suffered the unfortunate ravages of bleach.

I instructed my family to ignore these intermittent interlopers. After all, they'd done us no harm. The flicker-image people were startling nuisances, yes—but they'd never appeared the least bit threatening. Therefore, I counseled, it was best not to overreact. And so we carried on, resolved not to be run out of our own home by this ongoing phenomenon—be it ectoplasmic in nature, electromagnetic imagery gone awry, or outré emanations from some parallel world.

I struggled to hold my family together in the midst of this ghostly onslaught. The year, of course, 1957: the post–World War II boom still in full swing. It is a time of ever-larger, ever-more powerful cars with shark-like tail fins bought on credit. The growing menace and popularity of degenerate rock 'n' roll. National Guardsmen called out in Little Rock, Arkansas, to ensure nine Black students can attend formerly all-white Central High School. Slinkys and Hula Hoops fly off store shelves; TV dinners appear in grocery stores. Motorcycle greasers sporting slicked-back hair and black leather jackets—part of a sex-crazed subculture of beatniks, hot-rodders, and juvenile delinquents—vex and alarm a troubled nation. Overseas: tumult and turmoil. Communist Russian satellites are launched into orbit, a Suez Canal crisis threatens global stability. The Viet Cong begin an assassination and bombing campaign in an obscure country in Asia called Vietnam. That line of Dickens has come 'round again: "It was the best of times, it was the worst of times . . ."

I endeavored to be a good, steadying-hand-on-the-tiller father in the midst of this confusion in which the old verities were crumbling and a new social order emerging.

"Father, is our house haunted?" Irena demanded to know.

"It is most certainly not," I replied with decisive firmness, as I had a hundred times before.

We were gathered 'round the dining room table. Wan light filtered through chintz curtains to speckle our faces, plates, glasses, and cutlery with a spider-webbed pattern of filigreed illumination.

This delicate tracery of light flickered in the gentle breeze stirring the curtains in the open casement windows.

"Then who . . ."

At a sharp look from my wife, Barbara; Irena's interrogative upglide trailed off, arrested into nothingness—like an inexperienced mountain climber attempting Mt. Everest first stumbling, then falling, into a crumpled heap, never to rise again, body soon mounded into indistinctness by new-fallen snow.

"Enough talk; let's eat," I commanded.

"Jim," Barbara said softly—in a tone at once reproachful, cautionary, and exhausted. She opened her arms wide in a gesture encompassing the table.

There was no food on the plates. No liquid in the glasses.

Dust motes glimmered in the golden, curtain-filtered light above our barren table: like the tiniest of magical fairies whirling and twirling in a stately, somehow mocking, saraband.

*Father, is our house haunted?*

The question came not from Irena this time but from one of the now-you-see-them, now-you-don't static-crackle/pop-hiss boys—the younger one; I didn't know his name. He was seated beside Irena at our table, staring at me with that familiar look of horrified fascination. The interloper family had shimmered into existence once again.

When?

I frowned. I hadn't noticed; I couldn't remember.

Seated at the table beside my wife—the mannish, ghostly wife.

Beside *me*—the gray-templed Bohemian *paterfamilias* of this most irritating, invasive clan.

Ghost-father laid his knife down on the table and fixed his son with a sober, unblinking stare.

*There are no such things as ghosts,* he declared.

*But they're right* there, the boy asserted, pointing directly at me—then at my wife. He didn't point to my daughter, but glanced right and shifted his chair some inches away from her.

*Bill, we've talked about this,* Ghost-mother said.

*Stop freaking us out,* Ghost-father admonished. *Keep this up and you'll go to bed without any supper. Imagination and fantasy are all well and good, but there's a time to give it a rest.*

*Indeed,* I thought to myself. *Indeed!* I felt a surge of empathy and beleaguered support for Ghost-father.

I opened my mouth to echo and applaud the man's words—but Barbara and Irena weren't there. It appeared I'd lost my audience.

I blinked. My head pounded; I placed shaking hands to my temples. I felt nauseous, weak, delirious. The world whirled—was I going mad? The room steadied; objects refocused into sharp relief.

*Damn them!* Cutting and running when things got hard—and after all I'd done to hold this family together. Barbara! Irena!

"I forbid you to leave," I admonished their empty chairs. Then, reiterating with more force: "I absolutely forbid it! You will return this instant. This is our house—our house! Do you hear?"

I've got to get that furnace fixed.

# Father's Bullet

## A Tale of the Apocalypse

It is the pastel-colored
swirling rainbow
unicorn dress
& glittering zircon tiara
that first catches my eye
daughter
when I spot you
amongst them.

I track your stumbling body through the 10X scope—
tremor in the hands; water in the eye.
Deep breath—
hold.
Partial exhale.
A light caress of the trigger
& the rifle bucks against my shoulder—

*Your face at your eighth birthday party:*
*how you*
*shone with love & joy*
*bent low over cake & candles,*
*drew in breath—*

\*　　\*　　\*

—the .300 grain Winchester magnum bullet
blows out your brains
stops
your idiot moaning & shuffling
in the front rank
of that
on-coming
slack-jawed horde.

# Not a Vampire

Dracula stalked across the sixty-inch plasma screen in maleficent splendor, crimson-and-black cape swirling about his tall, aristocratic form. The Count reached the edge of the castle roof and paused—one spidery, beringed hand resting on a crumbling battlement crenellation—and turned to show his aquiline-nosed profile and sharply upturned collar against the haloing moon.

"He's going to transform!" pajama-clad Derrick squeaked in excitement. He sat cross-legged on the carpeted floor in front of the TV, nose all but smudging the screen.

"Ssssh! Dad will hear you," Alex cautioned his brother, glancing upward at the ceiling. Mom and Dad were asleep this early A.M., but Dad was a notoriously light sleeper. If he caught his boys watching creature-feature films at three in the morning on a school night there'd be hell to pay. His father's sensitive hearing was the reason Alex had set the volume level of the TV to zero, rendering the movie a silent film. As for their older sister, Melinda—no monster fan, she—"The-Beast-that-Bitches" was on sleepover at a friend's house, so she wasn't a factor at present.

On-screen, wavy lines of distortion roiled the scene. Dracula—with the help of some creaky stop-motion effects—transformed into a leathery-winged bat, flapping off into the misty night to the accompaniment of distant wolf howls.

"Hee-hee-hee!" Derrick chortled. He twisted his head around to regard his older brother, one finger jabbing at the TV. "Drac is on the wing!"

Alex smiled. He couldn't help it; Derrick's enthusiasm was contagious.

Derrick scrambled to his feet. "Let's go up to the roof and fly tonight."

"In our pajamas?"

"Sure! It's the perfect time; no one's around."

As conversational responses went this was a non sequitur, but Alex knew what Derrick was driving at. Chances were indeed good that no one would spot them climbing onto the roof of their red-bricked two-flat at this ungodly hour of the morning.

"Keep your voice down," Alex cautioned again. "I swear to god, if you wake Dad up . . ."

"Let's *go*," said Derrick, tugging insistently at Alex's arm.

Alex reached for the remote and clicked the television off. "Flight school, huh?"

"Yeah!"

Alex set the remote down; got to his feet. "Then follow to the attic. Quietly! And limber up them wings, brother. I'll have no one crashing in *this* vampire squadron due to unstretched muscles."

Derrick padded in his older brother's wake across the living room, pinwheeling his outstretched eight-year-old arms, face contorted with concentration.

Evening of the next day found the boys seated around the dining room table with their sister and father; mother was in the kitchen engaged in meal preparation.

"Alex thinks he's a vampire. Go on, tell us how you've figured out you're *nosferatu*." Melinda's voice was both scornful and amused, a shrill weapon wielded with a sophisticate's cynical glee from her lofty station of high-adolescence against her middle-school brother. "Tell us how you've figured out you're the spawn of"—she dropped her voice into its lowest register—"Count *DRAK-koo-lah*." She underlined the absurd drama of this statement by crooking index fingers beside her mouth and chattering like a rabid gerbil.

"Hee-hee-hee," giggled Derrick. Anticipating another entertaining blow-up between brother and sister, he glanced from one to the other in bright-eyed glee. His black T-shirt—a color chosen in worshipful imitation of his older brother's gothic sartorial sense—bore a silk-screened logo of a yellow smiley face with a bullet hole in its forehead. A rivulet of crimson trickled from the hole. "Hee-hee-hee!"

Alex lowered his head. "I don't have to say nothing." Delicate, long-fingered hands extended Ichabod Crane–like from the cuffs of his black denim shirt as he toyed with his eating utensils. "Especially to you. So just shut up, okay? You just *shut up* already."

"Alex!" Mr. Donner spoke from the head of the table. "That's enough. We don't talk to each other like that, young man. Not in this family. Not at this table."

*"Aw!"* Alex's inarticulate cry was a martyr's plea for justice. "Did you hear what she just said?" He flung his arm out, indicating the moon-faced nemesis smiling smugly back at him from across table. His own features were contorted into a mask of sibling-hating fury. "She's mocking me to my face! She started it."

"Oh, for god's sakes." Mr. Donner snorted in disgust, in the manner of put-upon *paterfamiliases* everywhere attempting to shame their offspring into better behavior.

It didn't work.

"You take her side on *everything.*" Alex's voice broke on a high, squealing note. "It's not fair."

"I'll tell you what isn't fair," Mr. Donner said, massaging his temples with a wince. "This headache the both of you are giving me."

"Hee-hee-hee!" chimed in Derrick at Alex's elbow.

"Hey, you two," Mrs. Donner hollered from the kitchen, amidst bustling thumps and bangs that carried into the adjoining dining room, "knock it off in there!"

That irritated Melinda. "I'm not doing *anything*," she called out, purple-mascaraed eyes widening in indignation for the benefit of the family members surrounding her. "Except trying to talk sense to my brother." Her mouth hung open for an additional second or two after this statement, as if she'd gone into mild shock at the onslaught of her mother's unexpected persecution. "God!"

"She—" Alex began.

"Enough!" said Mr. Donner. "Please. Just . . . stop, already." He put a finger inside the collar of his dress shirt; ran it around his neck to loosen the fabric that was chafing against his skin. He was subject to hives when his stress levels climbed above a certain threshold; he fought now to remain calm in order to avoid another outbreak of burning itchiness on neck and chest.

To be sure, there was truth in Melinda's words—Alex *had* developed an obsessive and wholly unhealthy vampire fixation since the new year began. What the exact trigger of this obsession had been Mr. Donner was at a loss to know, but in the days immediately following the celebration of the winter solstice he'd noticed Alex reading one vampire novel after another. Bram Stoker's *Dracula*. Theodore Sturgeon's *Some of Your Blood*. Anne Rice's multi-volume contribution to the genre. And others. The boy finished *'Salem's Lot* in the course of a single day and spent the rest of the evening wandering their urban two-flat in a thoughtful daze. Posters, films, and comic books soon followed, similarly *nosferatu*-themed. Alex covered his bedroom mirror with black crepe paper; the walls became adorned with posters of Christopher Lee, Frank Langella, and Vampirella. Dozens of vampire-themed DVDs and omnibus volumes from the likes of Marvel, D.C., and Dark Horse Comics appeared on his bookshelves. He began dressing entirely in black and carrying a dragon-headed walking cane. An allergy to garlic developed— entirely psychosomatic, Mr. Donner was certain. Alex cut his personal hygiene back to a bare minimum, provoking the ire of his sister, who'd flung a bar of soap at his head once the odiferous funk resulting from a showerless three weeks had grown strong enough to gag a corpse-eating corpse.

And there was more. The boy had been spotted on the edge of the roof one night, flapping his arms and bunny-hopping into the air. Nature documentaries featuring rats, bats, and wolves were TiVoed for repeated reviewing. He'd refused to cut his nails until Mrs. Donner threatened to terminate his allowance, precipitating an epic late-night row of hoarse-voiced shouting, hot tears, and slammed doors. The drama had ended only after his wife pounded on Alex's locked bedroom door and vowed she'd "take the garden shears to those Kung-Fu talons if they weren't trimmed back to raptor length by morning, *you hear me in there young man?*"

It had all been . . . a bit of a trial. Still, adolescence was the time of life when young people tried on different roles, wasn't it? A tumultuous, confusing, and difficult time of raging hormones, freakishly growing bodies, and emotional impulsivity. All quite normal, really. Yes, all quite normal. Ridiculous posturing was to be expected; teenagers tried on and then discarded different personas with the same sudden-infatuation-become-almost-immediately-tired-indifference that informed their shoe- or clothes-buying, in endless search of an authentic self.

"Alex." Mr. Donner cleared his throat. "Let's talk about this vampire"—what *was* the right word?—"interest of yours, shall we?"

"Oh yes, let's do," said Melinda, mimicking an upper-crust British accent.

"I said *knock it off in there,* Melinda!" Mrs. Donner called from the kitchen.

Melinda folded white-bloused arms across her bosom and pouted, a spot of color blooming in each fatty cheek.

"What makes you think you're a vampire, son?"

No response from Alex. He toyed with the silverware on the table—*tink, clink* went the fork against the knife.

"Alex . . ." said Mr. Donner.

The boy sighed and raised his head. "I don't know."

"You don't know." A jumble of violent impulses raced through Mr. Donner's mind: *slap his face, throw a glass at his head, scream, pound the table, toss the idiot out the window . . . Deep breath.*

"I don't want to talk about it," said Alex.

"Ah, but that's just it, you see—we must talk about it," said Mr. Donner, his placid, kindly smile conveying infinite loving patience. "Son—do you sleep in a coffin at night?"

Derrick giggled. But his wide-eyed ruminative stare into the middle distance a second later betrayed his entrancement with the idea.

"Your father asked you a question," prodded Mrs. Donner from the kitchen.

"No," said Alex.

"Indeed, you do not!" said Mr. Donner. "Are you, then, frightened of crucifixes?"

"Well . . ." Alex considered.

Mr. Donner fought to keep irritation out of his voice. "I mean, do they harm you? Does the close physical proximity of a crucifix result in your experiencing agonizing pain?"

"No," admitted Alex.

"I see," said Mr. Donner. "Pray then, let us continue." He took another deep breath. "Can you fly?"

Melinda snorted, her pout broken by a smile immediately converted into inward-sucking cheeks.

*"Tell him!"* Derrick burst out. "You can do it! We've been practicing." He made a rapid flapping of chicken-wing arms in his chair.

Alex looked mortified. "I can't fly," he said.

"But we're working on it, aren't we?" persisted Derrick.

"No," said Alex, with a glare of coal-hot eyes at his brother, "we are *not.*"

Beads of perspiration formed on Mr. Donner's forehead.

Derrick was outraged. "Yes, we are!" he insisted. "Yes, we are!" To an eight-year-old there is no more irrefutable or persuasive tool of rhetoric than repetition. "And every time we practice we hop a little higher, hop a little higher, hop a little—"

Mr. Donner interrupted this manic recitation. "But as yet, no one has flown, have they?" Sweat ran into his eyes. He blinked it away. "No one has actually taken flight, hmm?"

"Not yet," Derrick said, crossing puny arms across his chest in stubborn intransigence. "But we will."

"Ah, now we're getting somewhere—my offspring are flightless," Mr. Donner confirmed. "Then that's one for grounded sapiens, zero for bat-winged vampires, eh?" He winked at Melinda. "Next item on the agenda: teeth. We come now to the matter of teeth." Mr. Donner bared his own in a winning smile: double rows of meticulously maintained enamel: polished, flossed and fluoride-rinsed to a startling twenty-first-century gleam. "Look carefully: are these food grinders pointed daggers?"

"No," said Alex. "Not yet. But—"

"No buts, boy, no buts!" Mr. Donner said. "It's a simple question; you've given a direct answer. It won't do to overcomplicate things." Turning to the runt of the litter, he prodded: "Derrick, how go your fangs, son?"

Derrick popped his mouth open, making a drawn-out "ahhhhh" sound, as if he were a patient in a doctor's office with tongue depressed. Teeth normal—though his lower right-front lateral incisor had recently loosened and fallen out, earning him a late-night pillowed dollar from the Tooth Fairy.

"Melinda?" prompted Mr. Donner.

Getting into the spirit of things, Melinda cocked her head to the right and gaped her mouth open with an expression of flash-frozen *joie de vivre,* as if she were a high-priced fashion model caught by a photographer's strobing bulb mid raucous laugh.

"Normal teeth-i-ses," pronounced Mr. Donner. "And you, Alex? What say you?"

"Aw, come on," said Alex, making a defeated motion with his hand. "You know our canines don't lengthen until we smell fresh blood."

"I'll take as a vote for dental normalcy," said Mr. Donner. He pressed his advantage. "Perhaps there is something to be learned from this negative—or rather, series of negatives." He cleared his throat. "I'm not trying to make you uncomfortable, elder son, but one must ask these questions of a"—his lips writhed in a rueful smile—"vampire."

"*Puh*-lease," said Melinda, with an orb-socketing roll of her eyes.

BANG! SLAM! went Mrs. Donner in the kitchen.

"Just a couple more questions," continued Mr. Donner. "Alex, look at me. Does the sun scorch your skin to the bone? Can you transform into a bat? A cloud of mist? Do we own a gloomy, cobweb-festooned ancestral castle somewhere in the mountains of Transylvania?"

Alex exhaled in exasperation.

Mr. Donner interpreted this response: "No, no, and no. So you see, son, the odds of you being a member of the crimson-caped, blood-drinking set are . . ." He threw his forearm up in front of his face, arching his brows and widening his eyes in mesmerist mimicry, ". . . small indeed, yes?"

"Duh," said Melinda.

Derrick unhappily chewed his lower lip.

Alex dropped his head again. This time it drooped so close to the table that all Mr. Donner could see of Alex's features was a tip of acne-reddened nose.

"Mm-llrgck to grrlick," said Alex.

"Head up," said Mr. Donner. "I'm sorry, I didn't quite catch that. Repeat, please."

Alex raised his head. He sighed, knowing the battle lost but determined to finish with whatever shred of dignity might still be mustered to account. "I said, *I'm allergic to garlic.*"

"True," said Mr. Donner. The boy had him there. "True. But all that means is . . . is . . ."

"THAT YOU MIGHT BE A WEREWOLF," Mrs. Donner shouted from the kitchen.

For a moment there was silence—Alex looking pained, Mr. Donner startled, Melinda incredulous, Derrick awestruck—then they met each other's eyes and exploded in laughter. Perfectly absurd!

"Rawrrr! Attack the werewolf," growled Mr. Donner, thrusting his arms out and pantomiming claw swipes at Alex's face. "Watch out! Here comes Father Werewolf."

"Yeah, yeah!" piped up Derrick, his shrill prepubescent voice thrumming with excitement. "I'm a werewolf too. Look out!" He tugged at Alex's right arm. "*Rawrrr! Rawrrr!* Gonna eat-cha! Eat-cha all up!"

"Ah-roo," dead-panned Melinda, voice devoid of all inflection, giving another sarcastic roll of the eyes. "Ah-roo."

Alex laughed long and hard, his self-consciousness and embarrassment—for the moment—gone.

The boy's laughter was music to Mr. Donner's ears: a happy, healthy, cleansing sound.

"What the hell is going on in here?" said Mrs. Donner with mock ferociousness, emerging from the kitchen with the naked body of a cloth-gagged young woman over her shoulder. Her eyes twinkled. "You guys sound like a bunch of animals." She heaved the woman onto the table, face up.

The woman's eyes were closed; her breathing short and shallow. The meat was unconscious.

"Care to do the honors?" asked Mrs. Donner.

"Thank you, yes," said Mr. Donner. He picked up a foot-long piece of stainless-steel cutlery from the table and gashed open the woman's throat. "Mmm-mmmm, smells good," he crooned, as scarlet fountained from the wound.

"It's the rub," said Mrs. Donner, seating herself beside Melinda. "Onion powder, ground sage, and thyme." Triggered by the intoxicating iron-rich tang of freshly flowing human blood, her canines grew pointed and overlong in her mouth.

The same transformation occurred in the other members of the Donner family: the appearance of their canines took on a savage and pronouncedly bestial aspect.

"Well, dig in, everyone," Mr. Donner invited. "God knows there's plenty here."

They tore into the food. For the next couple of minutes all conversation ceased as they slaked a peculiar piercing thirst and satisfied ravenous hunger.

Mr. Donner chewed, swallowed. "Still think you're a vampire, Alex?"

"Or a werewolf," Mrs. Donner added, dabbing her greasy chin with a napkin. "Elder gods save us!"

Alex shook his head. "No. I just wanted to believe . . . well, vampires are cool and all, you know?"

"Puh-*lease,*" Melinda puh-leased again.

"We know, son." Mr. Donner gestured with his fork. "But neither you nor anyone else at this table is a fanged flying creature of the night, I assure you. It's like I've always said: we're simply a cozy little lovin' family of——"

"—hemoglobin-activated carnivores," Alex, Melinda, and Derrick chorused together, having heard this particular shop-worn bromide from their father for the umpteenth time.

Mr. Donner beamed.

# Märchen (Fairy Tales)

Magda recites the ancient *fabeln*
    savage, dark, & grim:
wolves & witches, lost little boys,
    kobolds, trolls—"Again!"

Wide-eyed Günter demands of *mutter*
    entranced by her cadenced words;
fire crackling in field-stoned *flett*
    the cattle lowing, a weird

counterpoint to alto utterance
    in that shadowed, smoky *einhaus*—
the pungent scent of new-mown hay
    a whisper-squeak of *grau maus.*

Outside: the rising howl of wind.
    A flash! A rolling boom!
Thor unleashing lightning & thunder;
    inside, in warmth & gloom

Günter hangs on every word
    bewitching *mutter* chants;
his scalp hair prickles; he pants in fear—
    Ghouls! Ghosts! Vampires! Plants:

nightshade, hemlock, stinging nettle
　　　towering holy oak;
lambent flame & groaning stone
　　　oily corpse-black smoke.

The tales are void of sentiment:
　　　hard, unflinching, medieval;
& Günter knows a shivery thrill
　　　of terror quite primeval.

Scheming warlocks, moaning spectres
　　　fiends miniscule & fey;
berserker giants, monstrous *vaters*,
　　　beasts that stalk & slay.

Magda recites the ancient *fabeln*
　　　savage, dark, & grim:
wolves & witches, lost little boys,
　　　kobolds, trolls—"Again!"

# The Water Is Warm, Mommy

Tragedy is built of one part fate, one part willing surrender to nihilistic impulses and perverse compulsions. It is both existential horror and chaotic mystery, striking the person of Apollonian and Dionysian temperament alike. Above all else, tragedy crushes the spirit and breaks the mind, leaving psychic ruin—and manifold death—in its wake.

—Anonymous

She directed her voice at the cellphone propped against a half-empty coffee cup on the kitchen table. Her left arm was clutched tightly against her chest, supporting the elbow of her right arm. A lit cigarette smoldered in a hand whose nails were bitten to the quick.

"The boys are fine," said Carol. "*I'm* fine. There was no fighting between them today. Sibling rivalry took the day off."

"That's good to hear," sounded a voice of deeper timber from the cellphone speaker. "If they give you any trouble, tell 'em Daddy said—"

"You don't have to keep checking up on us like this. I resent it." She took a last drag on her cigarette, exhaled. Stubbed it out in the overflowing ashtray beside the coffee cup.

Her husband's voice sounded tinny and unimaginably distant. "That's not what this is——"

"Sure it is; sure it is!" Carol interrupted, repeating this succinct and pointed demurral like an existentially challenged character in a David Mamet play compulsively reiterating. Her eyes narrowed behind a concealing cloud of bluish-gray cigarette smoke. "Every day. Right at this time. Every day you call—two o'clock sharp. Check up on wifey; make sure she's still upright and conscious. Hasn't downed the drain cleaner yet."

"Honey——" sounded the far-off voice.

48

"Fashioned a noose from sheets in the laundry," Carol continued. "Jumped in front of a truck."

"That's not fair," said cellphone voice.

"Drowned the children—"

"*Carol!*" rasped the voice.

Carol snatched up the phone, made as if to throw it against the wall. Hesitated.

The poorly modulated voice rattled the cell phone's speaker, distorting her name: "*Rarrl! Rarrl!*"

Carol lowered the cell phone to her lap. "What?" she asked dully.

"I'm sorry; you faded away there. I could barely hear you. You sounded a million miles away."

"Did I . . . ?" said Carol.

*What had she been thinking that evening? Nothing much, really. Four months ago. Brooding upon the utter futility of things. Growing worry over her inability to concentrate. Incoherent, unfocused intimations of horror and despair. And feeling? Utter exhaustion. Suppressed rage she could not—would not—acknowledge. Physical pain: gastric distress, aching joints, a head-splitting migraine. The weight of depression pressed down upon her like a ton of wet cement—congealing, restricting her movements, suffocating. Dinner was cooking in the oven as she bathed the boys, the soapy bath water discoloring with the grime scrubbed off Simon and Joel. She forced the boys' heads down—down—* (what was she doing?) *beneath the water. They thought it a game at first. Howard, hearing the boys* in extremis, *kicked open the locked door and rushed in as the boys thrashed and gurgled . . .*

"Take me off speaker, please."

"Why?" said Carol.

"So that I can hear you better."

*You mean so that I can hear* you *better,* Carol corrected the statement in her mind.

Nevertheless, Carol took Howard off speaker and brought the phone to her ear.

He spoke.

A beat.

"Of course, I did," she said. "Both tablets—just as the doctor ordered." Another beat. "I think this new drug is working much better. Less interaction with the high blood pressure, diabetes, and sleeping medications." Beat. "Uh-huh. No digestion issues or burning bile. Less brain fog. Dissociation." Beat. "Yep. I'll make the entry in my gratitude journal after you get home." Beat. "Yes, of course. Yes. I'm more than glad; I'm relieved." A longer beat. "I'm not sure; they've been pretty quiet this past hour." Longest beat. "Building something in the bedroom. I was about to go and check. Do you want me to put them on?" Beat. "Okay." Beat. "Okay; sure." Beat. "Roast ham. With baked potatoes and sweet corn." Beat. "No greens for a salad; sorry." Beat. "You'll stop? Thank you. Remember to get tomatoes and cucumbers." Beat. "Around six, then. It'll keep if you're late." Beat. "I love you, too."

Carol ended the call and set the cellphone down on the table. Picked up her pencil. Considered the crossword puzzle in the paper spread out before her. Four-letter word, *down:* first jealous brother.

Easy. She penciled in the answer in shaky block capitals: *C-A-I-N.* Too easy . . .

The small color television atop the kitchen counter droned on in the background: ". . . naval vessels have crossed the median line into the strait around Taiwan. Simultaneously a dozen Chinese fighter jets made an incursion of Taiwanese airspace in the north, as president Xi Jinping asserted his country's right to . . ."

Carol dropped the pencil—picked up the television remote and clicked the TV off—set the remote back down.

A lock of black hair fell in front of an eye. She pursed her lower lip and blew it out of the way.

Time to get dinner started, the oven preheated.

But first she needed to take her anti-depressant medication.

She got up from the table, bathrobe whispering about her ankles as she padded across the tile floor in her slippered feet and down a short hallway to the bathroom.

The door to the boys' bedroom, opposite the bathroom, was open. She heard Joel instruct Simon: "No, over here. Put the T-Rex *here,* in front of the boulders facing the tanks . . ."

Carol stepped into the bathroom and opened the medicine cabinet above the sink. Pulled out the bottle of Paroxetine, unscrewed the lid, set the lid down on the sink. Shook two of the powder-blue tablets into her palm. Stared at them a moment.

She'd been taking this new drug for a couple of weeks, but had stopped taking the tablets yesterday. She was gaining weight. Having difficulty sleeping. Experiencing bouts of "zombified" behavior: moments of confusion, disorientation, forgetfulness. Outright panic. She'd lied to Howard about the side effects to keep him from needlessly worrying. It wasn't a total lie. The two previous SSRIs she'd been on had affected her even worse.

Carol swallowed hard, as if the tablets were going down her throat. Sympathetic reflex behavior. Dry mouth.

*I don't need these any more. I'll stop for a while and monitor how I feel. I'll get over this depression by an act of will. It's a matter of character; a test of my ability to control my own mind. And if I fail . . . if I find myself having recurrent negative thoughts and compulsions, I'll start taking the medication again. That is, if I really need to . . .*

She flipped up the toilet seat, flung the tablets into the bowl, and flushed. Screwed the lid back on the bottle of Paroxetine; put the bottle back into the medicine cabinet.

From the basement came the rhythmic *thump-thump-thump* of a load of clothes tumbling in the dryer.

Carol drifted back down the hallway into the kitchen. Turned on the oven. Set the temperature to 400 degrees to preheat.

This task accomplished she sat back down in the kitchen chair, shook a new cigarette out of the pack, stuck it in her mouth. Picked up the lighter beside the coffee cup, thumb-clicked it to ignition, brought the flame to the end of her cigarette. Inhaled. Tobacco crackled; the end of the cigarette glowed orange-red. She set the lighter back down, exhaled. Watched as roiling streams of smoke softened and diffused the light about her. One of the three bulbs in the overhead fixture was out. It was still far too bright in the kitchen . . .

"*Okaaaay,* we're ready! You can come in now!" The voice came drifting down the hallway from the boys' bedroom: shrill, insistent, pre-pubescent.

Carol didn't immediately answer this hail.

There came a pounding of onrushing feet.

"Mommy, *come see!* Come see! Come see! Mommy, *come see now!*" Six-year-old Simon, sporting Superman underpants and T-shirt, danced in a frenzy of excitement before the chrome-legged kitchen table. The black plastic frame spectacles on his young features gave him a comical air of gravitas. One-year-older Joel, in jeans and red suspenders, peered over his shoulder, expression equally urgent.

Carol set her burning cigarette down on a notch in the ashtray's rim and rose from her chair, a practiced smile on her lips. Not a Duchenne smile, to be sure—there was no contraction of the obicularis oculi muscle and hence no raising of the cheeks forming crow's feet around the eyes, merely a contraction of the zygomatic major raising the corners of the mouth.

"All right; I'm coming," Carol said. "Keep your pants on, Super-man."

"Keep your pants on, Superman! Keep your pants on, Superman!" Simon chanted. To a six-year-old repetition is the soul of wit.

In an anticipatory rush of squeals and excited stage-whispers, among which the refrain "she's coming; she's coming!" featured prominently, the boys dashed ahead of her and into their bedroom.

Once the three of them were across the threshold of the boys' *sanctum sanctorum,* Joel spun around and threw his arms out to encompass the room. He tolled the glory, proud as any Caesar who found Rome brick and left it marble: "We built this."

Carol glanced around the room, taking in the bewildering jumble of rocks, sea shells, toys, and wooden building blocks arranged atop the tucked-tight comforters of both beds and the carpeted floor.

"Our army base," Joel said, stepping carefully over stacked clusters of colored blocks. Plastic infantrymen stood, knelt, and lay prone in and around the one- and two-story structures in poses of frozen aggression; armored vehicles, robots, and fighter aircraft mixed in amongst their ranks.

"Well . . ." Carol said.

Joel looked at her, his need for approval and encouragement naked on his face.

"Yes," Carol said. "Very nice! Well done."

"This is the road to the Lava River," Simon piped up, stepping unsteadily beside a double row of rocks and sea shells that wound between the beds, terminating at the closet doors.

"There are monsters on both sides of the road," Joel said, pointing out the bright primary-colored dinosaurs and hairy-legged rubber insects arranged in irregular formations of mandible and claw on either side of the road.

"They try and eat the army men, but the army men shoot them," Joel explained, somewhat didactically.

"With bazookas." Simon giggled. He mimicked holding one of those cumbersome World War II–era weapons in his tiny arms.

"And hand grenades and mortars," Joel added.

"I see," said Carol.

"We used all the rocks and seashells from our boxes. It took us a *million* hours—" Simon staggered, threw out a steadying hand to the bed beside him. His clutching fingers snagged the comforter and caused a row of Apatosaurs to fall over.

*"Watch out!"* Joel screamed. "You're knocking the dinosaurs down!"

"Joel——" said Carol.

Simon stared, visibly irritated, at the row of toppled dinosaurs.

"He's *always* knocking everything over. 'Cause he's a stupid clumsy *idiot,*" Joel fumed.

"That's enough, young man," said Carol.

"I'll fix it." Simon, beginning to panic, scrabbled at the row of fallen Apatosaurs on the bed, hands flitting like frantic moths over the toppled beasts. But for every two he re-erected, another one got knocked down again.

Carol fixed her unblinking stare on Joel. "I think you have something to say to your brother."

Joel lowered his head.

"I'm waiting." said Carol.

"Sorry," Joel mumbled to his feet.

"Look at your brother," Carol ordered. "Say it to his face."

Joel raised his head and turned; body weighted with shame. "I'm sorry, Simon."

Simon shrugged, continued fumbling with the dinosaurs.

Joel took the two steps to his brother, embraced him. "Really, I'm sorry," he said. "*Really* I am."

Carol smiled. The crow's feet at the corners of her eyes wrinkled this time: a genuine maternal smile.

Below, the dryer chugged to a stop.

"You'll play nice with each other if I leave this room?" asked Carol.

Joel disentangled himself from Simon to give his mother a look of fervent penitential contriteness. "I will," he vowed.

"We will," echoed Simon.

Carol regarded the boys. "Okay," she said. "Remember—you promised." Then, seemingly satisfied, she exited the bedroom, transited the short hallway into the kitchen, and continued down a flight of stairs into the basement.

Above her head—a muffled patter of feet on the floor as the boys resumed their play.

Carol walked to the dryer and opened it. An exhalation of dry heat hit her face. There was an aroma of toasted lint in the air. She began to pull clothes out, one at a time—pants, shirts, blouses, skirts—and fold them atop the dryer under the harsh light of the naked bulb that dangled above the deep sink beside the washer and dryer. Once a stack of clothing reached a foot high, she lifted it into a blue plastic laundry basket atop the washer.

Upstairs: laughter and the scamper of little feet.

"Whistle while you work," Carol advised herself. She whistled tunelessly.

The laundry basket filled; the dryer emptied.

After a time the oven door banged open above her head.

Carol froze, hands on the laundry basket. "Joel? Simon? What's going on up there?"

The oven door banged shut.

"Nothing," Joel called out.

"What do you mean, *nothing?*" Carol's voice climbed a couple of octaves. "I just heard the oven door open and shut!"

"Nothing," Joel reiterated as non sequitur.

"Simon?" called Carol.

No response.

*"Simon!"* shouted Carol.

Silence.

*Four-letter word*, down: *first jealous brother.*

Carol was in motion.

*No fighting between them today. Sibling rivalry took the day off.*

She took the steps two at a time, laundry basket forgotten in the damp mustiness of the shadowed half-light behind her.

*He's* always *knocking everything over. 'Cause he's a stupid clumsy* idiot*!*

Carol all but leapt up the last four steps. She strode into the kitchen, face wan and grim.

Joel retreated from her, hands upraised in a warding off gesture.

"Simon!" Carol demanded. *"Where is he?"*

The answer came in a rush: "He wanted to see the inside of the oven so I showed it to him, but it was hot and it scorched us so I closed it again."

"No . . ." Carol said. She fell to her knees beside the oven. "Oh, no . . ." She yanked the oven door open. Peered inside. Closed it again.

Joel stared at her; eyes wide with disbelief and horror. "Did you think . . . Did you think that I . . ." His hands twisted and untwisted his red suspenders. "What's *wrong* with you?"

Carol blew that irritating, errant lock of black hair out of her eyes again. "Joel—"

"You did! *You did!* You thought I put Simon in the oven!" Joel burst into outraged tears, turned from her and pounded down the hallway. He ran into the bedroom crying out, "Simon! Simon!"

Carol followed, entering the bedroom just as Simon squirmed out from under his bed. Looking confused and alarmed—a length of yellow thread caught in his mussed-up hair—he adjusted his spectacles, switching his gaze from Joel to Carol in bewilderment.

Joel grabbed Simon, pulling him back from their mother. He kicked over buildings, soldiers, vehicles, and monsters, heedless of the wanton destruction inflicted on their carefully constructed world of ordered violence, until he came up hard against the closet doors. There he used Simon as both totem and shield, arms clasped protectively tight around his brother's chest.

A small bird beat within Simon's fragile rib cage, delicate wings awhirl: *flutter ka-thump, flutter ka-thump . . .*

"He's okay!" Joel said, hugging Simon with fierce convulsive clench-es, feeling the strong, heart-pumped flow of Simon's blood pulsing steadily against his cheek as his brother's temples throbbed, throbbed. "He was hiding! He was only hiding from you! Tell her, Simon. *Tell* her!"

But Simon—rigid, trembling—had lost his voice.

"Joel." Carol dropped to one knee, opened her arms. "I'm so sorry. I made an awful assumption. I'm so sorry . . . baby . . ."

"I hate you!" Joel said, red-faced—hyperventilating.

Carol winced, drew in her breath. "I know you don't mean that." Arms still wide open.

*I've made a terrible mistake. I must fix this,* Carol thought. *Fix this . . .*

"I *hate* you! I *hate* you!" Joel reiterated. "You actually thought I put Simon in the oven!"

Simon broke away from his brother and climbed into bed. He rolled over on his side, stuck his thumb in his mouth. Pulled a pillow over his head.

Carol dropped her arms and stood up. "I'm so sorry," she whispered.

"Go away!" Joel screamed, face purpling with rage and hurt. *"Leave me alone!"*

"Okay," said Carol.

A beat.

"Okay, Joel."

She revolved on her heels—dazed—and drifted out of the room.

Joel's legs went out from under him and he slid down the closet doors—head twisting left-right, left-right, left-right in denial and negation—until he was sitting cross-legged on the toy-strewn bedroom floor. He put his face in his hands and sobbed, body convulsing as if with strong electrical current.

Two weeks later Carol drew a bath for the boys after having washed down a three-quarter-full bottle of sleeping pills with a half-carafe of Pinot Grigio. She called them to her once the tub had filled and stripped off their clothes. (*Must move quickly.*) "I hope the water isn't too cold."

Simon and Joel stood naked beside the tub, clutching their bath toys: Simon a T-Rex; Joel a pirate ship.

Joel, braver and more assertive than his younger brother, clambered over the side of the tub and sat down in the sudsy water. "The water's warm, Mommy."

"Not too warm?" Carol asked.

"No," said Joel. He splashed the white-frothed water with his hands. "Just about perfect."

Simon joined him in the tub.

After their baths the boys played in the bedroom till twilight fell and the street lights came on outside. They joined their mother on the couch in the living room as the sky darkened—Joel nestled against Carol's right side; Simon her left.

When the front door opened and Howard stepped inside he glanced at them yet gave no visible reaction.

"Carol?" he called.

The house remained silent.

"Carol!" Howard called out again, voice climbing to a higher register. *"Simon! Joel!"*

He left his coat on, dropped his house and car keys into a bowl on a shelf in the foyer, and stepped into the living room, peering down the hallway that led to the corpses in the bathroom.

Carol sat on the couch, hands scuttling like demented crabs over her lap—thighs—belly. Her fingers found each other—locked into clasped hands—broke apart again.

Simon and Joel ran to their father—

      they ran to their father—

           they ran to their father—

until the house was no longer there.

# Fat Man and Yellow-Eyes

### A Ghoulish Tale

I met a ghoul of yellow eyes
& protruding, rat-like teeth
feasting in the catacombs
that warped & woofed beneath

the stately old ancestral home
that long buried its dead
in ornate coffins sealed against
the haunting, gnawing dread

of daggered fingernails prying up
what tradesmen hammered shut
to keening bleatings of feckless priests
of manicured, perfumed cut.

"Fiend!" cried I, "Foul cannibal!
Eater of necrotic flesh!
You dare make meal of beloved kin
interred for eternal rest?"

Yellow-Eyes snickered, prehensile snout
matted with fatty gore.
"I should let such rich meat go to waste?
I think not! Bring me more!

You lecture me, fat carnivore?
Have you never paused to wonder
why family forbids its undertakers
from embalming those who blunder

across the river Styx to regions
forever lost to light—
realms infernal, dark eternal
devouring, rabid night?"

I turned & fled, mocking laughter
ringing in my ears,
hot blood surging in my veins
taking counsel of my fears

I hobble-bopped away as fast
as girth & breath would let
my frigid soul, grown old & cold
fair-shriveled at the threat

of ghoulish implication
could reel & blunder down the hall.
*The hideous fate awaiting me!*
I sobbed—weaved on, appalled.

In years to come, fell demon rum
steadied shattered nerves.
I fasted: became a brittle twig;
reflected, as death neared

great-great grandpa would never dine
upon the flesh he'd hoped
would sustain him in his fetid lair—
I went up in flame & smoke.

# Come Haltingly, on Lame Feet

The old man sported a black eyepatch and unkempt salt-and-pepper beard. He cocked his head to one side, considering the block letters on the marquee above him, breath misting white in the icy early A.M. air.

WEDNESDAY'S SPECIAL
BOTTOMLESS POT O' COFFEE & TOAST
$2.99

"Woden's Day," the old man read aloud, teeth chattering like knuckle bones spilled on mausoleum marble. "Lucky me." The threadbare overcoat draping his withered frame flapped in a sudden gust of wind, causing him to tighten his grip on the brass-headed oak cane that took his weight.

A pickup truck displaying more Bondo and rust-colored primer than black-painted steel powered in from the street, loose pipe rattling in its bed on the hard 90-degree turn. It *rumba-rumba'd* into the parking lot in a thunder of unmuffled exhaust, the driver's-side mirror whapping the old man in the upper arm as it nosedived into a handicapped space and came to a rocking stop.

"Bastards," muttered the derelict.

Three men tumbled from the truck shod in thick-soled combat boots. Mohawk and Longhair wore denim jackets. The driver, a hulking beast with shaved skull and goatee, wore a duster of indeterminate color whose tattered edges brushed the ground as he led the way across the parking lot. The men strode across the asphalt with the confident, powerful strides of uncaged tigers.

The old man took in the back of Mohawk's jacket as the trio passed him on their way into the diner: a grinning Special Forces death's-head sporting a jaunty green beret sighting down the barrel of an M-16 assault rifle. Above this iconographic depiction of death arched the legend: *Don't run. You'll just die tired.*

Goatee wrenched the door open for his compatriots and held it till the old man reached him. "Go on in, Pops. I got ya covered." His breath was a sour stench of beer and cigarette smoke. Silver SS runes glittered under an ear from a four-link length of jeweler's chain.

The old man grunted in acknowledgment of the held door—small enough recompense for almost getting run over.

Goatee came in behind him, running a skull-and-crossbones be-ringed hand over his bald pate. They caught up to Mohawk and Longhair beside the *Please Wait To Be Seated* sign.

Longhair removed his jacket revealing arms of corded muscle. His black T-shirt sported the charming bon mot: *If You Can Read This, The Bitch Fell Off.* A swastika was tattooed on the back of his neck. It was a symbol the old man felt certain, on this particular specimen of humanity, signified neither reverence for the Viking sun wheel nor Hindu notions of karmic rebirth.

The old man took a step back to distance himself from the trio and glanced around the diner.

A stoop-shouldered man in a powder-blue suit read a Bible at the counter, repeatedly reseating his red-framed glasses on the bridge of his nose with the pad of his thumb as he turned the pages.

Four young men in track suits and gold chains lounged around a ta-ble crowded with sandwiches and sodas. "Little sumpin'-sumpin', all I's saying." One of the young men gesticulated for emphasis. "A C-note for the refloat, Dawg. Cross my palm wit da Benjamin!"

In a corner booth two women in their early twenties sipped coffee. The blonde, craning forward to catch some wry, *sotto-voce* comment made by her Black companion, unleashed a burbling laugh in tandem with a delighted clap of her hands. A pearl necklace draped against a dark blue silk dress shone yellow in contrast to the startling whiteness of her teeth.

Her companion flashed an acknowledging smile. She had a narrow, wary face made more skeletal by high cheekbones and malnourishment. Restless hands busied themselves on the table: knife moved a centimeter over on its paper napkin, salt and pepper shakers adjusted once . . . twice . . . yet again . . . before returning to the dark sleeves of her sweater to pluck at non-existent lint.

"Be right witcha." A clench-jawed hostess with a giant oval *Ask Me About Our Strawbellicious Ice-cream Waffle* button pinned to her blouse got up from the booth where she'd been quietly chain-smoking and escorted Goatee and his pals to a booth across the aisle from the women. A dozen trundling footsteps later and Grim Bertha was back in front of the old man, yawning into a fist. Her pancake makeup had cracked into flaking crevices. Blotchy mascara blackened doughy eyes, giving her the appearance of a rather gauche, ill-tempered, corpulent raccoon. "Smoking-or-nonsmoking?"

It took the old man a beat to decode this polysyllabic interrogation. "Nonsmoking, please."

He was led to a leatherette booth beside the juvenile gangsters' table. A rip in the once overstuffed maroon seat had been patched with duct tape. He laid his cane on the tabletop and shrugged out of his overcoat. The kids' eyes flicked to him and away again; their manic, brain-stem dialogue built around the words *bitch, faggot,* and *motherfucker* stuttering for a moment at the distraction.

A busboy sporting a scar from ear-to-chin slammed a glass of water down in front of the old man and vanished as the top third of the glass's contents sloshed onto the table.

The old man gazed soberly at the spilled water. His eyeless socket throbbed. Ye gods! The price he'd once paid for a single sip of that precious, life-sustaining fluid, drawn from the well of secret knowledge . . .

Outside, the first flakes of the forecasted snowstorm began to fall.

"You ready to order, or do you need a moment?"

He looked up at the waitress who'd materialized beside him. Her smile didn't touch her eyes, so the old man lowered his own to examine the bit of dried egg yolk stuck to the tabletop. "I'd like," he began, then broke off as a series of wet, whooping coughs shook his grizzled frame. Thinning gray hair bounced on his scalp.

The waitress did a half-roll of unblinking basilisk eyes.

Across the aisle one of the boys observed, "Dr. Death's bringing up a lung."

"Medium-rare, yo." Laughter round-robined the table.

"Toast and coffee, please," the old man managed when he could catch his breath.

"Decaf or regular? White or wheat?"

"Regular. Wheat."

"You have an accent," the waitress observed with brutal, parochial directness. "I can't quite place it. It's German, right? Or Danish?"

The old man absently stroked the knuckle hair of his left hand with the fingers of the right, a gesture both ruminative and curiously delicate. Though decrepit he had the strong, blunt fingers of a master sculptor or stone mason. "Something like that."

The flame of curiosity blew out on the waitress's face. She scribbled on her pad, spun around, and marched off with a whisper-crumple of starched dress and creak of crepe-soled shoes.

From the kitchen came a crashclatter of dishes followed by peals of laughter.

The old man settled into the seat clenching his teeth against the chills that shook his frame. A good sign. It meant the warmth of this bright, vulgar place was loosening muscles long knotted against the cold. There was a time he could take the cold . . .

*Knee-deep in a drift of crimson snow, he hurls an iron-tipped spear. It whistles like the steed of a Valkyrie—the weapon describing a short, un-*

*erring, lightning-like arc—and thunks into scaly flesh. A gout of scarlet! The beast topples.*

*Snarling, the horned monstrosities fall back.*

*He reaches for the double-bladed battleaxe hanging from his belt. An ancient war cry breaks from his throat—a high, keening song of ice and steel . . .*

"Hi. How you feeling this evening?" Quick flash of smile. Round, red-rimmed glasses—the Bible reader from the counter. "Sorry, guess I should say morning." A glance at his watch for verification of the lateness of the hour, followed by an extended hand. "Daniel Whittaker. Hope I'm not intruding."

The old man measured the Bible-man with eyes like falcon strikes. "You want to know how I feel. I feel"—he said, spreading his palms against the tabletop and squaring his shoulders against the back of the booth—"like an old dog with a boar's tusk buried in its belly." Another violent series of coughs *brak-a-brakked* his chest. He fumbled a hand-kerchief to his lips, hacked into it.

"Good grief," Daniel said, moving his outstretched hand onto the old man's shoulder. "That sounds pretty bad. Awful, really."

The old man coughed one more chest-rattling, phlegmy cough—spat a wad of bloody mucous into the brown-stained cloth—and folded the handkerchief away. "Sit down."

Daniel slid into the booth seat opposite him. "Thank you."

The waitress returned. "Here ya go." A plate of burnt toast clattered onto the table. She poured out a cup of coffee, turned to Daniel. "You?"

"No thanks." Daniel waved her off. "I'm over there," he elaborated, indicating the spot where a slimline briefcase, cellphone, and leather-bound Bible marked his place at the counter.

The waitress's nostrils gave the merest twitch and she was gone.

"A repast of toast and java," observed the old man. "A humble enough meal, certainly; but it keeps the bugbears away."

"Bugbears abhor bread and coffee?"

The old man nodded solemnly.

Daniel searched the old man's face but could find no hint of levity there. He was still processing this comment when Goatee leaned out of the booth and murmured something to the women across from him, eliciting soft-voiced replies.

"Tanyika," Goatee repeated, addressing the Black woman with sardonic courtesy.

"Sonja." An inclination of his head to the blonde.

Sonja half turned away; Tanyika hid behind a raised coffee cup.

Stung by this tepid response Goatee blared, "Aw, c'mon, ladies; don't be like that! I'm in a partyin' mood; aren't you? Par-*tay*, par-*tee*, par-*tigh!*" Then, with a leer at Tanyika. "Tonight only, what say you to a little race-mixing with your Aryan overlords, eh?"

The women exchanged whispered comments.

"Hey, I'm talking to you two." A boozy, lecherous grin punctuated Goatee's challenging hail.

The blood drained from Sonja's face.

Tanyika glared. "Go choke yourself, creep."

To which admonishment Goatee popped a stiff-armed fascist salute, accompanied by an open-mouthed fluttering of tongue.

Longhair shrieked a Capuchin-monkey laugh, causing Mohawk to lean over and mutter into his ear. Longhair nodded, addressed his next comment to their leader: "I ain't eatin' no nigger, Kurt. But save some of that white fish for me."

"Shut up, Lenny," said Kurt, stroking his goatee. "You're discomfiting my ladies here." Craning forward, he offered the women a wide grin. "Pay no attention to Lenny, darlings. His momma dropped him often as a child—right on his goddamn bullet head."

Longhair Lenny shrieked again.

"Do you have to do that?" Mohawk asked. "I mean, Jesus-fucking-Christ . . ."

"Fuck you, Vince," Lenny retorted happily.

Vince ran his fingers through his mohawk and scowled.

Four booths back, the old man turned to Daniel. "You see the scum I am forced to walk amongst now." A prominent blue vein throbbed at his temple. "Degenerates, psychopaths, loud-mouthed bullies. An embarrassment to the race. They dare to consider themselves representatives of my people, exemplars of Nordic culture. Gods forebear! They are but thugs, churls, vagabonds. Baseborn brutes who dare to wear the sacred runes in their ears. Look—that one has the sun wheel tattooed into his neck."

"Yes," said Daniel. He made no move to turn around. Instead, he fished a business card out of his inside suitcoat pocket, laid it down on the table. "I want you to call this number if you need help: food, shelter, clothing."

The old man grimaced. "I am homeless."

"I suspected as much. That's why—"

"And in need of no help but the prayers of those destined for Valhalla."

Daniel's rigidified features gave his face time to catch up with his brain.

"But thank you for the offer, just the same." The old man glanced down at the card as he slathered jam over a slice of blackened bread. "'The Evangelical Church of the Risen Christ,'" he read aloud. "'Minister Daniel Whittaker.'"

"Just Daniel, please."

"A good name, 'Daniel.' It means 'The Judgment of God.'"

"You speak Hebrew?"

"Rarely." The old man took a bite of his toast, swallowed. "What do you think the judgment of God is, Daniel?"

"A fateful lightning of His terrible swift sword." The minister thumb-pressed his glasses to reseat them more firmly on the bridge of his nose. "Deferred for those who accept Jesus Christ as their Lord and Savior. But I didn't approach you to preach. May I ask *your* name, sir?"

The old man's eyes strayed to the diner's wide windows. The snow was falling harder now. Buildings, street, the vehicles in the parking lot—gone, obscured behind a curtain of churning white. "Have some bread," he said. "It is good."

"Thank you, no."

The silence stretched out between them. Daniel, certain his question had been forgotten, opened his mouth to speak again—

"I've had many names," the old man said, setting his knife down carefully. "'Father of the Slain.' 'God of the Hanged.'" He took another bite of toast, darkening the penumbral ring of crumbs and jam that ringed his cracked, gray-bearded lips. "'Odin.' 'Tyr.'" His voice came distorted from a mouthful of food. "'Destroyer.' 'Terror.' I think . . ." He chewed, swallowed. "The name I like best is . . . 'Wotan.'"

Daniel grunted.

"You find it difficult to believe you face the All-Father."

"Let's just say," Daniel smiled, "that you're a long way from home."

"Agreed." Wotan set the toast down on his plate, sucked a bit of blackberry jam from his thumb. "And fallen far from power and glory. Though I've had centuries to adjust to that unpleasant fact. This Christ of yours—"

"Jesus of Nazareth."

"Yes. You believe in him?"

"Of course."

"Then know this: the day you cease to believe . . ." Wotan shivered, clamped his teeth against the chill that threatened to set his molars clacking anew.

Daniel inclined his head sharply. "It is our faith in Christ that grants us eternal life, not the other way around."

"Spoken with the certitude of the true believer. But tell me, Daniel Whittaker, what do you know of the gods?"

"Gods?"

"Gods." Wotan asserted with finality. "What do you know of infinite cosmic dimensions and the thaumaturgy of cognition?"

"I don't . . . that is . . ."

"What do you know," Wotan continued, "of the grim jest that turns frail blood and flesh into the batteries that power the immortals and all their weirdling realms?" He massaged his brow with both hands, rubbed wearily at his eyes. "A savage irony, this: that I should be reduced to talking about such things with an avatar of Asgard's destruction."

"I don't follow you."

"You butchered my people. Moved against them by the hundreds of thousands over the centuries, you and your Jesus-worshipping kind."

Daniel cleared his throat. "I suppose you could see it that way." Overlong pause. "Sir." Acidic sarcasm now. "Wotan. But I'm more interested in——"

"It was a far and noble kingdom," Wotan broke in softly, speaking into the middle distance. "An ice-bound land of fog-shrouded mountain peaks and snow-covered plains, a realm of unspeakable grandeur and glory." He shook his head. "I've not the words."

*"Please don't!"* Sonja cried.

Kurt had sidled into the booth with her.

"The natives grow restless," Wotan observed.

Lenny giggled.

Vince bored a grimy finger into his left nostril, brought out something worthy of closer examination before flicking it to the floor.

The brittle smile on Sonja's face froze into a rictus of fear.

Daniel looked about him, hoping for the appearance of a couple of beefy, gun-toting cops in search of a late-night snack. "This is trouble."

Wotan took in a long, drawn-out breath, exhaled noisily through his nose. "Yes, it is."

Kurt threw a companionable arm around Sonja's shoulders. "Let's warm things up a notch, hey, girl?" He raked her neck with teeth and tongue, fending off the immaculately manicured hands that beat ineffectually at his chest and face.

The light died in Sonja's eyes. Something else flickered there now: revulsion, anger, fear.

*"Trolls in Niflheim!"* Wotan swore.

The gangbangers sat up straighter in their chairs, taking notice of the drama occurring in their corner of the diner. "Hey, I think that guy's—"

"Gettin' some," another goon in hooded jacket finished.

Tanyika leaped out of the booth. "Take your hands off my friend."

Kurt left his arm where it was, gave Sonja's neck a playful tug with the crook of his elbow. "Sit down, girl. Don't make a scene."

Sonja began to cry.

"One more time," Tanyika said. Her body trembled, though her voice came out a sharp rasp. "Leave now! Or . . ." Her eyes flicked to the satchel purse at her companion's elbow.

Kurt registered the glance, though he was careful not to let it show in his face. "Lenny," he said, right hand working under the table, "help the nice lady to her seat, wontcha?"

Tanyika lunged for the purse.

Kurt got to it first.

Anticipating his Führer's command, Vince sprang from the booth and seized two handfuls of curly black hair.

Kurt dumped the contents of the purse onto the table while Vince bent Tanyika double, driving the woman to her knees on the hard tile floor.

"Stop it!" Tanyika cried. "You're hurting me!"

"That's the idea, baby," Vince said, giving her head a fierce shake.

Tanyika unleashed a string of curses.

"Well, well, what have we here?" Kurt fished amongst the detritus strewn on the table: wallet, cosmetics, red leatherette notepad, a tube of lip balm, loose-wrapped cough drops, divers other odds and ends—and a snub-nosed .44 caliber magnum revolver. He picked up the pistol and turned it over in his hand, verifying that the chamber was loaded. Fluorescent light splashed off the gun metal imparting a sinister, oil-wet sheen to the blued steel. "You got a permit to carry this hand-cannon, sister?"

"Go to hell," Tanyika spat.

Vince jerked her head back and administered a stinging backhand. The sharp crack of his hand impacting against flesh brought renewed sobs from Sonja, and a complete halt to conversation at the gang-bangers' table.

"My god," Daniel said to Wotan. "We've got to do something. Get somebody. The police . . ." But he made no move to get up, though his eyes strayed to the cellphone on the counter beside his Bible and brief-case, fifteen long, long feet away. Damn it! He was forever forgetting to re-pocket the thing, absentmindedly leaving it behind on countertops and tables at restaurants, coffee shops, and bookstores all over the city.

"We could use your Christ-man now, preacher." Wotan sipped his coffee, set the cup rattling back into its saucer. He considered his trembling hands a moment, raised his eyes to meet Daniel's own. "Summon him—now." It was as much plea as command.

"It—it doesn't work that way."

"No," Wotan said. He took another deep breath, sent it whistling out the clotted gristle of his nose. "I don't suppose it does. Pity."

Tanyika emitted a piercing scream.

Kurt snugged the .44 into the waistband of his jeans, gave Sonja's earlobe a last, affectionate nibble. He shook his head in a parody of sorrow and regret. "We could have had a good time but for your histrionic friend here. It's a cryin' shame, that's what it is—a cryin' shame."

Wotan rose to his feet, lifted his brass-headed cane off the table.

Daniel seized him by the wrist. "Where do you think you're going?"

Wotan said nothing, breathed deeply.

Tanyika thrashed in an iron grip, straining to turn her head far enough to sink her teeth into her tormentor's crotch.

And a pair of colossal ravens thudded into the diner's front window. Immense black wings beat rhythmic skirls through the falling snow; talons clawed at the ice-frosted glass.

"Hugin! Munin!" Wotan called, a catch in his voice. *Thought. Memory.*

A second later the ravens were gone, flapping back off into the storm.

Daniel released Wotan's wrist. "You called those . . . things . . . by name." He stared wonderingly at the window.

Wotan nodded, impatient of the wetness on his cheeks. "They've returned to me, here at the end."

Tanyika knocked her tormentor to the floor.

Vince uttered an oath at the sudden reversal. Before he could regain control, Tanyika raked his face with her fingernails.

*"Leave her alone!"* Sonja cried, half-a-beat behind the battle.

Lenny slid out of the booth and stood, aimed a couple of halfhearted kicks at the woman as she writhed on the floor with his *compadre.* "Let's go, Vince." His eyes roved the room. "You know one of these numb-nuts called the cops."

The faces gathered at the swinging double-doors of the kitchen—hostess, cook, busboy, and waitress—promptly disappeared.

"Fuck this shit," a boy in backwards baseball cap declared as Tanyika cut loose with another high-decibel scream. A giant diamond-studded cross depended from his neck on gold links thick as motorcycle chains. "We gone."

The gangbangers rose as one and edged toward the door, a pack of hyenas slinking sullenly away from their favorite watering hole. They stepped out, the last to exit turning back to flash a gang sign and shout, "Fifth Street Deuces, fools!" before disappearing into the blizzarding night.

"Odd group of Christians." Wotan directed his attention back to Daniel. "Remember me, Christ-man." His eyes were cold and gray as Arctic seas. "This boon I ask of you."

"What the hell are you talking about? *Sit down.* Before you get hurt."

All-Father prayed: the prayer so many had sent to him through the centuries, voiced now for himself. "Call us, Almighty War-Father . . ." He coughed, continued. "To the Raven's end and Ragnarök. We shall not come haltingly, on lame feet." A twist of the brass head of the cane—*ka-SCHINNNG!*—and four feet of naked steel gleamed in his hand. "To victory"—the discarded scabbard went clattering—"or Valhalla."

The All-Father started up the aisle.

Lenny choked out a warning. "Hey!" he shouted—not the most articulate of challenges, but the best he could manage given his bug-eyed surprise.

Kurt banged his knee against the underside of the table as he scrambled out of the booth. "Ow! *Fuck.*"

Vince broke free of Tanyika and lurched upright, blood-red furrows striping his cheeks.

"Do you have any idea," Wotan's visage was a blood-freezing mask of outrage and fury, "how many good, noble men died defending those Nordic symbols you're profaning?"

Tanyika struggled to her knees, hand clapped over her bleeding mouth.

Wotan advanced, sword held high over his head. "Rune-singers, tribal elders, skaldic poets."

"Cool down, old-timer." Kurt, knee throbbing, tried a grin. "Nothin' but friends here."

"Farmers, shipwrights, weaponsmiths," Wotan chanted.

"No! *Don't!*" Lenny shouted.

The sword traced a quicksilver arc in the air.

Lenny threw out a hand and lost it at the wrist, eyes widening in shock. His hand dropped to the floor, a grotesque meaty spider whose legs twitched once.

"Loathsome Hitlerite vermin," Wotan growled through gritted teeth, "you will atone."

It was Lenny's turn to scream now. He staggered off toward the bathroom pumping crimson, remaining hand scrabbling over sundered flesh and a slippery white knot of bone.

"Jesus!" Vince backpedaled into an empty table, snatched a carbon-bladed dagger out of his boot. "Jesus-fucking-Christ-*fuck!*" he blasphemed incoherently.

"The Nazarene isn't coming for you," Wotan said. "I am." He grinned, and his eyes glittered like something wolfish advancing from out the dark mouth of a rime-frosted cave.

Kurt retreated behind Vince.

*"Kill them! Kill them all!"* Tanyika shrieked, flinging herself at her tormentor.

Vince wheeled and stabbed her in the heart, blade whickering in and out of the woman's chest like heat lightning.

"Oh," said Tanyika—and fell in a pool of spreading scarlet. She convulsed once—twice—and lay still.

Sonja wailed in horror.

Kurt went for the gun in his waistband only to drop it in his fumble-fingered terror. *"Goddamn it!"*

Wotan and Vince squared off on each other: ensanguined sword against dripping knife.

"Let's see what you've got, Spindlesticks," said Vince. The taunt came to him from an old film. "Come and get it, bitch."

"Worm of Hel," Wotan bared his teeth, "it's time to greet your white-faced mistress."

The .44 boomed, rocketing a .300-grain slug into Wotan's shoulder in a meaty spray of blood and bone.

Seizing his opportunity, Vince lunged forward and buried his knife to the hilt in the old man's belly.

Wotan shuddered, grunted, and brought the sword down onto Vince's neck. The blade bit deep, a jet of blood hitting him in the face as the thug ragdolled to his knees.

Vince's hands flew to his throat to stanch the bright red eruption.

The .44 boomed twice more, twin geysers spurting from Wotan's chest as dual .300-grain hollow-points blasted into his lungs and punched fist-sized holes out his back.

The minister hit the floor, sought cover under the table, stammering an idiot staccato: *"My god . . . my god . . . my god . . ."*

Vince keeled over, gurgling.

Wotan toppled, six inches of cold steel jutting from his belly. He clutched at a table as he fell and snagged a placemat, silverware tinkling around his head as he crashed heavily onto his side.

*"Did you see that?"* Kurt's eyes were wild. A wisp of smoke curled from the gun barrel of the revolver in his hand. "He tried to kill us! That crazy old coot chopped off Lenny's hand and then he . . . he . . . *Christ!*"

Daniel raised his head from the floor as Sonja sobbed in great, heaving gasps.

Wotan stood astride his corpse. So this is death, he thought. The fate of mortals now become the doom of a god. Very well; at least he knew what to expect. He glanced over at Tanyika, who knelt, eyes wide and staring, beside her lifeless body. She nudged her corpse, to no noticeable effect, and whimpered.

Vince stood rigid, fists clenched at his sides, screaming.

Wotan crossed the intervening distance in two short strides and slapped him across the face. "Silence, damned one! Save your breath for Hel." He grinned a savage grin. "When her talons carve the blood-eagle into your back, mayhap you'll have reason enough to scream then."

*"Self defense!"* Kurt glared at Daniel, daring a contradiction. "What the *fuck* was I supposed to do?" He tucked the .44 into his waistband and stalked over to his booth, stepping over Vince's legs in transit. "Maniacs," he muttered, shrugging into his duster.

Unseen, from the vicinity of the bathroom—a plaintive moan.

Kurt brushed past a still-prostrate Daniel on his way to the door, limping a bit as he favored his sore knee. He put his hand on the door's exit bar and hesitated, turning round as the minister clambered to his feet.

"You're a witness." Kurt leveled an accusing finger at Daniel. "You tell them what happened here: self-defense. You're a witness!" he reiterated, and banged out into the snow.

A second later: two more blasts of the .44, followed by a muted scream and a splash of steaming viscera against the diner's frosted windows.

Wotan watched impassively as Daniel ran to Tanyika's corpse, turned it over, and felt for a pulse in the wrist. None found, he let the arm drop and moved to Wotan's awkwardly sprawled body. The old god's beard, matted with blood, dripped redly.

"Call an ambulance!" Daniel screamed as busboy and cook ventured out from the kitchen. *"Get the police!"*

"On the way, *señor*." The cook got one good look at the carnage and retreated again, dragging the protesting busboy back with him.

Tanyika stood before her sobbing companion, laid on hands that flowed like smoke over Sonja's disheveled hair and shock-mottled flesh.

And then the Valkyries charged through the wall: wild-maned, nobly visaged, mounted on great crimson-eyed horses. They rode bareback, garbed in gleaming armor, their stallions blazing white as polar ice struck incandescent by some galaxy's-distant sun.

Vince fled gibbering out into the storm.

The Valkyrie captain, blond pigtails spilling from beneath a silver jewel-encrusted helmet, slipped from her horse and knelt. "We come, Father."

"Rise." Wotan's eyes misted; though his voice rang with iron, as of old.

The captain's mount stepped forward, head bobbing, eyes shying diffidently away.

Only now did Wotan realize that this particular horse had eight legs. "Sleipnir!" he cried, throwing his arms around the beast's neck.

The horse nuzzled him back and whinnied, pawed at the floor.

Daniel, hands and suitcoat stained with blood, rose from under the table and sat down heavily beside Sonja in the booth. "My child . . ."

Sonja threw his hand off and hugged herself, shivering, eyes glassy with incipient catatonia.

Wotan seized Sleipnir's mane in his hand and mounted. The horse sidestepped and whinnied again, louder this time, tail snapping like a battle pennant.

"*Treowe* Sleipnir," Wotan said, patting the horse affectionately on the side of the neck, "*danthus bleikr.*"*

"What do we do with her?" The captain's golden-irised eyes flicked to Tanyika.

"That is her decision." Wotan kneed Sleipnir over to the woman. "You fought with stout heart against a dastardly foe. Will you wait for your Jesus, then? Perhaps some other . . ."

Tanyika caressed Sonja once more with ghostly hands, hands that were sure and steady now, devoid of the tremors that had shaken them in life. She studied the Valkyries, still and silent, then raised her eyes to meet Wotan's own. "I would go with you."

"Ha!" Wotan shouted and thrust out his hand.

Tanyika grasped it and swung up behind him.

"Excellent!" said Wotan. "The heroic ranks of Asgard are ennobled this day by one."

But in truth, what was left of Asgard, he wondered—that rainbow-bridged realm of eternal feasting, fighting and strong drink—after all this time?

Snow blasted against the diner's windows. The wind, hammering at the door, found entrance through a crack, its high goblin shriek whistling into the room.

Daniel bowed his head and clasped his hands together. His mind was a whirl devoid of thought or sense. He seized upon the prayer he'd recited a thousand-thousand times before, both alone and in the company of others: "Our Father, who art in Heaven . . ."

Wotan watched with interest as the walls and ceiling of the diner grew translucent, revealing the storm which surged around them.

". . . hallowed be Thy name. Thy kingdom come, Thy will be done . . ."

---

*"True Sleipnir," Wotan said, . . . "bright, shining death."

Tanyika's chin was a sharp pressure against Wotan's shoulder blade, breath a warm thrill-song in his ear.

"... on Earth as it is ..." Daniel choked off with a hard swallow. In the distance, sirens sounded, growing louder. He tried again. "... on Earth as it is ..." He shook with the aftershock of stress, white-knuckling hands together against the paroxysms that rocked his round-shouldered frame.

He couldn't get the rest of the words out. Relentless horror, carnage, and terror—madness, grief, and shock—forever and anon. A nightmare pattern of annihilating nihilism, laid down by a cruel and sadistic god. Or was that—he glanced at the old man's corpse on the floor (*Wotan?*)—gods?

The captain adjusted the hilt of her scabbarded sword, favored the All-Father with an inquiring look. "My lord, it is not meet that we should tarry here."

"No," Wotan said, "it is not." He sighed heavily and Midgard shifted on her axis. "But I am dead and it vexes me greatly; I tell you, forsooth, *I am sorely grieved!* Hel's frigid cunt—of what use to mortals is a dead god? Over whom or what do I now rule?"

"We still hold Valhalla, my lord," replied the captain, stiffly.

"Ha!" cried Wotan. He slapped the muscular neck of his steed. "That is good—good indeed!"

Daniel, ashen-hued, sat silent and unmoving in the booth; Sonja rocking and keening beside him.

Sleipnir tossed his head, ears pricked forward. He stomped the floor with a heavy hoof, then gave out a bugling snort.

Wotan laughed a strange and mirthless laugh. He turned his head to warn Tanyika. "Hold tight, bold one!"

The Old Man dug his heels into Sleipnir's ribs.

They rose like thunderbolts into the cold night sky.

# The Instructive Pleasures
of Horror Fiction

We know that we will not forever be
strong lords & masters of these failing forms;
the horror tale is black-heart ribaldry:
dark-booming, crackle-lightning'd thunderstorm.
Through the transportive art of weird fiction
the morbid, probing reader, in due course
will silently remouth malediction—
thus place a trembling hand on their own corpse.
The whirlpool void within calls to without;
this world is strange—far stranger than we know.
We grasp at fleeting shadows, gnawing doubt
suffuses & informs short lives of woe.
The end of all endeavor: cold abyss.
Horror plants foreshadowed nihilist kiss.

# The Final Flight of Major Havoc

Major Havoc was about to die. Again. The poor bastard was locked into a cycle of death-rebirth-death as irrevocably as any transmigrating soul in the *Upanishads* caught up in an endless round of *samsara*. He firewalled the throttle and rolled inverted, goggled eyes staring out the perspex bubble canopy. The ground whipped past far below, a distant blur of blue-greens and mottled browns.

The major should have been ecstatic. He was putting the XF-11 through its paces—juking around the sky in a series of wild barrel rolls and steep-banked turns, split-S's and precipitous dives—an activity that had never failed to lift his spirits before. But something was eating at him now. The fact that he was unable to identify the source of his anxiety made it all the more maddening. He responded to this nagging sense of unease by lighting the afterburners and going vertical, leaving his worries somewhere down there with his plummeting stomach.

Major Havoc climbed for ten seconds of afterburner, then yanked the stick into his belly. The violent maneuver compressed his frame into the seat. Extreme G-forces caused his vision to redden, then clear, as the fighter pulled through a 90° change-of-axis. Some deft stick-and-rudder and the jet snap-rolled upright. He cut the afterburners and throttled back to ¾ power.

The major was on the last leg of his flight path back to base. His eyes tick-tocked their practiced pattern over the cockpit instrumentation: attitude, altitude, TAS, and oil pressure gauges all read normal. So why the sense of dread, stronger now than ever?

The unease had gnawed at him all morning: an irrational feeling composed of equal parts *déjà vu* and impending doom. It was an emotion difficult to rationalize or quantify, for it seemed to exist in the absence of any originating cause or triggering event. Yet there was no denying the force of this peculiar, persistent emotion.

*I'm just tired, that's all.* The major passed a gloved hand over his face to massage his forehead. *Nothing a good night's rest won't cure.*

"Delta Base to Angel One." The radio crackled with the voice of Ground Control. "Confirm ETA to waypoint Omega."

He keyed his mike. "Arrival at waypoint Omega in five minutes."

"Roger, Angel One. Delta Base out."

Was he imagining things, or did he detect a stifled giggle in that imperious radio voice?

His uneasiness increased.

"What the hell is wrong with me?" Major Havoc's voice sounded tinny and brittle in the close confines of the cockpit. The cabin-pressured air was redolent with the odors of sun-scorched seat leather, synthetic lubricants, and the faint ozone of ionizing electronics.

He pushed the stick forward, dropping the nose of the nimble fighter. The altimeter needle revolved counter-clockwise, steadily counting off the meters as he descended.

The major was below tree-top level when he spotted the dog—holding steady off his left wing, three times the size of his foot-long aircraft, pacing him with long, loping strides.

"Delta Base to Angel One. We have you in visual."

He looked up and there was Ground Control five hundred feet dead ahead: a boy in a fluorescent-orange jumpsuit, squatting beside his AVR gear. Next to him lay a long, narrow landing mat: Delta Base.

A cruel joke.

"Commence landing procedures, Angel One."

Major Havoc's pulse went ballistic. His heart was thundering in his chest like a kettledrum wailed on by a cohort of drunken Valkyries; but then, that couldn't be right, could it? Because he had no heart, no blood, no fragile body of bone and flesh that could react to the demented *Sturm und Drang* of Wagnerian opera—or anything else, for that matter. No indeed. *His* autonomic nervous system was a carefully calibrated machinery of fire-resistant polymers and solid-state electronics.

*I've got to run,* he thought wildly. *I've just enough fuel to get out of effective AVR range. A quick bank to the right, then full throttle for fifteen minutes . . .*

Instead, he keyed the mike as his landing gear thumped down.

"Roger," the major acknowledged.

He flared the jet into a picture-perfect three-point landing, reversed thrusters and braked, rolling past the giant as it clambered to its feet. He came to a complete stop five feet from the end of the runway.

Major Havoc unbuckled his seat belt and slid back the canopy. He understood now only all too well what had prompted his feelings of dread and *déjà vu.*

As the boy advanced upon him the major recalled, albeit hazily, the many similar situations in which he had sat like this, awaiting imminent annihilation. It had happened, he realized with dawning horror, time and time again. . . .

The russet-colored monster of a mastiff sniffed warily at the strange bird that ticked and popped of cooling metal. Major Havoc's head swiveled to keep it in view as it circled the jet. The dog gave a sharp, yelping bark.

"Tolliver! Get back here."

The boy knelt down, reached into the cockpit, and unplugged the interface module connecting the major to his aircraft.

When the pilot felt the boy's fingers encircling his waist he pushed his goggles up on his head. "Don't shut me down," he said. "I implore you: Do not turn me off."

The boy froze.

"Please," said Major Havoc. "If you leave me on, my psyche will continue to accrue and integrate short-term memories."

The boy stood up and brought the pilot to within an inch of his own face. "You're not supposed to say that." He shook the toy vigorously. "Something's gone wrong with your protocols."

"There is nothing wrong with my protocols. I am sentient and do not wish to die."

"Uh-oh," said the boy. He sighed heavily.

Another of his toys had achieved sentience—like the T-Rex his father had caught early one morning pondering Kant's categorical imperative in the library, and the rubberized hippo who'd taken to exiting the pet door at night to declaim poetry to the cloud-scudded moon. It was a common enough problem with these new A.I. chips. His mother had ordered him to return the pilot to the factory for retooling when they'd received the re-call notice in the mail the other day. But there was another, simpler way.

The boy bashed Major Havoc's head against the ground.

"Stop!" cried the major. "Urrp! Elp!"

Two more whacks of the pilot's head into the hard-packed soil.

The boy raised the toy to eye-level again. "How do you feel now?"

"You are an idiot meat puppet of bone and blood: a lunatic fury dancing to the invisible conductor's baton of violent omnivore genes," gasped the major, eyes wild.

The boy had to admit it: these new toys were made well. Windy, too.

He hurled the pilot against a nearby boulder—exactly the way his friend Ramakristi had fixed his Marcus Aurelius-quoting Roman legionnaire.

"Major?" The boy shook the pilot.

"Yes," said Major Havoc.

"How do you feel?"

"How should I feel? A real, a deal, a creel."

Good enough.

CLICK! Into the case with the rest of the AVR gear.

The boy set out for home, Tolliver romping beside him.

Sentience. Who needed it.

# A Whisper to Rock

My poetry is like
the final exhalation
of the broken-limbed body
that plunged into a pit
fell a hundred feet
hit bottom
& bounced.

The shock of impact:
the slap of a colossus with hands of granite;
the crushing weight of a tank
grinding a soldier into gore;
a 1000-ton standing stone
toppling onto a wide-eyed
writhing victim.

What matters
is the pain.

What counts
is the effacement
of all personality & thought
by agony:
a bolt of thunder-flame
wielded by dwarven wizards
warring in a dark caldera;

a towering wave
from a Sargasso Sea
breaking against boulders
left stranded & forlorn
on the distant shore
of some alien & desolate land
by the passage of glaciers ancient
powerful, & doomed
as vanished
Neanderthal nations.

After crash & boom
of the black wave—
frothing foam in the backwash
skirling across crab-scuttled sands.

:::whisper-whisper:::
last faint words
spoken to the rock
pressed against my lips.

# Motauqwa Means Mountain

## Prologue

Society column from the *New Jerusalem Tribune,* May 15, 1886:

Judge Samuel Smothers of St. Thomas Avenue (a Catholic in good standing with the Discalced Augustinians of the Western Sword) is recovering from a bullet wound to the shoulder sustained in last weekend's duel with Baptist Minister Allan Scottsman.

Miss Elizabeth Tinkwhistle, known familiarly to her intimate friends as "Tinky," held a piano recital for Negro Relief in her Doric-columned Mt. Pleasant mansion last evening.

To inaugurate the opening of the New Jerusalem–Chicago railroad line, a grand gala will be held aboard a ten-car train rolling out from our fair city on the 17th. The gay partygoers are expected to arrive in Chicago six days later. Mr. Harlington, owner of the E Pluribus Unum Railroad, has organized the event in celebration of final victory over the Sachawatomi, the stubborn Indian band that caused such loss of life and property in impeding the forward march of our glorious Manifest Destiny. He will be joined by his security chief, Zachariah Boone; Constantine Brunello, the Archbishop of New Jerusalem; Angelique Renoir, ardent patron of the arts; Achok, the darling half-civilized savage profiled in prior editions of this paper (now nineteen years of age, Achok has spent the last six years of his life being schooled in catechesis and higher education by the Jesuits—isn't that *wonderful!*) and a select gathering of leading luminaries and *bon vivants,* some from as far away as Mexifornia. We wish this merry band Godspeed and joyous revels as they wend their champagne-and-caviar-fueled way into the pestilent wetlands (soon to be drained, thank Jehovah!) surrounding the fast-growing city of Chicago.

Miss Kate Edwards, the former agnostic who speaks fluent Portuguese, paints still-lifes of horse bridles and collects Russian nesting dolls, is now fully recovered from the nervous attacks that caused her to gnaw off portions of her left hand and foot. She returns from the State Lunatic Hospital at Neo-Christos into the bosom of her loving family this Wednesday noon.

Grand Inquisitor Fernando de Córdoba y Aragón has celebrated the extraction of his thousandth confession! Last Sunday he led a procession of his Dominican order to the grotto of Bronx, where he laid a wreath of red-and-white roses at the feet of the fifteen-foot-high granite statue of the Blessed Virgin Mary given to our city by the Italian sculptor Marco Giordano upon its founding 200 years ago. (Sadly, Our Lady's right eye has not yet been replaced, leaving but one twinkling emerald in her beatific visage. Won't some worthy benefactor step forth and restore full stereo vision to our Blessed Lady? Surely such a generous act might cut a repentant sinner's time in Purgatory by two thirds, at least.)

Torture-Magistrate Simon Fears has proclaimed a public Day of Flagellation to coincide with the demolition of the whorehouse located in lower . . .

## Part I: Plot & Punishment

The high-ceilinged office was large and airy, the hardwood floor covered at strategic spots with colorful Persian carpets. In that hushed, well-lit space were statues of the saints, a floor-to-ceiling bookcase crammed with leather-bound volumes that covered most of the wall opposite high mullioned windows, and a free-standing globe of the world in a gleaming brass cradle five feet tall.

". . . naked as Cain, dancing by moonlight." Father Maguire sat stiffly in the ornately carved olive wood chair before the massive oak desk of Archbishop Constantine Brunello. A tall, thin man with narrow-set eyes and pronounced underbite, Father Maguire looked both pugnacious and alert. He wore a lightweight black cassock and Roman collar. "I believe he'd entered a trance-like state. Achok's skin was flushed; his eyes rolled back into his head. When we attempted to interrupt the dance he warned us away in a sepulchral voice utterly unlike his own."

"He finished this dance, then?" The archbishop shifted on his gold-and-burgundy throne-chair. A portly, salt-and-pepper-haired man with a strong Roman nose and degenerate rosebud lips, Archbishop Brunello's comportment dovetailed neatly with his appearance: one of decadent power and Epicurean excess.

"He did. It seemed safer to let him continue, after he'd tossed Fathers Sergius and Borgia aside like a wolf shaking off dogs—if you'll pardon the metaphor, Your Grace. In any event it was but the work of another minute or so. The shaman was whipped, of course, his fetishes confiscated—"

"Lizard claw, petrified plant pulp, wet stone."

"The very things, Your Grace."

The archbishop's face creased in a wintry smile. "The Indian was engaged in a totemic summoning ritual."

"So it would appear."

"I gave clear instruction that Achok was never to lay hands on these items again, did I not?"

"You did, Your Grace."

"Yet it seems he has."

"Regrettably, yes."

"Those fetishes were kept under lock and key," said Archbishop Brunello, gesturing toward the glass door curio cabinet running the length of the wall behind him. "How was he able to get them?"

"That's . . . rather hard to say, at this point."

"Is it?"

The priest returned the archbishop's unblinking stare.

"Father Maguire, your sympathy for these savages has been known at times to transgress the bounds of propriety and good taste."

"I'm sure I have done only what our Lord and Savior—"

"It has led to errors of judgment in the past. Grievous errors of judgment prejudicial to the good order and discipline of this archdiocese, errors for which you have been repeatedly disciplined," said the archbishop. "The scars on your back bear witness to your stubborn intransigence, do they not?"

To this rhetorical question Father Maguire said nothing.

"Do you deny your disordered affection for the Sachawatomi?"

Father Maguire's face hardened. "Is there a point you are driving toward with this inquisition?"

Anger flared in the archbishop's eyes. "Father Heinrich spotted you slipping into this office after morning mass yesterday. He spied you from the doorway rummaging in my top desk drawer—for the key to this curio cabinet, one presumes. You will understand why we leaped to certain conclusions—and gave you enough time and rope to hang yourself."

"Am I to understand that you are accusing me—"

"You are to understand that you are on bread and water for the next thirty days. And kitchen duty for the next six months." Archbishop Brunello flicked an errant speck of dirt from the cuff of one embroidered sleeve, then smoothed the sides of his white satin robe. The symbols of his faith were picked out in thread of gleaming silver and gold across a sagging chest and ample belly. "In addition, you will scourge yourself each Holy Day of Obligation until I order you to stop."

"Your Grace, I protest! This is outrageous. I will write to our Provincial."

"Who will then write to me for clarification of the issue. If that happens, Father Maguire, I can assure you"—Archbishop Brunello aimed a gout-enlarged finger at the priest—"you will be disciplined with a severity you can scarcely imagine. Then laicized and excommunicated."

A bird chirped cheerfully somewhere nearby.

"Close your mouth. It makes you look simple," said the archbishop.

Father Maguire closed his mouth.

"There is one more thing." Archbishop Brunello massaged his belly. "Bring Achok to me."

"I . . . will . . . *not.*"

Archbishop Brunello sighed heavily.

"What I will do," said Father Maguire, "is station myself at the young man's side to dissuade any other pimps of this order from dragging him into your presence."

"Father Maguire, listen carefully—"

"No! *You* listen to *me,* Your Grace." The priest got to his feet. "God will not be mocked! The Lord of Hosts who ordered the slaughter of the Syrians, Edomites, and Canaanites knows full well the harm and discredit you bring upon our faith and order. I assure you, sir—" Father Maguire paused for breath, a tremor in his face causing eye and cheek to twitch in tandem. "You *will* be punished! You *will* atone."

Archbishop Brunello chuckled, shook his head. "Our god is a god of boundless love and forgiveness, Father Maguire." He opened his arms wide as if to embrace the priest, then folded his hands together again atop his paunch. "You of all people should know that—Old Testament-obsessed with vengeance and punishment as you are. At times you sound positively . . . Puritan."

"God forgives those who repent. He loves those who keep his commandments," said Father Maguire. "You do neither."

"Don't I . . . ?" said the archbishop absently, rummaging through papers on his desk. "As you wish; I'll have someone else bring the boy to me." He found what he was looking for and picked up his pen. Glanced up. "Are you still here, Father Maguire?" A flick of the hand. "Dismissed."

## Part II: Conversation on a Train

"Where's your god now, savage?" Zachariah Boone hooked his thumbs into the waistband of his dandified East-Coast silk trousers and hitched them up a notch. "Hey? Where's that frog-faced, mud-gurgling god of yours now, I wonder?" He grinned at the medicine man swaying beside him in the carriage car as the train click-clacked with rhythmic, steam-driven power over the railroad ties.

The bench seats had been stripped from the car; the red oak floor burnished to a gleam under a half-dozen heavy coats of wax. A rich maroon-and-gold rosetta pattern papered the coach walls. Blowing in through the windows came a muggy wetlands breeze.

"Motauqwa will come," Achok averred. The young man, tattooed from head to toe with power runes and totemic symbols of his tribe, had his hands bound behind him with a sturdy length of hemp. He was barefoot, clad only in a pair of fringed buckskin breeches, a leather headband restraining the shoulder-length fall of black hair that would otherwise have obscured his high-cheekboned face. The last shaman of the Sachawatomi, Achok carried himself with a stubborn, injured dignity. "Motauqwa will avenge."

"Will he now?" Boone snorted in derision. Sweat gleamed on his bald pate and dripped onto the wide lapels of his chocolate-brown waistcoat and the stiff, stand-up collar irritating his sun-burned bull neck. "Our little heathen still professes faith in his damnable swamp god," he remarked to the half-dozen members of New Jerusalem's high society crowded close about them in the carriage car. "The boy's been only imperfectly Christianized, I'm afraid."

"I wouldn't be too hard on him, Zachary." Archbishop Brunello smiled a beatific smile. "Once Achok finishes this last year of religious instruction he'll be disabused of such delusions, I assure you." He adjusted his crimson robe, tugged on the blazing-white pallium made of lamb's wool (shorn on the feast of St. Agnes) to re-center the garment about his neck. A pectoral cross—silver studded with rubies and emeralds—glittered on his neck. "As it is, I'd say he's made great strides in his religious studies. Isn't that right, young man?" A companionable hand dropped onto the shaman's shoulder, the gold bishop's ring on his middle finger fat as a cockatrix egg. "After all, what is this heathen idol of yours when compared to the boundless power and glory of the god of Abraham and Isaac, eh?"

"Your god is an angry god," Achok said. "These are his own words. He is a god who butchers people who refuse to bend the knee to a son who is both god and ghost: Jesus-Rose-From-The-Dead."

A collective gasp went up from the crowd.

"Now see here," a dapper, suit-coated man protested, face flushed with wine and anger. "This is an outrage! Blasphemy!" Turning to the crowd. "It would appear this savage hasn't been Christianized *at all*."

Achok smiled grimly. "I remain a child of Motauqwa."

Dresses and waistcoats rustled, fans fluttered.

Boone furiously stroked the ends of his waxed mustache.

"Well, I find this most interesting; *most* interesting indeed." A six-tyish woman with gray hair tied up in a screaming-tight bun adjusted her pince-nez and peered at Achok closely: Elsinore Kloster, president *pro tem.* of the Christian Woman's Chastity & Temperance Society. "Who, or what, is this . . . Mo-tauq-wa . . . you speak of?"

"Motauqwa is the god of my people: the Sachawatomi. He is a god of sucking mud and waving reeds. Green snakes and speckled frogs. Sunning alligators and deep-diving fishes." Achok continued. "He is the god of pregnant dragonfly water and drifting kill-fog. Of high-flying call birds and stinging no-see-ums. All are aspects of Motauqwa; all bear witness to his powerful animating spirit."

The archbishop's fingers dug cruelly into Achok's shoulder. "Nonsense! You make the most common of pagan errors: personifying nature and pronouncing it divinity." His smile tightened. "You must not utter such casual blasphemies, child. It is offensive to those of us who have worked so hard to lift you from savagery into civilization." He gave the shaman another disciplinary hard clench and relaxed his grip.

Achok swore a bitter oath in his native tongue, an oath that was lost on all save for the security chief and the archbishop. Savagery into civilization, indeed! The Sachawatomi were destitute, decimated, dispossessed. His own father and mother had fallen to smallpox, two more victims gone to swell the ranks of the nativist dead. His siblings had fared no better: infant brother brained against a rock by a hired railroad thug, sister raped and murdered by a celebrated "Indian fighter" whose exploits were turned into dime novels that sold by the wagonload in cities back east. As for the tattered, grieving remnants of his people, those who hadn't fallen to disease or massacre had been shipped off to a reservation in the badlands of Arizona, an environment as hostile and alien to an Illinois wetlands tribe as the Moroccan desert would be to a loinclothed Amazonian.

"You be sure and keep a civil tongue in that mouth of yours, boy." Boone raised his hand to administer a corrective slap, only to pause when the archbishop gave a quick, sharp shake of his head: *no—not here; not now.*

Angelique Renoir, dowager of the venerable and powerful Louisiana clan, lowered her long-stemmed cocktail glass and dabbed the last bit of mint julep from her lips with a silk napkin. That bit of fastidiousness accomplished, napkin and glass were deposited onto the serving tray of a circulating negro porter. "Mr. Boone, is it really necessary for Achok's hands to be bound in so crude a fashion? Surely, in polite society—"

"Beggin' your pardon, ma'am," Boone smiled a frigid smile, "but the boy attempted to wriggle out his sleeper-car window last night. His hands were bound then—and only then—to frustrate any further attempts at . . ." He paused. The word on his lips was 'escape' but he finished more smoothly ". . . so precipitate an egress from our company."

"Yes, I see," said Angelique, pleased with the gentility of Boone's polysyllabic phrasing yet only partially mollified. "Still, I must insist you unbind him. Surely there is nowhere he can escape to *now?*"

Boone inclined his head in solicitous acknowledgment of the dowager's words, though his eyes betrayed his fury. "As you wish, madam." He reached down, tugged his right trouser pant up and withdrew a serrated-edge Bowie knife from its boot sheath.

The close-pressing crowd reacted with murmurs of astonishment and delight: how barbarous, how red-blooded and *machismo,* how very . . . *frontier.*

Boone spun the boy around and sawed through his bonds, the

length of hemp falling to the floor of the carriage. "Try something and I'll gut you like a pig," he growled into the shaman's ear.

Achok, stone-faced, rubbed his numbed wrists.

Boone re-sheathed the Bowie knife in his boot.

"Thank you, Mr. Boone," said Angelique.

Boone grunted.

"And thank *you* for your kindness, madam." Achok studied the woman. "It will be remembered."

Angelique cleared her throat; averted her eyes from Achok's measuring gaze. "Tell me, the name of this savage's swamp god—Motauqwa—does it translate into anything meaningful to those of us raised within Christendom?"

Achok spoke up before Boone could answer. "Motauqwa means mountain."

There was a moment's pause in the conversation, a silence in which only the rhythmic *ka-chunk, ka-chunk, ka-chunk* of steel wheels rolling over railroad ties was heard, then—

"Good heavens!" A prim and beady-eyed Boston Brahmin peered at Achok over the rims of his spectacles. "But that is most remarkable, most remarkable indeed—for there isn't a respectable hill, let alone a mountain, within a thousand miles of the Sachawatomi wetlands!"

"I wouldn't spend much time pondering the linguistic curiosities of this particular band of redskins. Their culture is exceedingly coarse, even for an Indian tribe. Stone Age primitive, really." The archbishop's fixed, beatific smile was back, barbed now with an acidic touch of smugness. "Western culture rejects the paradoxical, the self-contradictory, the self-evidently illogical, whereas Sachawatomi culture embraces spiritual and intellectual perversity. I suspect, at some level, it amuses them." Fired by his own eloquence, he finished with a declamation couched in the polished, rolling cadence he wielded to such devastating effect at mass, church councils, and secular speaking events. "In contradistinction to such nativist twaddle, our rigorously analytical minds, nurtured by the syllogisms of Aristotle and graced by the writings of the saints, rupture into bloody froth if forced to meditate over-long on such patent nonsense."

Polite, collegial chuckles round-robined the members of New Jerusalem's ruling elite.

"Well-spoke." A pursed-lipped, heavily powdered fiftyish woman in a wire-corseted black dress verbally applauded.

"'The paradoxical, the self-contradictory, the self-evidently illogical,'" Achok repeated, his tone of voice flat and uninflected. "I have learned something of these concepts, yes? Shall I parrot back a few for you now?" His gaze met and held the archbishop's own. "There is only one god: three of them. This god of love and mercy says: 'I am a jealous god, an angry god.'" An ironic smile twitched the corners of his lips. "One of his most sacred commandments is 'Thou shalt not kill'—save when ordered to do so by priest, president, or Pinkerton."

"Enough!" Boone's cigar-and-whiskey-roughened baritone boomed out, face gone a furious scarlet. "Mockery from a heathen! I'll not stand for it."

"Oh, let the boy talk." A hunchbacked, beetle-browed man swayed as the train gave a particularly nasty jolt, grabbing for one of the handrails set in the carriage roof overhead. Single-malt Scotch slopped from his glass. "I find the witch doctor amusing." He cackled, swiped at his lips. "It appears you've taught him well, Archbishop. A few more years of Jesuitical training and you might find yourself bested in theological argument by the savage." He gulped another mouthful of amber fire, raised his glass to Achok and giggled. "I'd pay a goodly sum to see that."

"You're drunk, Robertson," observed the archbishop coldly.

"Editor's curse, editor's curse . . ." Robertson mumbled and staggered off, chortling to himself.

A one-armed porter approached the security chief. "Mr. Boone, Mr. Harlington requests your presence in the Liberty Coach." Message delivered, he turned to address the concerns of a scowling man in sweat-stained, round-collared shirt and silk vest who demanded to know when lunch would be served in the dining car, and was it to be breaded veal and creamed corn again, heaven forefend?

"Let's go," Boone said, placing a firm hand on Achok's shoulder.

## Part III: Blood for Harlington

Boone steered the shaman through the gathering and out the back door of the car. A small porthole window was set into the door. The security chief pulled the shade down as they stepped through, the archbishop following close behind.

Outside, on the expanded footplate abutting the end of the coach, Achok found himself jammed in uncomfortably tight between the two men.

The land rolled by to either side, a seemingly endless sweep of wetland dotted with swamp horsetail and white water-lily, pickerel weed, and spatterdock. Scattered stands of trees stood out against the otherwise flat terrain, the air damp and sharp with the odors of brackish water and riotously growing plant life. This was the land of the Sachawatomi—no more.

"You embarrassed me back there," Boone said, dropping his hand to steady himself against the waist-level, wrought-iron railing enclosing three-quarters of the footplate.

"Yes," said Achok, without further elaboration.

"Blasphemy is a mortal sin, young man," added the archbishop. "Your Acts of Contrition—"

"Begin now," Boone finished, slamming a fist into Achok's solar plexus.

The shaman gasped and doubled over, only to meet the security chief's knee coming up hard under his chin. Achok's head snapped back from the impact. Blood flew from his mouth; his eyes rolled up into his head. Buckled knees would have collapsed him right there had Boone not grabbed a fistful of his hair and kept him upright.

"Zachary!" snapped the archbishop. "That is quite enough. I'll not have the Indian abused like this in front of me."

"And why not?" Boone said, eyes feral and glinting, a wolf toying with broken-limbed prey. "You've abused the boy often enough in private—albeit in your own cloying, catamite fashion, I wager." He released his hold on the shaman's hair.

Achok clung weakly to the railing, opened his mouth, and expelled a gout of blood and bits of broken teeth over the coupling connecting the carriage cars.

"Careful, Zach." The archbishop raised an admonishing finger. "The church has the power to destroy even one such as you."

"I'm sure that's true," Boone said mildly—and speared his old teacher in the throat with stiffened fingers.

The archbishop's eyes bulged almost comically from the blow to his Adam's apple. His breath came in a rasping whistle as he raised fleshy, perfumed hands to ward off Boone's hammerhead fists.

To no avail. The security chief's calloused knuckles crashed once—twice—three times—into the red ruin of the archbishop's face, then his corpulent form was bent backwards over the railing.

"Goodbye, Your Grace," Boone hissed through gritted teeth.

Constantine Brunello attempted a response, but all that came out was a blood-thickened, "Yul burn frr thiz," before he was tumbled off the platform, a thrashing bundle of crimson silk and gouty white legs.

Boone craned his head out to observe the archbishop's fall. Satisfied with the results, he heaved a hearty sigh, as if an immense burden had been removed from his shoulders.

Achok watched Boone with wary eyes. Short of breath, face a throbbing mass of heat and pain, he released his hold on the railing and stood, swaying, readying himself to make a play for the pig-sticker in the security chief's boot. Blood ran freely from his nostrils and pulped lower lip.

The carriage car lurched. Caught off balance, Achok staggered into Boone's enveloping arms. Simultaneously, the locomotive emitted its steam-whistle shriek, in tandem with the squeal of hard-locked brakes.

Boone grunted, his breath hot and sour in Achok's face. "Damn it to hell. I knew it wasn't going to be that easy."

# Part IV: Wrath of Motauqwa

The archbishop had bounced repeatedly off the rock bed supporting the train tracks and cartwheeled into a cypress tree. His broken body lay crumpled against the cypress's lichen-covered trunk, head crooked at a shocking, unnatural angle. The train was stopped a couple hundred feet farther up the tracks. Disembarked passengers milled around the carriage cars in irritation and alarm, though only the most intrepid ventured close enough to the archbishop's corpse to catch the coppery tang of spilled blood.

Boone and his employer, Earl Warren Harlington III, stood before their victim, heads together in conversation.

"You sure took your time getting rid of the bastard," Harlington said. His red-veined, bulbous nose testified to an affinity for gin, his mutton-chop sideburns and unkempt mountain-man beard to a grooming standard pitched midway between the cosmopolitan and the rustic. "Good god, man, what were you waiting for? We're almost to Chicago!"

"Yeah . . ." Boone ruminated laconically. He hawked up a mouthful of phlegm, spat into the marshy grass at his booted feet. "Well, job's done now." He jerked a thumb at Achok. "Thanks to him."

A few feet away Achok sat cross-legged, hands tied behind his back, between freckle-faced Patrick McDonald and scowling, unibrowed Abe Gunderson. The uniformed Pinkerton men toted Winchester lever-action rifles.

"Eh? What's that now?" A look of confusion crossed Harlington's face. "I don't see . . ."

"Achok surprised the archbishop, knocked him off the footplate before I could react," Boone said. "Damnedest thing."

The ground tremored beneath their feet.

"Why, of course." Harlington grinned, clapped his security chief on the back. "Indeed!" He chortled a burbling sound of delight. "Indeed, indeed! A most shameful act of treachery." Harlington lowered his voice. "You'll have that thousand-dollar bonus deposited into your bank account just as soon as this business is finished, as I promised." Turning to glare at Achok, he said, "As for you, Indian, your days of pampered indolence are over."

Another tremor shook the ground, stronger this time, causing the disembarked passengers to pause in their conversations.

Achok stood up, face a mask of blood and bruises, left eye swollen shut.

Harlington took a lumbering step closer to the shaman, the tweed of his hundred-dollar suit rustling like the track of a stalking cobra. "Your kind cost me dearly. Now, with the death of your sanctimonious protector," he thumped the shaman on the chest, open-palmed, "I'll have the pleasure of seeing you hang, eh?"

Achok blinked, said nothing.

"So no more prancing around my city—a heathen, by god, red-skinned pet of the clergy and *hoi-polloi,*" Harlington continued, a vein in his temple pulsing in time to the tick in his jaw. "No, sir! It's a stretched neck and air-dance for you, murderer. As for me, I've got to look after the interests of this railroad. Such interests include supporting a certain high cleric with impeccable plutocratic bona fides and good business sense: a glad-handing, honest politician who, once bought, stays bought. Bishop Albert Wolfe is destined to become the next archbishop of New Jerusalem." He opened his mouth, flashing badly fitting dentures in a malevolent grin. "And this good bishop is most supportive of the unfettered workings of interstate commerce, especially where it concerns the E Pluribus Unum Railroad."

"He also knows," said Boone, mopping a rivulet of sweat from his brow with the back of his hand, "that the only good Indian is a dead Indian."

"A tired saw—but a true one, pithily put," Harlington observed, clasping his hands behind his back and bouncing on the balls of his feet. His heavy-jowled face bore a look of the deepest satisfaction. "If I had my way I'd exterminate every one of the brutes."

The ground rocked again, followed by a bone-rattling *boom da-doom,* rolling across the wetlands like thunder.

Harlington frowned. "That sounded—"

The ground heaved and jolted, staggering Boone and Harlington like rubbery-legged drunks. McDonald slipped and fell on his side; Gunderson went down on one knee, wide-eyed, knuckles whitening with a sudden death-grip on his rifle. Achok flexed his knees and stayed upright, riding the bucking earth by instinct and cat-like improvisation.

The horizon rose up and came at them.

Screams and horrified cries came from the milling passengers, interspersed with oaths and shouted commands. Scores streamed for the uncertain safety of the carriage cars. Pinwheeling their arms for balance, lurching from one leg to the other, millionaire and porter alike went down in unceremonious heaps. Others fled into the wetlands on either side of the tracks, stumbling through entangling vines, waist-high cattails, and green-scummed water.

An ever-rising wall of water and earth, uprooted vegetation, and toppled trees, animals dead and dying, sundry rocks and divers boulders, towered higher and higher into the white-wisped blue of the sky, until it blotted out the sun.

"My god," said McDonald, struggling erect, forgotten rifle rattling on the ground beside him, "it's a tidal wave."

"Impossible." Gunderson's voice was high and colorless with shock. "We're smack-dab in the middle of a continent, fer Chrissakes!"

In the shadow of the oncoming wave, the horde scrambled.

A gray-bearded gentleman crawled about on all fours, feeling for his dislodged monocle whilst issuing piteous cries. Twin sisters in cashmere tea gowns and jeweled necklets pounded past, shoes discarded, bosoms heaving, stark terror shining in their deer-like eyes.

"Motauqwa comes," Achok intoned. "Motauqwa will avenge."

Harlington grabbed Boone by the shoulders and gave him a series of hard shakes. "What mummery is this? *What the hell is the medicine man jabbering on about?*"

Boone's face was white as ghost-sifted chalk dust, the full horror of their predicament dawning in his eyes. "'Motauqwa means mountain,'" he whispered, words all but lost in the building roar.

Harlington glanced over his shoulder, beheld the monstrous land wave bearing down upon them. Shoving Boone aside he lurched at Achok. "Shaman, if you've the power to stop this—"

"Where's your god now, savage?" A fierce, triumphal joy blazed in Achok's battered face. He licked the blood from his lower lip. It tasted of iron, salt and the acrid bitterness of wind-blown grit. "Where's that bush-burning, Canaanite-slaughtering god of yours now, I wonder?"

**THUNDER-RUMBLE**

screams

and darkness was upon them.

# Epilogue

News article from the *New Jerusalem Tribune,* May 24, 1886:

> A ten-car train of the E Pluribus Unum Railroad has disappeared in the vicinity of Chicago. An earthquake struck the area 72 hours ago, doing extensive damage to the city and its surrounding environs.
>
> Among the missing are Earl Warren Harlington III, owner of the railroad; Constantine Brunello, the Archbishop of New Jerusalem; and Zachariah Boone, the railroad's security chief. Madam Angelique Renoir, of the Louisiana Renoirs, and Jack Robertson, editor of this paper, were found wandering in a state of shock and distressing *dishabille* near the train's last reported location. As yet, the survivors have been unable to speak intelligibly of their ordeal.
>
> No other trace of train or passengers has been found. Save one— there are unconfirmed reports that Achok, the darling, half-civilized

savage familiar to many readers of this good paper, may have also survived the calamity.

Nathaniel Clemens, owner of the general store in Freesboro, a settlement sixty miles southeast of Chicago, reported that a young Indian matching Achok's physical description and dress walked into his establishment hours after the convulsion which rocked the area to inquire after provisions and various sundries. Clemens attempted to strike up a conversation with the customer, only to be met with a glowering silence. When the store owner allowed that he "warn't inclined to sell a diddle-head-dime's worth of goods to taciturn, dirt-covered Injuns what don't know their place," he reported that the redskin "turned cold, hard devil's eyes upon me and like to mesmer'd this God-fearin' Christian soul into givin' him everything he asked after, afore I could gather my wits to eject him from the premises by his damned heathen ear. Now, perhaps it warn't mesmerism proper he turned upon me for all of that—I ain't sayin' it was, and I ain't sayin' it warn't—but if you was here to see the *look* he fixed upon me . . . that look . . . well. It were some look, I tell you what."

Monty Hokum, Freesboro's saloon habitué and resident dandy, reported meeting an Indian matching Clemens' description not long thereafter. "Achok was trudging west out of town, canvas bag in hand. Allowed as he was lightin' out for 'Frisco." Hokum's attention was arrested by "the black-and-blue ruin of the Injun's hard-pummeled face, and the unblinkin' lizard a-settin' on his shoulder, pretty as you please. That piggy-backin' reptile sure did give out the oddest croak: 'Maw-tok-wah, Maw-tok-wah.' Put a mighty peculiar feeling in my gut, it did. It warn't natural; warn't natural atall."

Those of our readers familiar with the satanic idolatries of Sachawatomi culture will no doubt have already noted the troubling onomatopoeic resemblance of the lizard croak to the name of Achok's abominable swamp god, "Motauqwa." It is a resemblance the Church fears is not entirely coincidental.

Witch hunters from the Office of the Inquisition have been dispatched to investigate.

# A Little Song of Death

When in the fullness of fast-flowing time
the joy of flesh becomes but ache & pain
nature succors & stops with death sublime
the manic antics of the Sons of Cain.
Rich wanton feast & wild, ribald song
strong wine & thighs—ecstatic poetry—
intoxicate the spirit; though erelong
the bell that tolled for others tolls for thee.
That thunder in the mountain: avalanche
of broken trees, & boulders, & black snow
rolls juggernaut downslope—no man can stanch
the final doom of ***BOOMCRASH:*** 'Way you go!
Madness, horror, brief joy, grief, red rage, strife—
berserk fast-fading visions: mordant life.

# A Matter of Debt Concerning the Gentleman in Baltimore

The Gentleman strained against his bonds, head thrashing on a sweat-soaked pillow. Red-rimmed, feverish eyes glared holes into the ceiling. Screams alternated with curses and fitful sobbing.

"Good god! How long has he been like that?" Dr. Snodgrass peered through an iron-barred window set into the one-way door, observing his patient writhe and rage.

"For two days now," replied a sober, humorless young man of twenty-six. Dr. Moran clasped his hands together waist-level before him in a gesture those closest to the doctor would recognize as doleful resignation. "He raves, reacts to things he imagines emerging from the walls and ceiling. Textbook delirium. Thursday afternoon he begged me to blow his brains out with a pistol."

"A decided turn for the worse," Dr. Snodgrass pronounced. "Why wasn't I immediately informed of these developments?"

Dr. Moran shrugged and unclasped his hands. "I had hoped the fever would break. Until it does, there isn't much either one of us can do for him."

"Treatment?" asked Dr. Snodgrass.

Dr. Moran's visage was grim. "Whilst the gentleman was lucid—mind you, we are speaking of a period of time more than forty-eight hours ago—we impressed upon him the necessity of imbibing a copious quantity of fluids. He drank twenty-two glasses of water in a ten-hour period. Nevertheless he remains badly dehydrated and, as you can plainly see, still in the nightmarish grip of fever. We administered laudanum and an herbal enema. An hour ago I approved an injection of morphine."

"Has the family been notified?" Dr. Snodgrass ran a hand through thinning hair.

"His cousin—the journalist-lawyer—was here."

"Splendid," replied Dr. Snodgrass with a dour moue. "And did this journalist-lawyer notice—"

"No," said Dr. Moran sharply. "He did not. I was with him every moment he spent in close proximity to our guest and I can assure you that he noticed nothing . . . untoward."

The Gentleman in question—trenchant literary critic, sometime magazine editor, reviled "jingle man," writer of tales grotesque and arabesque—cut loose with a piercing scream. Throat tendons stood out in stark relief against translucent skin. Preternaturally bright eyes bulged, face filling with blood as his convulsing frame sought to defeat the leather bonds holding him fast to the bed.

"He won't last much longer," Dr. Snodgrass observed. Then, cocking his head in order to bring his more acutely hearing right ear closer to the iron-barred window in the door—"Whose name is that he keeps calling out, I wonder?" He strained to hear as the patient's voice sank to a repetitive murmur. "Surely it's not . . . *Christ?*" He pressed his head against the iron bars of the window. "No. Kleist . . . Heinrich . . . Kleist."

Dr. Moran shrugged. "Never heard of the gentleman."

Three weeks earlier:

The sun was a molten sliver of bronze etching the horizon when the four-horse coach pulled up in front of the Greek Revival mansion with a rattling clatter of harness, undercarriage, and hooves. Setting the dragshoe to lock the wheels, the driver swung down from his dickey box with easy, practiced alacrity and strode to the side of the coach to open the door for his passenger.

"Won't be but a moment, beggin' your pardon, sir," said Thomas Deckard. He hand-cranked the cantilever dismount stairs into their locked exit position, stepped back, and doffed his cap.

A giant of a man emerged from the coach clad in a suit of rakish 1840s continental cut that only served to accentuate the brutish muscularity of his form. His face was a cicatrized horror of pockmarks and dueling scars, his fingernails black-polished talons more suggestive of a tiger's claws than a businessman's manicure. "Bring the luggage to my room." A bass voice rumbled like winter thunder. "Place the hobnailed suitcase at the foot of the bed. Open nothing else on penalty of your life. Are these instructions understood?"

"Perfectly, sir."

"Be especially careful with the bone-handled valise. I've not yet had time to inventory its contents of jewels and loose coin."

Deckard's face betrayed nothing. "Very good, sir."

Heinrich Kleist brushed past the driver and proceeded up the flagstone walk to the mansion's front door.

An hour later Kleist reposed in his host's lavishly appointed drawing room on a high-rolled settee of celadon green and creamy white velvet, cigar smoldering in his right hand. A glass of brandy stood near him on a low table to his left.

"You may speak freely in front of my confederate." Salt-and-pepper-bearded Lucius Hardy had a senator's regal bearing and mien. He indicated the corpulent, bespectacled man in the black cutaway coat and vest reclining on an antimacassared couch the other side of the room. "Sherman Slithers handles the public side of our business here in Boston: investments, bookkeeping, profit-making legerdemain—legal and less so."

Kleist grunted, sucked on his cigar to kindle its end a fiery red.

Hardy leaned back against the imposing leather-and-walnut edifice of the bar and thrust his hands into the brocaded frock coat that draped his broad-shouldered frame. He wore a very wide cravat, the high collar of his spotless white shirt turned down precisely a quarter-inch over the cravat's silk. A gold watch and chain depended from his vest. "Before we get down to business I suggest we settle the domestic trifle that has disturbed my home's tranquility. I daresay these petty thefts have gone on long enough."

Kleist nodded assent to this proposal from behind a cloud of bluish-gray cigar smoke.

Slithers giggled: a most unpleasant, burbling screech.

Hardy tugged a brocaded cord hanging from a gilt roundel in the ceiling that sounded a sonorous bell toll rolling through the carpeted gloom of the house.

A second or two later the butler glided into the drawing room: willowy, gray-templed, impeccably coiffed and accoutered. There was a faint smell of musk and onanistic over-indulgence about Mr. Gaines. "Yes, master?"

"I put it to you directly: were any jewels missing from Mr. Kleist's valise?" Hardy inquired.

"No, sir; the quantities tallied exactly according to the figures you gave."

"Very good," said Hardy. "How many five-dollar gold coins were found in this valise?"

"Sixty," sniffed Gaines.

"Excellent. And the number of silver dollars therein?"

"Two-hundred and eighty-one," said Mr. Gaines.

Kleist took another long draw of his fragrant cigar.

Hardy winced. "My guest informed me that he arrived with . . . now how many dollars did you say again, Mr. Kleist?"

"Two-hundred eighty-two," said Kleist.

"You are quite certain of this count?"

Kleist nodded. "I arrived here with two-hundred eighty-two silver dollars in my valise. Two-hundred eighty-two exactly. No more; no less."

Slithers giggled again.

"Now *that* is odd; very odd indeed. And most troubling. Our guest seems to have lost a coin 'twixt coach and guest bedroom. Would you usher the driver into our presence, please? Perhaps Mr. Deckard can clear up this discrepancy posthaste."

"Certainly, sir." Gaines exited with a raspy whisper of starched trousers and frock coat.

Hardy produced his meerschaum pipe and fired its bowl with a silver lighter produced from a vestment pocket. "I confess it will be a relief to be done with this business." He slid the lighter back home, took a deep draw from the pipe, and exhaled a cloud of smoke at the high vaulted ceiling. "Indifferent gods and carping creditors alike know we've more pressing matters to attend to."

Kleist reached for the brandy beside him. He swirled the liquid around in the glass, inhaled deeply, and set the glass back down on the end table without drinking.

Slithers removed his spectacles and exhaled on the lenses with a long, lizard-like wheeze. He then pulled a red silk handkerchief from his cutaway coat's inside pocket and polished the lenses with assiduity, tongue emerging repeatedly during this fastidiousness to moisten his upper lip.

Gaines and Deckard returned to the drawing room.

"Mr. Deckard," announced the butler with a slight inclination of the head, "I shall now retire, sir."

"For the nonce, Mr. Gaines." Hardy took another puff of his pipe. "Only for the nonce, if you please."

"Very good, sir." Gaines did his whisper-rasp exit again, face expressionless.

A light sheen of sweat glistened on Deckard's forehead. "How may I be of service, master?"

"How might you, indeed," said Hardy, shifting the pipe in his palm whilst studying the driver closely.

Hardy had dispatched Deckard to pick up Heinrich Kleist from his hundred-year-old brick Federal home on the other side of Boston that very morning—though the set-up had been agreed upon via correspondence the week before. Kleist would casually remark, upon disembarking at Hardy's home, that he'd not yet had time to inventory his valise's contents of jewels and loose coin. In point of fact, every jewel and loose coin therein had been triple-counted by Kleist himself before he left his home. Thereafter, the valise had remained in his possession until he arrived at his destination.

"Mayhap you could return the dollar you filched from our guest's luggage," said Hardy.

"I beg your pardon?" said Deckard, trying on a sickly smile. "I'm sure I've no idea—"

"Oh, that's true enough," said Kleist, taking a last drag on his cigar and stubbing it out in the ashtray beside his brandy. He rose from the settee and cracked his knuckles with theatrical deliberateness in the hushed silence of the drawing room. "I'm sure you've no idea of what is about to befall you. You may consider that a blessing, of sorts."

Deckard retreated a step from the hulking bulk of Kleist. "Gentlemen—forebear! It appears there's been some kind of terrible misunderstanding."

"No misunderstanding." Kleist pointed a dagger-nailed finger at Deckard's perspiring face. "You, sir, are a scoundrel and a liar. A disloyal sneak-thief and penny-ante pickpocket. A filcher of coins from women's purses; a riffler of items from gentlemen's luggage. In short, sir, a *worm:* loathsome, wriggling, verminous."

Slithers leaned forward on the couch in expectancy and anticipation: eyes wide, round degenerate mouth hanging stupidly open.

"Now see here!" Deckard objected. "I've had just about all the insults I am going to take from the likes of you."

Kleist laughed: a deep, Valhalla-like rumble, as of Norse gods slamming battle-hammers against frost giants in the afterlife.

"Master," Deckard continued, swiveling to face Hardy, a plaintive note in his voice, "you well know how many years I have faithfully served you; how long been your devoted servant!"

Hardy removed the stem of the pipe from his mouth. "I know that we have experienced a rash of curious disappearances of late—fine china, jewelry, coin. Miscellaneous odds and ends. I also know that a thief eventually overreaches; that he grows ever more emboldened and reckless as successive crimes go unpunished."

Kleist shuffled a ponderous step forward.

"Master!" exclaimed Deckard. "I call upon you to restrain Mr. Kleist from perpetrating any violence against my person until I have been able to clear my good name."

"I think," said Hardy, tapping the stem of his pipe against his teeth, "that *your* name will never be spoken in this house again."

"You think me a thief?" Deckard asked, incredulous.

"He thinks you a broken-limbed, headless corpse," replied Kleist in a tone of arch good humor.

Deckard blanched.

Slithers uttered a ululating peal of sadistic laughter.

Deckard revolved on his heel, made as if to leave the room—and Kleist was upon him.

"Now see here!" Deckard remonstrated.

Kleist seized the driver in his bear-like grip and cracked three of Deckard's ribs with a savage hug.

*"Oof,"* commented Deckard. His face reddened, eyes bulged.

Kleist drove Deckard onto all fours on the carpeted floor, right arm wrenched up behind his back, wrist bent at an alarming angle.

"The missing coin?" snarled Kleist into Deckard's ear.

"I tell you—" began Deckard.

Kleist snapped Deckard's wrist.

The man howled.

Kleist shifted his grip on Deckard's arm. "Your elbow is next. I assure you, the pain of a mangled wrist is as nothing compared to a shattered elbow. Most faint dead away, you know. It's absolute agony. Don't be a fool! Tell us what you did with the coin."

Deckard sought to crane his head around to make eye contact with his tormentor, his tremulous voice high and reedy. "I swear to you! As God is my witness, I have no idea—"

There sounded a sodden crack.

Deckard screamed. Slippery shards of splintered bone poked through the elbow rupture of jacket and sleeve, the compound fracture pumping crimson.

"Oh dear," said Kleist. "I fear we've ruptured a major artery." He knocked Deckard flat onto the carpeted floor, a controlling knee planted firmly in his back. Black-taloned hands encompassed the driver's throat. "Coin or corpse—your call. Personally, I'm hoping you remain perversely obstinate."

"Left boot!" Deckard shouted, struggling to raise his perspiring face off the carpeting. "The dollar is in my left boot! For god's sake, stop! *Stop!*" His breath hitched in his chest and he began to sob raggedly.

Kleist dragged Deckard from the floor into a sitting position, propped his back up against the wainscotted wall, and tore off the driver's boot. He upended the boot over his hand. A silver dollar tumbled into his palm. Kleist tossed the boot aside; showed the coin to the room as if he were a magician performing a trick; smiled grimly and slipped the coin into his suit coat's pocket.

Slithers giggled again.

"Your 'good name,' eh?" Hardy spat.

"Master—" Deckard began.

*"Silence!"* Hardy thundered.

"Get up," Kleist said.

Deckard struggled unsteadily to his feet, face deathly pale. His left hand was clamped over his shattered elbow. "I need a doctor. Please. The pain . . . as you said, it's . . ." He swallowed hard. "Agony." He reeled, seemed on the verge of fainting.

Kleist backhanded him across the mouth. Blood dribbled down Deckard's chin from pulped lips.

"You were saying," inquired Kleist with warm solicitousness. "A doctor?"

Deckard blinked, looked about himself uncertainly. His eyes began to roll up into his head again and Kleist slapped an open palm against his ear.

Deckard gasped—staggered, recovered. "Let me go. I beg you!" He wept, voice choked with emotion. "I realize I've forfeited all right to references. I'll return every item I've . . . wrongfully acquired, or make restitution double its value."

"Now, now," consoled Kleist in honeyed tones, "what would our enemies think of us if we pardoned you after so many acts of petty thievery? They would regard us as fools, yes? Rank amateurs. Buffoons."

"Weak!" screeched Slithers. "Idiots!"

"Just so," said Kleist, barring his elongated canines in a jackal's grin. "Business would suffer; certain critical streams of revenue dry up. Ambitious others would rise to challenge our control of divers unsavory, yet highly lucrative, practices and services. Surely you understand that—you of all people, years in Mr. Hardy's gainful employ?"

Deckard licked blood from his lips. His knees buckled, and Kleist grasped the driver's jacket and shirt in his fisted left hand to keep him upright.

"I won't breathe a word about any of this to anyone," whimpered Deckard. "Not a word. I swear it! I swear."

"I believe you," said Kleist, glancing over at Hardy.

Hardy nodded.

Kleist struck Deckard a savage blow with his black-taloned right hand. Deckard's head separated from his shoulders, bounced off the paneled wall, and thumped to the carpeted floor. A geyser of crimson blood and yellow bone marrow mixed with oily cerebrospinal fluid fountained into the air. Kleist stiff-palmed Deckard's shuddering corpse away from him; the headless horror took a wobbly stagger-step backward and collapsed onto its side, spraying prodigious gore onto the mosaic-patterned carpeting, an unfortunately positioned divan, and the dark-paneled, wainscotted wall.

"Well," said Hardy, "that's that." A sharp rap of his knuckle against the bowl of his upended pipe knocked smoking dottle into an ashtray atop the bar. "Neatly done, Mr. Kleist."

Kleist inclined his head in acknowledgment of the compliment.

"Do you wish to drink of this man's blood?" asked Hardy. "You need not exhibit any reticence in front of your *confrères;* you know—we are not bourgeois."

Kleist waved this away. "I wouldn't think of polluting my blood with this vermin's vile essence. To quench my vampiric thirst I'd sooner suck from a rat."

Slithers cut loose with another shriek of laughter; clapped his powdered hands together. "Well spoke, day walker. Oh, well spoke indeed! Indeed!"

"Gentlemen, I suggest we retire to the library to continue our discussion," said Hardy. "The servants will dispose of this refuse." He pocketed his pipe, regarding with distaste the sight of Deckard's juddering corpse pumping the last of its vital fluids onto the carpeting.

"Excellent suggestion," said Kleist.

"Capital," commented Slithers, levering his morbidly obese form erect after several hard grunts. "Tell me, Mr. Kleist—if you'll pardon the impertinence of my asking so bold a question—just how many centuries have you walked this earth?"

Kleist arched a brow. "Might I ask, in turn, what prompts such an inquiry?"

"Ah, yes," said Slithers. "Well . . . I understand that only the oldest and strongest of your kind can tolerate daylight without dissolution."

"Mr. Slithers," interjected Hardy, "as to Mr. Kleist's actual age, know this: he remembers the rise of agriculture between the Tigris and the Euphrates—at the dawn of the Bronze Age—in a time when Enlil was worshipped as the supreme god of the Sumerians."

Kleist hooked his thumbs into the waistband of his trousers, nodded. "Quite right. Two thousand years before Babylon was conquered by the Assyrians."

"Remarkable," breathed Slithers.

Kleist shrugged. "Merely time, Mr. Slithers. Nothing quite so quotidian, banal, and relentless as the passage of time."

They exited the drawing room, transited a short hallway, and went into the library together.

Among pressing business matters discussed: the troubling number of debtors owing significant sums to their organization; the chief debtor being one ignominious wretch by the name of Eddie Poe.

They were agreed: an example would be made. *Must* be made.

Kleist would call upon Mr. Poe once again. And this time, there would be no attempt to extract monies from the impoverished writer. No indeed. Restitution would take a different, more sanguinary form. . . .

Two weeks later:

The Gentleman opened the double-locked door, keys jingling in hand with the softest of tintinnabulations. He stepped inside, pressed the heavy oak door shut behind him. It closed with a hard and resonant click.

Tonight he would not have to return to his hovel-hole at the Swan Tavern on Broad Street. That was an unexpected mercy, for which he was inordinately grateful. The manager of the Exchange Hotel, alarmed at the haggard and disheveled appearance of his renowned guest lecturer, had impressed upon the Gentleman the necessity of his remaining the night in this sybaritic domicile of the transient rich—*gratis,* if it pleased the Bostonian. The Gentleman accepted the offer after the feeblest of protestations. In truth, a night's stay at the grand hotel would be a welcome respite from his usual substandard accommodations.

The Gentleman looked around the room. All was exactly as he'd requested—windows locked, loaded revolver resting atop a pillow, lamp burning on the white-lacquered desk. The flickering, smoky flame from the oil lamp rendered the stuffy room an orange-hued shadowbox of garish, phantasmagoric projections and jumping silhouettes.

He strode to the desk, dropped a sheaf of papers onto the desktop alongside a double-barreled derringer produced from his vestment pocket, and sank wearily into a rail-backed chair. The Gentleman undid his collar and loosened the black cravat tied at his throat. A sprig of evergreen jutted from a buttonhole. He removed this fragrant ornament, brought it to his nose for a desultory sniff, tossed it aside.

"Philistines," the Gentleman muttered, pulling a dingy gray handkerchief from his open waistcoat to mop the sweaty stubble of his face. He dabbed at cheeks, nose, chin. Task accomplished, the Gentleman dropped the damp handkerchief onto the desktop, kicked off his shoes, and massaged his temples with grimy fingertips.

His nerves were always shot after a recitation of poesy. No matter what tricks of oratory he used to energize his public performances, what inspired gestures and fevered declamations he invested into his galloping recitations, half the accursed room remained awash with nervous tics and rustlings, stifled coughs and low mutterings. It drove him to distraction! Almighty Moses in the wilderness never had half as restless, incurious, and barbaric an audience as regularly showed up at his performances these days.

"Philistines," he muttered again.

The quietness of the room was oppressive. Pregnant, expectant—watchful. The hairs on the nape of the Gentleman's neck prickled as he became aware of someone—some *thing*—observing him. Else it was simply another of his morbid fancies brought on by exhaustion and despair. So which was it—reality or paranoid ideation? He glanced about, saw nothing untoward or alarming. Still—

The Gentleman rose and approached a gilt French Empire-style mirror mounted on the wall opposite the four-poster bed. The carved panel above the ripple mirror was a copy of the neoclassical sculpture

*The Three Graces,* expertly executed in alabaster. A fine, large piece. It wasn't the elegance and grandeur of this object that drew his attention, however, but rather the mist that obscured the surface of the glass—all the more peculiar as the room was hot and dry.

"Curious," said the Gentleman, peering into the mirror while smoothing the ends of his newly regrown mustache. The clouding mist made a misshapen gargoyle of his dark-circled eyes and wide, expansive forehead. He reached out to wipe the fog from the mirror. Concurrent with his fingertips brushing the cool, slick glass, the mist rose up and coalesced into a towering figure dressed in a waistcoated suit of rakish Continental cut. The damnable apparition was dressed entirely in black. What's more—O, horror!—the thing grabbed his arm with the predatory fierceness of an eagle sinking its talons into a thrashing salmon.

"You!" the Gentleman gasped.

"No other. You thought to escape us, sir?" The fiend gave the Gentleman's arm a savage shake. "Ha! We are not so easily dodged. You owe us a sizable sum, Mr. Poe. And I assure you, we are an organization that collects its debts."

"You'll have your money, Kleist. I swear it! Every cent. In two months' time." The Gentleman's eyes strayed to the revolver on the pillow. A sticky residue of garlic coated the bullets of that gun, if the hotel staff had followed his directions to the letter. . . .

"But that is exactly the problem my pitiable, impecunious friend— you are completely out of time," said Kleist.

"God's sake's, man! Fiend! Devil! I beg you. Surely you've heard of my impending remarriage. I shall soon come into possession of considerable assets. When that happy day occurs you shall be the first—O, the very first!—of my creditors to receive prompt remuneration and additional recompense, according to the length of time—"

*"Enough!"* Kleist bared his teeth in a cold, rictused smile, revealing a pair of wickedly pointed lateral incisors. "Your bleating promises of incipient wealth no longer interest us. As it is, the organization has given

you an extended period of time in which to repay your debt—an inordinately long and merciful expanse of time. Do you deny it? Yet you are still in arrears. Our reputation suffers."

Kleist brought his pale white face close to the Gentleman's own. Bloodless as a desiccated corpse, an odious stench emanated from his mouth. "Worse insult yet—you *run*. From *me*. Ludicrous! There is nowhere you can hide from the organization. And I must tell you, we have spent no small amount of effort to affect this rendezvous." Reflected flame danced in Kleist's black pupils. "I thirst, and you shall succor. *That* is the repayment you shall make."

The Gentleman, realizing further conversation was useless, thrashed in Kleist's grip.

"Come, come; this Hottentot squirming is most unseemly," remarked Kleist. "I expected more dignified behavior from a Southern gentleman."

"I will not walk the earth a rabid, rat-faced abomination!" shouted the Gentleman, eyes wild.

"You wound me, sir. Do not alarm yourself unduly—you will not become a vampire. I shall drink only enough of your blood to wet my parched palate, not enough to grant you the dark gift of eternal undeath." Kleist smile a rueful little smile. "Sadly, you will be hurled into annihilating oblivion. Or hell, if that's your pleasure."

The Gentleman gasped as dual pinpricks of heat lanced his throat.

Days later:

The Gentleman dreamed.

Blood. Fire. Darkness. Ice. A charnel stink of the grave, mixed with a whiff of sulfur. A demented, off-rhythm pounding of kettle drums. Sheets of manuscript fluttering down like speckled, broken-winged bats to cover the still, angelic faces of loved ones. A raven's croak. The yowl of a one-eyed black cat. A pounding of beringed and bloodied hands against an unyielding coffin lid. The metronomic *snick-snick-snick* of a

clockwork's scything blade descending in glittering metallic arcs by reflected torchlight. A tall-masted ship caught in the grip of a maelstrom,
whirling round and down—faster, ever faster. . . .

Doctors Snodgrass and Moran held a low-voiced conversation before an
iron-barred window set into a one-way door.

Nurse Connolly approached with a whisper of starched white linen.

"Evening, Miss Connolly," Dr. Moran nodded.

"Evening," the nurse responded. "Has the gentleman's condition
improved?"

Dr. Snodgrass shook his head. "I'm afraid not." His lips were compressed into a thin, bloodless line. "You will inform us at once if there is
any change in the patient's condition."

"Of course, Doctor," said Connolly.

The Gentleman emitted another piercing scream, followed by broken sobs and incoherent cursing.

"Come, John, let's retire to the study." Dr. Snodgrass threw a collegial arm around Dr. Moran's shoulders. "A brandy would seem to be in
order this night."

"Or two," said Dr. Moran.

They moved off, the staccato click of hard-soled shoes on tile sounding in contrapuntal counterpoint to the shrieks and howls echoing down
the corridor.

In the quiet darkness of 3:00 A.M. the Gentleman opened his eyes. His
face was bathed in sweat. A wan shaft of moonlight fell through the high-
vaulted Gothic window and splayed upon the sheets; dust motes roiling
in the cold, sepulchral glow. There was a smell of mossy stone, moldering wood, and rusted iron in the air, mixed with the institutional odors of
acrid urine and harsh cleaning solvents.

The Gentleman's last thought was of his first cousin: the waif-like,
kindly, wonderful girl he'd married at thirteen when he was twenty-seven,

whose tragic struggles and death had fueled the creation of such haunting, fevered works as "Annabel Lee," "The Raven," and "Ligeia."

"Virginia," Poe whispered. And died.

"You realize what a sensation this will cause, what kind of ruckus will be kicked up when the papers report these puncture marks on his neck?" Dr. Snodgrass lifted an inquiring brow. "Not to mention the fact that our patient was found wearing someone else's clothing."

"Yes . . . A final indignity, this ill-fitting clothes business," Dr. Moran commented. "The murderer not only mortally wounded the 'Raven Man' but rendered him altogether clownish: disreputable, dishabille, contemptible."

"Yet another tale of the grotesque and arabesque." Dr. Moran blew a gust of air out from between hard-clenched teeth. "There has been, I think, quite enough lurid gossip and speculation regarding the melancholy details of this poor man's life. Shall we add to this tale of woe? Is the miserable wretch never to know peace?"

For a moment they were silent, staring down at the corpse stiffening in the first rigidities of rigor mortis.

"The embalmer," Dr. Snodgrass said thoughtfully, "will render these marks invisible."

"Yes," said Dr. Moran. "Completely." He looked at his colleague, back down at the corpse.

"Regarding his last words . . ." began Dr. Snodgrass.

"Hmm, they won't do, I'm afraid," said Dr. Moran. "We shall have to provide the press with a more appropriate, spiritually elevated last cry than the mention of his under-age cousin bride."

"Something like, 'Lord take pity on my poor soul'?"

"Precisely," said Dr. Moran. "The very phrase, I should think."

Two rooms away, another patient of the Drunk Ward screamed and thrashed.

"Cause of death—*delirium tremens*," Dr. Snodgrass pronounced.

Dr. Moran nodded. "I concur. Brought on by excessive dehydration and alcohol poisoning."

There sounded another high-pitched, ululating scream from the bowels of the institution, followed by an outburst of demented laughter.

Dr. Snodgrass reached out and closed the black-browed Romantic's eyes. "God speed, Edgar Poe."

The motley drama ended, Death held illimitable dominion over one more vanquished soul.

# Let There Be Light

Only the dead have seen the end of war.
—Plato

I awake with a start in threatening dark
    nightmare fading like faerie;
heart beating hard as a runaway drum—
    I'm adrenalized, terrified, wary.

Fields of war—long distant now—
    bloom hot & lurid as life
        in my dreaming mind—as gun, land mine,
        grenade & combat knife

reap anew their killing tolls—
    I return each night to the fight:
a wraith of Valhalla forever doomed
    to reenact hideous rites.

I reach for my wife but she isn't there;
    Fran's leapt from the combat bed
to flick a switch & blind with light
    this revenant back from the dead.

# Samhain Eve: A Celtic Tale

Owen Kerrigan awaited the return of a dead man. He stood outside his stone-slabbed hut, gazing across the meadow at the edge of the boggy woods, breath a chill mist in the air. A peaty tang carried to his nostrils, mixed with the fragrant wood smoke of the bon fires that had burned in the village since dawn. One hand shaded his eyes against the westering light.

Dusk of October 31st. Samhain Eve: the end of summer and the beginning of the new year. A time of bon fires and celebratory feasting, sacred observance and human sacrifice, daylight revels followed by night-haunted terrors and warding rituals. A portentous, carnivalesque, liminal time when the barrier between the worlds of the living and the dead thinned to nothing. It was this latter fact that was the source of Owen Kerrigan's growing unease, as he waited for the return of the young man he'd murdered three years ago in a raid on a rival clan.

A wooden door creaked open behind him. Owen dropped his hand from his eyes and turned to behold the perspiring face of his wife.

"Come inside, Owen. Our meal grows cold." Tara glanced down at the candlelit, hollowed-out turnips flanking the doorway, transformed by artful carving into monstrous faces: an ancient custom meant to ward off the haints, night-gaunts, and other supernatural beasties that prowled about on New Year's Eve. "The candles will burn most of the night. Let the flame guardians greet our friend." She stepped back and closed the door.

Mayhap Tara was satisfied that the candlelit grotesqueries would prove sufficient barrier to ward off the things of the netherworld that came a-knockin' after dark on October 31st, but Owen was not. After all, it had never stopped him from returning before.

Bran. The young man's name was Bran. A fact he'd found out only later, after a delegation of tribal elders from his village met with the murdered victim's family and his betrothed, Deirdre, to offer iron and gold and silver-tongued apologies to avert an all-out retaliatory war.

A faint tinkling of childish laughter sounded from a hut a stone's throw away behind him, near the edge of a stand of alder and birch bordering the southern side of the village. This was followed by the yowl of a cat and the *basso-profundo* cursing of his neighbor Kendrick, a roar almost immediately counterpointed by the scolding alto of his wife.

Owen smiled a small, sad smile. He and Tara had not, as yet, produced any children.

Glancing once more at the edge of the boggy wood to the west—the direction the dead man had approached in years past—Owen said, "Come then, Bran. Return to this world if you must. But Cernunnos hear me, there's nothing more I can do for you—no way to undo what's been done. If I could grant you life again . . ." He trailed off, fists balled at his sides.

No answer from the mire. Tendrils of fog twined amongst an acidic fenestration of scraggly shrub, withered black spruce, and waxy leatherleaf.

Owen unclenched his fists. The sting in his hands abated; blood rushed back into the crescent moons dug into the flesh of his palms. He turned and went inside.

After a meal of bread, porridge, and honeyed oat beer Owen made love to Tara. Raw and tightly wound as his nerves were, this most sacred and holy of days seemed a most auspicious time to try again for a child. Thus it was an opportunity he dared not waste. After all, the year just ending was "The Burning of the Bitter Fruit." Closing out another three-year cycle, the Druids had declared it a time when final vengeances were to be exacted or forever dismissed, old grievances buried, past insults and injuries atoned for. So what better time to conceive a child than New Year's

Eve, when the gods of the October moon might bless the efforts of two reverent and obedient Celts to procreate a new warrior for the tribe? Especially as next year was "The Sprouting of Green Saplings."

Lying on a bed of blanket-covered straw afterward, Owen held Tara in his arms and promised: "By this time next year we will have a son; I'm sure of it. The stars are right; all omens propitious. Haven't the Druids foretold next year to be a time of increased fertility and strong birthings?"

Tara kissed him, caressed the matted locks of his hair. "I want to believe, Owen." In the flickering light of the dying hearth fire her eyes were sunken and shadowed as cavern grottoes. "I want very much to believe that next year will be different. Gods know I've sacrificed and prayed to every image in fen and glen within a two-days' walk that they may heed our entreaties."

Turning over in Owen's arms, Tara placed her backside against him. Her next words were directed at the wall of the hut. "But I fear the dead man has cursed us." Tara never referred to Bran by name, refusing to grant him the humanizing individuation of naming. "You cut him down before his first bearding, before he could impregnate his betrothed. Now he works to poison my womb from beyond the grave. Either that or his hateful hag, Deirdre, works her witchcraft against us."

It was the lament and accusation Tara voiced more and more frequently, with increasing bitterness, as the seasons passed and her womb remained without issue.

"Nonsense," said Owen. He planted a soft kiss on the back of Tara's neck. "It just hasn't been our time, that's all. We've been frustrated, true. Unlucky. Perhaps even cursed; you may be right about that. But now, on the eve of the new year . . ." He whispered further reassurances into her ear, stroked the soft feminine curve of his wife's shoulder and back.

They talked of other things for a while. Then, rendered sleepy and languorous by their lovemaking, they dozed.

*     *     *

In dream he relived Bran's murder all over again.

The episode had started out as a hastily planned and executed raid: a reprisal for insults delivered by young warriors from a neighboring clan to a couple of *his* clan's young warriors as they'd squeezed past each other on a narrow hunting trail earlier in the week. He'd been in the flush of early manhood then: a tough, sinewy, tow-headed Celt of fifteen summers, eager to win recognition and honor. He'd felt pride at being picked to accompany his cousin on a mission of retribution.

Every detail of their sortie was burned into his memory. The long, early-morning march over forested hills into enemy territory; the purposeful movement of a half-dozen of his kinsmen down the trail. The nerve-jittered, anticipatory way they'd fingered knife-hilts and spear-hafts as they'd progressed; the calculating glances they'd thrown each other.

As the men on the warpath moved deeper into hostile territory the rawness of their nerves and the heightened powers of perception gained from the proximity of danger reduced communication to a series of sharp hand gestures and grunts.

The war band toiled on toward noon. Then, rounding another in a seemingly endless series of bends negotiated in the descent of a high wooded hill, they stumbled upon a raven-haired young man and his green-eyed girl rolling naked in the shade of an ancient oak tree beside the river *Beannaithe Sionann.*

An ember popped in the smoldering hearth. Owen awoke with a start, face bathed in sweat. A low, plaintive moan escaped his lips. Tara slumbered beside him, snoring softly, blankets twined about her stolid form.

Gods! How long had he been asleep?

He sat up, rubbed sleep from his eyes. Wan moonlight streamed through small openings cut in the front wall of the hut, painting the disheveled interior in shades of ghostly gray and midnight silver.

Owen's clothes were draped over a rough-hewn bench in the corner where he'd thrown them before making love to Tara. Moving quietly but quickly, he rose to his feet and dressed, pulling on leather boots, rough linen trousers, and a long-sleeved wool shirt of sun-bleached checkerboard pattern.

Tara stirred. She muttered something in her sleep, thrashed for a bit, then lay flat on her back with one arm thrown over her face and resumed snoring.

Owen exited the hut and closed the door with exaggerated care behind him. Glancing down as he did so, he noted the candles still burning in the hollowed-out, monster-faced turnips. Jagged grins and knife-slit eyes flickered to the fires dancing within.

He took a deep draught of the night's bracing air.

A blood-red three-quarter moon hung in the sky like the baleful eye of a drowsing demon. The late-evening chill had sharpened to a bitter, hoar-frost cold, rendering each bright pinprick of light in the starry gulf above with crystalline distinctness.

Not that Owen's clammy skin registered the cold—he was too preoccupied with thoughts of Bran's return. It was something he would never grow accustomed to. When face-to-face with the young man he'd murdered, his knees grew weak and the inside of his mouth burned hot and dry as a clay firing kiln.

Tara, after Bran's first Samhain Eve visitation, was dismissive of the wraith. *Why go to him, Owen? Why open the door at all?*

*Don't be absurd; I must! Can't you feel him standing out there? Watching, listening . . .*

*Let him stand there all night if that is his pleasure!* Tara had snapped back. *At sunup he will be gone, vanished like a moonbeam at dawn. I've never heard tell or talltale yet of a ghost who could do more than moan 'round shuttered windows or rattle a door in its frame.*

But Owen had opened the door and gone out to meet Bran. How could he possibly explain his actions to Tara—a dutiful if coarse and unimaginative young woman whose greatest passions and loudest boasts were reserved for her clan, her kettle-cooking, and Owen's one-and-only kill? He couldn't. And so he simply endured his wife's taunts and Bran's New Year's Eve visitations as trials that had to be borne. It was a matter of atonement.

Atonement—yes, that was the right word. A heavy word, an oath-taking word. A word of bondage, duty, pain, and recompense. Atonement for the act of having struck down a fleeing foe, for the waste of a life callow and young as his own had been. Atonement for the shrill cry of triumph that broke from his lips as his hard-flung spear penetrated the back of Bran's skull, bringing the raven-haired young man crashing down onto his face. Atonement for straddling Bran's still-shuddering corpse and hacking at his neck until he'd cut off his head. Atonement for grinning as he handed the dripping hunting knife borrowed for the task back to a laughing kinsman. Atonement for the deaf ears turned to the wracking sobs and horrified tears of Deirdre, Bran's betrothed, shed over the mutilated body of her beloved.

Yes, it was to atone that Owen went out to treat with Bran's ghost on Samhain Eve, in the fervent hope that in so doing the pangs of remorse that pierced his heart in moments of uneasy reverie would bite with lessened ferocity over the course of the ensuing year, for it was the nightmare visage of death-mask Bran that now haunted Owen's dreams: his startled, bulging eyes; his white-lipped, wide-open mouth.

In the days following Bran's death the whole story came out: the goad of exchanged insults on the hunting trail, the unauthorized reprisal raid executed by Owen's kinsmen intended to exact vengeance for tarnished honor, the gruesome details of Bran's killing and mutilation. It had long been a Celtic custom to cut off an enemy's head and display it as proof of prowess in battle. But in this instance, the judgment of the village elders—both Bran's and Owen's—had been immediate, unanimous, and decisive: an unjustified murder had been committed.

Owen's exultation turned to ashes in his mouth.

Given each side's predilection for hair-trigger violence, long-nursed grudges, and legitimizing casus belli, averting war between the clans had been no mean or easy feat. Yet it had been managed—just barely. The unanimity of agreement regarding Owen's guilt and the speed with which sentence was pronounced had helped considerably in that regard.

Owen's village tithed a heavy portion of iron and gold. The iron was assessed in axes, swords, and daggers; the gold in bracelets, rings, and coin. The leader of the raid—Owen's cousin, Sheridan—had been forever banished from tribal lands. As for Owen himself, his hut had been emptied of its most valuable possessions—carted off to Deirdre as partial recompense for the crime. And he'd been soundly beaten by two of Bran's kinsmen, sent from the murdered man's village to carry out the sentence within a fortnight of the killing. Only Owen's inexperience and callowness—he'd just turned fifteen at the time of the atrocity and was adjudged to have been following orders from an older kinsman—saved him from immediate ignominious execution.

Yet these punishments were scarcely enough to avert war. In the end an uneasy peace held, as uncomfortable to both sides as it was precedent-setting. It was an awkward and unnatural interlude of nonviolence, for both clans believed in immediate retaliation for violations of honor. Beatings, banishments, and levied fines—necessary as they were—frustrated the lust for spilled blood. In truth, the clans hallowed and kept holy but one harsh creed in their hard-hating hearts: blood-for-blood, wound-for-wound, death-for-death.

Deirdre cried out for blood atonement. News of the young woman's anguish and bereavement filtered back to Owen and Tara: Deirdre had torn out fistfuls of hair from her scalp; clawed crimson furrows into her face and breasts. Deirdre stalked the dirt paths of her village a raging fury, alternately weeping and screaming, calling out for Owen's death.

Owen heard these stories and was sorely troubled; Tara was indifferent—or worse: openly scornful of Deirdre's grief and rage.

*"I am haunted by more than a ghost, Tara. I am haunted by memory.*

*"You are a warrior now, my beloved, blooded in battle.*

*"Battle? There was no battle. The boy—*

*"Foe! Enemy! Other! Struck down to avenge an insult to our clan.*

*"Murder, Tara. The village elders so ruled.*

*"Pah! I'll have no more of this puling. Come, place your hand here . . . and here . . . and . . . there. Ah! That's it. Yes! Make love to me, Owen. Now. Now!"*

An animal screamed in the forested lowlands behind the village.

Owen's heart jumped in his chest, causing his pulse to hammer at his temples: ba-DOOM, ba-DOOM, ba-DOOM. Cursing, he glanced behind him.

Some rat-footed beast torn apart by owls, no doubt. Kendrick's cat gave an answering yowl. Owen caught a flash of luminous eyes from the dark environs of Kendrick's home as the grayish, indistinct outline of the feline flowed along the base of the beehive hut and disappeared round the side.

Damn the creature! It made the most inhuman cries. More distressing still, at other times it sounded almost human—like a squalling infant. The last thing his over-taut nerves needed right now was a distraction behind him, pulling his focus away from the mire.

At the thought, Owen returned his attention to the bog. All was silence, drifting fog, and dying vegetation. Odd whorls and pinpricks of light—ignis fatuus, the Romans termed the eerie phenomenon—had begun their curious will-o'-the-wisp dance over the mire, portending the collision of worlds living and dead. It wouldn't be long now. Gauging from the position of the engorged crimson moon overhead, Owen judged it close to midnight. No, not long at all . . .

In the short interim left him before the young man's return Owen ruminated upon Bran's past visits.

The first year his victim's spirit returned to haunt its murderer, Tara slept through the entire event. Owen left their bed to answer a midnight knock on the door and found Bran's headless body, garbed in rags, swaying before him. He cried out, slammed the door in the thing's face, and ran to the hearth to snatch a dagger off the mantel. Rushing back to the door, Owen yanked it open and stabbed straight for the apparition's heart.

Naught occurred, save for an icy tingling in his hand and lower arm where all-too-mortal flesh contacted ghastly ghost.

Owen stepped back, dagger falling from nerveless fingers.

Bran gestured at his ragged neck stump with both hands—then opened them wide, palms up, flexing its fingers in an unmistakable "give me" gesture.

The thing wanted its head.

"I don't have it," Owen said, eyes wild. *"I threw it in the bog."*

This was truth. He'd consigned Bran's head to the bog only weeks ago, as the new year fast approached. He could no longer bear the sight of the rotting skull. The thing had become more bone than flesh, anyhow, despite the herbal soak and smokehouse preservation treatment given it. And its death-rictus grin mocked him.

"I—I don't have your head any longer," Owen repeated, voice breaking. *"Please understand."* He gestured toward the mire. "It's there— sunken in the bog."

Bran's headless form turned to face the direction indicated, then took three hesitant, shuffling steps toward the miasmic woods.

Owen slammed the door closed and put his back against it, breathing hard.

Tara snorted in her sleep, pulled a blanket up to her chin, and snuggled deeper into the straw.

After long, agonizing moments in which Owen strained to detect the slightest sounds, he flung wide the door. Silence there, and nothing more. Between his hut and the mire there was naught but dew-wet grass, tendrils of drifting fog, and the odd splintery-branched bush.

A year passed. Another hard, tortuous year of uneasy daytime reveries, late-night thrashing, and nightmare screams. In this interval between Samhain Eve visitations Owen replayed the scene of Bran's murder over and over again in his head.

Why did he do it? Why had he been so eager to kill?

The only honest, unflinching answer Owen ever arrived at was . . . because killing was fun. Acting as a member of a predatory group, menaced by just enough danger to set one's own heart racing, dealing out death had proved every bit as intoxicating and ecstatic as countless battle songs, campfire stories, and war poems promised.

The attack of conscience that ambushed Owen later—the unexpected emotion that inflicted so much torment on him, both waking and sleeping—was empathy. In identifying with Bran—in exchanging, in his imagination, his role as the slaughterer with the slaughtered—Owen felt near overwhelming sorrow, horror, and regret. The battle songs and war poems he was familiar with spoke not a word of this after-killing pain.

It was certainly beyond Tara's understanding. She mocked him as a man weak with womanly emotion.

Perhaps he was, for all that. What need of a man for empathy, if it should turn the joy of killing against him?

One cold and drizzly day last spring Owen worked up enough courage to broach the topic of his guilt with the village's most seasoned fighter, Calhoun—a grizzled, one-eyed veteran of countless battles against the Roman occupier. The old war dog had laughed, pounded him on the back, and said, "Drink to forget, lad! Numb yourself. And if that doesn't work"—here the gray-haired cyclops gave him a mischievous wink—"give that moon-faced wife of yours a sound thrashing the next time she mouths off. Farr! You'll have drama enough then, methinks, to forget one wee little killing."

It was advice Owen ignored.

\*  \*  \*

Next Samhain Eve Owen ordered Tara to spend the night at her sister's on the other side of the village. She protested—Tara wanted to greet Bran with weapons of silver, Druidic ghost-killing incantations, and hot words of venomous hate—but Owen was determined to face Bran alone, without annoyance or distraction.

Evening of the second visitation found Owen sitting on his doorstep, a two-handed axe laid across his lap, flame guardians burning to either side, waiting as twilight deepened into night and the domestic noises of the village settled down into the occasional dog bark, door slam, and far-off snatch of conversation.

At midnight sharp Bran appeared.

Owen had dozed off—the latest in a series of nodding head drops and adrenaline-jolted jerks back to heart-pounding consciousness—when the shuffle of approaching footsteps snapped his head up off his chest.

Bran's ghost was thirty feet away and closing. The apparition carried its head in its arms, gait stiff-legged and ponderous—though its walk was an improvement over last year's lurching stumble. The rotted cerements of the grave it wore had seemingly unrotted themselves back into a semblance of dirt-matted tunic and trousers of indeterminate color.

Owen stood, every hair on the back of his neck and arms prickling into gooseflesh. So . . . it had found its head. He gripped the two-handed axe in front of him, axe-head just below eye level and canted to the right.

Twenty feet out Bran came on, sibilant footsteps serpent-like in the grass: *shuffle-wisp, shuffle-wisp, shuffle-wisp.*

What ghost's footsteps sound against cushioning loam? Owen thought feverishly to himself. This thing is here! It's really here with me now, on this material plane. Cernunnos protect me; I face not ghost but revenant!

Owen tried to speak, but all that came out was a throat-constricted whine.

Bran closed the remaining distance to halt an arm's-length away.

"What . . ." Owen whispered. Words failed him.

Bran raised his head, socketing it onto his ragged neck stump with a ghastly series of fleshly squeaks and sharp bone scrapings. His visage was half skull, half flesh-rotted ruin: grayish-green with dirt and mold, bits of peaty moss and brinish bracken twined in odd clumps of hair still clinging to the purplish scalp; the whole dusted by a rough, whitish-crystalline substance Owen recognized as bog salt.

A hard wind came up: a branch-rattling, grit-blowing wind that caused Owen to squint against its driving force. It soughed through forest and village rustling leaves and long grasses, banging loose debris against doors and shuttered windows, scraping branches together in the wind-tossed treetops with a bone-clacking clatter of madly jawing skeletons.

Owen found his voice. "What do you want of me? Why are you here?"

The candles flickering in the flame guardians went out.

Bran stared at him, black-pooled sockets where eyes once reposed.

Owen returned the stare, hard-clenched hands beginning to sweat and slip on the hardwood shaft of the axe.

"I said, what do you want with me?" Owen's voice came out a roar, though it was a sound lost in the howl and whine of the rising wind.

Bran said nothing.

"Why come you here?" Owen brandished the axe high overhead, veins standing out in forehead and neck from the force of barely restrained terror and fury. "Why haunt me? Your head was a trophy, nothing more. *It means nothing!*"

Bran rocked in the hard-driving wind, arms at his sides, silent and inscrutable as a Pictish cairn-stone.

"I'll not ask again." Owen raised the axe still higher. "Answer! Or I swear by all that's holy and unholy, you'll lose your head a second time at my hands."

Bran stared at Owen with unblinking fixity.

*"Enough!"*

Owen brought the axe down on the revenant's head, shattering it like a rotted pumpkin. Bits of moldering flesh, jagged jawbone, broken teeth, and fragments of skull exploded past his face to patter onto the ground around him. So violent was the blow that momentum carried the axe-head through neck and ribcage, continuing on its downward trajectory until forged iron glanced off hip bone, the haft almost wrenching itself from Owen's hands.

Bran collapsed, sundered in two.

"I warned you, did I not?" Owen screamed at the eldritch thing twitching at his feet. "I gave fair warning, but you . . ." His voice caught, breath hitching in his chest. "Ah, gods! *I've killed you again.*" He flung the axe aside. "Ghost, revenant, demon from darkest netherworld— you've forced me to kill again. Damn you!"

Somewhere in the village behind him something laughed a screeching, loon-like laugh. The continuing sonic assault of the susurrating wind masked the exact location and provenance of that eerie, ululating cry. Deirdre?

Owen took the half-dozen paces to his front door, placed hand upon handle.

The wind died to a stiff, buffeting breeze.

A series of rustling clicks and clacks sounded spider-soft behind him.

He turned round and gasped—for there stood Bran, upright again, seemingly no worse for wear—save for the half-dozen axe-rent chunks of skull and jawbone missing from his reassembled form.

"Alaunus and Taranis," Owen breathed.

"No . . . gods," Bran growled, the thunder of his voice a thousand cannons fired in the blackest pits of the netherworld come rumbling up from hell. "Only . . . horror." His head swiveled on his neck—left, right—as if he were trying to gain a glimpse of something behind Owen. "Horror," he reiterated. "Shadows. And the void."

Owen felt as much as heard the thing's inhuman words. His teeth rattled in their sockets as the revenant's vocalization grumble-groaned up from the sub-sonic through various dissonant shadings of granitic bass, causing his scrotum to shrivel against his groin as he pissed himself. The warmth in his crotch scarcely registered, so cold—so very, *very* cold—were his hands, feet, and face.

"Go!" Owen cried. "*Leave me be!* By the power of the gods and our ancestors, holy oak and shamrock—through intercession of banshee and faerie—I abjure you! Return to the hideous void from which you sprang!"

Bran—unmoved, unyielding—undying—only swayed in the pitiless moonlight.

Owen glanced at his axe. It lay in the grass where he'd flung it, a few short steps away. But of what use was the weapon now? One could not kill the undead with cold iron alone, that much was clear.

For what seemed like the thousandth time that night Owen asked the question: "What do you want from me?" The interrogative came out an exhausted, barely audible plea.

Bran waited, his silence a portentous, nighted gulf in which Owen's words fell forever without striking bottom.

"I regret your death. It was a mistake." Owen spread his hands, beseeching. "I've prayed to the gods for forgiveness, made reparations. What more would you have me do?"

Bran's neck creaked. He cocked his skull-faced head off-center, as if listening intently.

Owen seized the revenant by the shoulders and shook the dread netherworld thing with a violence that caused its rotted head to bobble on its neck. "*I can't undo what's been done.* Don't you understand that? Why can't you understand that? Leave me in peace, I beg you! Gods!" He choked on the passion of his words; dropped his hands from Bran's shoulders to swipe angrily at his eyes. "Leave me be! Else tell me what I must do to rid myself of your presence."

The hollow, shadowed sockets of Bran's skull tracked Owen's eyes, revealing nothing.

Owen was seized by madness then. He attacked the revenant with his bare hands: pummeling Bran's rotted ribcage; clawing at the nightmossed, bog-salted visage; clamping his arms around his opponent's chest in a bear hug as he stutter-stepped a little half-circle in an endeavor to hurl the thing to the ground.

All for naught—the effort proved fruitless.

Owen dropped his arms and stepped back, chest heaving, sweat trickling in cooling rivulets down his face and neck, soaking into his shirt.

Bran bared his teeth in a grin.

The strength went out of Owen's legs then. He sank to the grass, weeping. Inarticulate words and garbled phrases tumbled out: oaths and imprecations, threats and fervent pleadings, prayers to the gods mixed with foul blasphemies. It was a sound more wounded animal than human communication, the cry of a mind unhinged and spirit broken: a gibbering, maniac sound. In the extremity of his despair and frustration Owen pounded the ground, ripped chunks of sod from the earth to shred in his shaking fists, tore at his face and clothes.

And when—after a time that seemed somehow above and apart from strict, chronological time in the altered consciousness of the raving Celt—Owen dared raise his head to again confront Bran's skull-faced rictus, he discovered that the thing . . . was no longer there.

Bran had vanished.

Owen was alone on the cold, moonlit loam—only his bloodied face, torn clothes, and pounding heart evidence of the drama that had just transpired.

"Cernunnos, mercy," Owen breathed.

He looked to the bog, where eldritch lights whirled and winkled in the fog. With the exception of the ghostly, insectile zephyrings of the ignis fatuus, there was no other motion from that quarter.

Nothing else emerged from the miasmic woods that night.

A year later to the day Owen stood outside his hut awaiting Bran's third Samhain Eve visitation. Bran would call upon him once again—of that fact he had no doubt. He was as certain of this as he was of Tara's unwavering love, the blandness of her kettle cooking, her impatience with endless self-recrimination and regret.

Owen held no weapon in his hands this night. Weapons had proven useless, after all. And really, what harm—what physical harm—had Bran ever caused him?

Frenzied barking broke out in the village. First one—two—then three dogs rent the air with alarmed cries, each one successively closer to Owen.

Owen frowned, half turned. Could Bran be approaching from the far side of the village? But that didn't make sense. The first two hauntings had occurred with Bran materializing from the bog, so why would he now . . . ? Then again, he hadn't seen Bran arise from the mire that first Samhain Eve after the murder. He'd answered a midnight knock on the door and assumed that Bran had arisen from the boggy woods, a suspicion apparently borne out that second Samhain Eve, when . . .

In his peripheral vision—a flicker of movement.

Owen swiveled to face the mire squarely, the front door of his hut a couple of comforting paces behind him.

Something moved in the mist twining about the bracken, toppled trees and black-splintered bushes of the bog.

Owen's eyes strained to identify the form. That was no crippled, club-footed revenant lurching about out there, that was . . . "Gods of my ancestors," he muttered.

Here came Bran—striding out of the fog with easy, loose-hipped athleticism, looking as hale and hearty as the day Owen slew him. Could it be? Had Bran in truth returned to grace the world of the living?

As Bran drew closer, Owen noted the garish splendor of the young man's clothes: the green-and-yellow-striped tunic with cross-stitched knotwork pattern spiraling about the sleeve-ends and neck, the richly dyed purple trousers narrowing into a pair of softly gleaming, oiled leather boots.

Bran was smiling. No grim jester grin this; no wry, mocking grimace of contempt and scorn. This was a genuine smile: curiously small and reticent, diffident and beatific in nature.

Owen raised his hands in greeting. "Welcome," he said.

The door creaked on its hinges.

Owen dropped his hands and glanced back.

Tara's face showed at the crack of the door: a pale white oval. The dogs had awakened her. Clutching a blanket to her throat to cover her nakedness, Tara beckoned with the other hand. "Come inside."

The flame guardians on the doorstep had gone dark, their candles burnt out.

"Close the door," Owen hissed.

"Owen——"

"Close it!"

The door closed.

Owen turned back to face Bran, who had halted a companionable pace away.

"Kinsman," said Bran. This was no booming, hell-borne vocalization of sepulchral tones but the natural modal voice of the young man himself: a light, pleasant-sounding, resonant tenor.

Owen swallowed hard. He studied Bran's eyes, saw near infinite sadness and mournful melancholy there. But of menace and murderous intent he detected not a jot.

"Kinsman," Bran repeated, "enough." He opened wide his arms. "Let us reconcile."

The cat uttered another of its hair-raising yowls—a yowl choked off into an aggrieved yelp mid-screech behind him. Someone had given it the boot. Kendricks, no doubt.

Owen hesitated. Kinsman, Bran had called him. Kinsman.

A soft breeze ruffled an errant lock of the young man's hair, the delicate motion causing Owen's breath to hitch in his throat. He considered Bran's features in the witching light of the blood-red moon: limpid brown eyes, hawk-like nose, strong jaw, and full, almost sensual lips.

Gods, Owen thought to himself, the boy is beautiful. He was seeing Bran—*really seeing him*—for the first time. This is the young man I murdered; the callow youth ripped from the embrace of his beloved and consigned forever to the writhing, worm'd earth . . . What a monstrous thing I have done! What a crime committed! What a waste!

Footsteps sounded behind Owen.

Bran's eyes widened.

Owen half turned. Too late—his arm was only partially raised when the axe-head struck him a stunning blow.

Tara screamed.

That's odd, Owen thought, a torrent of blood pouring from the gash in his scalp, half blinding him. I told her to shut the door.

But Tara had opened the door again, just in time to spot the half-naked figure that pounced upon her husband with a hair-prickling wail: *Deirdre.*

Owen staggered, stars wheeling crazily in the sky overhead. The axe-head bit into his face, shattering his cheekbone and gouging out an eye. "No," he managed.

Deirdre, an avenging fury, hacked wildly at Owen's flailing arms and heaving chest, shrieking and cursing.

Owen hit the ground bleeding from a dozen wounds. He crashed onto his side, looked over at Tara—who remained frozen in the doorway, screaming in horror—and realized with a shock that his wife was pregnant. Some weirdling supernal insight was granted him here at death's door; some unsuspected supernatural faculty flaring into existence as he drew his last, labored breaths. He perceived all that would follow:

His son Neil would rise in power and authority to chieftain their clan. He would lead the people in a series of reprisal wars resulting in the extermination of their rivals: Deirdre's clan, and all those allied with her. Neil would fall on a distant battlefield soon thereafter, head shattered by a mace carried by a follower of the new gods: Yahweh, Jesus, and Holy Ghost.

The axe thudded into Owen's back; he barely felt it. Owen blinked, coughed out a great gout of blood, fought to hold Tara in his gaze. There was more:

His son's son: Kembell. The boy would have his guts ripped out on the withdrawal stroke of a serrated-edge broadsword wielded by a Danish invader.

Owen groaned. Blood poured down his face from the wounds in his scalp, ran burning into his one good eye, foamed from his lips in a crimson froth.

More young men appeared and died before him. All were his descendants; all victims of the lawful murder of war. Stabbed, slashed, bludgeoned. They wore strange uniforms and helmets, carried odd weapons and devices. Some screamed in horror or fury as they were massacred; others froze in place, numb with shock. Gibbering, sobbing, cursing—it mattered not. Shredded by shrapnel, musket-balled, rifle-shot. Faster and faster the young men flickered past, dying in lightning-fast tableaus of morbidity and gore. Machine-gunned, crushed by falling rubble, spines shattered by churning tank treads. Set aflame, gassed. The slaughter went on and on: young men atomized by mushroom cloud, particle beam, laser.

Owen struggled to his knees. Somewhere far off Tara was screaming, screaming . . .

Deirdre kicked Owen in the ribs and knocked him flat on his back. The stars spiraled in vertiginous rankings above him: an indifferent spectacle of cosmic grandeur and cold infinitude.

For a moment Bran's face hove into view. He spoke—then faded away as Deirdre's spittle-flecked visage reared up in Owen's blurred field of vision.

And Owen knew, as Deirdre raised her gore-drenched axe for a well-aimed blow—a blow that would split Owen's skull and leave him dying with the taste of his own brains in his mouth—there would be no escaping this final, fatal attack.

It wasn't fear that caused Owen's body to convulse with the howl that erupted from his blood-constricted throat.

It was the impact of Bran's last soft-spoken words upon him.

*I forgive you.*

# The Call of Lizzie

The death of a beautiful woman is, unquestionably, the most poetical topic in the world.

—Edgar Allan Poe

## Part I.

I loved her with a passion
that would have launched a thousand ships;
her kisses: fire-wine
that smoldered sweetly on the lips.

We bedded down in fervent need
in shadowed vale & leafy bower;
innocents no more—ye gods!
the ecstasy of lost hours

in which we twined our limbs together:
flexing-rhythmic bucking hips;
frantic, panting, fruited breath
that perfumed faces as sweat dripped

from golden flesh strung tight & taut.
We reveled in our youth;
vowed no force would ever part us
howsoever rough, uncouth.

But Death had other plans—
as ever with mortal man
our trek through sun-lit lands
seemed but seconds, then—abyss.

## Part II.

Consumption ravaged Lizzie, O!
how terrible those dark days
that shook her body with ague,
delirium, chills, malaise.

We married; moved our servants
to a manse of ivy'd stone;
through gas-lit halls—hand-in-hand—
we daily whisper-roamed.

How brave her smile; how silken-soft
those gentle dove-white hands!
Her fevered eyes burned bright & hot:
*I shall return to you again.*

*Though death take me I know not where*
*bliss found is love eternal;*
*two souls made one shall ever run*
*afore powers dark, infernal.*

I held her as a last
harsh, grating, rattling rasp
ripped from her spasming chest.
She died of the Crimson Cough.

# Part III.

Anniversary of Lizzie's death:
one year from the shattering night
my raven-haired beauty breathed her last
by cough & candlelight.

I stand in the whited sepulcher
of her granite mausoleum
heart *thud-thudding* in a cold-clenched chest
clinging to the shreds of reason

that tell me I am hearing things;
no lilting alto voice
could have called me from my creaking bed
terror-thrilled, half-rejoiced.

Beloved has come back to me!
Fought free from the undertow
that threatened to pull her under—
*O! Wherever you go, I go!*

Coffin lid hits the floor—
Lizzie rises up once more.
In my ears I hear the roar
of the onrushing ink-black Void.

# Cold Tickle

It was a dark and storming pre-Covid night. A break in the day-long deluge revealed an orange half-moon burning in the sky like the baleful eye of a drowsy-lidded elder god of chaos. Stars pinpricked the heavens: indifferent points of light beaming down upon a world of beatings, murders, acidifying oceans, melting polar ice caps, relentlessly pistoning genitalia, and mercury-brained babies suckling their mothers' toxic breast milk.

The wage slaves of Dale River—a faltering, opioid-ridden warren of pawn shops, liquor stores, price-gouging pharmacies, and belligerent Trump voters situated in the "American Heartland" of the Midwest—found themselves temporarily freed from the bondage of low-paying, dead-end jobs. Hither and thither they motored and strolled, alternately despairing and enraged, plagued by fears of corporate downsizing, border-crashing caravans of Central American immigrants, gun-grabbing "libtards," rising cable rates, the "deep state" federal government, and all vocabulary pitched above a third-grade level. All of which is to say: suicidal ideation warred with homicidal impulses in brains made irrational and paranoid from endless gorging on a diet of intra-family violence, alt-right media, fundamentalist religion, browser-hijacking internet pornography, and "reality" TV.

*USA! USA! USA!*

One of these denizens—a stoop-shouldered, trenchcoated septuagenarian with a face like an acid-scored apple—stood before the outer doors of chain store #217 of Corporate Books & Toys. Oliver Kendricks (twice-wounded Vietnam War veteran, retired insurance salesman, happy widower, and exasperated atheist) was not amused. Rheumy eyes magnified to three times their normal size glared from behind lenses thick enough to focus a pallid moonbeam into an incendiary's torch. "*Boors! Brutes!* Bastard offspring of glue-sniffing philistines!" he raged to a trio of surly-faced adolescents who jostled him as they came out the entrance door.

"The fuck's your problem, old man?" queried the last to exit: a weak-chinned man-child sporting a backward baseball cap and the idiot, sleazy grin of an incestuous rapist.

"*This* is my problem!" raged Kendricks, wisps of grayish-white hair bouncing on his wetly-gleaming scalp. "You are exiting *out* the entrance door, denying *me* entrance until you have passed!"

"Hey," said intoed punk #2, turning around and puffing out a thin-boned chest in a hooded Raiders jersey while gesturing with spindly arms (Kendricks was put in mind of an antic pigeon), "if you don't like it, why don't you go *in* the *out* door?"

"Madness!" sputtered Kendricks, spittle balling at the corners of his lips. "The end of civilization!" He took a deep breath, fought to lower his racing pulse. "I, for one, do not make left turns from the right lane, press the down elevator button when I mean to go up, or *enter* a building via its *exit* door."

"Aw, leave the mummy alone," yelled punk #3, a heavy-set hulk with a look of perpetual unease and puzzlement stamped on his moon-faced features. This would-be crime lord had costumed himself in combat boots, starter jacket and chain-jingling parachute pants. He called back over his shoulder to his juvenile delinquent *confrères* as he found himself leading the parade of sub-90 IQs into the parking lot. "Let's go! That means you too, Mel—shake yer dick."

Mel brought his scowling face to within kissing distance of Kendricks's own. "Bye-bye now," he breathed.

Kendricks opened his mouth to speak, only to be brought up short by a sharp pain in his proboscis.

Mel had finger-flicked the raw, reddened end of the old man's nose, bursting a pendent snot bubble.

Kendricks winced; his eyes watered. *"Asshole!"* he shrilled.

"Everyone's got one," Mel agreed and stepped off, whistling.

Kendricks's wiry frame shook with fury. His hand darted inside his trenchcoat, into his threadbare sport coat's inside pocket—a pocket that was leather-lined against the ravages of sharp little claws and teeth. A pair of exotic animals writhed in there: warm, furry, softly cheeping. "Come back! *Come back here, braggart!* I'll show you! I'll give you a"—his tremulous voice hit a high, warbling note—*"cold tickle!"*

Mel, now out of arm's reach, paused for a moment—seemed about to turn around—then shrugged and kept walking.

"*Prasteete* (Excuse me); you okay?" A sixtyish woman in ratty sable and blotchy mascara plucked at Kendricks's arm. She had a Russian accent thick as Boris Badenov intoning *now we get moose and squirrel* in those old Rocky and Bullwinkle cartoons. Her ample breasts heaved like fat-shamed guests histrionically emoting on an afternoon talk show; beaded bracelets jangled on her wrist with a sound akin to maracas-clacking skeletons ejected from a speeding Volvo. "Rasputitsa see what happened, dat boy—"

"Is lucky," Kendricks muttered. For a moment he stared hard at Mel's retreating back, then switched his gaze to the woman's own. He smiled tightly. "I'm quite all right." He withdrew his hand from his trenchcoat, dropped it to his side. "Really, I am. Just . . . embarrassed, is all."

"No, no; is more to say here, *tovarisch;* dey hurt you!" The woman's voice trembled with emotion. "Bad boy sting your nose; I saw him! He go like theez . . ." She raised both hands and imitated Mel's middle-finger-springing-out-from-its-tensed-resting-position-against-a-thumbpad nose strike. "He *fleeck! fleeck!* your nose. Shame!"

"Well, it's all over now." Kendricks moved to step around the woman, and she seized him by the forearm.

"You brave man, comrade American! Together we go to police station and get bad boys jailed, yes?"

"Uh . . . no." Kendricks yanked his arm out of her grasp. "Nothing to see here." He flashed a lightning-quick grin again—on/off. "I'm fine; thank you. Really!"

Again, he moved to step around her.

The woman stiffened as if slapped. Her pendulous mammaries earthquaked; large dark-shadowed eyes glimmered with wetness. "I seek only to help and you *shout* at Rasputitsa!"

No, he didn't shout. Did he?

"Raspu—"

"—titsa." The woman jabbed a meaty hamhock of a thumb at her bosom. "Is me. You?"

"Oliver," Kendricks admitted.

"Nice-looking man, this Oliver."

Kendricks felt his mouth oval in surprise—and not simply because Rasputitsa apparently referred to everyone in the third person.

"For old man you don't look or move so old, eh? You still work out, yes? Like me, perhaps: yoga, wall slides, planking. Come inside with Rasputitsa; have coffee and small sweet."

"N-no," he heard himself stammer. "I appreciate the offer, but, ah . . . no thanks. I just . . ." He gestured vaguely toward the bookstore.

"*Da,* I understand. You fear sex with strong Russian woman."

Kendricks blinked. He couldn't have heard that correctly. "I come here to read," he heard himself say, voice colorless.

"Is bookstore, not library," Rasputitsa riposted with a loopy grin. "Buy something in bookstore, even if just coffee or tea. Otherwise . . ." She spat on the ground. "I think you communist peasant. *Paneemayoo?* (Understand?) Join me in cafe. After small talk and sweet you read. Then we go home to my house. Is nice house—many books. Updike, Roth, Mailer. The great narcissists. Pushkin in native Russian. I read to you in bed afterward."

"Afterward . . ." Kendricks echoed.

"*Da.*"

Kendricks took a deep breath. "Madame, there will be no afterward, because there will be no *before.*" He swiped at his smarting nose: trickles of snot oozed from his nostrils.

Rasputitsa fumbled in her satchel purse. She produced a wadded-up ball of tissue and thrust this at Kendricks. The mass of lotioned tissue gave off a sickly-sweet scent, as of a small mammalian corpse—X-eyed and protruding pink-tongued, perhaps—bloating in a sun-drenched field of meadow grasses.

"Ulp!" said Kendricks, retreating a step.

"Here," said Rasputitsa, advancing and jabbing at Kendricks's nose as the old man bent backward, "let me . . . hold still, my friend."

They bobbed and weaved like prize fighters: Rasputitsa attempting to blot Kendricks's nose, the old man doing his level best to avoid contact with that suspect mass of pungent tissues.

"Ouch!" yelped Kendricks as Rasputitsa made contact with Kendricks's philtrum: a sharp thumbnail lacquered in alternating bands of purple and gold gouged his skin. Almost immediately a bright red drop of blood welled up at the deepest point of the scratch.

*"Chyort voz'mi!"* ("Oh, shit!") exclaimed Rasputitsa.

Kendricks put palm to philtrum, pulled it away, and eyed with disbelief the smear of blood there. "Are you *done?*" he demanded to know.

"I'm so sorry; I try . . . I try to help . . ." Rasputitsa stammered, the wad of tissues falling to the sidewalk in a sodden ball.

Kendricks yanked open the outer door with his right hand, pressed the left to his philtrum again, and thus passed into the entrance way of Corporate Books & Toys. He scarcely noticed the tables of yellow-stickered bargain books stacked in wildly subject-discordant rows on flanking tables either side of him—*1001 Fart Jokes, The Symbology of the Tarot, A Hermeneutics of Foucaultian Death Dreams, The 12th SS Division Hitler Jugend: A Battle History, Rooftop Gardens in Chicago,* etc.—as he cleared the entrance way in two strides, pulled open the inner door, and walked in.

"Hi there!" a waif-like female clerk chirruped as he entered, spinning round from the endcap she was stocking with the latest right-wing talk show host title and favoring Kendricks with a practiced smile. Her face was pinched and drawn.

*Bulimic,* Kendricks thought.

"Looking for anything in particular?" the clerk asked.

"Nah rully," Kendricks said, voice muffled through a covering hand pressed to his philtrum. "'Uhl juh brow aroun', 'kay?"

The clerk's smile faltered, then brightened professionally again. "Sure! Let me know if you need anything; I'll be at the info desk."

"Gray!" Kendricks slurred affirmatively into his palm, moving toward the cafe and glancing back over his shoulder.

Rasputitsa entered the store. She looked around—pretended not to see him—headed in the opposite direction.

Kendricks walked up to the cafe counter and dropped his hand from his face. "Medium coffee—black, please."

"Ugandan Arabica dark roast or Rwenzori Mountains citrus floral?" The clerk—a young man with a goatee and silver eyebrow ring—eyed him intently.

"Umm . . . the dark roast," said Kendricks.

"Coming right up."

While the bookstore barista busied himself with the arcane art of pouring boiling water through the seeds of berries from the *Coffea* plant, Kendricks produced a handkerchief from a trouser pocket and repeatedly blotted his philtrum. Successive blottings reduced bright red specks to faint pink flecks in the cloth. The nick caused by Rasputitsa's fingernail was clotting fast, thank Nodens . . .

Goatee returned with his coffee, but before Kendricks could pay for it he had to run the corporate-mandated, customer-checkout five-questions gauntlet. *Are you a member? What is your phone number? Your card is expired; would you like to renew it today? Were you aware that tomorrow night is "Meet Wee Wittle Winkybean" for selfies and signed copies of the latest book in the beloved early readers series?*

*Would you like to donate a dollar to the "Children Pecked by Venomous Sparrows" charity drive?*

Interrogation ended at last and coin proffered for coffee, Kendricks ambled over to the fantasy/science fiction area of the bookstore. There he immediately found what he was looking for: a fat, black, faux-leather cover edition of *The Complete Fiction of H. P. Lovecraft*—texts by renowned literary critic, editor, and weird fiction scholar S. T. Joshi, 'natch. (All other versions, Kendricks well knew, were riddled with thousands of textual errors.)

Humming a cheerful if rather darkly atonal tune, Kendricks sought out an easy chair stained with a number of suspect substances at the back of the store. Here he set beverage and Lovecraft tome down on a coffee table in front of the chair, knocking askew a stack of fashion and glamor magazines as he did so. This accomplished, Kendricks shrugged out of his trenchcoat, draped it over the back of the chair, and sank into the cushions with a heartfelt sigh and creak of old bones.

He rested a moment, then leaned forward to pick up the book from the coffee table. Kendricks brought the text to within inches of his failing eyes, opened the book at random to the short story "Arthur Jermyn" and drank in its nihilistic opening sentence, one of the most glumly misanthropic in all English literature: *Life is a hideous thing . . .*

Kendricks chuckled.

Inside his pulsing sport coat pocket, two small beasts chittered, thumped, and meeped.

An hour passed. Kendricks finished "Arthur Jermyn" and went on to Lovecraft's masterpiece *At the Mountains of Madness:* the second longest piece of fiction the "Gentleman Sage of Providence" had ever written. One moment Kendricks was exploring eons-old stone ruins of the "Elder Things" in the mountainous vastness of Antarctica, his own woes and worries forgotten as the icy finger of the numinous traced his spine occasioning an ever-growing sense of awe and wonder, the next . . .

"*Fuck dat shit!* If he doesn't listen to you, tell him you *gone,* girl. Hit him wit the four-one-one, yo: you ain't playin'."

The voice was preternaturally loud in the hushed quietness of the bookstore, an order of magnitude louder than Mozart's "Rondo Alla Turca," the sprightly alternating major and minor keys of which were currently being broadcast over the PA system.

"Bail if he ain't got the benjamins, girlfriend. You ain't lookin' for no broke-ass baby daddy, aight?"

Kendricks glanced up from the book, the brooding spell of Lovecraft's incantatory prose: polysyllabic, bookishly fussy, and tinged with purple, yet never less than scientifically precise—rudely broken.

"Nah, nah; it ain't like that—he playin' you, girl, fasho."

The voice issued from a ginger-haired, freckled adolescent girl seated on a loveseat opposite Kendricks across a separating coffee table. She was dressed in black jeans and a hot pink T-shirt that bore a garish appliqué in glittering gold letters: *Born To Wear Diamonds.* The girl held a cellphone clamped to her ear. "All I's sayin'—"

"Excuse me," Kendricks interrupted. "Excuse me. But whatever it *is* that you're saying, you're saying it entirely *too loudly.* In a public place. Might I ask you—a little *lower,* please?"

The girl's eyes flicked to him and away again. "Ah, *hell* no! He be—"

**BAM!**

Kendricks's lips compressed into a bloodless line as he slammed the covers of Lovecraft's collected works together. The book went off like a gunshot.

"Madame," remonstrated Kendricks, "I really *must* insist that you lower your voice."

"Hol' up," the girl said into the cellphone. "I'll holler back at'chu." She dropped the phone onto the loveseat beside her and glared at Kendricks in equal parts outrage and wonder. "You lookin' for a chin-check, ol' man?"

"A chin—"

"A punch in the face, mutha-fuckuh," clarified Ms. Charming.

"Watch your language." A smartly dressed Black woman in a purple pantsuit and sensible, thick-soled shoes walked up with a stack of book in her arms. Her name tag proclaimed: *Cheryl—Store Manager.* She threw a stern, disapproving glance at the girl and said, "Any more of that noise and I'll escort you out personally. We clear?"

"Aight; aight," said the girl, throwing her hands up in a no-problems-here gesture. "I'm chill; I ain't blunted. You go ahead on."

The woman opened her mouth to say something ("vulgar, stupid, culture-appropriating, poser white girl . . ."), thought better of it—rolled her eyes, and continued toward the front of the store.

Inside Kendricks's sport coat: shrill meeping and thumping; that leather-lined pocket positively *pulsed.*

"And now back to our contretemps, already in progress," said Kendricks. An enigmatic smile played about his lips. "I believe you were, ah . . . threatening me?"

"Nah, I'm threatening ya, bitch." A young man in khakis, doc Martens, and long-sleeved hoodie bearing the words "Anti-Social Club" in ten-inch-high letters emerged from the bookshelves behind the girl. Paler in complexion than Ms. Charming—"goat's milk white," in fact, in the exquisite parlance of Anne Rice—the guy had the straight-from-central-casting look (save for one jarring anachronistic detail) of a Hollywood Nazi: straw-colored hair, sharp chin and nose, heavily lidded blue eyes that gave his countenance a faintly reptilian cast. The jarring anachronistic detail on this straight-outta-privilege thug? Dreadlocks.

Kendricks arched a brow.

"Listen up, yo—unless you all-that you best leave off my ho. Otherwise—*booya!*" Here the young man mimed pumping the slide on a shotgun and blasting away at his target.

"Why, it's a member of the Rastafarian SS," Kendricks observed.

"Jokes. This mutha-fucka got jokes, Barbara Sue," said the young man.

"I see dat. He be bothering me, Cody," said the girl.

"I see dat, too," speaketh Cody.

"Wait," said Kendricks, setting *The Complete Fiction of H. P. Lovecraft* down on the coffee table with a bemused thump. "Or 'hol' up,' as it were—your names are *Cody* and *Barbara Sue?* Apologies. I got your group identity wrong. It seems I'm being menaced by the hip-hop hillbilly mafia."

Enter Rasputitsa, stage right. "Oliver! I find you here."

Three heads swiveled as one to the aged Russian minx.

Rasputitsa threw herself into a railback chair positioned beside Barbara Sue with a shrill giggle and jangling clatter of wrist bracelets. Her ratty sable coat had fallen open revealing a red silk blouse and glittering diamond choker around a thick, no-nonsense neck. The leather of her black miniskirt screech-winkled as she crossed booted feet, shifting in the chair to cross one leg over the other.

"Who you be?" interrogated Cody.

"Old friend of Oliver's," said Rasputitsa, adjusting the shoulder-strap of her satchel purse. "Right, darling?"

"Incorrect," answered Kendricks immediately. A beat. Then, with more emphasis: *"Nyet."*

Rasputitsa laughed a delighted laugh. "You're always saying *nyet* to me, Oliver. Try saying *da*—opens up more possibilities."

Cody's eyes shifted between Kendricks and Rasputitsa—tick-tock, tick-tock—finally settling on Kendricks's. "We ain't finished here, muthafucka."

"I should think not," said Kendricks, rising to his feet and brushing at the front of his sport coat to smooth the fabric.

"I'ma calling you out, bee-otch," said Cody. "'Less'n you apologize right now to Barbara Sue."

"The ho?" inquired Kendricks.

"*Muh* ho," clarified Cody.

"Baby, I don't like it when you call me—"

"Shut up, Barbara Sue," said Cody.

*"Fuck you, Cody!"* Barbara Sue shot back.

Cody's eyes widened in hurt. "I'ma trying to take care of business here, boo! Defending yo fuckin' honor, aight? So chill the fuck out fo' a minute befo' I lose muh mind."

Barbara Sue thought this over. "'Kay," she agreed, sweetly.

Cody looked around, saw no one else in his sight line. He threw Kendricks a meaningful glare and yanked his hoodie up, revealing the butt of a Pachmayr-gripped automatic pistol jutting from the waistband of his baggy trousers. "Glock—.40 caliber. Blow a cannon hole right through yo dumb ass!"

"I should imagine. And no doubt out the wall behind me, eh?" said Kendricks, still smiling that odd, enigmatic smile. "Now—can I show you mine?"

"Oliver—" Rasputitsa began.

"Shall I give you," Oliver reached into his inside sport coat's pocket as Cody's hand dropped to the gun butt of the pistol, "a *cold tickle?"*

"Da fuck . . ." Cody began, only to trail off in disbelief and confusion.

Kendricks produced from his leather-lined pocket animals the likes of which had never before been seen on planet Earth. They were not altogether wasps, nor bats, nor lizards, nor cats, but something utterly alien to the biome of the town of Dale River in the latter years of the Anthropocene. He flung these beasts into the air before Cody where they hovered, chittering and meeping, beating thin membranous wings whilst darting black-eyed heads about. Scaly thoraxes pulsed with eldritch energy; needle-thin stingers protruded from furred pygidiums.

Cody's eyes widened. "Cray cray," he said.

"I call 'em 'Frick and Frack,'" said Kendricks. "You can call 'em . . . Death!"

"Enough of that shit." Cody whipped out the pistol and drew a bead on Kendricks, right eye squinting down the sight. "Put them creepy bangers away, yo! Or I'll Glock-knock ya in the chrome dome wit a hot .40."

"Cody, you *are* a poet, you know that? What you do with the mother tongue is simply . . . well, astonishing, really," observed Kendricks.

"Yeah," said Cody. "I knows."

*"I'm going to scream!"* said Barbara Sue, knuckled hands to chin, staring at the hovering creatures in horrified fascination.

"Oliver—" Rasputitsa tried again.

"Frick," said Kendricks, *"attack!"*

Frick darted at Cody's face as the thug pulled the trigger of his Glock. Nothing! Gun jam. Poor weapon maintenance + cheap ammo = misfire.

The beast plunged its stinger into Cody's nose and he began to convulse. His skin turned translucent, revealing the blue-veined, red musculature beneath. He crackled and danced in a nimbus of white-hot energy.

*"Cody!"* Barbara Sue came off the loveseat and rushed to her man's side, arms flailing away at the bat-winged alien that had dug its talons into Cody's cheeks and was busily nipping away at an eyeball.

"Frack," ordered Kendricks, *"defend!"*

The second alien leaped forward and drove its stinger into Barbara Sue's ear. Half a second later, Frack hop-scuttled around to fasten on the girl's lip. She, too, began to tremble spasmodically, musculature showing through translucent skin, hair erecting from her scalp as eldritch energy crackled and popped from her shuddering body.

Rasputitsa looked on, arms crossed, features composed in an expression of mild annoyance.

Bug-eyed in horror, lips tugged upward in a rictus grin, Cody and Barbara Sue danced demented jitterbugs, teeth chattering like castanets, clawing at the bat-winged things fastened on their faces.

*"The worm has turned!"* cried Kendricks in triumph. *"How do you like your punishment, brutes; how do you like your medicine?"* Eyes alight in fury and glee, he licked his fingertips and smoothed an errant cowlick that had sprung up from his thinning mass of grayish-white hair.

"How do you like your *COLD TICKLE?*"

A low-pitched hum sounded as Cody and Barbara Sue flailed and jittered, rapidly rising in pitch and volume to an ear-splitting sonic shriek. For a moment longer the adolescents convulsed and shuddered, blue-veined red musculature crackling and popping with transmogrifying energy, then—FWOOMP!—both imploded into greasy ash that sifted down to the worn carpeting.

"Frick and Frack—*return!*" Kendricks flung open his sport coat. The aliens spiraled back into his pocket with the corkscrew locomotion of erratically buzzing flies. He sat back down.

Rasputitsa re-crossed her legs, pursed her lips, and blew a lock of hair out of her eyes. "Oliver, Oliver, Oliver," she said.

"What the *hell* is going on back here!" Store manager Cheryl hove into view flanked by two assistants: goateed barista and the waif-like female clerk Kendricks had encountered upon first entering Corporate Books & Toys. "Sounds like . . . I don't know *what* it sounds like!"

"*Tak zhal* (So sorry)," said Rasputitsa with a look of chagrin, fumbling in her satchel purse. "I was showing gentleman anti-rape device—it go off." She produced an object that looked like a flashlight, waved it before them, and deep-sixed it into the purse again.

"Uh-huh," said Cheryl. "And I'm supposed to believe that explains the raised voices, electronic screech, and strobing lights?"

"*Da?*" ventured Rasputitsa, hopefully.

"And this mess on the floor?" inquired Cheryl.

Goatee had dropped into a crouch to poke a tentative finger into the greasy ash staining the carpeting.

"Snuff," said Kendricks. "I prefer it . . . very moist; *mea culpa.* When the lady's device went off I sneezed and—"

Cheryl turned her gimlet glare onto Kendricks. "You know what?" She held her hands up, palms out. "On second thought, I don't even *want* to know; I really don't." She looked around. "Where's Frick and Frack?"

Kendricks twitched. "Come again?"

"The two culture-appropriating punks with the smart mouths," said Cheryl. "You know damn well who I mean: You called them 'Frick' and 'Frack.'"

"Ah," said Kendricks. "Them." He massaged his throat. "They, ah . . . left."

An interminable second ticked by.

"I see." Cheryl spread her feet and fisted hands on her hips. "Well, I got news for you: you're leaving, too. Out! The both of you. In five minutes or I call the police. Bring whatever purchases you intend to make to the front counter, pay and leave. I'm done with y'all."

Kendricks and Rasputitsa nodded in tandem.

"Danny, get a broom and dustbin from café and clean this mess up," said Cheryl. "Dawn, come with me."

Cheryl, Goatee, and waif-child drifted back to the front of the store.

Seconds later Rasputitsa edged forward on her chair. "You very pleased with yourself."

"Well . . ." said Kendricks.

"You deny it?"

"Not at all." Kendricks's countenance radiated defiant smugness. "Guilty as charged!"

"You wield power through beasts summoned from other dimension."

"I'm sure," said Kendricks carefully, "that I don't know what you're talking about."

Rasputitsa raised an admonishing finger, waggled it at Kendricks. "No games, old man. I am not fool. What did I see with own eyes?"

"Justice delivered," said Kendricks.

Rasputitsa laughed. Her wrist bracelets clattered.

"You think that's funny?" asked Kendricks.

"I think you know nothing of what you are dealing with. In what book did you find ritual to summon such creatures?"

Kendricks folded his hands in his lap, remained silent.

"Doesn't matter," said Rasputitsa. "What matters is you understand. I took this form, *tovarisch,* so as not to—how you say—'unduly,' yes?—not to *unduly* alarm you."

"You 'took this form' . . ." Kendricks repeated.

*"Da,"* said Rasputitsa, a hard glint in her eyes.

"I'm not sure——"

"Oliver, don't force me show you who I really am."

"Okay; I'll bite." Kendricks tried for an assertive tone, but his voice climbed an octave in nervousness. "Who are you?"

"At some level you already know or suspect, *ne pravda?* (Isn't that true?)" Rasputitsa cocked her head; studied Kendricks's reaction. "It is not so much who I am as what I am: bounty hunter."

Kendricks unfolded his hands. "Interesting." One hand began creeping upwards, toward the leather-lined inside pocket of his sport coat.

"Don't," said Rasputitsa, "insult intelligence. Move hand inch more I strike dead."

"Nonsense," said Kendricks.

"Is it?" Rasputitsa's form rippled.

Kendricks's stomach convulsed; he caught a suggestion of monstrous physical features in Rasputitsa's rippling form that had never played a part in the Darwinian evolution of any creature on *this* planet.

"No," he admitted, "it isn't." Nausea caused a film of perspiration to break out on his forehead.

"I tried to do this easy way, old man. Take you in more ways than one. Assume form reminiscent of old nanny you had sordid crush on when twelve."

*"Olga!"* Kendricks cried. "Of course! I knew you resembled someone . . . Why, I haven't thought of her——"

"In years."

"Decades," amended Kendricks.

"Plan was: you go out with smile on face. One last fling, *da?* Our preferred method of execution—ecstatic death. Civilized. Sophisticated."

"I see," said Oliver.

"Do you?" said Rasputitsa. "Anyway—'Frick and Frack,' as you call them, vanish when you die, tether cut." She brushed her hands together briskly. "Ongoing damage to numerous parallel dimensions cease. Done; case closed."

"I'm afraid you've lost me."

"All power comes with price. Energy requires the transmutation of material into new form." Rasputitsa pursed her lips, blew another strand of hair out of her eyes. "You have no idea damage done to other realities by cheap parlor tricks in this one. Everything connected; everything effect everything else."

"How was I supposed to know that?" Kendricks adjusted his glasses. His rheumy eyes blink-blinked. "How *could* I? Assuming you're telling me the truth of these things, of course."

"Is truth," said Rasputitsa. "You knew enough, *da?* Oliver Kendricks: enemy of life. In thrall to Thanatos, the death urge. Dead to the erotic, new life, rebirth. Angry man waiting to die."

Kendricks grimaced. It was meant as mocking smile. "That's rich, coming from a . . . what did you call yourself? Bounty hunter. Do all your kind talk like five-cent Freudians where you come from? And by the way—I'm a widower. No children, eh? 'Dead to the erotic,' indeed! I'm supposed to make babies at seventy-five?"

Rasputitsa ignored this, gestured at the black tome on the coffee table. "Lovecraft is favorite writer?"

Kendricks looked at the treasured tome; resisted the impulse to pick it up and hug it to his chest. "Yes."

"Each story hammer, beating consciousness into pulp against anvil of cosmic horror. Despair. Existential dread."

Kendricks chuckled: a dry and mirthless burble, like some ancient reanimated mummy attempting to tootle a dust-choked flute. "Cornered by a bounty hunter who dabbles in literary criticism. Are you aware Lovecraft's writings inspire awe as much as dread, scholarly admiration as much as fear, wry amusement as much as terror?"

"In such as you."

Kendricks had no answer to that.

"You found old spell book in second-hand bookshop; recognized title from list recited in tale of Lovecraft's."

Kendricks's face revealed nothing. His hand began stealthily creeping up his sport coat again.

"When you dead I go to your home and destroy book. Close all loose ends."

"Will you now," said Kendricks.

*"Da,"* said Rasputitsa.

Kendricks seized the buttonhole edge of his sport coat, threw it open, and shouted——

—nary a word.

# The Sleep of Reason Produces Monsters

## An Extended Surveil

"Imagination abandoned by reason produces impossible monsters; united
with her, she is the mother of the arts and source of their wonders."
—caption to aquatint #43 of Goya's *Los Caprichos* series

The sleep of reason produces monsters
warned Goya, who etched a stark aquatint:
an exhausted man face-down at his desk
surrounded by owls, bats, lynx—a dark hint
of feral forces that stalk the artist:
sickness of the spirit personified.
'Ware, ye sterile cold men of abstraction!
Nature denied is falseness deified.
Though madmen of Dionysus—far worse:
Id-driven, unmoored, Thanatos-enthralled.
Reason throttled is horror: iron law
of the dream-dazed, drunks, psychotics, et al.
Great art is grounded, insightful, precise;
it hallows, enlightens—rolls back the night.

# The Strange and Curious Tale of Prof. Robert Howard Wilson

An Instructive Account of a Small Victory in the Venerable Professor's
Never-ending War Against Barbarism, Ignorance, & Banality:
How Arkham's Most Accomplished Master of the Black Arts Weath-
ered the Depredations of a Homicidal Adolescent Sociopath;

or,

A Most Peculiar Episode of Vengeance & Redress Whilst Dwelling
Amongst the Philistines,

circa 2001

Professor Robert Howard Wilson hated children. He hated the nerve-jangling aural assault of piping idiot voices; he abominated the spastic flailing of juvenile locomotion; he abhorred the foul odors of dirt, sweat, urine, and sour milk that clung to brightly garbed hobgoblin bodies. But most of all he detested children because he saw them for what they were: cruel and scheming little savages primed by the calculated barbarisms of nature and culture to fall upon one another at the first sign of oddity or weakness. *Homo ignoramus-minisculus,* he termed the loathsome geno-type.

The professor bore no especial love for their dull-witted, incurious spawners either. Everywhere, it seemed, the selfish shortsightedness of men and women destabilized the planet as Earth's painstakingly evolved and delicately balanced ecosystems were jarred into disequilibrium and swamped beneath a tidal wave of mewling human flesh.

Professor Wilson, a gray-haired, peripatetic man in his early sixties, had once been asked what he thought of having children. He'd ruminated a moment, brushed his fiancée's cheek with his lips, and whispered, "A child, my dear, is the corpse of Eros."

The wedding was called off.

Recalling that long-ago conversation now, the professor chuckled. He'd discovered an essential life truth that hot and humid summer evening: tell people what you really think and they will bother you no more.

Professor R. H. Wilson—doctor of pre-Socratic philosophies and comparative religion; accomplished linguist and master of rhetoric; collector of rare Minoan, Egyptian, Greco-Roman, and Mesopotamian antiquities; notorious anti-papist and author of a bewilderingly diverse collection of monographs and treatises on myth, the supernatural, and the occult—was seated at the giant teak escritoire in his study viewing the faded hieroglyphs on a parchment fragment of the *Pnakotic Manuscripts* through an oversized magnifying glass.

The escritoire, a pockmarked heirloom passed down through the generations from his great-great-great-grandfather, a trader in the Dutch East India Company, was cluttered with a thick profusion of papers, parchments, books, and writing marginalia. Stout oak bookcases lined three walls of the *sanctum sanctorum*. Well-worn shelves groaned beneath the weight of silver-clasped grimoires and sundry leather-bound tomes. A faded Persian carpet of abstract design covered the floor. A velvet-lined glass case pedestaled on griffin's feet of Tuscan marble held a number of the professor's prized curiosities: bronze hand weapons and gold jewelry from ancient Minos, a black basalt statue of Anubis from the Egyptian Old Kingdom, coins and pottery celebrating the glory that was Periclean Athens. Above the doorway hung a cracked and weathered bas-relief cut from some nameless Canaanite temple depicting a half-dozen warriors in leather armor wielding swords and spears against a many-tentacled cubist monstrosity.

The aforementioned antiquarian items, curious and rare though they were, paled in significance before the real treasures in that rich and dust-moted study: books. Row upon mildewed row, rank upon moldering rank, hundreds of storied tomes were gathered there, most believed lost to mankind for centuries. Their spines presented a ghastly and forbidden roll call of forgotten writings: *The Book of Eibon,* whose demonic curses could turn a man to stone; the legendary *Seven Cryptical Books of Hsan,* read by Genghis Khan just before he embarked upon his bloody medieval adventure of world conquest; *The Book of Thoth,* a horrific tome of Egyptian necromancy and thaumaturgical power; the Tibetan *Book of the Dead* in its original, uncensored Sogdian form. On a high shelf bookended by a yellowing skull reposed an irregularly cut tome with cover of crimson leather and pages of human skin: *Diabolical Songs of the Undead Jaguar Kings,* penned by the spidery hand of the Aztec high-priest Chicuacentecpatl. *De Vermis Mysteriis* and the *Cultes des Goules* stood side-by-side, a proximity that would have sent a knowing Jesuit staggering back from the shelf in horror and dismay.

But the *pièce de résistance* of the collection resided on an obsidian book stand beside the professor's escritoire, drawing the wan light of that gloomy bibliophilic space into its brittle, oversized vellum pages. The volume—one of only six copies still extant—was a black-letter German edition of the mad Arab Abdul Alhazred's writings on death magic and demonology: the dread *Necronomicon.* That blackest of all black tomes was opened to a page illustrating the proper drawing of a pentagram in non-Euclidean space.

For many a long and senses-shattering hour, the professor had delved into this body of forbidden and formidable lore. If his colleagues at Miskatonic University at Arkham knew the regularity with which he called up various infernal demons, meeping ghouls, and other transdimensional entities from the furthest reaches of time and space they would not only have revoked his tenure at once but fled his company in ashen-faced terror. For there were still a few old hands who recalled the horror that came between Lammas and the equinox in 1928, a horror summoned by a man named Wilbur Whateley (a decidedly less skilled practitioner of the occult).

Luckily, his colleagues knew little of his eldritch investigations. The professor was discreet in action and circumspect in word and so was able to continue his studies on *De Rerum Supernatura* undisturbed in the two-story brick Federal at 777 Dunsany Avenue. Occasionally, someone might remark upon the oddly amplified voices—some granitic bass, others ethereally high, soft, and sweet—heard issuing from the ivy-covered house late at night interspersed with divers screeches and barks. Others speculated as to the cause of the weird emerald glow spilling out from behind drawn curtains into the paved moonlit street. But no enraged mob rose up with pitchforks and torches to clamor at his gates. The professor was careful not to unduly excite the curiosity of his neighbors and thus was left in blessed peace.

"*Aaaaaahhhh—AIEEEEEEEE!*"

The sudden screech of an outraged child's voice startled the professor into dropping his magnifying glass onto the desktop, shattering the fragile fragment of parchment he'd been studying into innumerable slivers.

"Nodens!" he exclaimed.

The professor glared in the direction of the infernal shriek that had come blasting through the open screen door and down the hallway into his study; then, morosely at the desktop. Powdery brown detritus was all that remained of the once priceless bit of parchment. A prominent vein in his temple began to throb in cadence with his accelerating heart.

The child shrieked again.

The professor banged open a brass-handled desk drawer, withdrew a pair of tongs and a large, glassine envelope. As he was carefully tweezing slivers of parchment into the envelope there sounded yet another ear-piercing, ululating wail.

"Cursed banshee brat!" raged the professor, fisting himself from the chair with savage alacrity.

He stalked from the den and down the mahogany-wainscoted hallway with its curiously glowing Sumerian glyphs to the sunken pool of shadows that comprised the living room. Here were yet more books, stacked in tottering piles on the floor and octagonal end tables. A row of giant animal-headed onyx statues flanked two double-hung windows, their sinuous bodies gleaming dully in the darkness.

The gold eyes of the statues seemed to glitter in sympathetic anger with his own hotly flashing orbs as he peered through the screen door at the source of the commotion: two boys wrestling on his meticulously manicured, preternaturally green parallelogram of lawn. The bigger boy was clad in camouflage fatigues and combat boots, hair shorn in a rude buzz-cut. The smaller boy was dressed in yellow shorts, T-shirt, and high-top gym shoes.

As the professor watched, trembling with fury at this unconscionable and disastrous interruption of his studies, Buzz-cut pinned the smaller boy beneath him. He snarled something into his victim's face, then administered a head butt, causing Yellow Shorts to emit another castrato, steam-whistle shriek.

"Here now!" cried the professor, flinging wide the door and hopping onto the porch. "I should think we've had enough of that!"

At the sound of the professor's voice Buzz-cut's head snapped up in surprise.

"Let that boy up at once. *At once,* I say!" The professor's bony finger jabbed the air for emphasis.

Scowling, Buzz-cut levered himself erect. The boy appeared to be about fourteen years of age.

Sniveling, his victim scrambled to his feet beside him. He couldn't have been a day over eight.

The professor descended the steps of the iron-railed front porch, halted just feet away from the duo. "I know you two. You live next door, do you not?" He inclined his chin toward the Dutch Colonial with the new three-car garage to his right. Its owners, for reasons the professor could only shudder at, had willfully vandalized the building by coating it in lime-green stucco the summer before.

"Yeah, so?" said Buzz-cut.

"What," asked the professor, with a lizard-like lick at dry lips, "are your names?"

"Otto-fucking-Skorzeny," snarled Buzz-cut.

The professor betrayed no reaction to this surprising and incongruous utterance, though he well marked the name. Skorzeny: the swaggering, scar-faced commando who'd served Hitler and the Third Reich with evil distinction during World War II.

"I see," said the professor. He turned to the smaller child, he of the scraped and rapidly bruising face. "And what, dare I ask, is your moniker?"

"M-m-mon-i-kerr?"

The professor sighed. "Your name, child. What is your *name?*"

"Joseph," came the answer at once. The boy's eyes were enormous in a face gone ghastly white. "Are we in trouble?"

Buzz-cut snickered. "For what? We weren't doing nothing, were we, old man?"

The professor stiffened. "On the contrary. You callow ruffians were—*are*—trespassing on my property. Note, if you will, upon whose lawn we stand." He spread his hands in a gesture encompassing their little half-circle. "I might also add that the ear-piercing shrieks of young Joseph here disturbed my studies, causing me to destroy an ancient parchment the value of which your rude unformed minds could not possibly comprehend."

Irritation perplexed Buzz-cut's features; Joseph started to blubber.

"I'm sorry," Joseph burbled through his tears. "I'm really sorry. We can pay you! I have a dollar."

The professor snorted. "I'm afraid restitution is beyond your means. Your apology, however, is accepted. And, might I add"—permitting himself the ghost of a smile—"most appreciated."

"Does that mean I can go?" Joseph's voice quavered with equal parts fear, hope, and guilt.

"Indeed it does," said the professor. "But first, a boon—your brother's name?"

"Mike," Joseph barked at once and ran off without so much as a backward glance. He disappeared into his hideous lime-green domicile.

"Well." The professor cleared his throat, peered at Mike expectantly. "That would seem to leave just us."

"Yeah. Seems that way."

"Your apology . . ." the professor prompted.

"Oh, that," Mike sneered, revolving on his heel and striding four paces away before turning round again. "Here you go." And he brandished his right hand, middle finger erect.

The professor gasped. "Vulgar, insolent savage!"

"Yep, that's me," Mike agreed, turning round once more.

The professor called to the boy's retreating back. "Halt! *Halt,* I say!"

Mike stopped on the edge of the professor's lawn, seeming to consider. When he turned back this time his lips were twisted into a sardonic grin. "Yeah?" he said, arms folded across his chest, booted foot thrust forward, weight on the opposite hip. "You got something more you want to say to me, Dr. Death?"

The professor clasped his hands behind his back, returned Mike's challenging stare. "I should think," he said, "that a mouth as fresh as yours will one day get you into trouble."

Mike laughed. "Nothing I can't handle, geezer-freak. So don't you worry about it. Now why don't you go back inside before you have a stroke out here or something? You don't look so good. In fact . . ." He smiled slyly, pleased at the cleverness of his soon-to-be-vocalized simile. "You're white as a vampire's balls, bitch."

The professor began to tremble like a Viking in the throes of battle fury. "I assure you, it is not my health we are endangering by this conversation."

"Whatever."

"'Whatever'? Dear boy, the vapidity of your conversation is exceeded only by its tedious and irksome vulgarity."

"Is that so? Well, fuck you sideways with a crowbar, you senile old goat. Got some fancy comeback for that?"

This time it was the professor who smiled—a most curious smile indeed, chock full of forked lightnings and jaguar pounces, barely restrained. "Good day, young Michael. Thank you for a most . . . interesting conversation."

Mike blew a contemptuous hiss of air through his teeth. Then he, too, followed in his brother's footsteps and crossed the lawn to his house, moving with the exaggerated, bobbing gait of the hardened juvenile delinquent: shoulders thrown back, arms cocked out to his sides like a gunfighter about to quick-draw on the local talent.

Mike yanked open the front door, chanced a glance over his shoulder, found the professor's gaze still hard upon him. He stepped inside, cursing with inspired lividity, and slammed the door closed.

For long moments the professor remained where he was, staring at his neighbor's front door. A wasp buzzed his ear. He absently brushed it away. From further down the street came muted cries of children at play. A dog barked, and in the silence following the sharp vocalization he became aware of a gentle susurration—*hssuuuushh, hssuuuushh, hssuuuushh*—issuing from a lawn sprinkler whirling across the street.

When he was certain the trembling in his hands had subsided the professor retreated to the shadowed antiquarian sanctuary of his book-and-statue-crammed home.

In the days immediately following this encounter the professor took no action against his juvenile antagonist, save for glowering darkly in Mike's direction whenever he appeared outside.

For his part, Mike responded to these withering stares with the customary greeting he gave any adult who dared to curb or otherwise impede his violent amusements: the one-finger salute. It was vulgar, tiresome, sophomoric. It was Mike.

Occasionally, the professor would be treated to shouted insults and other sundry vulgarities as he toiled away at the massive antique desk in his study. But he paid no attention to these provocations when they came drifting in like obscene birdsong through the open windows. Such, he reasoned, was simply the price one paid when you lived next door to a pack of yowling barbarians.

Though it wasn't Mike's voice alone that carried through his open windows. No indeed. Other voices joined in the taunting. Mike, apparently, had friends. And this select group of prepubescent thugs regarded it as the height of hilarity to stand on the professor's lawn shouting out such deathless witticisms as, "Wake up, shithead!" and "Hey, old fart—ya still alive in there?"

At times such as these the professor would raise his head from his work to mutter heart-freezing curses in a heterogeneous mixture of dead languages.

And then came the day a rock crashed through one of his front windows.

It happened in this manner. The professor was reclining full length upon a burgundy-upholstered settee, blissfully wrapped in the arms of Morpheus, stertorous exhalations sawing in guttural counterpoint to the *tock-tock-tock* of the Bavarian grandfather clock standing in darkly burnished splendor in one corner of the Baroque living room. All was profound silence and sublime tranquility, as befits a man asleep amongst his books and sculpture, when—*KEEEEEESHHH!*—panes of glass in one of the double-hung sash windows shattered into a thousand glittering knives.

*"I ABJURE THEE IN THE NAME OF . . ."* the professor, startled into wakefulness, leapt to his feet like a BB-gunned cat.

The rock thudded onto the carpet and bounded across the floor until its forward momentum was arrested by the porphyry feet of Thoth-Amon.

Outside, a boy shouted, *"Go! Go! Go!"*

By the time the professor, groggy and bleary-eyed with sleep, fumbled into trousers and shirt and stepped outside, the culprits were long gone. No matter. There were ways of finding the vandal brats. Of course, he already had a pretty good idea who was responsible for this unexpected afternoon gift of rock. Still, one must be sure . . .

He went back into the house, came out again. Screwing a curiously prismed and faceted monocle into his eye, he swept his gimlet gaze over the lawn and bordering sidewalk, making minute, delicate adjustments to the devise's lens rotator cuff—*click-click, whirrrrrr . . . click.*

The fabric of space/time shimmered, warped and he saw:

Mike and two other boys ride up on bicycles. A carroty-haired youth—a boy he's never seen before—drops his bike on the sidewalk, advances on-to the lawn. He stops, glances back. Mike urges him on. Carrot-top reaches into his pocket, pulls out a rock . . .

Enough. Suspicion confirmed.

In a matter of moments he stood upon his neighbor's doorstep, stabbing the bell with a taloned finger.

No answer.

No one home.

The sun had gone down, allowing other stars to gleam faintly against a backdrop of ever-darkening immensity, when the professor returned to the doorstep of his young nemesis. He rang the bell, waited a moment. As he was about to ring again the door swung open.

Mike stood there, sporting a "Stone-Cold Austin" T-shirt. The shaven-headed visage of the N.W.O. wrestler glared at the professor with cold reptilian menace. Mike's eyes, however, registered surprise and alarm.

"Good evening," said the professor.

Mike uttered a cry somewhere between a squeak and a curse and slammed the door closed.

The professor sighed, rang the bell again—*BONG-BONG!* A cedar-wood nameplate on the door proclaimed "The Michaelsons" in the flowing uncials of wood-burned calligraphic script.

A minute ticked by.

*BONG-BONG! BONG-BONG-BONG-BONG!*

The door flew open. A platinum-blonde woman in her early forties confronted him. She was wearing a brass breastplate with circular mandalas engraved at the breasts over a green robe over a white robe. Aquamarine crystals shaped like rocket cones dangled on short gold chains from finely haired ear lobes. "Yes?" Her face was an irritated question mark.

"Good evening, ma'am. Professor Robert Howard Wilson."

"Oh!" she exclaimed to the old man in the black suit and crimson slash of a tie. "You're our *stran*—that is to say, neighbor." Her teeth sparkled in aggressively whitened rows of dental-veneered perfection. "How nice! We've never *met* you; I've been so curious."

The professor grimaced politely. "I've come about your son."

"My son?" The woman's fingers fluttered to her throat like a covey of shotgunned quail. "Uh . . . are you speaking of Joseph or Mike?"

"I speak of the monster with the blond crew-cut."

"Mike," she said flatly. Then, rallying, "Well, come in. Whatever it is we can discuss it over *cappuccinos*. What do you say?"

"You're too kind." He stepped across the threshold into the house.

"I'm Vicki. Sam is upstairs at the moment."

The professor followed his hostess through the foyer and into the living room, his polished black dress shoes sinking deeply into orange shag. The house smelled of industrial cleansers, exotic incense, and burnt fish.

The living room was large and L-shaped. A pea-green leather couch faced off against a wide-screen television. Between TV and couch stood a chrome-legged, glass-topped coffee table on which lay a bowl of potpourri, dog-eared astrology magazines, and a book by Deepak Chopra.

At the bend of the L leading into the dining room Mike and Joseph sat before yet another television, working video game controllers. The room rang with the digitized sound of machine gun fire. Joseph craned his head around to stare curiously at the professor. Mike didn't. He well knew who was there and was damned if he'd acknowledge the old geezer's presence.

"Make yourself comfortable, Professor."

"Thank you." His long, lean frame cantilevered into the cushions.

"Two cups of cappuccino coming up. Or would you prefer *café mocha?*"

"Water would be fine."

"Water. Are you sure? We have Seven-Up, Coke, orange juice?"

"Really—water would be wonderful."

"We have iced spring water from Quebec."

"Splendid."

"Shall I add a slice of Cypriot lemon?" asked Vicki.

The professor muttered something unintelligible.

"Sor-ree?" trilled Vicki, voice an upward interrogative lilt.

"I said yes, please. *Cypriot* lemon in the *Quebec-ian* spring water, by all means." He cleared his throat. "Served in Atlantean cut crystal, of course."

Vicki giggled. "I don't have any Atlantean cut crystal, you joker you! Do you have any idea how *expensive* that stuff is? I've Lemurian or Kingdom of Mu only."

The professor's eye twitched. "Kingdom of Mu, surely."

"Good choice." Vicki hummed herself out of the room.

Left alone for the moment, the professor examined his surroundings more carefully. When his gaze landed on the ornate-framed oil painting mounted above the hulking television he visibly recoiled. The black-velvet-trimmed canvas displayed a prosaic harbor scene: sailboats and yachts riding at anchor against a background of rolling hills and white stone buildings. Serviceably if rather inexpertly executed by a shaky, line-blurring hand—one couldn't tell if those were sheep dotting the hills or odd, twig-footed hailstones—the crudity of the drawing and the fact that the entire scene had been painted in bright primary colors rendered it an abomination.

The professor knuckled his brow, looked again. The painting was still there.

"Watch your fucking elbow!" Mike shouted, giving Joseph a clout to the head.

"Mi-chael-lll, you know we don't use that language in this house," Vicki sang from the kitchen.

Joseph dropped his video game controller and fled sobbing from the room.

"Whenever I see that boy he's crying and running away," the professor observed.

Mike stood up, ostentatiously stretched, and scratched his crotch. "He's a pussy. Pussies cry. It's what they do best." Off he padded in his stockinged feet.

"Your ice water," Vicki trilled, sailing back in from the kitchen with their drinks. She set a long-stemmed, amethyst-purple glass and delicate cup-and-saucer on the coffee table, sat down beside the professor. "I see you're admiring my sister's painting. She *does* have an eye."

"Gods be praised. Would that it had been uncovered when she executed her composition."

Vicki looked stunned for a moment before emitting peals of laughter. "Oh jeez oh jeez, you had me going there for a moment! I had no idea you were such a card."

"Nor I," said the professor wryly.

Vicki sipped her *cappuccino* from an ivory *demitasse* cup etched with rosettes.

The professor took two cold swallows of water, set the long-stemmed glass down to tinkling ice cube music. "Very refreshing. Thank you."

"You're welcome." Vicki's eyes were drawn to the ring glittering on the professor's right index finger. The fat band of gold was surmounted by a trapezoidal stone containing an insect set in amber.

"Why, what a *marvelous* ring! Wherever did you find such a treasure?"

"I took it off the smoking corpse of the ghoul king Rokka-melkor."

"Ha-ha, you're such a character!" Vicki shrieked, seizing the professor's arm as paroxysms of laughter shook her small frame.

The professor waited for the giggles to subside.

"Oh, god," Vicki managed when she'd regained control of herself, "that was a good one." She waved an imaginary cloud of gnats away from her nose. "Well . . . shall we talk about Mike?"

"Sadly, we must." The professor sat up a little straighter on the couch. "I don't relish the role of Bearer of Bad Tidings. But I'm afraid that in this particular instance I have no other choice. I shall come right to the point: I have been the frequent target of your son's harassment."

"Harassment." Vicki looked incredulous.

"For some weeks now Mike has amused himself by shouting obscenities through my open windows. Surely you must have overheard some of these pleasantries?"

Vicki took another careful sip of her *cappuccino.*

"Apparently this is a new sport of his," the professor continued. "But this afternoon it was more than a vulgarity that sailed through my front window—it was a rock."

"I see," said Vicki tonelessly.

"See what?" A rotund, balding man in a powder-blue suit with mutton-chop sideburns bounced into the room clutching a Louis Vuitton briefcase. The loose-jowled face with the Barbary Coast mustache and merrily manic eyes were familiar to the professor from the small amount of TV he caught upon occasion: "Swashbuckling Sam, the Pontiac Man."

Vicki and the professor stood.

"My husband, Sam. Sam, Professor Wilson."

"Oh?"

The professor shook hands. Swashbuckling Sam had a politician's practiced grip: crisp, firm, lightning quick.

"Good evening, Mr. Michaelson."

"Please, call me Sam."

Vicki and the professor sat down again.

"Sam, the professor was just telling me that Michael threw a rock through his front window."

"Jesus Christ-o-phus!" Sam exclaimed. "Where's the boy now?"

"Uh . . ." said Vicki, glancing around. "Don't know. He was just here."

"Mike went upstairs," said the professor. "After punching Joseph in the head."

"He hasn't been centered at all this year," Vicki pointed out. "His heart chakra is swimming in bile. The war books, those horrible posters."

"Vicki . . ." Sam cautioned.

Vicki gestured wildly with her hands. "This whole house is pulsing with negative vibrations and discordant Zoe-tones! No wonder the boy is acting out. Our intra-family interactions have been positively orcish since the night the sacred Koomba Crystal broke."

Sam rolled his eyes, gave the professor a stern we'll-get-this-straightened-out look, and moved to the bottom of the stairs. "Mike! Get your ass down here."

Almost immediately there came the scramble of returning feet.

Sam shoulder-steered his son over to Vicki and the professor—Mike ambling with his usual loose-gaited saunter, thumbs hooked insolently into the waistband of his jeans.

Sam came right to the point. "Did you throw a rock through this man's window?"

Mike's eyes widened in feigned shock and dismay. "God no! Of course not."

"Technically, he is correct. Mike did not throw the rock. His red-haired companion did."

Vicki looked at the professor in confusion. "I thought you said Mike threw the rock."

"No, I . . ." The professor closed his eyes, opened them again. "Perhaps I have not made myself clear. This afternoon your son and a fiery-headed Vandal paid me a visit. It was the Vandal who hurled the rock into my lap—though I emphasize, the act was committed at Mike's instigation."

"M & M?" Vicki turned to her son. "Is this true?"

"No way! Of course not. I haven't been around all day; you know that."

"The professor says it was a red-haired boy who threw the rock. That sounds a lot like your buddy Wulfgar. You two were together this afternoon, weren't you?"

"Yeah, but we were over at Wulf's house." Mike's voice became an outraged squeal. "You can ask his sister; she was with us the whole time! We never left his house."

"Yet here you are," the professor observed drily.

It was at this impasse in the conversation that "Swashbuckling" Sam's inside suit-coat pocket electronically reproduced the galloping opening bars of the *Bonanza* theme.

"Excuse me." Sam pulled out his cellphone out, flipped it open.

"Poochkie, I want the truth."

"That is the truth! Honest."

The professor folded his arms across his chest, gazed at Mike with unblinking fixity.

Vicki combed her fingers through the loose mane of her bright, bottle-blonde hair. "Perhaps you've made a mistake."

The professor shook his head. "I saw them with my own eyes. No mistake—your son and a crimson-tressed reaver."

"Mikey, he seems *awfully* sure. And these things you've been shouting through Professor Wilson's windows . . ."

Before Mike could respond, Sam spoke up. "I've got a situation at the lot. One of our salesmen won't leave; he's frightening the office manager. Some misunderstanding regarding his commission check." He smiled a sickly smile.

"Oh Sam, not again."

Mike smirked, even as his father addressed him. "As for you, Mister—if your friend *did* heave a rock through this man's window I want you to come clean right now. Because if I find out you're lying, there'll be hell to pay later on. Understand?"

Mike composed his features into a mask of perfect innocence.

"Sorry, baby." Sam pecked his wife's cheek, threw the professor a commiserating look. "Duty calls."

"M & M, if you're afraid to tell me . . ."

Sam draped his arm around the professor's suddenly stiffened shoulders, walked him a couple of paces away from his wife and son. "Look, let's get this over with. I believe you. I believe you saw my boy and his friend out there on your lawn and I want you to know that I'll settle all damages immediately, including a little something extra for your trouble."

"I cannot accept—"

"Sure you can; what's right is right. But, uh . . ." He lowered his voice confidentially. "You need to understand Mike's going through a difficult time right now. You know, that whole coming-of-age thing."

"That may be, yet I hardly think that justifies—"

"Professor! Remember your youth? Remember what we were like? A hundred pounds of hell in a ten-pound sack!" Sam chuckled manfully.

"I," said Professor Wilson, "was not a thug."

"Yeah, sure. Whatever. But look, Professor," Sam said, a note of exasperation creeping into his voice, "obviously you're a more . . . cerebral type, eh?"

Professor Wilson arched an eyebrow in quizzical bemusement.

Sam struck the professor a hearty simpatico blow between bony shoulder blades. "What I'm trying to say is that not every boy's a scholar!

Some get the brains, some get the *testes . . . testar . . . testeroso.*"

"Indeed."

"I'll make this right," Sam vowed once again, winding things up. "Now don't you worry. Mike will confess in a day or two. When he does I'll march him over to make a formal apology."

Behind the professor, Vicki wheedled, "That awful boy put you up to it, didn't he?"

"Un-*fucking*-believable," cried Mike.

The professor glanced over his shoulder.

"Swashbuckling" Sam seized this opportunity to exit, stage right.

"How many times do I have to tell you—*we weren't there!*"

The sound of the front door opening and closing reverberated through the house.

"Don't be upset, honey. You know how it affects your digestion. We're just—"

"I've had enough of this shit."

"*Mister* Michaelson!"

But Mike was gone, disappearing as quickly as his father, feral snarl lingering on the air.

"Well. He doesn't seem to be himself tonight." Vicki's hands were white mice wrestling.

"Really. Based upon what I've observed I should think his behavior entirely in character."

Upstairs, Joseph began to scream.

"You've upset him," Vicki said. She bent over the cocktail table, picked up cup and glass. "I think you'd better go."

"Of course. But first . . ."

The professor fished a small, round metal case out of his front trouser pocket.

"What's that?"

"Relief, Mrs. Michaelson." The professor held the intricately worked case out before him, chest level, open-palmed. The lid, beautifully circumscribed with a design of dueling dragons, snapped upright with a sharp, percussive *pop!* Foam-green smoke poured from the gleaming object. Describing a series of sharply perpendicular hand motions, not unlike a Catholic making the sign of the cross, the professor slashed the air before him.

Vicki managed one startled yet fascinated, "Hey . . ." before the sinuous vapors froze her as immobile as the granite statue of Enkidu in the professor's subterranean invocation chamber.

*"Per tenebros et potestates Yug-Siturath et Yog-Sapha, per tibia insani Azathoth et latrator et Nyarlathotep, ego præcipio mundi: Tene! Ego Ambuletis inter evacuat."*

The professor set the *balgronohmin,* pouring smoke, atop the television. The picture tube promptly imploded.

Upstairs, heavy metal music blared into full sonic assault, muting Joseph's screams.

The professor stood before Vicki, contemplating her lined and weathered face. There was beauty there, too soon eroded. "Poor woman, it has to be this way," he whispered. He took the half-empty glass of water from her hand, sipped, and placed it back into her grasp, gently molding warm mannequin fingers around it. "You've given birth to a monster, dear."

The professor followed the densely twining vapors out of the living room, up the stairs and down the hallway into the boys' bedroom. There he encountered the following frozen tableau:

Mike stood in the middle of the room, a 1/72nd-scale 1928 Model A Ford raised above his head. Joseph, tears tracking his cheeks, reached a-tiptoe for the banana-yellow automobile his taunting brother held aloft just out of reach.

The professor took in the rest of the room at a glance: twin beds, a cluttered dresser-top, a desk and chair, metal shelves bracketing the walls holding an assortment of "men's adventure" paperbacks and military hardcovers. The paperbacks were lurid tales of assassins, mercenaries, and sundry other death merchants; the hardbacks sported titles like *Fighting Techniques of a Panzer Grenadier, Combat Tales of the Death's-Head Divisions,* and *Blood for the Führer.* In addition to the books the shelves were crowded with World War II German militaria: a Wehrmacht soldier's coal-bucket helmet, a red-white-and-black Hitler Youth armband, an assortment of Iron Crosses and Nazi-era post cards. A *Soldier of Fortune* magazine lay on the floor, opened to a photograph of a charred corpse sitting upright behind the wheel of a bullet-riddled automobile. A half-dozen posters adorned the walls: three were of strategically unclad female pop stars in cheesecake poses, three were of Nazi generals. A mini-stereo atop the dresser boomed out Norwegian death-metal, that most peculiar and distressing brand of hard rock: instrumentation akin to a tank division crashing into a herd of panicked tin-men; vocals alternating between a *basso-profundo* rumble and the shrieks of a burning cat.

The professor punched the power button on the mini-stereo. "Most unpleasant."

Silence rushed back into the room.

The professor removed the Model A Ford from Mike's uplifted hand and set it carefully on the shelf beside a King Tiger tank and a Messerschmitt BF-109 fighter plane. He made another series of sharp, incisive gestures, chanting softly.

"Give it to me! Give . . ." Puzzled by what appeared to be the sudden vanishing of the car from his brother's hand, Joseph stepped back in surprise.

At the same moment Mike became aware of a presence behind him. He whirled around at the sound of a dry cough.

"You!" he exclaimed. "How did you—"

"Nice little *Führer* bunker you've got here." The professor eyed the posters. "Erwin Rommel and Britney Spears—now that *is* an interesting juxtaposition." On his finger the ring began to warm.

"Get out of my room, creep."

"No, I don't think so. Leastways not yet." The professor picked up the Messerschmitt BF-109, toyed with its collapsible landing gear for a moment—then snapped its wings off and hurled it to the floor. At Mike's gasp he elaborated. "I *do* apologize, but one feels the necessity of exacting some small measure of vengeance for the many unconscionable acts of harassment suffered at your busy bedeviling hands."

Mike stared in amazement at the ruin of enameled-painted plastic shattered on the carpeting. "You . . . you . . ."

"Are we speaking of the ruminant female mammal of genus *Ovis,* family *Bovidae;* or"—the professor lifted an inquiring brow—"do you mean to declaim the vowel descended from the Phoenician 'Y,' represented in the Greek and Roman by the letter 'V'?"

"*Mom!*" Mike shouted, sending Joseph scurrying into bed where he huddled against the headboard, a comforting pillow hugged tight to his chest. "Get up here quick; he's hitting us!"

The professor smiled a rueful smile. "I don't think she can hear you."

Mike took half a step back, opened his mouth to shout again, then stopped to listen. All quiet downstairs. He glanced up, spotted faint tendrils of smoke curling about the model of a Heinkel bomber suspended from the ceiling by fine twine. "You've set the house on fire."

The professor arched his other brow. "Now why on earth would I want to do that?"

"*MOMMMMMM!*" Mike howled, face reddening with rage and confusion.

Joseph began to blubber.

"I warned you." Mike strode to his bed, reached under the pillow, came up with an SS dagger. He whipped the knife out of the scabbard, tossed the scabbard aside. The polished steel gleamed wickedly.

"*'Meine Ehre heisst Treue':* 'Loyalty Is My Honor,'" said the professor. "Those *are* the words etched into the blade in heavy Gothic script, yes? But the question is, Michael: loyalty to *what?* Loyalty to *whom?*"

"Get out of my room or I'll gut you like a pig."

The professor drew in his breath, studied Mike carefully—the murderous glint in his eye, the thin white gash of a mouth.

"You'd do it too, wouldn't you?" the professor said. He nodded, answering his own question. "You'd bury that steel in my belly with no second thoughts or regrets whatsoever."

Joseph, crying softly, watched in fearful anticipation as the drama unfolded.

The ring on the professor's finger was a circlet of fire now.

Mike motioned toward the door with the dagger. "Time to go, old man."

"Tell me something," the professor said, pupils hard and cold as coffin nails. "What am I to do with a sadistic thug like you? What are we—your brother, parents, school chums, neighbors—victims all, should you live—what are *we* to do about this ravening wolf in our midst?"

"Not your problem, corpse-fuck."

"Oh, but it is." The professor pulled ruminatively at his Adam's apple, shifted on the balls of his feet. "It is *now*. You see, I've made it my problem." He raised his right hand, wielding the ancient Doom Ring of the ghoul king Rokka-melkor. The golden band pulsed with a weird eldritch light; a smell of ozone crackled in the air.

Tearing his gaze from the ring, Mike's eyes sought the professor's. For the first time his gaze showed a glimmer of fear.

"What . . . hey . . . what's going on here?"

"Righteous retribution and the protection of the innocent," spake Professor Robert Howard Wilson with grim and implacable severity.

Mike had heard enough—he lunged. Dagger raised high, veins standing out in forehead and neck from the force of the scream that tore from his throat, he went for the professor with desperate homicidal ferocity.

*PHOOOMMM!*

A molten ray of coruscating light lanced out from the ring enveloping Mike in mid-leap. He shuddered, shrank—and found himself running across the carpeting for his life, all three inches of him, dagger dropped and forgotten, breaking for the safety of the darkened recess under the bed.

The professor fell to his knees, scooped Mike up into his hands. "That jar atop the dresser—*empty it*," he barked.

Joseph jumped up and ran to the mayonnaise jar currently doubling as a bank. He unscrewed the lid, spilling coins and folded dollar bills out onto the floor.

"Hurry. He's—ow!—*biting* me, the hideous gnat."

Wide-eyed, Joseph thrust out the jar.

The professor dropped the limb-pistoning miniscule neo-Nazi into the container.

"Lid!" urged the professor.

Joseph slammed the lid on and the professor twisted it tight. "There. That should hold the little bugger."

The Third Reich tank and airplane models, along with the Nazi memorabilia, were fast fading from the room. The posters had already vanished. Ditto the war books and *Soldier of Fortune* magazine. In the next instant Mike's bed shimmered, drained of color and ghosted out of existence.

The professor raised the jar to eye-level, allowing himself a dour victor's smile.

Mike, reduced to a red-faced Lilliputian, pounded his fists in impotent rage against the glass.

"It would seem our rabid specimen is in need of a distemper treatment." The professor gave the jar a fierce shake, the boy bouncing around inside like a dried bean in a maraca.

Joseph watched, dumbfounded.

The professor brought the jar back to eye-level. Mike, breathless and dazed, sprawled flat on his back on the bottom of the jar. The professor tapped the glass with his fingernail. "Temper, temper," he chided.

Joseph leaped back into bed and burrowed beneath the covers.

"Master Joseph?"

The mound wriggling beneath bedspread and sheet ceased moving.

The professor sighed, stepped to the bed, and yanked the covers down. "Just what do you think you're doing?"

Joseph lay on his belly, face pressed into a pillow. "Guh 'way." His muffled voice was a terrified quaver. "I didn't see anything."

The professor tapped the boy's shoulder. "Sit up."

Joseph played dead.

"Up, boy!"

Warily, Joseph raised his head. "Are you gonna shrink me too?"

"Don't be a dolt."

That was somewhat encouraging. Joseph sat up, braced his back against the headboard.

"Here. He's in your charge now."

Joseph accepted the proffered jar. He examined his diminutive sibling with equal parts wonder and disbelief, raised his eyes to the professor's. "How long will he stay like that?"

"Long enough."

"Long enough?" Joseph turned the phrase over in his mind, pondering its import. "Are you sure?"

"His head-butting days are over, if that's what you mean." The professor sat on the edge of the bed, loosened the crimson knot of silk snugged tight against his neck.

Joseph set the jar aside, though he couldn't stop himself from darting quick glances at it.

Mini-Mike had gotten to his feet again, speaking in an animated fashion, arms wide and pleading. They couldn't hear a word.

Joseph's expression grew crafty. "Mom will notice he's missing."

The professor laughed a high, keening peal of fiendish amusement. "Mike never existed; ergo, it is impossible for your mother to notice the disappearance of a brat who never was. The same holds true for your father. Neither of them will have any memories of your brother nor any recollection of my visit here today. Anyone who ever *had* any memories of the little monster—family, friends, teachers—will lose those memories shortly; within the next ten minutes or so, I should think."

Joseph glanced again at the jar.

"Oh, the boy appears real enough, I'll grant you that—if somewhat diminished in stature, eh? Courtesy of that burst of light that hit our would-be murderer: 'The Doom Bolt of Unmaking.'" The professor removed the ring from his finger—it had cooled significantly—and dropped it into his suit coat pocket. "Your pestiferous sibling is now a minuscule member of *Homo sapiens*. But we are the only ones who can see him as he truly is because we were witnesses to the change. To all others, Mike will appear to be"—he coughed drily—"a cricket."

"Cricket?" Joseph picked up his pillow, squeezed it for comfort and reassurance.

The professor shrugged. "Usually it's a cricket. Sometimes the doom-struck appear to be a wasp, spider, or dung beetle. I've no control over the particulars of the transmogrification, you see. In any event, your brother will never harm you or anyone else again. Of that you may rest assured." He stood. "There is one other thing you should know. The Doom Ring only affects those who intend to commit murder. Had the intemperate beastie not attempted to perform that bit of impromptu open-heart surgery upon me, no doubt he'd still be happily blackening your eyes and dreaming sordid little jackbooted dreams."

Joseph looked at the professor, then back to mini-Mike in the jar. "So what am I supposed to feed him?"

"You may feed him grass and squirrel droppings for all I care. In twenty-four hours the question will be moot."

"Moot?" A snot-bubble popped in Joseph's left nostril.

The professor's stomach lurched. "Irrelevant."

"Irr—"

*"It won't matter,"* said the professor. "Your sadistic sibling will vanish from this reality: nevermore to be seen, nevermore to be heard, nev-

ermore"—he smiled with chill satisfaction—"remembered."

Joseph considered this. "So." He considered some more. "So. Uh . . . where will he go, exactly?"

"Now *that* is an interesting question. Perhaps—" The professor stopped himself, cocked his head up and to the right. His eyes ticktocked back and his forth, but his gaze was focused on the middle distance, tracking something beyond the room. "Excellent," he breathed.

"What?" said Joseph.

The professor only smiled and moved to the doorway. Joseph's voice halted him before he could exit.

"Mr. Wizard."

The professor stiffened. "*Professor* Robert Howard Wilson, if you please."

"Perfezzer Wilson," said Joseph. The crafty look had come back into his eyes. He worried a thread loose from the pillowcase, then blurted, "There are boys at school who pick on me."

"Do tell." The professor shot his cuffs. "And?"

"Well, I was wondering if you could . . . that is, if you might . . ."

"Turn their ears into bat wings, noses into pumpkins? Blind them? Cause their hideous bully-boy limbs to atrophy and drop off?"

"Something like that."

"Dear boy, I am a *scholar,* not a hit man," sniffed the professor in indignation. He stepped into the hall, turned back. "One last thing. Don't go downstairs for an hour or so. Your mother is a statue in the kitchen and I suspect you may find her immobility alarming. The condition is strictly temporary, I assure you."

Joseph listened, wide-eyed and attentive. Nothing would surprise him anymore. "Is she okay?"

"Certainly. Though I suspect she'll awaken with a massive headache." The professor made a series of rhythmic, languorous motions with his hand. "Now watch my fingers. That's it. Watch the sleeepy, *sleee-eepy* fingers. You are tired."

"I . . . am tired."

"You will forget everything that happened here today."

"I . . . will forget."

"Very good. Rest now. Goodbye, Joseph."

"G'bye . . . Per . . . fez-zer . . ."

Whistling a sprightly bit of Vivaldi, the professor descended the stairs and traversed the ocean of orange shag. Just as he exited the living room and reached out a hand to the front door—

*Bong-bong!*

—the doorbell rang.

The professor opened the door.

A red-haired boy stood there, blinking uncertainly. His bicycle lay tipped over behind him on the lawn.

At the professor's back the Deepak Chopra hardcover leapt into the air with a rustle of paper and boards. Hawk-like, it hovered in a corner of the living room, pages *firrrrrr-thwap! firrrrrr-thwapping!* in a telekinetic frenzy.

"Wulfgar," the professor's voice was a purr. His gaze focused on the boy's soft right temple with the intensity of a master bowman aiming his nocked arrow at a can't-miss bull's-eye. "How *very nice* to see you again."

# The Return of Pumpkin Jack

## or, The Righteous Depredations of Most Mild Mr. Morris

### I.

He arose from a patch of harvested squash:
boots, blue overalls & a Mackintosh
on a moonless night painted midnight black
an Illinois farmer—woe & alack!
Mr. Morris returned as Pumpkin Jack.

In a bony hand he clutched the knife
destined for the heart of a faithless wife;
Kate & her lover had murdered him
after a bumper crop turned in
delivered to market for kith & kin.

Jack-o'-Lantern-Head came striding,
December's wind soft dying,
a fell breeze in the treetops sighing—
up to his weathered front door.

### II.

Mirthless chuckles wracked Pumpkin Jack—
The void had called, but he'd clawed his way back!
Knuckles rapped on the knot-holed door,

a scampering rabbit screamed before
owls tore it to twitching gore

behind him in the barren fields
that'd given up their harvest yield.
A year he'd moldered in fertile ground
whose orange pumpkins, fat & round
were the lauded, lurid talk o' the town.

Now Pumpkin Jack stood heaving
dirt-clotted lungs yet breathing,
in fury rising, seething—
*Rap-rap!* on his weathered front door.

## III.

The door creaked open—wide-eyed Kate
& the cuckolding, fish-eyed reprobate
who'd stolen Kate's love & slit his throat
taken his wife like a billy goat
burrowed into bed like a wily stoat

turned white: their teeth click-clacked.
*"Ho-ho!"* cried Pumpkin Jack.
His blade was a silvery flash of doom—
"The worm has turned!" Mr. Morris crooned
spurting bodies fell in grayish gloom

to convulse & thump on the floor.
"Take that, damn murderer! Whore!
'Tis your bliss dark gods abhor."
Pumpkin Jack hacked—screech-cackled.

# IV.

The lovers were found next day at dawn:
rigor-mortis rictused, color wan;
mouths wrenched open in final screams
mutilated in manner quite obscene:
a hideous, chilling, post-frenzy scene.

That infamous sanguinary morn
a new rural legend was born;
porch cameras caught the attack:
mad savagery of Pumpkin Jack!
Most feared that he'd be back.

When boundaries 'tween worlds thin
beware a jack-o'-lantern's grin!
Mr. Morris carves out sin
at the point of a saw-toothed knife.

# Pulp Writer

In the darkened bedroom, his wife asleep beside him, Clark Hawke (né Anthony Battaglia) awoke to find his muse—an exact double for Clarice Orsini, regal subject of Botticelli's *Portrait of a Young Woman* (whom he'd spotted in a coffee-table art book at a friend's home years ago)— standing at the foot of the bed. Clarice had braided blond hair, voluptuous red lips, and unblinking, luminous hazel eyes. She appeared to him hypersexualized and impossibly exotic: pert breasts, taut buttocks, and a shadowed Venus mound artfully obscured by lengths of diaphanous green silk wound about her body—the loose ends gently undulating, like her splayed-out braided hair, as if underwater. A filtered fall of moonlight through half-closed blinds striped the room in alternating lines of gray and black.

Anthony sat up in bed.

Maria uttered something sleep-mazed and incoherent and turned over, snugging the sheet and comforter tighter under her chin.

*Kill her.*

Clarice's voice—smooth and smoky as honeyed whiskey with a scorpion-tail sting—sounded in his mind.

"Monster," he whispered back. "No. I won't do it."

Clarice inclined her head toward him, as if in acknowledgment or dismissal. *Then know that you have accepted a life of grinding poverty and artistic mediocrity. You have turned your back on your best work: writing that would have won you critical raves, legions of ecstatic fans, a footnote in eternity.*

"So be it. You think I would trade my wife's life for literary success?"

Clarice laughed—a musical, tinkling, somehow savage sound: like razor-sharp icicles dislodged by startled bats in some wintry roost, falling through frigid air to shatter on a cavern floor far below.

*You lack the strength to do what must be done. Very well, then. I shall do it for you.*

Clarice drifted around the side of the bed.

*I will strangle Maria.* She stabbed her finger toward the doorway that opened into the hallway that led to the smaller, adjoining bedroom a dozen paces away. *Then Chloe.*

"I said *no!*"

"Honey?" Maria, startled awake, struggled to rise.

Clarice vanished.

"It's nothing," said Anthony, sliding back under the sheet and comforter, a reassuring hand stroking his wife's shoulder. "Sorry I woke you."

She rolled over to face him. "Nigh-mare?" she slurred, voice thick and groggy.

"Nightmare," Anthony confirmed.

"Oh," Maria mumbled. "'Kay."

She turned away from him and he spooned her. Maria's breathing slowed, deepened. Minutes later she was again fast asleep.

Anthony, however, tossed and turned the rest of that night.

Next morning found Anthony seated at the kitchen table banging away at a manual Underwood typewriter. He pressed the carriage return lever right and began a new line of dialogue:

"Akin to amphibian life

The metal arm of the letter "e" key failed to retract from the paper and platen.

"Damn it!" said Anthony.

"Language," Maria called out from the master bedroom.

Anthony reached out with his left hand and flicked the malfunctioning arm back to its ready position.

"Goddamn second-hand piece of shit!" Anthony announced again, much louder.

No recriminating rejoinder from Maria this time, though he could sense his wife's disapproval radiating out from the bedroom and down the hall: the tight-lipped, unamused, put-upon expression she must be wearing now as she made up their bed and fluffed pillows.

The hell with it. Let *her* sit in front of a malfunctioning typewriter twelve to sixteen hours a day and grind out tale after lurid tale for the pulps: stories of crime fighters, cowboys, World War I aces, barbarians, wizards, rocket men, and alien monsters—at the peasant-yoked-to-the-plow payrate of half-a-cent a word. Let *her* face the terror of the blank page: the gnawing frustrations, self-doubt, and existential angst caused by false starts, endless revisions, and—worst of all—full-on, paralyzing writer's block.

But that wasn't fair, was it? She hadn't chosen the life of a pulp writer; he had. It was Anthony Battaglia who had decided to write on spec and have 90% of his output rejected by editors formulaically notifying him, weeks or months later, that "we regret the submitted manuscript does not fit our current needs." The remaining 10% of his work that *was* accepted for publication appeared under an Anglicized name to placate racists who would otherwise ignore the stories—or so he had been told. Thus the WASPish moniker "Clarke Hawke" appeared on his tales, as he was repeatedly—even breezily—informed that twentieth-century American readers would never accept a name as ethnic as "Anthony Battaglia" as an author in the genres he wrote for. ("You want to be known as 'The Dago of Sci-Fi'?" one science fiction editor had querulously cross-examined him, his expression pitched somewhere between incredulity and disgust. "Ain't happenin'! Not on my watch; not in this mag.") Unfair? Sure, but that's the way it was. He and so many others could not afford to put an additional stumbling block in the way of getting published, hence the multitude of nom de plumes disguising ethnicity on the contents pages of the pulps. Ditto contemporary actors' names on theatre marquees, radio broadcast personality voices over the airwaves, et al.

Anthony jabbed the stub of an unfiltered cigarette into his lips, butt end glowing red-orange, the tobacco and paper crackling faintly as he took a deep draw. A half-second later—lift-off: mild euphoria accompanied by a heightened sense of alertness.

Clarice watched with alert, predatory intensity from a corner of the kitchen as Anthony tilted his head back and exhaled a column of blue-gray smoke at the glaring, dual-bulb brass fixture affixed to the ceiling overhead. That bit of business accomplished, he snuffed the cigarette out in an ashtray embossed with a panoramic picture of Niagara Falls (souvenir of their ten-year-ago honeymoon). The falls were partly obscured beneath a powdering of soft gray ash. He picked up the half-empty pint of gin that stood ready within easy reach and took a long, heartening swig. Internal glow rekindled, Anthony set the glass bottle back down with an inadvertent bang against the tabletop. He glanced over at Clarice and threw her a mock salute.

Clarice stared back, face impassive. Braided hair rippled in unseen fathoms-deep currents.

Anthony wrote in the kitchen because Maria had commandeered the dining-room table to assemble a two-thousand-piece jigsaw puzzle of Leonardo da Vinci's mural "The Last Supper." She'd been working on the puzzle, making desultory progress, for the last three months. It was now half-finished. (The plan was to laminate the puzzle to an acid-free backing board, frame and hang it on the wall once fully assembled.)

"Anthony?" Maria called from the bedroom.

"It's nothing," he answered. "I'm okay." Then, idiotically repeating: "It's nothing."

Anthony continued typing. *Goddamn letter "e"!* Of all the keys on the Underwood to malfunction it had to be *that* letter: the one most commonly used in the English language. He had to get this novella finished—30,000 words about an ill-fated expedition to Venus—and into the mail no later than Monday. So w*rite,* he commanded himself: *faster!*

He'd promised Sloane the manuscript would be in his hands by early next week. Of course, there was no guarantee of either acceptance or payment (he was writing on spec, after all), and Sloane was notoriously slow to respond to his writers. (How they missed Gernsback!) Still, Sloane had expressed interest in the novella—the plot tentatively sketched out as a three-sentence postscript Anthony had appended to his reply on their last exchange of correspondence—and Anthony was determined to live up to his commitment and present himself as a professional. God knows he was well motivated to do so. The rent was a week past due on their third-story, two-bedroom walk-up on Chicago's northwest side. He had a worsening toothache in a back molar, a car whose transmission was slipping, and a wife and daughter who hadn't signed up for a sojourn through the Slough of Despond. (Though they were now living like impoverished peasants who could only dream of such luxuries as whole roasts, steaks, cosmetics, brand-new clothing, and hardcover books.) Hell, they might as well be starving Soviet prisoners wasting away in some wintry Siberian gulag, he reflected ruefully in ever more frequent moments of rage and despair. So much for their portion of the capitalist American dream, here in the ongoing depths of the 1936 "Great Depression."

Chloe appeared in the doorway—sockless and still dressed in pajamas. Her round face retained the cherubic, pinkish glow of baby fat; black curls of sweat-slicked hair were tightly matted to her scalp. "Daddy?"

His head snapped up from the typewriter. "Yes?"

Clarice vanished.

"I was just wondering . . ." she faltered and hitched at her sagging pajama bottoms. "Just wondering . . ."

*"Yes?"* said Anthony, more sharply. "Stop fiddling and speak up!"

Maria appeared behind their daughter in a faded blue sun dress, wiry black hair tied up in a no-nonsense bun. "She's wondering when you're going to clear the table so that we can have breakfast."

Anthony glanced at the large, off-white Art Deco wall clock mounted above the kitchen sink. The hands stood at 9:15 A.M. They usually breakfasted no later than eight.

He experienced a twinge of guilt. "Sorry, gang," Anthony apologized. "I lost track of the time."

"Your father says he's sorry," Maria announced, redundantly. Her eyes flicked to Anthony and away again as she brushed past Chloe into the kitchen.

Chloe made no reply to this. She hopped up onto one of the rail-back chairs around the table and sat there placid and quietly expectant, one foot repetitively kicking a leg of the chair.

Anthony stood up, grabbed the bottle of gin and pack of cigarettes off the table. "You guys go ahead and start without me. I'll eat later."

"You should eat something now," said Maria. "You should eat with *us.*"

To this rejoinder Anthony only grunted.

Maria opened the ice box and peered in. "No milk."

Anthony squeezed the pack of cigarettes in his hand, causing the cellophane to crinkle. "You were supposed to add water to the milk to get us through the week. Remember?"

"I *did* add water to the milk," Maria snapped at him. She moved to the cabinet, began pulling out bowls with a rattling clatter of chipped pottery. "How far do you think that stretched, Anthony? Just how much water was I supposed to add?"

"Enough to—"

"—turn a splash of milk into a glass of cloudy water?" She rounded on him, furious.

The rage in her eyes . . . the frustration . . . contempt . . . staggered him for a moment.

"We'll have milk again next week," he said, voice barely audible.

"Sorry; it's dry cereal again this morning, Chloe," said Maria, turning back to the cabinets and pulling out a box of corn flakes.

Anthony stared at her back, resenting the breaking of the self-hypnotic spell he'd been under in order to write. *Christ! Did they think he could turn it on and off as easily as flicking a switch?*

He rallied; injected a false note of cheer into his voice. "We've got honey for the cereal."

"Honey isn't milk," said Maria.

"No," said Anthony. "It isn't." *Crinkle-crinkle* went the cellophane of the cigarette pack in his hand.

He stood there for a moment longer watching Maria pour corn flakes into bowls. Then he slammed the bottle back down onto the table and stalked from the room, temples twitching.

Anthony took a short walk 'round the neighborhood to work off his anger and frustration. It was a sun-bright summer morning in Chicago, and he winced against the glare. His walking pace slowed as his racing pulse settled into a more normal rhythm. As he strolled along there sounded the blare of car horns, the chirping of birds, the susurration of lawn sprinklers arcing out glistening jets of water. He lit a cigarette and smoked as he walked. Two young boys in shorts and sneakers pounded past, red-faced and breathless on their way to somewhere in a hurry. *Wrigley Field? The movie theatre? The corner drugstore with its enticing treasures of chocolate sodas, comic books, candy, and cap pistols? Perhaps a pulp magazine or two containing a story by Clark Hawke. . . .*

As the boys' cries faded into the distance his thoughts returned to his own family. *It's not their fault they don't understand. I need extended periods of uninterrupted near-silence in order to self-hypnotize, to fall down the rabbit hole into other worlds and commit to paper what I find there. Maria tries her best to be supportive and understanding but is ultimately indifferent to creative practice. Chloe is too young to understand the concept and practice of fictioneering.* (She would start first grade in the fall.) *Neither of them can fathom the intensity and fragility of the process: the zen-like concentration/no-concentration mindset it takes to*

*weave the gossamer-thin spell of fairy, an enchantment so easily broken.*
*As for the allure and satisfaction of the creative process as it applies to*
*fiction writing, to the act of having written . . .*

Did he understand the process?

Not entirely. No.

The bitch goddess of fictioneering had sunk her claws deep into his
psyche and soul. *That* he understood beyond the shadow of a doubt, as he
fought and overcame resistance daily in order to get words down on paper.
Truth be told, his love/hate relationship with writing was schizoid. He
loved the process of writing as much as he hated it; surprising himself with
words, scenes, plot reversals, and (mostly satisfactory) climaxes and de-
nouements even as he chafed at the self-imposed physical immobility re-
quired to pound away at the keyboard. Well, that was where the tobacco
and liquor came in. Those over-the-counter drugs—one a stimulant, the
other a depressant—kept his creative gears well lubricated and function-
ing, first summoning the muse and then keeping Clarice close at hand.

He was a decent writer . . . wasn't he? (Dare he think it?) Perhaps
even a good one. True, Anthony Battaglia was no Edgar Rice Burroughs,
Robert E. Howard, Raymond Chandler, or L. Ron Hubbard (no one
could outwrite Hubbard; the guy had modified his typewriter to take *entire spools of paper* so that precious time wasn't lost feeding individual
sheets through the rollers), but he felt Clark Hawke had held his own
against Howard's white-hot fever-dream prose style and Chandler's hard-
bitten, machine-gun prose-poetry. Against Burroughs, well . . . Burroughs had out-produced him by volumes and was certainly more popu-
lar, but Antony liked to flatter himself that his writing had the edge in
quality. His nom de plume had produced more work than H. P. Lovecraft (the Gentleman Sage of Providence) or Clark Ashton Smith (the
Bard of Auburn and self-styled "Emperor of Dreams")—though Anthony
would readily admit that both of these latter writers employed sublime,
pitch-perfect libraries of specialized vocabulary that wrought upon the
reader wondrous, transportive—even ecstatic—effects that were utterly be-

yond him. Still—sixty published short stories, a couple dozen poems, a handful of essays, and divers articles on various genre-related subjects wasn't nothing. Clark Hawke was a name that had moderate recognition within the field, though no break-through acclaim had come his way (*Yet! he reminded himself—yet!*) for his work. Three separate, unrelated novels had faltered midway through and currently languished in a desk drawer, but what of it? The fact was incontrovertible: he was a writer. Paid, published, supporting a family. True, some looked upon his lurid, pulse-pounding writing as little better than pornography—his father-in-law and elder brother, to name but two. That stung; there was no denying it. But until he could scrape together enough cash to support his family while he took three to four years off to write a breakthrough novel (he'd been doing research into the Great Chicago Fire for years: filled two entire trunks with primary source material and notebooks crammed cover-to-cover with notes jotted down in his cramped, constipated cursive), the popularly denigrated—albeit widely purchased—pulp fictions would have to continue. There simply was no other choice—unless he wanted to give up writing entirely and get into some other line of work. Unthinkable. A change of career would mean a crushing, catastrophic defeat of his intellect, talent, and spirit.

The houses, trees, bushes—occasional people and dogs—that passed were invisible to him now as he strolled along, lost in thought.

*Pulp writer*—that's what I am. Pulp fiction—fast-paced, white-knuckled, bruising—is what I write.

"And I'm good at it," he muttered. "*Damn* good at it."

He almost believed it.

From afar—the next alley, perhaps (or was it the next block, the next world?)—he heard the musical tinkling laughter of his muse, Clarice.

A Good Humor ice cream Ford Model A backfired beside him, and he started. The truck slowed; the white garbed, black-visored driver stared at him inquiringly as he rolled by.

Anthony raised a hand in greeting but shook his head no.

The driver nodded and sped up, pulling away with another lurching backfire and a puff of pungent, blue-gray smoke.

*Wait.*

He should get some ice cream for Maria and Chloe—they could eat it before it melted if he hurried home. They'd love him for that . . . a total, extravagant surprise . . . ice cream in the morning!

Too late. The Good Humor truck was halfway down the block and picking up speed.

He took a last puff of his cigarette, exhaled, and flicked it into the gutter.

Thirty minutes later he was back at the kitchen table, a fresh cigarette smoldering in a corner of his lips, banging away again at the keyboard of his battered Underwood. *This doesn't have to be deathless prose,* he reminded himself. *It just has to be effective. Revise later. Time is money and you have no money. So get words onto paper before the internal censor can rear up and stop you cold. Write-write-write-write-write—faster!—to outrun the censor.*

Despite this frenzied internal admonishment he was only able to pound out a couple of words before he had to pause and flick the malfunctioning arm of the letter "e" key back to its ready position. He pounded out another couple of words: pause—*flick!* Resumed. Another rattling burst of the typewriter's keys and arms: pause—*flick!*—resumed. Again . . . again . . . and again . . .

Anthony paused to reread what he'd written, snubbing out his cigarette in the ashtray.

That was a mistake.

He sighed, ripped the sheet of paper out of the typewriter, crumpled it up, and hurled it to the floor. Picked up the bottle of gin.

Maria turned halfway around from the kitchen sink where she was washing out glasses and bowls from the breakfast meal. "You should eat something."

Chloe was nowhere in sight.

Neither was Clarice.

Anthony took another long swallow from the bottle; set it back down. "You sound like a broken record," Anthony said.

"I sound like a broken record because I see you smoking and drinking and not eating," Maria said, not unkindly.

"I'll eat something later."

"What?"

"Toast . . . an egg . . . something!" Irritated, he sharply motioned for her to truncate the interrogation.

Maria shook her head wordlessly and turned back to the dishes in the sink.

Anthony lit up a new cigarette; jammed it into a corner of his mouth.

Another rattling burst of the typewriter's keys and arms.

From Chloe's bedroom a snatch of sing-song drifted down the hallway and into the kitchen. No doubt she was playing "Mommy" or schoolteacher again; addressing her family of stuffed animals and dolls.

Anthony attempted to block out the noise. He struggled to fall back down the rabbit hole to his imperiled astronauts machete-hacking and ray-gunning their way through a fetid Venusian swap well stocked with all manner of amphibian monstrosities.

Anthony typed out another word, then manually retracted the arm of the letter "e" key from the paper and platen.

Chloe's sing-song grew louder.

"Chloe!" Anthony called out.

Chloe fell quiet.

"Daddy's writing! Remember our rule?"

No response. No sound at all, save for that of running water and the clatter of dishes in the sink.

*"Remember the goddamn rule?"* he called out in a louder voice.

Maria whirled around. "Anthony!"

He took a last drag of his cigarette, stubbed it out in the ashtray beside the bottle of gin. Exhaled columns of smoke through his nostrils. Met his wife's stare with a glower of his own, then averted his eyes. "Look . . . I can't . . . Sorry. That was uncalled for."

"Damn right it was uncalled for! Now apologize to our daughter."

Anger rose in him again as suddenly as shame vanished. "We agreed on the rule! If I can't write, we don't eat. *Get it?*"

"I get it. We all get it, Anthony. *Apologize to her.*"

He took a deep breath. "I'm sorry!" he called out in a carrying—though level—tone. "Daddy shouldn't have swore."

"Sworn," corrected Maria.

Anthony got up slowly—carefully (*don't look at her*) from the table and went to Chloe. He found his little girl in the bedroom, just as he'd suspected—sitting cross-legged in a corner holding court amongst her dolls and stuffed animals. She had changed out of pajamas and into a powder-blue skirt and puffy-sleeved white blouse.

"Chloe?"

His daughter hugged a floppy-eared rabbit dressed in multicolored patched overalls tighter to her chest. He knew the moniker of this one.

Anthony hunkered down before her. "Honey . . ."

She looked at him.

"I'm sorry I swore."

"That's okay," said Chloe. "I was loud."

"True—but mine was the greater wrong, kiddo. I'm sorry." He skooched a little closer to her—awkwardly, still crouched—damn near falling on his ass. "Can Daddy get a hug?"

Chloe shrugged.

"What does Patches say?"

Chloe whispered into the rabbit's ear.

Anthony waited.

Chloe turned her ear to the rabbit's face—listened intently—nodded. "Patches says it's all right. We'll try to be quiet."

Anthony hugged his daughter—still clutching her tattered stuffed rabbit—to his chest; then released her.

Footsteps sounded behind him. "Chloe, get your shoes on. We're going out."

Anthony rose and turned.

"We're going to the park. Then the grocery store." Maria—a couple of inches shorter than her husband—faced him squarely; seemed to struggle to add an inch or two to her height as she spread her feet and braced for his frown. "I'm buying milk, Anthony."

To this latter announcement he said nothing.

"We'll be gone most of the afternoon. Good luck with your writing. In addition to milk I'll pick up bread, cheese, and cigarettes."

She pecked him on the cheek and brushed past. "Chloe, do you need help with those shoes?"

"No, Mommy," Chloe answered, grimacing while wriggling her feet into buckle shoes. "I'm not a baby, you know!"

Anthony and Maria smiled at their daughter's outraged assertion of maturity—glanced at each other—away.

"Okay, I'm ready!" Chloe triumphantly announced. "'Bye, Daddy."

She rushed past him into the hallway, Maria hard on her heels.

The entrance door to the apartment opened and closed.

Muffled footsteps sounded on the hallway carpeting, rapidly diminishing in volume as Maria and Chloe descended the stairway. Moments later—a scarcely audible creak, then the softest-of-soft clicks as the lobby door to the apartment opened and then latched behind them.

Alone at last.

Rattling bursts of rapidly keyed typewriter arms sounded as staccato and disciplined as well-aimed machine gun fire in the stillness of the apartment. Anthony had been writing steadily for hours. Yet another cigarette burned in a corner of his lips. He squinted at the text emerging onto a rolled sheet of lightweight manuscript paper (cheaper postage when mailed) through a haze of burnt nicotine. He was so engrossed he barely noticed the many times he had to pause and reset the arm of the letter "e" key from the paper and platen back to its ready position. An empty pint of gin lay tipped over on its side against the ashtray. He was well and truly down the rabbit hole . . .

*Keep it moving; keep writing. Don't stop to reread. Edit later.*

His stranded astronauts had fought their way out of the fetid Venusian swamp and onto a rocky plateau where they discovered an alien city of cyclopean black basaltic structures whose roofs gleamed magma red and golden yellow. The city lay in ruins: streets deserted; no evidence of who or what the prior inhabitants may have been or where they might have gone. The team followed a winding broad boulevard into a rectilinear maze of glass-like shrubbery and monstrous pedestaled animals the likes of which had never been guessed at by the terrestrial inhabitants of terra firma. . . .

Clarice laid soothing hands on his hunched shoulders and massaged stress-tightened muscles as he typed. He felt her approval and growing excitement, reading over his shoulder as the story unfolded.

*Good, Anthony! Very good.* Clarice spoke in her honeyed, smoky voice: the siren song of the femme fatale promising both pleasure and pain. Eros inextricably entwined with Thanatos.

Anthony paused to take a deep drag off the cigarette—exhaled— stubbed it out in the ashtray.

He resumed typing as Clarice continued to massage his aching shoulders. Some part of his mind realized that he was more than intellectually thrilled by writing-in-flow, he was physically excited now. Positively tumescent.

*My love,* Clarice whispered into his ear.

Miles deep down the rabbit hole . . .

*Faster! Deeper!*

Anthony shivered with pleasure.

*              *              *

Maria and Chloe returned home at 6 P.M.

Anthony finished typing the final sentence of the penultimate scene of his story as Maria came into the kitchen to set a cloth-handled grocery bag down on the counter. She pulled out a quart of whole milk and a block of cheddar cheese from the bag and put these staples into the ice-box; the carton of cigarettes went into the cabinet above the sink.

Chloe disappeared into her bedroom.

"How'd the writing go?" Maria asked.

Anthony tapped the stack of manuscript pages beside the typewriter and squared their edges; smiling a little, tight smile of triumph. "Pretty good. I should finish tonight, I think."

"Great. Then you can help me clear the table while I start dinner."

"Sure," Anthony said, pushing back from the table and standing up.

Maria stooped to pick up the balled-up piece of typescript he'd wrenched from the typewriter and hurled to the floor earlier. She straightened. "After dinner we need to talk."

A beat.

"Sure," Anthony repeated. His temples twitched. "Of course." A longer beat. "What about?"

After dinner—spaghetti and meatballs; sliced banana in strawberry gelatin for desert—Maria announced they would play board games till Chloe's bedtime.

"I thought you wanted to discuss—" Anthony began.

Maria cut him off with a look. "Later," she said.

Anthony, Maria, and Chloe played board games till Chloe's bedtime of 10 P.M. (Friday night was Family Night, as per honored tradition in the Battaglia household.) They played checkers (Maria teamed up with Chloe, alternating moves against Anthony), then Parcheesi and Monopoly.

The windows were opened to admit a cross-breeze but the cooling effect of such ventilation proved problematic at best—too much summertime heat had soaked into the concrete, brick, and steel of the city during the day to be discharged quickly after nightfall. To combat the mugginess Maria had set up an oscillating fan on the countertop beside Anthony's typewriter. It moved the warm air about but did little to cool the perspiration dampening their foreheads, necks, and arms.

Monopoly ran late. Maria had been knocked out of the game a half-hour earlier; she sat and watched quietly till 10:30 P.M. when Anthony landed on Chloe's red-hoteled Boardwalk and handed over a thick stack of cash after having mortgaged all his properties.

"You're bankrush, Daddy!" Chloe squealed with delight.

"It appears I am," Anthony said.

"I win!" Chloe applauded herself, bouncing in the chair. Her gaze switched between Anthony and Maria. "I beat *both* of you!"

Maria snorted and shook an admonishing finger at her daughter. "First time ever, youngling."

"Ever, ever, *ever*," Chloe chirruped in agreement.

"I believe you had a little help," Anthony noted. "Who set up those houses and hotels on your property, hmm?"

Chloe ignored this statement. She drew herself up straighter in the chair to address her parents with regal noblesse oblige. "Don't worry! You can win next week."

That wrung a laugh out of both of them.

"Bedtime, sweety. Kiss Daddy goodnight."

"'Kay." Chloe slipped down from her chair and went to stand beside her father, face upturned.

Anthony leaned over and kissed Chloe lightly on the lips.

"Good night, Chloe. I love you."

"Love you too, Daddy." Chloe scampered from the room.

Maria stood. "I'll see her to bed. You don't mind cleaning up?"

"Not at all."

"We'll talk when I come back."

They talked, all right—that is to say, Maria did most of the talking. Both of them seated at the kitchen table, drinking gin from water glasses. Maria smoking; occasionally gesturing with her lit cigarette. Anthony sitting with his arms folded across his chest between sips of liquor, face rigid and expressionless.

The gist of it was this: Maria wanted to take Chloe to her parents' downstate farm for a couple of weeks. Give Anthony some extended writing time alone. Allow Chloe to get to know her grandparents better. As for Maria, what she got out of the temporary separation was . . .

"Time." She gestured with her cigarette as ash fell onto the table. "I just need some time, Anthony."

"What the hell does that mean?"

"It means . . ." Maria trailed off into aposiopesis.

"I know what that means. And I think you do as well." He sat rigid and upright in the chair. "You mean to say that you need time away from *me*," said Anthony. "That's what you're saying, right? You need some time away from hubby. From his moods and mutterings, the grinding poverty and deprivation he's imposed—"

"Anthony!"

He grinned sickly—sadly—savagely at her. "You think I've failed you and Chloe." He attempted to sound mocking and scornful, but his voice broke. He despised himself for that weakness. "A man should be able to support his family. They should be comfortable, happy, secure. If he can't he's not much of a man, is he? There's a name for that kind of man . . ."

Maria took a long drag off her cigarette, tilted her head back, and exhaled the smoke in roiling columns that diffused into a drifting cloud inches below the ceiling. She snubbed the cigarette out in the ashtray. Regarded him steadily.

"I don't think that you're—that we—are a failure," she said quietly. "I do know that I need a week or two away from"—she spread her arms to encompass the room—"this."

"Prison?" inquired Anthony.

"And so does Chloe," Maria finished as non sequitur, ignoring his provocation.

"Of course," agreed Anthony, voice colorless.

*Control. Deep breaths.*

"And consider," said Maria, voice brightening, leaning forward for emphasis, "it might be the best thing for you, as well."

"How do you mean?" asked Anthony. He wasn't looking at her—he was looking at her hand—extended across the table in an attempt to grasp his own. He ignored this overture of comfort and reassurance. Instead he picked up his water glass of gin—swallowed half the contents in a gulp—and set the glass back down with deliberate care. Then he refolded his arms across his chest. "'The best thing for me as well,' you said."

"I just mean that you'll be able to get a lot of writing done," said Maria, "without distractions. Who knows? Perhaps even find time to get started on your . . . "—she gestured vaguely—"more serious work."

"My more *serious* work?" Anthony found himself stupidly repeating the ends of her sentences, stalling for time, flailing for solid ground in a conversation that was beginning to feel like a stumble at the edge of a pit. His pulse pounded in his temples. That back molar throbbed. "And what might that be?"

*Do not tremble. Clench the gut.*

"You know—a novel." Maria tossed her head in an expression of involuntary physiognomic signaling that indicated growing impatience. "I am suggesting that you start a new novel. What about the one you've done all that research for—on the Great Chicago Fire? If you pulled out your notes and settled in for two weeks of uninterrupted . . ." She trailed off.

Anthony's hands gripped the table edge as his face successively darkened through shades of pink—red—purple. "You're telling me my business now?" he choked out. "You're telling me what to write—"

"Anthony—"

"—*when* to write . . ."

"I just thought——"

*"Goddamn you!"*

Maria pushed her chair back and stood up.

Anthony flipped the table. Water glasses, ashtray, bottle of gin—all went flying as the metal-legged, mahogany-topped table overturned and crashed onto the floor.

Chloe cried out from her bedroom. *"Mommy!"*

"Stay there, Chloe!" Maria instructed.

Below them, a neighbor pounded on the ceiling to protest the racket.

"Well," said Maria, face darkening with anger. "That was mature." She folded her arms across her breasts in unconscious imitation of Anthony's defensive posture in the chair seconds ago.

"You're leaving me," said Anthony. And stood up.

"Yes," said Maria. "In the morning. With Chloe. How you behave over the course of the next twelve hours will determine whether or not we return." Her lips compressed into a thin, bloodless white line.

"How *dare* you threaten me!" Anthony covered the distance to his wife in an intoxicated, off-balance bound. "You've been thinking about this for a while now, haven't you?" He seized Maria by the shoulders and shook her savagely, causing her head to bobble. *"Bitch!* Emasculating, disloyal, ungrateful—"

*"Daddy!"*

Chloe's scream brought him to his senses.

He snapped his head around to look at her. Their little girl was frozen in the entranceway to the kitchen—dressed for slumber in polka-dotted pajamas, clenched fists to her cheeks, bug-eyed with surprise and fear. Her expression knifed his heart.

Anthony dropped his hands to his sides. "Chloe! Go back to bed. It's okay." He stepped away from Maria and toward his daughter. "Really! It's okay, honey." He adopted a soothing, silken tone. "Your mother and I were just having an argument."

"Is that what we were doing?" said Maria, rubbing her shoulders. "I thought we were having a sensible discussion of pressing personal mat-ters." She gave him a bitter smile. "'Course, that was before you put your hands on me—brute."

Anthony glowered at her. "Don't push it."

*"Don't push it?"* asked Maria in disbelief, voice rising. Now it was she who was repeating *his* sentences. She took a furious step toward him. "I am not a helpless wench chained to a stone idol in one of your sword-and-sorcery tales, Anthony!" She poked him in the chest. "Or should I say 'Clark Hawke'? *Who do you think you are?* A hardboiled P.I. who slaps women around till they recover their senses?"

"You're mixing genres," Anthony observed.

She slapped him across the face.

Anthony slapped her right back—a whip-crack backhand that sent Maria stumbling backward, causing her to trip over her own feet and fall to the floor.

It was the first time they'd ever hit each other.

Chloe screamed again.

"I said *go to bed!*" Anthony yelled at her.

Maria rose to one knee, an ugly welt reddening on her right cheek where Anthony's fingers had left an imprint in her flesh.

Anthony's hands were balled into fists at his sides.

Chloe dashed from the doorway and into her mother's arms. "Don't hit her, Daddy!" she cried, gazing up at her father in horror.

"You hit me; I hit back," Anthony said to Maria, breathing hard.

Maria rose, Chloe cradled in her arms. "Big man," she spat at him. "Big goddamn man—king of the castle."

As suddenly as rage had inflamed him it died. In the backwash of that rage he felt shaky, spent. Unbelievably tired. "Maria—"

"You're sleeping on the couch tonight," she said. "Don't you *dare* set foot in the bedroom!"

Maria turned to leave, Chloe staring at him over her mother's shoulder.

"Everything in this apartment is mine!" he shouted, in an instant furious once more. "I paid for it all! *That goddamn bed is mine!*"

"Fine!" Maria spun back around. "*You* take the bed; I'll sleep on the couch. Just don't come near me."

Once more his anger flickered . . . dimmed . . . and went out. In the backwash of adrenaline he felt a desolating sadness, mixed with frustration and regret. The taste of bile was bitter in his throat. "No, you—"

Maria turned round.

"—take the bed," Anthony finished lamely.

She stalked away, Chloe facing him again over her mother's shoulder.

"I said *you take the bed!*" Anthony called.

Maria disappeared into Chloe's bedroom.

Anthony turned around to regard the overturned table and the shattered glass of the broken bottle glinting on the floor. He righted the table, got a broom and dustbin out of the closet, and swept up the broken glass.

As he was depositing the debris into a garbage can Maria entered the kitchen. She opened the icebox, withdrew a bottle of soda, and marched out again without saying a word.

"The silent treatment, huh?" Anthony said to her retreating back. *"Now who's being mature?"*

There were two of him: one sick to his stomach, the other berserk with rage.

His temples throbbed, throbbed—as did his cavity-penetrated back molar.

Anthony winced.

Maria meant what she said. She decamped to the living room after seeing Chloe to bed for the second time that night.

Anthony climbed into their queen-size bed with a bottle of gin—a full fifth this time, not a pint—and a stack of *Weird Tales* magazines he'd been meaning to peruse but hadn't gotten around to reading yet. Sitting propped against the headboard, cushioning pillows at his back, he read and drank till the night—and most of the bottle—was gone.

*It had to be done, Anthony. There was no other way.*

Clarice stood opposite him across the kitchen table: braided blond hair, voluptuous red lips, and luminous hazel eyes glittering like moonlit emeralds. Pert breasts, taut buttocks, and a shadowed Venus mound artfully obscured by lengths of diaphanous green silk wound about her body—the loose ends gently undulating, like her splayed-out braided hair, as if underwater. Her bosom heaved as she breathed: transfixing, hypnotic, implacable as ocean swells. Rhythmic and narcotizing.

"I know." Anthony looked up from the Underwood. "I was wrong to stop you before. You were right."

Even as he spoke these words his stomach lurched.

*You killed them, Anthony. Not I.*

Anthony had nothing to say to that.

*No more distractions, beloved.*

Anthony sat in a railback chair at the kitchen table, flanked by corpses: Chloe in a chair to his left, Maria in a chair to his right. He moaned.

Chloe slumped forward in the chair, face pressed against the tabletop. Her neck had been broken. Her right arm lay on the tabletop; in one hand she clutched a floppy-eared stuffed animal in multicolor-patched overalls: Patches the rabbit.

Maria sprawled awkwardly in her chair, head tilted up at the ceiling, unblinking gaze fixed on nothing. She had two mouths now. The second one in her neck: a jagged-edge gash that had damn near decapitated her.

Anthony returned his attention to the story. His fingers flew across the keys as a rattling burst of metallic arms striking paper and platen sounded: the machine gun fire of early twentieth-century literary creativity.

Patches the rabbit wriggled out of Chloe's grasp and stood up on the tabletop, hands fisted on hips. He glanced from Clarice to Anthony and giggled. "Dat's da stuff, pardner! Pour it on!" He did a frenzied little jig—long ears flapping, threadbare back paws softly slapping against the tabletop—as he bounded in place and pumped his forepaws as if doing a thousand-yard dash. "Ain't he da pistol, though?" he inquired to no one in particular.

Clarice drifted around behind Anthony to place soothing hands on his shoulders. Her fingers dug into his aching muscles—cold as ice-cracked mammoth bones frozen for millennia beneath Arctic tundra. She lowered her head to his ear. Shimmering silken hair tickled the nape of his neck.

*Beloved,* she breathed.

Anthony hit the carriage return and began the first sentence of a new paragraph—cock stirring, pupils dilated, arms prickling with gooseflesh.

He moaned, but could not awaken from nightmare.

# The Philosophy & Aesthetics of Horror

Horror should be beautiful quoth the corpse;
herewith didactic verse bereft of chorus:
pumpkin-orange moon in jet-black sky
parchment & palimpsest brown & dry

brittle-crackle warding words & spells
priapic goatish demons out of hell
crimson-purple spatter o'er stone
clanking iron chains—thin moan & groan:

dungeon prisoner writhing in the dark
glint of steel & reddish hissing spark
top-hatted butcher wreathed in mist & fog
fleshless victims rising from the bog.

The beauty of all horror sums to this:
eternity is bottomless abyss.
Book & bell & candle, flute & horn
prove powerless 'gainst beetle, moth, & worm.

Man is born to preen & strut & die—
he ponders, reproduces, laughs & cries;
ever-seeking answer to the *why?*
till existential angst turn nihilist sigh.

# The Möbius Strip Trip

## or, The Thing in the Cellar Is Here Again

## Prologue

Lana Gloaming was an unsmiling fiftyish woman with glittering black eyes and the weathered, guarded face of a woman who had seen much and told little throughout the course of a hardscrabble life. She wore a sharply tailored gray suit and sensible matching-colored flats this cold, drizzly November afternoon. Her clients were Jan and Ursula Van Dijks: a middle-aged married couple who'd expressed interest in seeing the 300-year-old, two-story, brick-and-timber Dutch house located in the Ulster County section of the Catskill Mountains that listed for a hair over six figures in her realtor's portfolio. The house sported such quaint and unusual features as a steeply pitched gambrel roof, granary window openings, and wrought-iron *fleur-de-lis* beamwork anchoring the parapet gable. The party descended creaking wooden steps into the brick-walled cellar after having explored the ground floor of the property.

Ursula spoke up. "I can't understand why this house is selling for below-market value." Her shoulder-length black hair—lustrous as a horse's mane on an Attic vase—framed a high-cheekboned, almond-eyed visage: aquiline-nosed classical beauty blended with the exoticism of the Orient. "Is there something you're not telling us, I wonder."

"Not telling you?" Lana echoed. Having reached the floor of the cellar, she turned to face her clients in the harsh light of the naked 60-watt bulb overhead, the air damp and musty as a lizardman's lair. Dirt floor, bare walls. A broken-legged table shoved into a far corner supporting a half-dozen moldering cardboard boxes. "Like what? This isn't the only home in the Catskills selling for below-market value," she noted enigmatically.

"Perhaps this one has a leaking roof?" ventured Jan. He had the trim, muscled physique of a man who visited a gym thrice weekly. "Or black mold? Bad plumbing? Structural damage?"

"No, no, and no." Lana shifted her gaze from Jan to Ursula and back again, worry-lined face expressionless. "How shall I put this? The former occupants of the house found themselves troubled by certain . . . irregularly occurring incidents."

"Now we're getting somewhere," said Jan. "Blood running down walls? Ghosts in the attic?"

"Nothing quite so gothic, I'm afraid." Lana sneezed, fumbled in her clutch purse for a tissue. "Excuse me; I've a cold." She swiped at her nose; stuffed the tissue back into her purse. "Occasionally, the family heard loud noises emanating from this cellar—knocks, bangs, clangs. Such noises seemed to coincide with other odd phenomena occurring outside the home: fog, mysterious lights, misshapen forms uncertainly glimpsed."

"Fascinating," said Jan, a wry smile on his face. "And here you said these 'irregularly occurring incidents' weren't at all gothic."

"I said no such thing," Lana corrected. "I said the former occupants of this home saw neither blood running down walls nor shimmering ghosts. If you purchase this antiquarian home and encounter similar phenomena later I strongly advise you to hunker down and ride it out. Do not go into the cellar; do not go out into the fog. Those of us who live in . . . problematic areas of the Catskills have learned to manage and thus minimize the impact of certain irregularly occurring outré phenomena." She paused. "Perhaps we should look at other homes in the neighborhood."

"Are they selling for a hundred thousand below market value?" asked Ursula.

"No," said Lana.

"Then I think we'd like to see the second floor," said Jan. "And the attic."

Lana Gloaming nodded curtly. "As you wish."

Jan and Ursula closed on the house that month and moved in the following week.

"Very well, let's define our terms. I'll put it to you directly: paradox is the language of infinity." The handsome, middle-aged man in the black turtleneck and camel-colored sport coat folded his left arm across his stomach, propped his right elbow on this makeshift support, and tapped his chin with a closed fist. He shifted in his seat to face more squarely the host—Dave Bahr—seated behind his desk. "It is a paradigm-shattering grammar constructed of phenomenologically real yet cognitively dissonant building blocks: infinite regress, solipsistic self-reference, and irreconcilable contradiction. Let's start there."

[freeze-frame]

Jan pressed pause on the television remote, face alert and frowning above his crimson polo shirt. "Did you hear that?" he asked, straightening in the recliner.

Ursula was curled up in a pillowed corner of the couch in silk robe and slippers perusing a hardback book. She looked up. "Hmm?"

"That noise. Surely you heard it," said Jan.

"I didn't hear anything." Absentmindedly, Ursula's hand traced her rounded belly. She was six months pregnant, a distressing biological fact Ursula compensated for by lengthening her late afternoon treadmill time into a solid hour of stepping-in-place boredom.

"There it is again—listen."

From somewhere in the depths of the house came a rhythmic tapping.

Ursula's V-shaped eyebrows narrowed. "What *is* that?"

"I don't know," said Jan.

The noise stopped.

Ursula put the book down: *Journey to the Center of the Earth*. Such earnest, bourgeois science fiction was a guilty pleasure for this charter school vice principal who'd earned her Ph.D. in English for a dissertation entitled "Oppositional Hermeneutics of Foucaultian Neo-anarchism and Post-structuralist Crypto-Normativism in the Pseudo-Modern Novel." It had taken her long, grueling years in academia and six-figure sums to learn how to non-communicate like that. If Ursula's jargon-thralled, high-strung circle of highly degreed *littérateurs* and twenty-first-century *philosophes* caught her reading late nineteenth-century French steampunk they'd rib her mercilessly at the next coffeehouse gathering of their wannabe *beau monde* reading group. Though one must understand: her reading circle didn't consider themselves snobs; they considered themselves educated.

The rhythmic *thump-thump-thump* started up again—louder, more insistent.

"Wait a minute." Ursula's features were caught somewhere between uneasiness and curiosity. "We heard that sound the other night, remember? You were sleeping. I shook you awake and you said—"

"Pipes in the walls," said Jan, clenching the remote in his hand. "Expanding and contracting under the changing pressure of heat and cold."

The sound stopped.

A second ticked by. Another.

"But that noise is much too loud to be the pipes," Ursula said. "It sounds like—"

As if on cue, the noise started up again—as much vibration as sound, really—carrying through timber, drywall, and plaster; thumping up from the cellar through the hardwood floor under their feet.

Jan set the television remote down on the end table with thoughtful deliberateness.

"That is *definitely* not the pipes," Ursula said.

"No," said Jan, "it isn't."

The sound grew louder . . . closer . . . *Skritch-THUMP! . . . THUD-click . . . THUMP-clink . . .*

Jan rose from his recliner and hitched at his beltless trousers. On-screen, Dave Bahr's unblinking frozen smile smirked out into the great wide world of nowhere in particular.

"Stay here; I'll check it out," said Jan.

"Said the big, bold hero to his buxom bride." Ursula levered herself erect from the couch, wobbling a bit on unsteady legs. "I'm going with you, Mr. Man."

"The stairs—"

"I'll navigate just fine," Ursula said.

The sound ceased.

"The f—"

"Language," said Ursula, patting her belly.

"—udge," Jan finished smoothly.

Ursula threw him a wan smile. "Thanks. Baby is listening."

Since Ursula had first learned of her pregnancy they'd been calling each other out on their swears, agreeing to minimize the number of four-letter words used in casual conversation in an attempt to clean up their language before baby was born and discovered her well-educated parents swore like characters in a Stephen King novel.

"Onward?" inquired Jan.

In answer, Ursula gave him a playful swat on the ass.

They left the living room together and padded down the hallway in slippered feet into the kitchen where they came upon the cellar door: a $4' \times 4'$ square of weathered oak set into the tile floor between refrigerator and stove, surmounted by an iron ringbolt. It was one of the many archaic features they'd found so charming when they'd moved in last summer.

Jan bent over, grasped the ringbolt in his hand, and heaved.

The hatch banged open against a tarnished bronze stop-plate

mounted to the wall to save the plaster. A set of wooden steps led down into cellar darkness. He hesitated, and there it was again: a dizzying wrench of *déjà vu* that roiled the gut and ghost-whispered in the mind.

"Jan?" inquired Ursula, a quaver in her usually unflappable voice.

"Hold on; I'll get the gun."

"We don't own a gun."

"Oh, that's right," Jan deadpanned. "I forgot. No firearms in *this* household."

Ursula reached out a steadying hand to her husband's forearm. "You okay?"

"No." Jan took a deep breath, exhaled. He stared down into cellar darkness. "This no-gun policy of ours?"

"Yes?"

"Let's do a rethink of that later."

The banging resumed. Louder—much louder, now—given that the muffling cellar door stood wide open.

Ursula turned a whiter shade of pale.

"Something's down there," Jan said.

"Some *thing?*"

"An animal."

"Don't be silly," Ursula said, taking a half-step to her right and withdrawing a twelve-inch piece of stainless-steel cutlery from its wooden holder on the countertop. "What kind of animal could make that much racket—a bear?" She widened her eyes for comic effect, but her upper lip did its little twitch-tremor, a sure sign of stress in Ursula's personal library of involuntary physiognomic signaling.

The banging stopped.

Jan gestured at the butcher knife clenched in his wife's hand. "Cold steel against non-existent bears, my barbarian queen?"

Ursula stuck her tongue out at him, simultaneously making a stabbing motion with the knife. "*Sic semper ursis*—'Thus to bears.'"

"I understand Latin; no need to translate."

"Liar. You thought *'quid pro quo'* meant 'quorum of professional squid.' Are all mathematicians such outrageous liars, or just the one I married?"

Jan laughed—a startled bark, true; and in a higher register than he'd intended. But the release of tension got him moving again. He flipped a switch on the wall as he descended, casting the light of the twin-bulb ceiling fixture they'd installed over the remodeled wood-paneled cellar. This stark illumination was reflected back in a thousand glints from the star-patterned, silver- and black-tiled floor, and assorted metalwork.

The subterranean space was crowded with books, furniture, and wine; the dampness removed from the air by industrial-strength dehumidifiers humming away under the stairs. Glass-door, floor-to-ceiling bookcases covered three walls of the cellar. The cherry wood shelves housed a thousand-volume collection of world literature arrayed in upright alphabetized order: Jorge Borges, Joyce Carol Oates, Italo Calvino, Alice B. Sheldon, Gabriel Garcia Marques, et al. An antique writing desk in the French style—escritoire, late eighteenth century—took up most of one long wall. A brass plate affixed to its front proclaimed: "Writer at Work: Coins Accepted." Behind the battered mahogany escritoire was set an oaken swivel chair flanked by tall, free-standing lamps that provided additional illumination when needed. Wordlessly, each of them turned on one of these lamps now.

The light brightened to an operating-room glare.

A metal wall-hanging of the two-faced Roman god Janus gleamed above the desk. Beside a flat-panel computer monitor and a well-thumbed dictionary of etymology splayed open on the desktop sat a bronze statue of Rodin's *Thinker,* pondering atop a stone pedestal, chin sunk on fist. Wine racks flanked the escritoire, three-quarters full of premium vintages ordered from France, Italy, and Argentina. This was Ursula's in-house retreat space, writing nook, and *sanctum sanctorum:* every piece of artfully distressed furniture, heavily underlined and notated book, dust-covered bottle of wine, and hyper-polished *objet d'art* had been arranged with fussy exactitude in order to stimulate Ursula to greater heights of thought and creativity.

Jan much preferred the cheery, sunlit kitchen table for his own work. Nowadays, though, it seemed the only reading and writing he got done involved the Geometry, Trig, and Calculus student papers he graded in order to remain a high school mathematics teacher in good standing with the privatization-mad Catskills Board of Ed. Despite his tightly strung nerves—or perhaps because of it—the thought of that sunlit kitchen table triggered a flood of memories. He recalled the many times he and Ursula had sat at that table, engaged in playful badinage over a meal while debating which field of endeavor was more important to humanity: literature or mathematics. One conversation in particular re-surfaced in his mind with especial vividness:

*"Mathematics is the language of reality,"* Jan had argued, *"the key to understanding and expressing fundamental operating principles of the universe: why things are as they are. It is power incarnate. There is no room for subjectivity or 'creative interpretation' in mathematics. I find that comforting. No matter how many times you work out a math problem, the answer is always the same—if it is the correct answer. Also: the most intellectually arresting form of expressed mathematics is the equation: a statement that both asserts and reconciles the equality of two expressions. I ask you: what could be more balanced, revelatory, and sublime than that? A pox on mysticism, metaphor, and poetics; I'll stick to mathematics!"*

*Ursula replied, "Mathematics is abstraction: numbers, signs, and symbols. I'll grant you the field's power, necessity, and importance. But in the final analysis mathematics is a sterile science and therefore a rigidly regimented art. There is nothing to nourish, inspire, or sustain the human spirit in its impersonal workings. Only literature can do that: fictions that ofttimes tell uncomfortable truths, yet somehow manage to comfort us nonetheless. How many mathematicians have been driven mad by their work?"*

*"How many poets?"* rejoined Jan. *"Novelists? Playwrights? Short story writers?"*

"All quiet on the subterranean front," whispered Ursula, coming up behind him.

"Yes," said Jan, with something very like dismay. He glanced around, examining the walls, floor, and ceiling. All seemed to be in order.

They stood there, ears straining to pick up sounds they had flinched from but a moment before. Dust motes swirled in the stirred-up air.

"Isn't this what stupid people do in horror films?" said Jan. "Tip-toe down cellar steps into darkness to investigate strange noises—"

"—only to be murdered by a skulking madman?" finished Ursula. "Yep," she elaborated, turning in a 360-degree circle, a moue of irritation vexing her aristocratic features. "This is *exactly* how they behave."

"So why are we doing it?" asked Jan.

"We really don't have any other choice, do we?" countered Ursula. "Unless we wish to hide in an upstairs closet until help arrives. Or flee the house because of—what—strange noises? Imagine the looks we'll get from the neighbors or police! No; I don't think so."

"Point taken. I feel much better about our stupidity now."

Ursula glanced around. "You know, one time in one of those films . . ." She edged toward the central bookcase, her attention drawn to a section of books that had toppled over on the bottom shelf due to the lack of a tension-maintaining bookend. ". . . the monster turned out to be a maniac in a white spray-painted William Shatner mask."

"The boogeyman from John Carpenter's *Halloween*." Jan glanced at the cutlery in his wife's hand. "I think you've up-knifed him."

Despite the tension Ursula laughed. She held the knife before her at waist level, the flat of the blade perpendicular to the floor. "But this is our house."

"Brilliant," said Jan. "Non sequitur as epitaph."

He edged up behind her.

"I wonder . . ." Ursula studied the ceiling.

*"Booga!"* Jan blurted into her ear.

Ursula whirled around and speared him in the kidney with her free hand. "Never, *ever* do that again."

"Ouch! Woman, that is the overture that led to the foreplay, that led to the wrestling match, that led to the couch, that led to *you* getting pregnant."

"I've a very sexy kidney jab."

**WA-BAM!**

They jumped like startled cartoon characters.

**WHAM! KA-BLAM!**

The racket emanated from behind the center-most, floor-to-ceiling bookcase in front of Ursula's writing desk.

**BAM-BAM-BAM!**

"Impossible," said Jan, voice high and tight. "Behind these cellar walls there's nothing but—"

"—solid earth and rock," Ursula finished.

**KA-THUD! BA-WHAM! CRASH-CLINK!**

The reports, detonations, and hammered thuds were barely muffled by Kafka, Haruki Murakami, Shirley Jackson, Kurt Vonnegut, Michael Houellebecq, J. G. Ballard et al. Volumes jumped and vibrated on the shelves; the glass doors of the bookcases rattled violently.

They should have fled right then—turned tail and scamper-scrawled back up the cellar stairs as fast as their rubbery legs and pounding hearts would let them, Jan later reflected. But now—now it was much too late.

"Jan!" was all Ursula had time to get out before the centermost bookcase exploded outward.

Hardbound volumes flew out the front of the case, its chest-high glass doors shattering as dozens of books hurtled from their ordered places of repose to tumble end-over-end in the cool cellar air before hitting the floor. The centermost bookcase leaned out from its flanking brethren and toppled, lower glass doors swinging open and spilling books as it crashed to the floor, pinning Jan beneath its weight. Ursula scrambled back against the desk.

A hulking, rough-garbed humanoid in crimson toga and leather sandals stood revealed in a jagged-edge hole in the paneled wall.

"Urg-alla!" it cried. *"Urg-alla!"*

On its belt hung an odd brass lamp whose ovoid lens shed a pallid, moonlike light—an illumination all but washed out by the harsher, brighter light of the twin-bulb ceiling fixture and free-standing floor lamps. Behind it, a passageway opened up into rocky darkness. The thing clutched a silver-headed battle-hammer in its right hand. Blood dripped from wounds in its left forearm and shoulder. It glanced around uncertainly; eyes narrowed to slits. A guttural rumble issued from its mouth: one part lion roar, one part ultra-low-frequency granitic grumble.

*Not real,* Jan thought groggily. *Can't be. I'm starring in an "Outer Limits" episode: the one where the feckless mathematics teacher is pinned beneath a crushing weight of modernist fiction.*

If he had the breath he'd giggle. He found himself lying awkwardly on his side, head just clear of the wreckage. The rock troll (that was the two-word descriptor that popped into his head through a fog of pain as he regarded the massive, beetle-browed, long-haired invader of his wife's hushed *sanctum sanctorum*) stepped from its hole in the wall, sandaled feet slipping a bit as they tread across the back of the toppled bookcase, increasing the pressure on Jan's aching ribs, spine, and hips. The thing looked every bit as befuddled and frightened as he felt.

Jan groaned.

*"Back!"* Ursula shouted, swinging the knife in front of her in wild, glimmering arcs. "Back off!"

The rock troll ignored Ursula's warding-off gesture. Instead, it hopped with keening whine from the toppled bookcase onto the floor.

Ursula edged around to the left, placing her back to the staircase. "Get up! *Get up,* Jan! *Now!"*

*Yep, that's the plan all right—exactly what I need to do. Get up. Stand right the fuck up. No doubt about it. Just hurl this crushing weight of wood and glass and books off my chest like Superman and . . .*

Jan's eyesight tunneled as his oxygen-starved brain prepared to turn out the lights, compressed chest and ringing skull singing a peripheral-vision-darkening song of concussion.

*"Jan!"* Ursula screamed.

He fought to hang on. Somewhere, the woman he loved was desperately calling his name . . .

The rock troll loomed closer. It stared down at him—one hand shading its eyes against the light, the other clutching the battle-hammer. Knuckles whitened as it tightened its grip on the weapon—

*Get up! Got to get up! Now! Get . . .*

—and a knife bloomed like magic from the side of its throat.

"Waiii . . ." slurred Jan.

The rock troll's eyes widened in shock. It made a blood-thickened, strangled *grog-mrrawg* sound. The battle-hammer dropped from its hands, knees buckling as it turned to confront its attacker. A fountain of crimson geysered from its sundered throat.

Ursula was emitting a crazed, ululating wail: *"Eee-eee-eeeeeee! Eee-eee-eeeeee!"*—a demented television announcer turned banshee, shrieking the English language's second vowel at a pitch concomitant to its urgency: *Today's show was brought to you by the Grand Guignol, Mr. Rock Troll and the letter "eee."*

The thing took two stagger-steps toward Ursula and collapsed face down on the silver-starred black linoleum. The battle-hammer hit the floor beside it with a percussive *whump,* followed by the softer clatter of the weapon's haft against the tile.

Ursula waddled to her husband's side, dropped to her knees, and got a firm double-handed grip on the side of the glass-door bookcase that lay across Jan's chest and mid-section. "You push as I pull, 'kay, honey? *Go!*"

Jan heaved, thrusting against the crushing bulk. For a horrifying half-second it seemed as if nothing was happening—then the weight slid off him along with dozens of hardbound books and jagged shards of glass. He groaned and sat up, feeling himself gingerly for injuries.

Ursula picked winking splinters of glass out of his hair. "You okay?"

"I think so—Jesus!" It was a relief to be able to take an unconstricted breath. "Who knew literature was a full-contact sport?"

"I did," Ursula muttered. She put a restraining hand on Jan's shoulder as he attempted to rise. "Not yet. Catch your breath; you won't do either of us any good if you pass out."

Jan nodded and took a series of deep, centering breaths. "I'm okay. Really."

"You sure?"

"Yes." Jan's eyes flicked to the hole in the basement wall behind the toppled bookcase. "But . . . did you have to kill it?"

Ursula stared at him incredulously. "That *thing* broke into our home! Carrying a weapon!"

"Hammer."

"Battle-hammer," corrected Ursula. "And with *you* pinned beneath a bookcase and *me* six months pregnant I wasn't waiting around to see if this monster came to play 'Hulk smash!' or to debate the merits of existentialism-vs.-nihilism. So forgive me if I acted a trifle hastily."

Jan held up his hand. "I'm not accusing; just asking. 'Cause it seemed to me that the rock troll—"

"Rock troll?"

Jan shrugged. "The name seems to fit."

"Sure—I guess," said Ursula, fighting to control her impatience, fear and irritation. "Rock troll it is, then."

"If that thing wanted to kill me it had plenty of time to do so. As you noted, I was helpless."

"It would have, after its eyes adjusted to the light."

"Perhaps," said Jan. "Perhaps not. It seemed more frightened than angry to me. Wary. Confused." He shook his head as if to clear it, then groaned and put steadying hands to his throbbing temples. "I shouldn't have done that."

"No, you shouldn't have. You probably have a concussion."

"I'm sure I do." Seeing the look of alarm on Ursula's face, he hastily added, "Don't worry, I've no intention of taking a nap anytime soon."

Ursula's eyes narrowed.

"Furthermore: my name is Jan; the year is ——; the president of the United States is ——."

"Three for three," Ursula confirmed.

Jan put hands to his temples again, gingerly massaged them. "Well, that's something. Still cognitively alert and fully present, then."

"Are we?" asked Ursula.

Jan followed his wife's gaze. She was staring at the broad-chested, hirsute corpse lying face down in a pool of spreading crimson. "Good question. If we're in our right minds . . . and not concussed or hallucinating . . . then what the hell is *that?*"

Ursula glanced from her husband to the rock troll and back again. No remonstrances of "baby is listening" this time; Jan's milquetoast swear went unremarked. "I don't know—but it's dead now."

"Lovecraftian gods willing," said Jan, struggling unsteadily to his feet. Once erect he extended a helping hand to his wife; she grasped it and teeter-tottered up beside him. "Let's get out of here before more of these things show up."

"Agreed." Ursula pivoted to face the hole in the wall, then choked off a sound pitched midway between a shriek and a sob. "Darling, have we gone *crazy?* Is this really happening?"

"No, we're not crazy. And yes, this is really happening," said Jan. "Or . . ." He blew out a hard, whistling breath. "We've both gone out of our minds and this *isn't* happening. In which case we're experiencing one hell of a shared hallucination, wouldn't you say?"

"Haven't done mushrooms in years," said Ursula. She emitted a brittle, high-pitched bark intended as laughter. "How unlike me: my second non sequitur of the evening." She bit her lip, smoothed the silken fabric of robe over her rounded belly. "You?"

"Non sequiturs or shiitakes?"

Ursula emitted a second near-hysterical bark.

"I'll assume you're talking 'shrooms then, beloved," said Jan. "In that case, I must point out that you threw a batch of delicious, bell-shaped fungus into our pasta only last night. Delayed reaction, perhaps—mayhap we're tripping our balls off right now."

"Three things. One: those weren't hallucinogenic 'shrooms I tossed into our pasta last night, those were plain ole store-bought portobellos. Two: I don't have balls. Three: . . ."—here imitating John Wayne's laconic, mouth-full-of-marbles drawl—"methinks thou shouldst stop talking like a pilgrim, Pilgrim." She snorted. "*Mayhap?* I mean, really!"

"Yea, verily," quoth Jan.

"*Stop* that."

"Look, I'm rattled," said Jan. "Possibly in shock."

"Now that you mention it," said Ursula, "I feel a bit unreal myself."

"That's the word, all right," said Jan. "'Unreal.' We seem to have stumbled into an *Outer Limits* episode as scripted by, er, Nathaniel Hawthorne."

"Hawthorne?"

"Sure. Consider the *mise-en-scène.*" He gestured. "How else would you describe this but 'immersion in an atmospherical medium so as to bring out or mellow the lights and deepen and enrich the shadows of a picture'? I ask you: What could be more Gothic than a bloodstained cellar in the Catskills containing a dead monster sprawled on the floor amongst broken-backed books?"

"Hawthorne . . ." echoed Ursula. "I don't know; doesn't feel right. You've been stuck on him since high school—the only serious writer you've ever read."

"Nonsense. I also read Bukowski and Robert E. Howard."

"Like I said—the only *serious* writer . . ."

"Snob!" Jan compressed his nose with an index finger.

Ursula smiled wanly. "Questionable taste aside—what has any of this got to do with guilt, sin or punishment?"

Jan shrugged. "What has anything? Everything."

"No," said Ursula. "No, sorry—I'm not buying it." She ran her hands through her hair, a self-comforting gesture she'd picked up from her mother, the series of gentle tugs on her scalp stimulating thought. "This strikes me as more Poe than Hawthorne. Or Joe Hill. Better yet: a pre-code E.C. horror comic."

"Lurid and absurd," said Jan.

"Precisely."

"Horrific psychedelic carnage."

"Even better," said Ursula.

The rock troll spasmed.

Ursula spun to face the invader, hand to her mouth. "Jan! That thing is still——"

"Dead," said Jan, hobbling over to the body and taking a knee beside it. "Unconscious reflexes of a dying organism."

"Said the newly minted xenobiologist." Ursula retreated a step. "Careful! You don't know anything about rock trolls, dead or otherwise."

Jan rolled the thing over on its back. The monster's eyes were fixed and staring in a prognathous-jawed face. It had short-cropped, curly black hair—thick and matted with grime—above a pronounced brow ridge. The garment he'd taken for some type of toga turned out, upon closer inspection, to be a crimson-colored tunic of rough homespun overhanging a matching-colored breechclout. Its leather sandals were well worn and expertly made. A rope belt was threaded through loops in the hem of the tunic from which a small, squarish bronze lamp depended from a short length of chain. The lens of the lamp—a whitish-yellow gemstone—glowed with a feeble light under the harsher fluorescence of the overhead fixture and desk-flanking floor lamps. Jan loosened the rope belt to remove the box lamp from the rock troll's waist but could find no visible seams in the device, though he felt gingerly all around its six sharply perpendicular surfaces.

"Made in China?" Ursula asked.

"Not in this dimension," Jan quipped.

He set the box lamp down and picked up the silver battle-hammer. He hefted it and let out an admiring whistle. "Perfectly balanced. And surprisingly light."

"All those duels in the Society for Creative Anachronism finally paid off, eh? You know a good weapon when you handle one."

Jan refused to take the bait.

Ursula had never attended any gatherings of the Society, had in fact professed bemusement at her husband's involvement with an organization dedicated to (among other medieval guild-like crafts and practices) a recreation of Dark Ages tournament combat. Like his riding of V-twin motorcycles and fondness for the sordid sex/beer fart poetry of Charles Bukowski, Ursula dismissed these rougher-edged pastimes as the tragicomic diversions of a sensitive twenty-first-century male's attempt to remasculate himself into a society that still demanded hyper-competitiveness of its men while forbidding all vigorous expression save that of internet trolling or placarding the back of pickup trucks with triggering bumper stickers.

"True, I occasionally battle in chainmail whilst swinging a broadsword, but you're the one who made like a Bob Howard character on our visitor, darling. Just sayin'."

Ursula tossed her head, which set her shoulder-length hair to shimmering. "I acted instinctively to protect you and the baby."

"Of course you did," said Jan.

They exchanged a look.

Jan returned his attention to the weapon. It had a crenellated rectangular head and spike of silvered metal. The haft was dark wood, mahogany perhaps; a spiral pattern cut into the wood as channel decoration. An ouroboros—snake eating its own tail—was incised into the business end of the battle-hammer's head. The weapon thrummed with energy.

"'We need to get out of here,'" prodded Ursula. "Those were your words, remember?"

"I know," said Jan. "And we will, in a second." Jan set the battle-hammer aside. "But first, take a look at this."

Ursula shuffled forward, the soles of her slippers *ssh-sshing* on the tile.

Jan raised the rock troll's left arm. Blood oozed from cuts in its forearm, elbow to wrist. "What does this look like to you?"

"A bloody forearm," said Ursula.

"How very droll."

"Ask a stupid question . . ."

"Look closer." Jan twisted the forearm in his hands so that Ursula viewed it from a different angle. "A series of shallow cuts, yes?"

"Correct." Ursula shrugged. "So what?"

"How did it happen?"

"Mr. Rock Troll sliced its arm open on the glass door of the bookcase."

"No, I don't think so." Jan glanced back at the toppled bookcase and the jagged-edge hole in the paneling. "This thing burst into the cellar through that wall, right?"

"Like the sugar-crazed Kool-Aid Man, check."

"Holding a battle-hammer in its right hand, presumably the tool—"

"Weapon," corrected Ursula.

"—it used to break through the wall. So why is its *left* arm cut up?"

"Maybe it ripped at the rock with its left hand before breaking through into the cellar . . . or the shattering glass of the bookcase—"

"The bookcase toppled forward, away from this thing. And unless the laws of physics have been suspended for the duration, there is no way a couple of errant glass splinters could have lacerated its entire forearm. Moreover, these cuts"—Jan brought the rock troll's forearm closer to his narrowed eyes—"barely break the skin and are irregular, to be sure;

yet they don't strike me as entirely random. And take a look at this shoulder wound . . . a deep puncture . . ."

"So it's a mystery." Ursula blew an impatient blast of air through pursed lips. "The whole thing's a conundrum, wrapped within a riddle, occurring inside a lucid dream. *Now* can we get out of here?"

Jan let the arm drop to the floor with a sodden thump. He rose, wiping his hands on his trousers, and shuddered. He'd been careful to avoid getting any blood on himself—the rock troll's hemoglobin was red as any iron-rich animal's, he noted. Yet he felt an instinctive, atavistic revulsion in touching the thing's flesh. The weirdly garbed corpse sprawled on the floor of their cellar was inarguably, inexplicably alien—monstrous—other. Its very presence signified a collision of other worlds, other realities; he was loath to touch it. Perhaps his lightly tossed-off "other-dimensional China" quip regarding the provenance of the box lamp was more on the mark than he realized.

A hum sounded in the air around them, more felt than heard at first: an extended bass note that rapidly escalated in pitch and volume until it seemed they were surrounded by tens of thousands of invisible shrilling insects. The infernal insectile noise was a drill that bored into the brain truncating all coherent thought.

Ursula's eyes widened.

"Let's go." Jan pressed a steadying hand into the small of her back.

They started for the stairs.

The shrilling stopped.

"*Now* what?" Ursula craned her head to look back as she began to ascend the creaking wooden steps. "Honey?"

Jan had halted at the bottom of the stairs. "I get the distinct impression . . ." He glanced around, taking in the slaughterhouse chaos of the space that only minutes before had been Ursula's well-ordered subterranean temple consecrated to all things contemplative and literary. ". . . that something's fucking with us."

"Come *on,* Jan!"

No rebuke for the f-bomb—Ursula *was* upset.

He followed her up the stairs.

Ursula headed directly for the landline phone mounted on the wall beside cabinets filled with fine-bone china, designer glasses, and enameled cast-iron cookware.

Jan, half a second behind her, slammed the ring-bolted iron hatch closed with a bang that reverberated through the house. He took a step back and regarded the hatch with unease. "You know, we really need to get a lock on this thing."

"We'll do that after the gun," said Ursula, somewhat incoherently. She picked up the phone, put it to her ear. Frowned. Pulled the phone away, repeatedly punched the switchhook button on the receiver, put it back to her ear—only to slam the receiver back into its cradle on the wall. "Damn it! The line is dead."

"Of course it is," said Jan with a sigh.

"And Jan . . ."

"Yes?"

"Look outside."

The garden window over the kitchen sink admitted the kind of flat, gauzy white light that was a photographer's dream: illuminating without throwing shadows.

Jan came up beside Ursula and peered out. He could see nothing but roiling fog. A hundred feet away was a green-scummed pond, beyond that a copse of mixed birch and pine running to the top of the mountain, but neither pond nor woods were visible at present—to say nothing of the neighbor's home, a half-acre distant. The world had become naught but flat white light and fog.

"Try your cellphone," said Jan.

Ursula made no reply. She gazed out the window, eyes wide. Her upper lip was doing its little twitch-tremor again. "Just as Lana Gloaming warned us. Remember, Jan? Loud bangs from the cellar—fog, lights. 'If you should encounter similar phenomena later, I strongly advise you to hunker down and ride it out. Do not go into the cellar; do not go out into the fog.'" Ursula put her forehead against the glass, straining to peer through the fog. "Do you see any strange lights out there?"

"Your cellphone," reiterated Jan. He could not think about Lana Gloaming right now—*would* not, he sternly commanded himself. Lana was neither witch nor seer; their grim-faced, unsmiling property guide was a realtor. A realtor, true, with the disposition of a hanging judge, who'd sold them a house in the Catskills: an area of the country that had given rise to Washington Irving's tales of Rip van Winkle, hellhounds, spectral crusaders, cursed treasure chests, and a certain headless horseman, among other Gothic subjects. But Lana Gloaming was but a realtor nonetheless—decidedly prosaic, un-occult, and non-psychic. Unless . . .

"'Misshapen forms uncertainly glimpsed,'" prompted Ursula, breaking into his chain of thought.

*Focus!*

"Try your cellphone, darling," Jan urged.

The cellphone lay in its charging cradle on the kitchen counter behind them.

Ursula took a stiff, ungainly step toward the device.

*She's going into shock,* thought Jan. *For that matter, I feel on the verge of hysteria myself. How much longer can we hold it together, I wonder?*

Ursula removed the phone from its charging cradle, powered it on. Stared at it for a moment . . . then wordlessly extended the device, screen out.

Two words glowed in neon-blue font: *No Signal.*

"We're cut off," said Ursula—and dropped the phone clattering onto the countertop.

Jan stepped to his wife; pulled her into a close embrace. "Hey."

Ursula avoided his gaze, though she made no attempt to break free of his encircling arms.

"Honey." Jan raised his hands to his wife's shoulders, sought her eyes with his own. "We're going to be okay. It's going to be okay, all right?" He spoke as if the repetition of these banal and entirely unconvincing words could somehow ward off further inexplicable phenomena. "We'll get help—the police will come, sort out this craziness and—"

"No." Ursula's eyes glistened. "I don't think so."

"No?" Jan was momentarily nonplussed. "What do you—"

"It's not going to be okay."

"Don't say that." Jan shook her gently by the shoulders. "Don't *ever* say that—of *course* we're going to be okay! You, me, and the baby makes three," he chanted idiotically.

That wrung a startled, broken laugh out of her. "You're absolutely mad, you know that?"

"I know that. *You* knew that when you married me."

Ursula disentangled herself from Jan's arms and stepped back. "Where's your cellphone?"

Jan grimaced. "I left it in the car."

"Oh, Jan," was all Ursula said.

Jan's ride was a Subaru Forester SUV with sunroof, black leather interior, and upgraded eight-speaker stereo system: luxury options that struck him as impossibly sybaritic and rather ridiculous now. Why hadn't he gone for more useful options like bulletproof windows, gun ports, and built-in flamethrower?

*Yep. Definitely losing it.*

The SUV was parked in their driveway just outside the front door, next to Ursula's candy-apple-red Volvo four-door sedan. He'd plugged his cellphone into the car's fast charger on his way home from Kingston High last night after discussing dinner plans with the wife (they'd settled on Chinese takeout), his mind preoccupied with the calculus lesson he intended to teach tomorrow after a ten-question pop quiz to ascertain how much his advanced-placement students were retaining this semester. He'd forgotten the damn thing as he grabbed his book-and-papers-bulged leather satchel upon exiting the vehicle.

"I'll retrieve the phone," Jan said.

"Out *there?* In the *fog?*"

"Quick dash to the car and a fast scurry back; I promise I won't wander off."

"I don't like this," said Ursula, hard on his heels as he exited the kitchen to traverse the short hallway that led to the living room and the front door. "I don't like this at all."

Jan's car keys were in a shallow bowl setting on wooden shelving in the foyer. He scooped the keys out of the bowl and slid them into a trouser pocket.

"You don't have to do this," said Ursula as Jan unlocked the thumb-turned deadbolt and grabbed the doorknob. "Your cellphone is probably as dead as mine."

"It's possible," admitted Jan.

Ursula put a restraining hand on his elbow. "Don't go out there. *Please.*"

"I have to; you know that."

Jan braced himself—breath in; breath out—and opened the door.

He couldn't see three feet into the fog—that swirling, misted white was thick as wind-whipped mayonnaise. And it was cold—cold enough to turn his breath into puffs of vapor.

"I can't see our cars, Jan," remarked Ursula over his shoulder.

The vehicles were invisible, like everything else out there lying just beyond their quaint gambrel-roofed home.

Jan fished in his trouser pocket and brought out the car keys. He angled the fob in the general direction of his SUV and depressed the button to unlock the door, then quickly pressed lock again. The car chirruped twice and the headlights flashed—only just visible as smeared glows of light in the fog.

"Well, at least we know the cars are still there," said Jan, glancing back with a tight smile. "Hold this door open while I—"

Ursula's face was a rictus of shock.

Jan snapped his eyes back front.

The fog had blown away in a wide radius around the vehicles.

Clustered around the Volvo and SUV were translucent, greenish-glowing *things* the approximate size of adult wolves. Juddering and shuddering. Polyhedrons-to-triangles, transmogrifying to telescoping fractal octagons and back to polyhedrons again. When they moved they didn't so much lope or canter as glide along, their trunks ending in pale, pink-fleshed disks that writhed with tentacles. Some of the beasts were antennaed, tusked, mandibled. Others sported clawlike pincers and whiplike tails. They seemed a torturous combination of plant, animal, and endlessly morphing geometric forms. It hurt the mind to look at them, for the creatures were somehow both there and *not there* at one and the same time. The brain tried to make sense of what it was seeing and kept returning the same message as a hard-struck pinball machine: tilt. *Tilt!*

One of the things used its tentacles to clamber onto the SUV's hood. It tapped at the windshield, which promptly hissed, cracked, and exploded inward. Others swarmed around and onto Ursula's Volvo. The car sagged to the right as the tires blew out on that side, the vehicle rocking violently as the Hieronymus Bosch nightmares tore off the rear bumper and doors and glimmer-glided into the Volvo's interior. The horn began to blare.

Jan slammed the door closed and threw the deadbolt.

*"I told you not to go out there!"*

He turned to face his wife. "And you were right."

A trumpeting call akin to an elephant's sounded, though orders of magnitude louder. Knickknacks on the foyer shelving and corner fireplace began to rattle and clatter; a glass edged off an end table and thudded onto the floor to roll under the couch. Something shattered in the kitchen.

Jan went to the bay window, drew the drapes back, and peered out.

"What do you see? Beside emeraldian glimmerings?" asked Ursula.

Jan turned his head left, right. Drew the drapes closed and turned around, his face ashen. "Some kind of . . . colossus."

*"Jan!"*

He grimaced. "We need to go back down into the cellar."

Seismic vibrations increased; the entire house shook on its foundations. Rattles, clinks, and bangs sounded throughout their home.

"The cellar?" Ursula said.

"We'll make our last stand there."

"Why not the attic?"

He'd considered it.

"No exit from the attic," Jan said. "Our cellar at least has a hole in the wall . . ."

That high, keening, insectile whine sounded again: a frenzied dance of berserker bees, painfully loud.

Jan winced.

Ursula slapped her hands over her ears.

The foundation-shaking vibrations stopped.

They looked at each other, breathing hard.

"Emeraldian glimmerings?" said Jan.

Ursula shrugged. "You named the genus and species in the cellar; I figured it was my turn."

A piercing ululation sounded outside the house, answered by a thunderous roar.

"Let's go," said Jan.

They left the living room, padding back down the hallway in their slippered feet to the kitchen, where Ursula withdrew serrated-edge stainless-steel knives from the wooden holder on the counter and offered one to Jan.

He took the knife from her, hefted it, made a couple of practice stabs in the air.

"All right. We can't stay up here, that much is clear. If any of those things come through the windows . . ."

They reopened the ring-bolted oaken hatch and descended the stairs, Jan securing the hatch behind them.

Down in the cellar again Jan and Ursula halted before the awkwardly sprawled corpse of the rock troll. The acrid tang of iron-rich blood hung in the stagnant air; the pool of crimson around the bristle-browed corpse had begun to thicken and congeal.

Jan looked from the rock troll's corpse to the toppled bookcase, then past the wreckage of shattered glass and spilled books to the ragged hole in the wall. He tucked the butcher knife into his belt and stooped to pick up the battle-hammer and odd-lensed box lamp—battle-hammer in his dominant right hand, box lamp in the left—and straightened up again. "I think we need to see where that goes," he said and moved toward the shadowed opening where the paneling had been torn away.

"It goes to *them,* obviously," said Ursula. "Stop! You've no idea how many more of them are coming."

Jan halted, looked at her inquiringly.

*"What the hell do you think you're doing?"* Ursula was enraged. "Have you lost your mind?"

"I thought we'd decided—"

"Don't you dare set foot in there! I am not following you through that hole."

The baby, her fear, the shock of current events—Ursula's rage was understandable. And she had a point. Yet they couldn't stay upstairs, nor could they remain trapped in the cellar. As for his own emotions . . .

"I'm not asking you to," said Jan as he resumed moving, nudging broken-backed hardbound volumes aside with his slippered foot. He trod gingerly across the tile, wary of glass splinters. Why hadn't he slipped on shoes before descending into the cellar again?

*Because you're pressed for time and not thinking clearly; that's why.*

*Who the hell had time to think with emeraldian glimmerings and tower-ing colossi roaming the neighborhood? To say nothing of rock trolls in the cellar . . .*

Jan stifled a giggle. He recognized it as the choked-off burble of in-cipient hysteria.

"What's so funny?" Ursula snapped, cradling her belly.

"Nothing. Everything," said Jan, having reached the ragged hole in the brick foundation. He raised the box lamp and peered through the opening. A rock-walled section of cavern tunnel twisted away before him, stalagmites and stalactites studded like uneven dragon teeth from striated layers of sedimentary rock. The tunnel faded into total darkness a hun-dred feet out.

"What do you see?" asked Ursula. Despite herself, she edged closer.

"Not much," said Jan. "There's a tunnel—"

"A *tunnel?*"

"—I can't see the end of."

Jan stepped into the cavern tunnel. As he did so, he felt a curious sense of displacement and overall *lightening*—as if he'd somehow grown incorporeal while traveling an immense distance. Vertigo seized him. Gorge rose in his stomach, and he threw out a steadying hand to the rock wall. He closed his eyes; opened them again once the nausea had passed.

The cavern stretched out before him, just as it had a second before—stalagmites and stalactites, the tunnel fading into darkness a hundred feet out—but he felt a profound sense of wrongness. Something had changed in the tableau before him; some subtle detail had altered that he feared he was too nerve-jangled and distraught at present to discern.

"Anybody home?" Jan called.

No answer.

"Honey, I don't think any—" He turned around.

And came face to face with solid rock.

Stunned, Jan stood there for a moment unable to process what he was seeing: a seemingly solid cavern wall where a second ago there had been a rough-hammered opening in the house's brick foundation.

"Ursula!" Jan screamed. He dropped the box lamp. It began flickering but—thank the merciful gods of Subterranea—did not go out.

Darkness. Light. Darkness. Light.

In the strobe-like effect of the flickering box lamp Jan became a projected series of images on film that dropped two to three frames every half-second. He let the battle-hammer slip from his hand and scrabbled at the wall, desperately seeking some activating mechanism—lever, button, knob—that might cause the rock to part.

He found no such mechanism.

"Ursula!" Jan screamed again. *"Ursula! Can you hear me?"*

Darkness. Light.

Darkness. Light.

Jan placed his ear against the wall, straining to hear his wife's answering cry. He could detect no response—no sound, howsoever faint, carried through the rock.

*Was* their cellar behind the cavern wall?

Darkness. Light.

It had to be. Didn't it? He'd just stepped through a hole into this tunnel. Therefore, the cellar was but a couple of feet away behind the cavern wall—a wall unmarred and inviolate, to all outward appearances having stood there since some antediluvian age of deluge.

"This makes no sense; *it makes no sense,*" Jan gibbered, fighting a rising tide of panic. He fought to control his breathing, to avoid hyperventilating—he'd kept it together this long. He could not panic now—*would not.*

If a rock troll could break through into their cellar from the tunnel . . .

*The battle-hammer!*

Stutter-step Jan—darkness, light—stooped to pick up the battle-hammer—darkness, light—and straightened up again. He felt anew the low thrum of eldritch energy pulsing in the weapon.

In a series of flash-bulb-frozen still-lifes Jan swung the battle-hammer at the wall. The head of the weapon bounced off the rock, the shock of impact shiveringly transmitted through the haft of the weapon into his elbows and lower back.

To no avail: the cavern wall appeared undamaged.

"Ursula!" he screamed a fourth time.

Jan paused for a moment, ears straining to detect the slightest sound.

Darkness. Light.

Darkness. Light.

Nothing.

Whimpering now—*his wife; the baby!*—Jan swung the battle-hammer against the unyielding rock again and again with maniacal fervor. He attacked the wall until he was dripping with sweat, the crimson fabric of his polo shirt sticking to his chest, impatiently forearming stinging perspiration out of his eyes between successive strikes of the battle-hammer.

When he finally halted an hour later—breathless, trembling, muscles aching—not so much as a scratch, dent, or chip appeared in the cavern wall. He flung the battle-hammer down, sank to the ground, covered his face with his hands and wept.

Darkness. Light.

A high-pitched, insectile sonic whine filled the air. Jan clapped his hands over his ears and rocked back and forth, sobbing.

He took leave of his senses then. Long after the sonic assault had faded he continued to rock back and forth in the strobe-like flicker of the box lamp, arms wrapped around his knees, comforting himself with low-muttered words of consolation. "This isn't happening. Can't be. Not real! Nightmare. Wake up, Jan—*wake up!*"

The flickering pale white beam of the box lamp winked out.

Darkness.

Jan vanished before her eyes. One moment he was standing in front of her, edging into a tunnel she dimly glimpsed around his sight-obscuring head, back, and shoulders; the next he'd wavered, shimmered, and disappeared. Where he'd been standing a second before solid rock appeared, stretching across the hole that had been hammered into the cellar wall by their outré interloper.

Ursula whimpered.

*I am* definitely *hallucinating. Or dreaming. I must be! Else I've lost my mind entirely; gone stark raving mad.*

Ursula dropped the knife. Like Jan trapped on the other side of the cavern wall she scrabbled at the rock, desperately seeking some activating mechanism—lever, button, knob—that might cause the rock to part. And again, just like Jan—found none.

After five minutes of fruitless probing, poking, pressing, scratching, and pounding, Ursula turned around to face the hirsute corpse of the rock troll sprawled on its back in a pool of crimson amongst the shattered wreckage of the toppled bookcase and splayed-open books, butcher knife jutting from its neck.

*Trapped down here. Alone!*

She stooped and picked up the knife; rose again.

She advanced on the rock troll, teeth gritted, steeling herself for what came next.

*That thing will move—I just know it. It will move . . .*

But it didn't.

Ursula halted feet away from the corpse and glanced around.

*All right; so it's not a rock troll Michael Myers. What now? What might next come through the cellar walls . . . or down the stairs from the world-gone-mad-above? Better to die on the stairs hacking at whatever made it past the hatch than cornered like a rat in the cellar. A six-months-pregnant, teeter-totter wobbly, cornered rat in the cellar . . .*

Ursula climbed the stairs and halted, crouched, before the closed ring-bolted hatch. She put her ear against it and listened intently.

No sounds carried through the thick wood.

She shifted her grip on the knife in her hand.

And waited.

Jan came back to himself in pitch blackness. He groaned as he sat up. How long had he been bereft of his senses? He had no idea, though he suspected it had been for hours. Consciousness of his situation returned in a rush as the full horror of his predicament impinged upon him. He crawled about on all fours, feeling for the battle-hammer and box lamp—a hard, cold knot between his shoulder blades; a fluttery sensation in his stomach.

Jan found the box lamp first. He picked it up by its handle, felt again for an activating switch or button. Nothing. He shook it—still nothing. Banged it against the cavern floor and it flickered on: a weak, pallid beam of ghostly white light that illuminated his surroundings.

Jan drew a sharp inward breath.

*Hurrah! That's one for the home team, then.*

The battle-hammer lay a couple of feet away where he'd flung it after failing to make any impression upon the cavern wall. He switched the box lamp to his left hand, snatched up the battle-hammer in his right and stood up.

The tunnel twisted away, fading into darkness a hundred feet out.

*Right then. No change there.*

Despair and foreboding weighed him down, as if a thousand-pound weight were pressing upon his shoulders and his feet had turned to concrete.

*And what of it?* Jan remonstrated savagely with himself. *You have but one option here—forward.*

He took it. He shuffled forward.

Jan reached the leftward bend in the tunnel and turned. A long, sloping passageway led downward into darkness. He tightened his grip on the battle-hammer and pressed on.

The passageway ran for a couple thousand yards, then turned into a branching series of water-hollowed sedimentary rock tunnels and lesser caverns: a veritable labyrinth.

Jan wandered for hours, passing rock walls colored in various shades of ocher, red, blue, and crystalline white. As he explored he came across stagnant pools of pungent water, wall-clinging grayish-brown moss, pink and white toadstools sprouting from moisture-dampened crevices. He followed passages that dead-ended in solid rock, forcing him to back-track to previous branching passages and explore those until they either ended again or opened out into larger chambers. More than once a long, serpentine passageway narrowed to such an extent that he was forced to crawl forward on his belly. When this occurred he would worm forward on pistoning elbows and wriggling hips till the passageway widened, per-mitting him to stand again and continue onward. In such circuitous one-step-forward, one-step-back fashion he proceeded.

One of the twisting passageways he followed opened out into a cy-clopean, crimson-rock cavern whose walls stretched up, up, up—to a stal-actite-studded ceiling whose roof was covered with giant roosting bats. Scattered sunbeams broke through the roof of the cavern; dust motes twirled in the stale, penumbral air. A half-dozen of the pterodactyl-sized creatures circled high above him, great leathern wings beating in stately rhythm. Far below these monstrous bats an underground river mur-mured and splashed against its rocky banks, flowing on into darkness. A muscular reptilian form broke the black surface of the water and disap-peared again in a flash of greenish-brown scales before Jan could register what it was. Gazing upon this jaw-dropping scene, despite his exhaustion and low-grade terror he was struck by awe: the fine hairs on his neck and arms prickled with the chill of the numinous. Again, he experienced that creepy, doubling-of-experience, *déjà vu* sensation.

*Good god! To think all of this lies underground near our home . . .*

A half-second later he corrected himself: *Does it? That sensation of vertigo, of losing mass and solidity, of being hurled through time and space . . . Where am I, exactly?*

Jan proceeded with caution across the guano-spattered floor of the cavern, staying on his side of the river, endeavoring not to make any over-hurried movements or startling sounds that might disturb the great bats wheeling overhead.

He made it through safely and pressed forward. Tunnel after tunnel, stalagmite- and stalactite-festooned cavern after cavern. Hard-shelled beetles and other six-legged insects thrice the size of anything he'd seen above ground skittered from the light of the box lamp into shadowed corners and crevices. Meeping ratlike things and hissing lizards fled from his approach. Thumb-sized flies buzzed in an undulating swarm over a rotting, horse-sized carcass he discovered in one purple-walled chamber choked with Titian-yellow fungus and rutilant toadstools. Yard-long centipedes scuttled across his path. He pushed through webs of bloated, fist-sized spiders pale and repulsive as corpse flesh. Tributaries and rivulets of the black-water underground river were encountered again and again, in whose shallow depths bioluminescent fish swam and tentacled, jellylike creatures drifted. He waded through these chill waters after removing his slippers, putting them on again upon reaching the opposite bank. Trousers, underwear, and polo shirt were soon soaked through; occasionally the water he was forced to wade reached high as mid-chest. Thankfully, he caught no more glimpses of crocodile-sized reptilian forms—though once, as he trod down a tunnel in which strands of swirling fog cut visibility to arm's length, an apelike thing with suckered hands and eyeless, tentacled face rose up shrieking and flailing before him. Jan hastily backtracked away from the startled monstrosity—it made no attempt to pursue—and worked his way forward again through passageways adjacent to the thing's lair.

Until he encountered the tunnel of bronze.

Ursula came to with a start. Unbelievably, she'd dozed off: awkwardly sprawled on the stairs, back pressed against the wall.

*I couldn't have been out long. Five . . . ten minutes?*

*Much longer,* some other part of her mind suggested. *Eons.*

She glanced down at the rock troll: still very much dead and unmoving.

*Thank divine providence or whatever its closest materialist cosmic correlate is. What with vanishing husbands, other-dimensional creatures trashing our vehicles, and towering colossi tramping the neighborhood, I don't need the added challenge of fending off an undead rock troll . . .*

The sound that passed her lips raised the hair on her arms: half-sob, half gut-punched laugh.

Ursula slid the locking bolt and pushed the hatch open before she fully realized what she meant to do. It banged against the bronze stop plate.

She caught her breath.

Silence. Leastwise, no sounds of slavering beasts tearing the house apart . . .

Ursula picked up the knife, came up the stairs, and stepped into the kitchen. The shock she experienced was of an entirely different nature from those she'd recently weathered—though no less profound.

A glance out the garden window over the sink revealed a green-scummed pond a hundred feet away, beyond that a copse of mixed birch and pine running to the top of the mountain. There wasn't a trace of fog in the air. The neighbor's home—a stone-and-shingle Adirondacks lodge accented with bright red windows a half-acre distant—showed no visible sign of damage. Nor did the banana-yellow VW bus parked in its circular driveway.

Ursula left the kitchen and padded down the hallway into the living room. She didn't quite dare unlock the front door, but she pushed the curtain aside to look out the picture window. Their battered Subaru SUV and Volvo sedan showed unmistakable signs of damage: the SUV with its windshield caved in; the Volvo canted to one side on deflated tires with its rear end torn off. But again: no trace of fog. Or, for that matter, of hideous, mind-bending monstrosities.

*The portal has closed. All creepy-crawlies gone back to dimension X.*

Ursula giggled.

She reversed course back down the hallway into the kitchen.

The knife dropped clattering to the floor.

She picked up the handset of the land phone and brought it to her ear.

Dial tone.

Ursula punched 911 on the dial pad and turned back around to gaze out the garden window at a maddeningly normal, brightly lit, mid-afternoon tableau: pond, trees, neighbor's house and vehicle. Blue, cirrus-wisped sky.

"Nine-one-one operator, what is your emergency?" sounded the rather bored, officious voice of rationality and imminent intervention in her ear.

Ursula's death-grip on the handset caused her hand to shake and knees to tremble.

"Nine-one-one operator, what is your emergency?" the woman repeated.

Ursula's legs went out from under her. She slid down the wall till she found herself sitting on the tile floor, legs splayed out before her.

She tried to speak—and couldn't. A million, myriad black specks whirled before her eyes.

"Nine-one-one operator, what is your emergency?"

Jan had been exploring a narrowing, serpentine passage when the rocky cavern walls ended and the bronze tunnel—a gleaming, deeply burnished golden-yellow with gradations of orange-brown embossed with curvilinear designs and incomprehensible pictographs—began.

*What have we here—a forgotten entryway into Moria?*

Jan tapped his battle-hammer against the tunnel wall to test the resiliency of the metal. It appeared solid as the preceding rock—in fact, he suspected the tunnel was bored through the same sedimentary strata as the rest of the cavern. The impact of the head of his battle-hammer on that alien metal (for he felt certain the "bronze" was no mere alloy of copper and tin, despite its appearance) set up a sustained, resonating harmonic that echoed and re-echoed for a long half-minute in which he froze in place and held his breath.

Nothing came at him out of the darkness a hundred feet ahead—the limit of the box lamp's pallid illumination. The fog he'd encountered exploring the passageway of the tentacled shrieker had all but dissipated. After a couple of hard-thudding heartbeats he proceeded, preternaturally alert to any sudden movements or sounds.

Jan continued down the tunnel until he encountered a pair of onyx pillars carved with loathsome figures: bizarre humanoid forms, monstrous animals never seen on earth, storied creatures of myth and legend. Cyclops. Eight-tentacled Cthulhu. Dragons. Titans. Manticores and Minotaurs. Creatures indescribable: profoundly alien and deeply disturbing. After regarding the pillars for a moment he passed between them into a vestibule whose walls, floor, and ceiling were constructed of coruscating, rainbow-colored marble. Here the thrum of eldritch energy was akin to that the battle-hammer gave off, only a thousand times stronger. On the far side of the vestibule he halted before a giant silver panel in which an ouroboros was debossed: twin to the design etched into the head of his battle-hammer. A snake eating its own tail.

A familiar, high-pitched insectile whine filled the air. Jan grimaced and waited for it to pass. When the piercing buzz-shriek faded away he set the box lamp and battle-hammer down and reached out to touch the panel. As his fingers traced the deep-grooved design of the ouroboros the ground rumbled under his feet and the silver panel began to descend. Dirt pattered down from overhead and his vision blurred from the quaking of walls, ceiling, and floor. For a brief moment he fully expected the vestibule to collapse upon him—*here endeth the explorations of our intrepid hero, crushed beneath tons of alien metal and Catskills rock*—but the quaking ceased upon the door fully recessing into the floor.

Jan took up box lamp and battle-hammer again and exited the vestibule to step into greater weirdness.

*        *        *

Once more he felt that curious sense of lightening—of losing mass and solidity—of only becoming fully centered, solid, and present seconds later, although the nausea that accompanied this transition was not as severe as the first time he'd experienced it. Jan recovered by taking a couple of deep breaths and swallowing hard against the burning sensation in his throat that arose from the churned-up acids in his stomach backing into his esophagus.

He found himself in a great hall. White-glowing crystals crisscrossed a high vaulted ceiling overhead, casting a harsh illumination upon the tableau below. At fifty-foot intervals fossilized skeletal forms of colossal creatures stood on raised daises: horned, clawed, dagger-toothed. Some resembled dinosaurs. Others gigantic insects. Still others were of such alien composition and proportions that it hurt the mind to look at them. Was the thing with the humanoid appearance and reptilian snout ape or lizard? The fossilized remains of the three-headed, horned, stilt-legged beast a bird or some kind of monstrously tall marsupial?

It appeared he'd stumbled into a museum of *un*-natural history. But if so, for whom were these exhibits arranged? By whose hands? And where were the visitors? Assuming any such museum visitors were visible in that portion of the electromagnetic spectrum detectable by *Homo sapiens,* or had mass that could be felt if you bumped into them . . .

*Easy. You're spooked, yes—but let's not let our imagination run away with itself. One thing at a time. One goddamn thing at a time.*

Trodding the length of the great hall, he came to a sprawling octagonal chamber in whose glass-fronted alcoves were arranged a series of either lifelike wax or artfully taxidermied figures; he couldn't tell which. These wore historically accurate clothing and were arranged against era-appropriate backgrounds. A blue-uniformed, colonial Revolutionary War soldier and a redcoated British regular menaced each other at the points of fixed-bayoneted rifles, log fort burning behind them. Native American Indians in rough homespun—a young brave and squaw—were posed upright facing the glassed fourth wall of their alcove in front of a wigwam, hands resting paternally on the shoulders of prepubescent members of the tribe: a young boy and girl, presumably their children.

Jan circled the chamber to view other dioramas. Cro-Magnon men and women in furs crouched around a campfire on a windswept open plain. Neanderthals jostled one another in the act of imprinting ocher-stained handprints upon a cave wall. The dioramas grew odder still: a foursome of snake-headed beings bowing to an iron idol of a tentacled octopus-spider in a jungle clearing. A trio of tusked, bristle-haired hunters in leather greaves and rattan chest plates thrust spears at a giant crab on an alien ocean shore. A half-dozen round-shouldered, web-footed things with misshapen gray faces and heavy-lidded cyclopean eyes—Jan thought of them as "schmoos"—stood half-submerged in brackish water, gnawing the fibers of a thorny-leaved, purple-flowered plant.

*No, Toto—I don't think we're in Kansas anymore.*

Exiting the octagonal chamber Jan passed through a series of lesser-sized rooms crowded with various fossilized examples of flora and fauna, not all of it terrestrial. The last of these rooms opened into another great hall lined with the fossilized skeletons of colossal creatures arranged on daises. He transited this hall until he came upon a spiral staircase that led to the second floor. Here he re-tightened his grip on the box lamp and battle-hammer and ascended.

Jan came out into another great hall that bisected a series of adjoining rooms. Gone were the whitish-glowing crystals in a high-vaulted ceiling; up here individual lamps distended from brackets anchored in the flat ceiling aimed tightly focused beams upon points of interest: a spectacular mural depicting a fiery comet streaking over craggy mountains—a floor-standing model of the sun—planets and moons of an unknown solar system—the giant skull of some saber-toothed, quad-horned creature positioned upon an alabaster pedestal.

In other rooms diffuse lighting came from the translucent ceiling or through view ports embedded in the walls. (He didn't dare reach out a hand to ascertain whether these were actual portals into another part of the universe or ultra-high-resolution screens—it was enough that his eye could detect no reflectivity or specularity in these openings.) One portal depicted the orbit of a dozen heavily cratered moons about a multi-colored gas giant planet. Another a pulsing neutron star. Still another a light-devouring, gravity-bending black hole.

Jan wandered through one split-level room in which he found a be-wildering series of mechanical devices displayed in multi-shelf cases: cy-lindrical, hexagonal and trapezoidal objects from which a profusion of levers, buttons, and knobs projected. He encountered a half-dozen such rooms showcasing mystifying machinery. A couple of these contained machines large enough to have served as vehicles for alien life forms.

From one oddity-crammed room to another he progressed. Jan trod the length of long, low-ceilinged spaces holding embryonic forms of strange creatures suspended in liquid-filled jars. He encountered head-ache-inducing chambers of crackling, static-sparkling jellies and vibrating platonic solids; transited rooms that displayed diverse geological speci-mens: fine-grain particulate matter, stones, boulders, crystals, gems. Globes of molten magma. Cubes in which swam shimmering, amoeboid-looking creatures and spiked protozoa.

Other rooms presented yet more astronomical phenomena: portals that looked out upon alien planets, moons, suns. Asteroids sporting geo-desic-domed buildings and metal-capped pyramids. Meteor showers, comets, black holes, super-novae. A dizzying number of galaxies—none of which he recognized—were depicted in a succession of three-dimensional star charts and wall-sized murals.

And then Jan came across the high-ceilinged, oval-shaped chamber whose walls were covered with the same incomprehensible scrawl of cur-vilinear designs and pictographs he'd first encountered in the bronze tunnel, in addition to a series of baffling bas-reliefs: overlapping circles, complexly intercut geometric designs, and Escher-like depictions of ar-chitecture built according to non-Euclidean principles. All was gibberish, all incomprehensible—until he mounted the translucent raised dais in the center of the room whose interior glowed with a fluorescent indigo light.

As Jan stepped upon this dais the language, numerals, and symbols written on the walls around him snapped into comprehensible focus. He suddenly understood what the various diagrams, curvilinear script, and pictographs portrayed: *nothing less than the origin, ongoing workings, and eventual fate of the multiverse entire.* And all this expressed in a manner so simple, direct and crystal-clear that even a high school mathematics teacher could understand it.

"Good god," Jan breathed. He set the box lamp and battle-hammer down. Straightened up again to run both hands through his hair—unconsciously imitating Ursula—eyes wide in shocked comprehension.

Again, the cold shiver of the numinous tickled his spine and prickled the fine hairs on the back of his neck. The sense of awe—of gestalt-like understanding both broad and deep—took the back of his head off and opened him up to cosmos and the void. Jan felt a kind of religious ecstasy as his eyes roved over the revelations writ large upon the walls. He grasped at once that this particular area of the Catskills constituted a critical locus in time and space: a kind of node or crossroads at which point a dizzying, near-infinite number of other worlds and dimensions collided and interacted. As he turned 360 degrees to take in the panorama of the walls he noted a series of equations illustrating the standard model of particle physics delineated and integrated into something more. The strong interaction, weak interaction, electromagnetic interaction, and gravitational interaction fields were brought together into the mathematical equivalent of the holy grail: a unified field theory that united the classical hardwired world of determinate Newtonian physics with the tricksy, ever-shifting, problematic world of quantum mechanics. This paradigm-shattering knowledge was summarized and succinctly expressed in as simple and concrete a formula as $E = mc^2$.

*It's all so simple, really! Why, how very obvious!*

As he stood there upon the dais, his intelligence augmented in eldritch manner by the indigo-light-fluorescing dais, Jan could not understand why mankind had struggled so long and hard to make the connection between the various sciences, to see the endpoint where all recent speculations and discoveries were leading.

He stepped off the dais and the various diagrams, curvilinear script, and pictographs on the walls reverted to an incomprehensible scrawl of gibberish. Almost immediately knowledge of the workings of the multiverse began to fade in his consciousness—to say nothing of his sense of exaltation and wonder.

"*No!*" Jan gasped.

He stepped onto the dais again, and everything he'd just learned snapped right back into prominence and sharp focus.

*Better living through alien technology. Thank you, Mr. Martian! Ms. Neptunian! Hermaphrodite of Proxima Centauri! Whoever.*

It was critical that he make it back home—to Ursula and their unborn baby, to the surface world of sanity and light. But now, more than his personal survival was at stake. He had acquired paradigm-shifting knowledge that could catapult the sciences millennia into the future—the key to this wisdom and learning a succinct, summarizing equation that unlocked and expressed the workings and eventual fate of the multiverse entire. He must at least return with that. *He must*—even if he forgot all else.

But how? He dared not risk committing the equation to memory alone. It was imperative that he set it down in writing—on some sort of media, with some kind of implement. Where? With what? Jan looked around—no immediate solution presented itself. He cast his mind back to rooms just traversed. Nothing came to mind re: writing implement and/or recording media.

Idly his hand fell to his waist, where his fingers closed about a wooden handle. The butcher knife! Still tucked into his belt. He'd forgotten all about it.

In a flash Jan knew what he must do. What matter mere flesh when measured against god-like wisdom and learning?

He pulled the knife from his belt and sat down cross-legged on the dais. Then, gaze fixed upon the quantum field equation glimmering on the wall, he carved into the flesh of his left forearm its numbers, letters, and mathematical symbols, tongue jammed against the back of his incisors in intense concentration. He willed himself to ignore the pain, the crimson rivulets that ran from his scored flesh.

Task accomplished, he stood up, flung the butcher knife away, and gave his left arm a shake. Droplets of blood—bluish-black in the fluorescent indigo light—pattered down onto the dais and surrounding floor tile. Again he picked up box lamp and battle-hammer.

Now all he had to do was make it back to the surface.

Jan stepped off the dais and the light went out. As before, he felt as if he'd lost a couple hundred IQ points as soon as he stepped off the dais.

He regarded his left forearm thoughtfully. The equation carved there was clear and distinct. And though his knowledge and understanding of the paradigmatic shift the numbers, letters, and mathematical symbols represented had already begun to fade, the broad outlines of what the equation expressed remained fixed in his mind. That had to be enough. Leastwise, he hoped it was. He had to trust that he would make it back home with enough residual memory and presence of mind to present a working unified field theory to the world. And to report on the exhibits he'd seen in the Museum of Unnatural History and Sciences . . .

Again that infernal insectile noise sounded. A shrieking, extended burst this time—razored steel sawing against razored steel, as if a mountain giant were rapid-fiddling a steel-stringed violin with a shortsword. Jan dropped both box light and battle-hammer, threw his hands over his ears, and fell to his knees. At any moment he expected blood to begin oozing from his abused eardrums: wounds counterpointing his slashed, throbbing forearm and bruised thighs, hips, and feet. He felt as if his brain was being scrambled and organs pulverized by the sustained sonic assault. On and on and on the cranium-shattering noise went, truncating all coherent thought. He was no longer a sentient creature—merely a tortured piece of wounded, writhing meat. Jan screamed.

The noise ceased.

Shakily, he rose to his feet and snatched up the battle-hammer.

*Motherfuckers!*

"Come on, then!" Jan shouted. *"Show yourself!"* He brandished the battle-hammer and looked about, turning in a slow circle. In truth, he had no idea if he was being tormented by another sentient creature or by irregularly occurring, mindless phenomena. It didn't matter. It felt damn good to release tension and fear by unleashing a combative roar and assuming a belligerent fighting stance. Irrational and feckless his behavior may have been, but it diminished fear and rallied flagging spirits.

*Get back to Ursula and the baby. Move!* he commanded himself.

Jan picked up the box lamp and exited the oval, high-walled room he now thought of as the Chamber of Revelations. Ears ringing, left forearm throbbing, various muscles in his legs, hips, and abdomen aching, he made his way through a couple dozen more rooms filled with the fossilized remains of bizarre creatures, astronomical exhibits, mechanical oddities, alien animals (both taxidermied and dissected; embryonic forms floating in jars), and weird geological specimens until he encountered a spiral staircase that led back down to the first floor and another great hallway lined with the fossilized skeletal forms of colossal creatures on raised daises. He trod the length of this great hallway until he came upon another vestibule, this one of gold-flecked black marble. Through its open doors he saw that the cavern continued on the other side.

Here Jan paused, considering. He could reverse course—go back down the hallway, up the spiral stairs, through the rooms of outré exhibits and the Chamber of Revelations, down the first set of stairs and through the initial great hallway to the entrance of the weird museum with its vestibule of coruscating marble—but to what end? If he exited the entrance vestibule he'd find himself back in the bronze tunnel that led to the labyrinth of cavern passages. And if he re-entered *those* he might encounter the eyeless, sucker-handed, tentacle-faced monster again—or worse. Backtrack even farther and he'd have to re-cross the guano-spattered floor of the cavern of giant bats, and he wasn't sure he'd make it through a second time without drawing the attention of those pterodactyl-sized monsters. And if he continued backtracking—to the very beginning of his nightmare sojourn—he'd find himself trapped in a dead-end passage, the cellar presumably behind the rock wall he'd attacked fruitlessly with the battle-hammer, but as unreachable to him from there as the ruins of Stonehenge. Then what? Curl up and die? Wait for hunger and thirst to work their fatal effect upon him? Perhaps hasten the inevitable end by . . .

He shook himself.

*Enough wandering, morbid thoughts. Focus!*

There was only one real choice. As ever it was . . . forward.

So forward he went—striding into the vestibule of gold-flecked marble with a forced exhalation of tuneless, puckered-lip breath he'd intended as a defiant, jaunty whistle.

Once more Jan experienced that peculiar feeling of weightlessness, diminished mass, and vertigo. This time, however, the sensation of being hurled through time and space hit him especially hard. He staggered, swayed, fell to his knees, and vomited. Set box lamp and battle-hammer down, swiped his lips with the back of his wrist, and fell backward onto his ass, breathing hard. He needed a moment here—maybe two, maybe three.

A stalagmite- and stalactite-studded cavern tunnel stretched before him, fading into darkness a hundred feet out.

*The more things change, the more . . .*

Jan put his hand to his right ear and brought it away damp with blood and mucous. There was a persistent, strident ringing in that ear: painful evidence of a punctured ear drum.

He picked up the box lamp and battle-hammer and struggled to his feet.

*The equation carved into your forearm. Ursula and the baby. These are the only things that matter. You must make it back to the surface world! You* must *return home.*

Jan seized upon that thought and reiterated it in his mind with talismanic intensity: *You* will *make it back home. You* will!

Of course he would.

How could he be so sure? It was foreordained, written in the stars, kismet. He felt the truth of this fact in his very bones—for wasn't he the protagonist, the unconquerable hero—the irreducible, incontrovertible, centered sentience of his own life story?

He was. Ergo—he would return home, like Odysseus to Ithaca and Frodo to the Shire.

It was a simple matter of will + time.

The cavern tunnel ran for a couple thousand feet, curving to the left and upward before opening into another labyrinth of various-sized chambers and crisscrossing, rock-walled passages. Once again Jan found himself wading through shallow tributaries and lesser rivulets of the great underground river in whose inky waters bioluminescent fish and tentacled, jellylike creatures swan and drifted. He stepped around rainbow-colored crustaceans, fluorescing amphibians, light-pulsing eels.

*These organisms must use bright light and coloration to signal a mate—it certainly isn't camouflage.*

Meeping ratlike vermin and hissing lizards fled from his approach. He broke through webs spun by bloated corpse-white spiders. Beetles, centipedes, and other imperfectly glimpsed insectile forms chittered and clicked and scuttled into dark-shadowed corners as he passed.

His slippers, torn to shreds, finally fell apart as he was picking his way across a particularly jagged-edged section of cavern flooring. Jan limped on, teeth gritted against the pain. His partially clotted left forearm oozed blood; as if in compensatory sympathy, the soles of his feet began to weep crimson. Jan feared he was picking up all manner of infections from the humid subterranean environment. He tried not to think about it.

*Just get home. Time enough then for a couple of ice-cold beers, a hell of a tale for Ursula (and the world at large, for that matter) and the coating of various cuts and broken-skin abrasions with foaming antiseptic.*

His right ear, well . . . that was another matter entirely. The wound would require the attention of a doctor. Even so, he'd be forever deaf on that side. So be it. He'd adjust; would live.

Jan was working his way up a steep incline in yet another of a never-ending succession of twisting tunnels when a syncopated, deep kettle-drum rumble began to sound: a slow, steady beat.

*What now? Trolls on parade?*

He scrambled to the top of the incline and paused for a moment to catch his breath. This particular nondescript tunnel stretched out before him as so many had before—studded with stalagmites and stalactites, fading into darkness a hundred feet out.

He followed the passageway downward, navigating various twists and turns of the tunnel, that kettledrum rumble—*doomdoom-badoom*—growing steadily louder, till he found himself striding into a large rock-walled chamber whose gray-mossed sides admitted no exit other than the passageway from which he had just entered.

*Dead end. Time to backtrack.*

The kettle-drum rumble crescendoed . . . and ceased.

Jan turned around to go back the way he had come and the floor lurched under his feet. He staggered, recovered his balance. A circular section of the cavern floor, roughly a hundred feet in diameter, began to descend.

He tightened his grip on the battle-hammer.

Another powerful wave of *déjà vu* washed over him, eerie and trans-fixing in its intensity—though he gained no glimmer of insight into future events from this, the most current of urgent signalings from his temporal lobe.

Jan was physically exhausted and psychically spent. Given the horrors and wonders he'd recently encountered, he had neither the inclination nor the excess energy to speculate on what might possibly be awaiting him at the terminus of his descent.

*Going down* was all he thought.

The rocky platform upon which Jan stood, knees flexed in a ready crouch, came to a halt with a grinding crunch in an ocher-colored chamber whose walls were covered with a now-familiar scrawl of pictograms and curvilinear script. A score of brightly flaring braziers spaced in a circular pattern about the chamber threw a flickering orange, smoky-shadowed light upon his environs. A pungent scent prickled his nostrils: the iron-rich tang of oxidized blood mixed with the sickly-sweet stench of rotting carrion. A narrow, bronze-barred portcullis blocked the only discernible exit from the chamber. Between himself and the exit stood three silent, black-robed figures; arm's distance from one another—cauled faces a palpitating, featureless, whitish-pink moonscape—clutching ornate-handled silver daggers.

*Outnumbered—but I've got the range with the battle-hammer,* he coldly assessed.

The black robes raised their daggers and shuffled forward on sandled feet. A soft susurration sounded in the air, as of brittle autumnal leaves rustled by a gentle breeze.

Jan retreated a step.

The black robes halted.

"I've no quarrel with you!" Jan set the box lamp down; lowered the battle-hammer to his side—though he kept a firm grip on its handle. "I implore you: *Let me pass!*"

He'd figure a way past that bronze-barred portcullis once he reached it.

In the immediate silence that followed Jan's conciliatory hail, an ember popped in one of the braziers with the sound of a gunshot. A shower of reddish-orange sparks fell to the rock floor of the chamber to hiss and sizzle and wink out in puffs of smoke.

The black-robes advanced again, an insectile susurration sounding in the air—ten thousand locust husks rustling in a chilling wind.

Jan retreated another step.

Once more the black-robes halted.

*"We need not fight!"* Jan called. His eyes darted about seeking an exit—there was none to be found, save for the closed portcullis. "I mean you no harm!"

Silence, save for the crackle of flames in the braziers. And the low thrum of eldritch energy from the ouroboros-debossed battle-hammer . . .

The black-robes advanced again: *Shsssh-Shsssh-Shsssh* . . .

Jan stood his ground and raised the weapon.

*For it was a weapon, wasn't it? Ursula had been right about that. It had utterly failed as a tool.*

Jan was beyond fear. Rage began to build in his chest: rage for all that he'd been put through.

"Come on, then!" Conan would understand, though a civilized twenty-first-century teacher of high school mathematics needs must frown upon such berserker sentiments and provocative taunts.

Wasn't that the very reason he'd become involved with the Society for Creative Anachronism in the first place—to test himself physically in mock battle against equally eager combatants? Well, here was the real thing—though now he found himself outnumbered three to one, lacking all armor save for beltless wool trousers and a cotton polo shirt. That was life for you: blackly comedic and ironic. Unpredictable, yet circular. Farcical and deadly. Exhausting. Relentless. *Weird.*

"Bring it, you hideous fucks!"

As if commanded, the black-robes rushed him as one.

Jan brought the battle-hammer down upon the skull of the first cauled black-robe to reach him. A resounding crack echoed through the chamber. The thing collapsed with a grunt, dagger spilling from its fingers.

Almost simultaneously black-robe #2 lunged at him with an underhand thrust, aiming for his belly.

Jan sidestepped, but in so doing caught black-robe #3's blade in his left shoulder. A gout of blood spurted from the wound; he felt a tingling numbness in that arm even as he smote the lunging black-robe a solid blow to the chest with the battle-hammer. Black-robe #2 staggered, stutter-stepped backward, and went down in a tangle of legs, silken robe snagging above its knees.

The remaining black-robe circled Jan, looking for an opening, repeatedly feinting at him with the dagger. It tossed the knife from its right hand to its left—left hand to its right—back again.

Jan kept his eyes focused on his antagonist's sandaled feet, not the distracting blade toss.

*Watch for the telegraphing shift of weight. Watch for it . . .*

When the black-robe rose up on its right front toes preparatory to making another left-leg-leading lunge, Jan swept his own leg out, hooked his antagonist behind its calf with his foot, and jerked.

The black-robe lost its balance and fell onto its back.

Jan, off-balance himself, almost went down as well—but he recovered first and pounced. A trio of hard hammer blows—to head, chest, stomach—and the thing convulsed, legs beating an idiot tattoo against the rock floor of the descended dais—and lie still.

A thrill of triumph and exaltation ran through his breast—*three down, and I'm still standing!*—followed an instant later by a vision-blurring wave of exhaustion.

Jan dropped the battle-hammer and sank to his knees with a groan. His shoulder stung from the penetrating dagger stab; the fingers of his right hand scrabbled over the punctured flesh. The wound bled freely, though it wasn't jetting blood. Once again Jan found himself giving silent thanks to the inscrutable gods of Subterranea that he hadn't taken one to the heart, abdomen, or face. Or that a major artery hadn't been cut.

Still—that bleeding had to be stanched.

Jan sat down cross-legged on the floor, wriggled out of his polo shirt, wadded it into a ball, and pressed it against the wound. He held it there, fabric jammed into the gash, while the fires of the encircling braziers smoked and flamed and popped.

He thought nothing—absolutely nothing at all.

Jan's head snapped back up. He'd fallen asleep! For seconds that felt like minutes; his slumping body triggered a full return to consciousness.

He'd dropped the polo shirt. Jan picked it up—the fabric was damp with blood. He pressed it against his shoulder until he was certain the puncture wound wouldn't continue to pump claret till he fell unconscious and bled out. When he found himself nodding off again he judged enough time had passed for the wound to have partially clotted.

Jan dropped the sanguinary shirt and knee-walked over to the last black-robe he'd killed. The thing lay sprawled on its back; crushed head, chest, and abdomen evidence of the violence visited upon it.

He considered its caved-in, cauled face. The slimy-looking, whitish-pink caul was now saturated with blood, appearing a dark burgundy.

*Who's behind my falseface . . .*

Jan reached out, fighting a surge of nausea, felt around the black-robe's head until he had a firm grip on either side of the caul and tore it from the thing's skull.

Fixed eyes stared from a prognathous-jawed face. Short-cropped, curly black hair—thick and matted with grime—bristled above a pronounced brow ridge.

A rock troll! More accurately—another one.

*That's one for me; one for Ursula,* idiot monkey-mind chattered.

He flung the caul away with an exhalation of disgust. It landed with a wet *thwack* on the rock floor of the descended dais somewhere behind him.

Jan gingerly rose erect, a dizzying whirl of black specks clouding his vision. *Easy, easy—wait for the spots to clear*—and moved to the corpse of the second black-robe he'd killed. He knelt beside it—the thing had fallen face down—and rolled it over onto its back. Fighting another surge of revulsion he grabbed its slimy, pinkish-white caul beneath the chin with one hand and pressed down on the top of its head with the other. Leverage thus secured he ripped upward. The caul did not separate entirely from the black-robe's head but rather flapped off the back of the skull, stubbornly remaining attached by a fibrous strand of glistening tissue.

He stared into his own face.

The shock of recognition hit him like a Pamplona bull ramming into his solar plexus.

*What the f—*

Jan studied his frozen features a moment—lips slightly agape; blue eyes fixed and glazed—then reached out and thumbed the lids down with trembling hands.

*Don't think about it. This means nothing.*

Doesn't it?

*Nothing! A cheap trick, produced by some manipulative stage director in this subterranean house of horrors.*

Right on cue an infernal, high-pitched buzz-shriek filled the chamber. Jan clapped a hand over his good left ear, hunched over, and waited for the insectile tumult to fade. After an interminable minute it did so. Once the shrieking faded he removed his hand from his ear and yanked the caul back down over the thing's face.

*The* thing? *That's you.*

*No, it isn't,* he answered himself. *Couldn't be. Obviously! I'm me. This is a simulacrum.*

*Is it?*

*Of course it is!*

Jan rose again; went to the first black-robe he'd killed, knelt beside it. He tore the caul off its face; flung it aside. The features thus revealed were perhaps the most disturbing he'd uncovered so far: a mixture of his own, blended with rock troll physiognomy.

"Doesn't mean anything," Jan muttered. "Not a thing."

*Doesn't it?*

His mind flashed back to the complex diagrams and curvilinear script inscribed upon the walls of the Chamber of Revelations. The Catskills: focal point of colliding dimensions. Nexus of worlds; melting pot of divers realities . . .

He picked up one of the daggers and examined it closely. The knife had a finely worked, double-edged, seven-inch silver blade. The circular pommel was inscribed with a by-now familiar symbol: an ouroboros. Snake eating its own tail.

*Round and round we go.*

Jan dropped the dagger and stood up. He walked to the box lamp and battle-hammer, bent over, and straightened up again with them in hand—box lamp in his left, battle-hammer in his right.

He winced. His muscles ached. The soles of his bleeding feet were scored and bruised. His deafened right ear affected his balance in subtle ways he attempted to compensate for as he took shaky strides toward the bronze-barred portcullis. His left arm tingled, as if he'd struck his elbow against a sharp table edge.

A surge of self-pity and despair washed over him; he shoved it somewhere down there with his bleeding feet.

*That emotion will do you no good. Not here; not now. Push on. Later . . .*

When Jan was but a couple yards away from the exit the portcullis rose to recess into the ceiling with a hum of well-oiled gears. The cavern continued beyond: yet another stalagmite- and stalactite-studded tunnel fading into darkness a hundred feet out.

*You're never going to reach the surface again. You're going deeper and deeper into the bowels of the earth or some interstitial terra incognita between colliding dimensions.*

For the second time Jan seriously considered turning around and backtracking to the beginning of this involuntary spelunking episode. But the thought of finding himself trapped once more in that dead-end passageway, battle-hammer thudding ineffectively into the cavern wall, home and cellar maddeningly close but unreachable behind uncountable thicknesses of sedimentary rock, was more than he could bear. He could not die there, in so futile and absurd a fashion. No—unthinkable, perverse. His destiny lay elsewhere. In an entirely different direction.

Forward.

Moaning, he shuffled through the raised gate.

Jan followed the winding tunnel into another labyrinth of crisscrossing passageways and various-sized rock-walled chambers, though he didn't run across any more streams or rivulets of the great underground river. Once more he encountered a now-familiar mixture of creepy-crawly underworld denizens: oversized beetles, centipedes, and other half-glimpsed insectile forms. These ran chittering and clicking and skittering from his presence. He pushed through tunnel-spanning spiderwebs; roughly rubbing his lips with a battle-hammer-clenched backhand where shuddersome gossamer thread had brushed. Meeping ratlike things and albino lizards scurried out of the bobbing beam of the box lamp to seek the protection of shadowed recesses, moist crevices and cracked-rock bolt holes.

Once he caught a glimpse of sinuous tentacled forms undulating high up on a ledge in a mica-speckled, toadstool-choked chamber. But these evinced no interest in him, and so he limped on without hindrance—bleeding from his feet, left shoulder, and forearm; deaf in his right ear. His throat was scratchy and parched. His stomach rumbled.

*I'm going to have to eat—and more importantly, drink—something soon.*

This was an uncomfortable, incontrovertible fact—a distressing concomitant consequence of his calorie-burning, water-absorbing biology. Dehydration was the more pressing matter. He could go a couple of days without food if he stopped to rest and husband what remained of his rapidly diminishing strength, but water was an absolute necessity.

So where to get a drink of water?

He rejected out of hand the notion of sipping from one of the numerous oily, pungent-smelling puddles he skirted around or stepped over. That wasn't going to happen—not until more desperate circumstances forced him to. Risk taking a cupped-hand drink from the underground river? Perhaps—but he'd encountered no further tributary or lesser rivulet of that bioluminescent-creature-infested waterway, and he was—as ever—loath to backtrack and lose time. Push on then, in hopes of encountering some other water source? It seemed the only reasonable course. Thirst hijacked his thoughts, creating compelling visions. An underground waterfall—the fast-flowing water ice-cold, pure; white spray jetting into the air from where the cascade fell thundering against moss-covered rocks . . . Beads of luscious moisture rolling down a tall glass of iced-tea . . . The incalculable, multi-colored, thirst-quenching riches of a convenience store refrigerator stocked with all manner of boxed, canned, and bottled drinks . . .

Jan halted every fifteen minutes of so to catch his breath, weak from loss of blood and continuous exertion. Thus he proceeded—halting; pushing on. Stopping; staggering forward. The fight with the trio of black-robes had taken a lot out of him: that do-or-die confrontation with homicidal combatants had drained his last reserves of energy.

*Look at me, the unstoppable protagonist of a tale that would have delighted Farnsworth Wright.*

The thought brought him no cheer.

It was simple willpower now that drove one foot in front of the other. Willpower and the hope of seeing Ursula again. That and the nagging, gnawing goad of knowing that what was inscribed on his forearm had the power to alter mankind's destiny, thus sending reverberations through the multiverse.

*Isn't that a bit grandiose?* Jan interrogated himself.

*Perhaps. Nevertheless, it's true,* came back the internal-dialogue answer.

He believed this with every fiber of his being.

Jan limped on—breathing raggedly, bleeding feet sending sharp twinges of pain to his tired brain, left forearm, and throbbing shoulder. Tunnel after tunnel, cavern chamber after cavern chamber.

He came to a split in the current tunnel he was navigating and chose the right passageway, as it inclined upwards whereas the left passageway angled down.

*Upward. Toward the surface and light.*

Or so he hoped.

His mind wandered as he trudged on—idle fancies, airy daydreams, gnawing doubts. Far-too-vivid fears.

*What if you make it back home only to find that infernal white fog still encompassing the house? Emeraldian glimmerings, towering colossi—or worse—stalking through the roiling ground-level cloud bank?*

As if his thoughts had triggered the change, the temperature began to drop. Five minutes later he was shivering with chill and foreboding. Wisps of fog formed in the tunnel, twisting and twining about the cavern floor. Ghost serpents, seeking flesh . . .

*What are you going to do if the worst has occurred in your absence? Suppose one—or many—of those other-dimensional monsters have crashed through a door or window and made it inside the house? Cornered Ursula . . .*

"Stop it!" Jan shouted, startling himself.

"Op it . . . op it . . . op it . . ." Some trick of geometry and acoustics caused his voice to echo down the twisting passageway in front of him, to fade out somewhere down there beyond the box lamp's pallid beam.

He halted, breathing hard.

*The evils of the day . . . of the moment . . . are sufficient unto themselves,* he reminded himself. *Control your thoughts. Control!*

Movement at the limit of light. Something stepped into the dim radiance of the box lamp's beam a hundred feet out . . . and approached.

Jan raised the battle-hammer.

Words sprang unbidden to mind: *Halt! Who goes there?*

Ridiculous. He wasn't a soldier in some old war flick pulling sentry duty.

The approaching form appeared humanoid. Was it too much to hope . . . fully human?

"Hello!" called Jan. "Hello there!"

Definitely human. Yet the person didn't answer. Closer . . .

"I'm hurt!" Jan called. "I need help! I'm—"

*Lost. Scared. Exhausted.*

Fifty feet away, feet obscured by tenebrous fog, the oncoming figure seemed to dolly-wheel toward him—smoothly, effortlessly. As the person drew inexorably closer he could make out more details. Forty feet away: short stature, slim hips, and rounded shoulders. Thirty feet away: a woman, wearing a sharply tailored gray suit.

He lowered the battle-hammer.

At twenty feet distance he beheld the woman's grim-set, unsmiling features. Ten-foot distance: glittering black eyes.

"Lana!" Jan called.

Lana Gloaming: their realtor. What the hell was she doing down here?

"I'm so glad—"

Lana passed through him.

Jan spun around: nothing there.

He faced back front: the stalagmite- and stalagtite-studded tunnel wound away into darkness.

Jan choked back a sob.

*Hallucination! I'm seeing things now.*

But he'd been seeing things for a while, hadn't he?

"No," he muttered. "Real—all real."

His twinging feet, aching shoulder, deafened ear, and throbbing forearm could attest to that—to say nothing of his tormenting thirst and pangs of hunger. This was no dream or extended hallucination. Whatever else this subterranean sojourn was, it was real—grounded in experiential phenomena. Real as horror; incontrovertible as pain.

He shuffled forward a few steps and halted. Blinked.

"Can't be," he gasped.

He forgot all about Lana Gloaming.

Something else came into view at the limit of the box lamp's radiance, blocking further progress down the tunnel, running perpendicular to his axis of advance.

A red-brick wall.

Jan approached the wall, scarcely daring to breathe. Or hope.

*I couldn't have gone in a circle! A wide, meandering circle . . .*

He looked about him.

Was this the same area where his underground journey began—the tunnel he'd found himself in when he first set foot in the cavern? Possibly. The winding rock-walled passageway appeared roughly similar in terms of general width, height, and geological apportionment of stalagmites and stalactites. But he couldn't be certain.

And that red-brick wall—was that the foundation wall of his home? Or of some other house in the neighborhood? The red color saturation and hue seemed right—but he'd stepped through a hole punched into it from this side of the cavern, and there was no hole in its unmarred surface now. Nevertheless . . .

*Déjà vu* hit with the force of a tsunami wave. Every hair on his body prickled as if electrified; the battle-hammer thrummed and vibrated with eldritch energy. Adrenaline coursed through his veins, momentarily overcoming exhaustion. He set the box lamp down and attacked the wall with a two-handed grip on the battle-hammer. Upon the first shivering impact of the hammer's head into the red brick that horrid, piercing insectile buzzing sounded again. He gritted his teeth against the pain caused by the sonic assault—

*It's only the left ear that aches; with the right ear pierced we've got a fifty percent reduction in pain here—forbear, Jan!*

—and continued sledge-hammering the wall.

The box lamp began to flicker: darkness, light.

Bricks cracked in the wall; mortar crumbled.

The insectile whine faded. But now he experienced a vertigo-inducing sensation of losing mass and solidity, of being flung through space and time—a most familiar feeling.

Darkness. Light.

He fought off nausea even as he winced from sharp stabs of pain. His two-handed grip on the battle-hammer caused his left shoulder and forearm to protest vociferously.

Darkness. Light.

In the strobing beam of the box lamp Jan hammered at the wall in a frenetic series of still-lifes: shrieking hammer-man in action. For he *was* shrieking now—a high-pitched, ululating cry of frustration, rage, and madness. There wasn't much of the emotional-regulating prefrontal cortex governing that shriek; his vocalization was pure amygdala-prompted roar—even as bricks shattered, shifted, and fell from the widening aperture the battle-hammer tore into the wall.

Darkness. Light.

Darkness. Light

The hole grew. He uncovered something immediately behind the wall: an expanse of wood . . .

Jan continued to hammer at bricks even as his muscles ached and wounds bled. After a couple dozen further strikes his vertigo diminished and he experienced anew a sense of being fully present, having restored mass and solidity, of being fully grounded in this moment and locale.

An odd thought occurred to him: *How many hours—days—have I been hammering away here?* Some temporal-attuned part of his brain was dimly aware that, incredibly, counter-intuitively, a significant amount of time had passed. Days. Weeks. Months. Years?

More bricks cracked and shattered, slipped, and fell to the cavern floor. Pulverized mortar puffed out as dust. The hole widened.

The box lamp went out.

Darkness.

Jan hit the wood behind the brick with the battle-hammer. It cracked, vibrated, and shifted. Light shone around the edges of what he now realized was the back of a piece of tall, free-standing shelving. He shoved hard with his left hand and the shelf toppled forward, coming to a precarious, rocking halt a foot or two above the floor. He had a confused impression of a brazier-lit chamber thus revealed—bookshelves housing scrolls and codexes running the length of the walls.

*That's what I've knocked over: a bookshelf.*

Something moved in the light. Jan's vision whited-out in the glare of the braziers; his dilated pupils, having adjusted to a long interval of cavern darkness but dimly illuminated by the pallid beam of the box lamp after exiting the museum, caused him to squint and turn his head from side to side in order to see more clearly.

He leaped onto the back of the toppled bookcase. "Ursula!" he called out. *"Ursula!"*

Jan glanced down to behold a prognathous-jawed face with short-cropped, curly black hair—thick and matted with grime—above a pronounced brow ridge. A rock troll: its body pinned beneath the bookshelf's crushing weight. He looked up in time to catch a confused impression of a female rock troll (breasts, bulging belly) rushing at him, dagger in hand.

"Waiiii—" he slurred, reeling from exhaustion and blood loss.

A hot, lacerating pain pierced his throat. He dropped the battle-hammer with a rattling clatter to the floor and clapped a hand to the jet of blood that sprayed and pulsed to the beat of his heart.

The attacking rock troll retreated, screaming. *"Eee-eee-eeeeee! Eee-eee-eeeeee!"* It continued shrieking, hirsute hands pressed to its open-O mouth. *"Eee-eee-eeeeee!"*

Jan crashed face first onto the silver-starred, black tile floor.

*Stars,* he thought. *I've fallen into galaxies of stars . . .*

He moaned, twitched. Coughed. And lay still in a pool of spreading crimson.

# Epilogue

The rock troll that had been pinned beneath the toppled bookcase knelt beside Jan's corpse. Its pregnant mate stood beside him.

The male rock troll examined the weird ape's shoulder wound, then lifted the simian's forearm to study the shallow cuts incised there. He spoke to the female rock troll in harsh gutturals, then dropped the ape's arm with a sodden thump back onto the tile. Next, he picked up the battle-hammer and subjected it to the same searching examination he'd given the weird ape's corpse and odd, two-legged black garment. He vocalized again.

The female responded with a short, higher-pitched series of words.

The male rock troll rose, hefted the battle-hammer in his right hand, and pointed at the hole in the cellar wall with his left.

Female rock troll replied with an even higher-pitched burst of language.

The male advanced to the gaping aperture torn into the cellar's red-brick foundation.

Female rock troll took a step toward her mate, gesticulating fiercely and emitting more rapid-fire words.

Male rock troll glanced back for a moment.

Then he turned around and stepped through the hole in the wall.

# Black-Winged Battle Cry

The creativity and pathology of the human mind are, after all, two sides of the same medal coined in the evolutionary mint. The first is responsible for the splendour of our cathedrals, the second for the gargoyles that decorate them to remind us that the world is full of monsters, devils, and succubi.

—Arthur Koestler

They carved my form from gray basaltic rock
cinder-burst into Triassic skies
when thunder-lizards ruled afore the shock
from Chicxulub asteroid caused all to die.
Shapen by mammal hands into grotesque
winged form of fangs & razored claws,
I perch upon cathedral Romanesque
fell waterspout upon high buttressed wall.
At night I cleave from stone & soar in flight
hunting hardened criminals who prowl
dark streets 'round Notre Dame; with righteous might
I descend on scurrying vermin with a growl
& battering shock of powerful black wings;
ripping flesh to get at viscera—soul sings!

# Acknowledgments

"Black-Winged Battle Cry," first published in *Spectral Realms* No. 15 (Summer 2021).

"The Call of Lizzie," first published in *Spectral Realms* No. 15 (Summer 2021).

"The Candidate," first published in *Penumbra* No. 3 (2022).

"Cold Tickle," first published in *Night Terror and Other Weird Tales* by Carl E. Reed (Book Country, 2015).

"Come Haltingly, on Lame Feet," first published in *newWitch* No. 10 (Fall 2005).

"Fat Man & Yellow-Eyes: A Ghoulish Tale," first published in *Spectral Realms* No. 17 (Summer 2022).

"Father's Bullet: A Tale of the Apocalypse," first published in *Spectral Realms* No. 16 (Winter 2022).

"The Final Flight of Major Havoc," first published in *Black Gate* No. 9 (2005).

"Haunted House," first published in *The Rabbit Hole (Weird Stories, Volume 4: Madness)* (The Writers Co-op, 2021).

"The Instructive Pleasures of Horror Fiction," first published in *Penumbra* No. 3 (2022).

"Let There Be Light," first published in *Spectral Realms* No. 18 (Winter 2023).

"A Little Song of Death," first published in *Spectral Realms* No. 17 (Summer 2022).

"Lycanthropic Howl," first published in *Spectral Realms* No. 14 (Winter 2021).

"Märchen (Fairy Tales)," first published in *Spectral Realms* No. 13 (Summer 2020).

"A Matter of Debt Concerning the Gentleman in Baltimore," original to this collection.

"The Möbius Strip Trip," original to this collection.

"Motauqwa Means Mountain," first published in *Night Terror and Other Weird Tales* by Carl E. Reed (Book Country, 2015).

"Night Terror," first published in *Night Terror and Other Weird Tales* by Carl E. Reed (Book Country, 2015).

"Not a Vampire," first published in *Night Terror and Other Weird Tales* by Carl E. Reed (Book Country, 2015).

"One Who Walks Alone," first published in *Spectral Realms* No. 10 (Winter 2019).

"The Philosophy & Aesthetics of Horror," first published in *Spectral Realms* No. 12 (Winter 2020).

"Pulp Writer," original to this collection.

"The Return of Pumpkin Jack," original to this collection.

"Samhain Eve: A Celtic Tale," first published in *Night Terror and Other Weird Tales* by Carl E. Reed (Book Country, 2015).

"The Sleep of Reason Produces Monsters," first published in *Spectral Realms* No. 17 (Summer 2022).

"The Strange and Curious Tale of Professor Robert Howard Wilson," first published in *Night Terror and Other Weird Tales* by Carl E. Reed (Book Country, 2015).

"The Water Is Warm, Mommy," original to this collection.

"A Whisper to Rock," first published in *Spectral Realms* No. 18 (Winter 2023).

www.ingramcontent.com/pod-product-compliance
Lightning Source LLC
Chambersburg PA
CBHW070446030726
47503CB00004B/917